The Kiss Quotient

"A riveting, compulsively readable romance that brims with feeling and warmth." —*Entertainment Weekly*

"Hoang's witty debut proves that feelings are greater than numbers, no matter how you add things up." —*People*

"With a deft hand, Hoang crafts an honest and thoughtful look at the challenges Stella's neuroatypicality poses while never losing sight of who Stella is as an individual, especially as her relationship with Michael evolves into something far beyond the scientific." —*Harper's Bazaar*

"Helen Hoang's *The Kiss Quotient* is an absolute delight—charming, sexy, and centered on a protagonist you love rooting for." —BuzzFeed

"Hoang writes Stella with insight and empathy."
—*The New York Times Book Review*

"Hoang does an amazing job of crafting a vividly romantic tale filled with depth, humor, and a universal sense of humanity." —*New York Times* bestselling author Emily Giffin

"In just under twenty-four hours, I devoured *The Kiss Quotient* by Helen Hoang, and it was AWESOME. Adorable, sexy, smart. Exactly the book I wanted to read!"
—*New York Times* bestselling author Christina Lauren

"I devoured *The Kiss Quotient*. It's one of the best books I've read in a very long time. It has everything—it's funny, sad, poignant, and impossible to put down."
—*New York Times* bestselling author Christine Feehan

"This is such a fun read, and it's also quite original and sexy and sensitive."

—New York Times bestselling author Roxane Gay

"*The Kiss Quotient* had me under a spell the moment I met the hero. I was excited, in love, and couldn't wait to get back to this book every time life forced me to put it down. A rare and riveting love story."

—New York Times bestselling author Penelope Douglas

"An unexpectedly sweet romance that left me with a huge smile on my face. I dare you not to fall in love with these two characters and their story. Helen Hoang's debut is quite simply delightful!"

—New York Times bestselling author Nalini Singh

PRAISE FOR

The Bride Test

"With *The Bride Test*, Hoang has once again shown readers the importance of representation in literature, while also creating a sexy, compassionate story about the power of love and the enduring American dream."

—The Washington Post

"Everything you want a romance novel to be."   —NPR.org

"Hoang sheds light on a rarely represented segment of society, literally rewriting who is deserving of the leading role in a romantic novel."   *—Vogue Hong Kong*

"*The Bride Test* is positively delightful. . . . It's smart, honest, and achingly romantic, just as sexy as it is sweet."

—Taylor Jenkins Reid, author of *Daisy Jones & The Six*

"Helen Hoang is a master of building characters that feel relatable."

—*New York Times* bestselling author Christina Lauren

"Prepare to fall in love all over again. . . . *The Bride Test* is a charming love story that is equal parts sexy and sweet."

—PopSugar

"Refreshingly real."

—*Marie Claire*

"A heartwarming contemporary romance."

—OprahMag.com

"From the author that rocked the lit world with her 2018 novel, *The Kiss Quotient*, comes an equally addicting read that is perfect for summer."

—*Women's Health*

"Hoang writes with the kind of humanity that we all should embody: the kind that makes you believe that there is still an abundance of good left in the world at any given moment."

—Shondaland

"This new quirky, heartwarming romance will make you believe in love again."

—*Woman's Day*

"You're not just reading a fun novel, you're also reading a novel that's giving visibility to groups that aren't often written about."

—Betches

"A charming novel about the different forms that love can take."

—*New York Post*

"Helen Hoang's books . . . are both delicious love stories and also deeply personal."

—*Glamour*

BERKLEY BOOKS BY HELEN HOANG

THE KISS QUOTIENT

THE BRIDE TEST

THE {Kiss} QUOTIENT

{HELEN HOANG}

JOVE
New York

A JOVE BOOK
Published by Berkley
An imprint of Penguin Random House LLC
penguinrandomhouse.com

Copyright © 2018 by Helen Hoang
Readers Guide copyright © 2018 by Helen Hoang
Excerpt from *The Bride Test* copyright © 2019 by Helen Hoang
Penguin Random House supports copyright. Copyright fuels creativity, encourages
diverse voices, promotes free speech, and creates a vibrant culture. Thank you for buying
an authorized edition of this book and for complying with copyright laws by not
reproducing, scanning, or distributing any part of it in any form without permission.
You are supporting writers and allowing Penguin Random House to continue to
publish books for every reader.

A JOVE BOOK, BERKLEY, and the BERKLEY & B colophon are
registered trademarks of Penguin Random House LLC.

ISBN: 9780593337219

Jove trade edition / June 2018
Jove mass-market edition / April 2021

Printed in the United States of America
3   5   7   9   10   8   6   4   2

Book design by Kristin del Rosario

know you hate surprises, Stella. In the interests of communicating our expectations and providing you a reasonable timeline, you should know we're ready for grandchildren."

Stella Lane's gaze jumped from her breakfast up to her mother's gracefully aging face. A subtle application of makeup drew attention to battle-ready, coffee-colored eyes. That boded ill for Stella. When her mother got something into her mind, she was like a honey badger with a vendetta—pugnacious and tenacious, but without the snarling and fur.

"I'll keep that in mind," Stella said.

Shock gave way to rapid-fire, panic-scrambled thoughts. Grandchildren meant babies. And diapers. Mountains of diapers. Exploding diapers. And babies cried, soul-grating banshee wails that even the best sound-canceling headphones couldn't buffer. How did they cry so long and hard when they were so little? Plus, babies meant husbands. Husbands meant boyfriends. Boyfriends meant dating. Dating meant *sex*. She shuddered.

"You're thirty, Stella dear. We're concerned that you're still single. Have you tried Tinder?"

She grabbed her water and gulped down a mouthful, accidentally swallowing an ice cube. After clearing her throat, she said, "No. I haven't tried it."

The very thought of Tinder—and the corresponding dating it aimed to deliver—caused her to break out in a sweat. She hated everything about dating: the departure from her comfortable routine, the conversation that was by turns inane and baffling, and again, the *sex* . . .

"I've been offered a promotion," she said, hoping it would distract her mother.

"Another one?" her father asked, lowering his copy of the *Wall Street Journal* so his wire-framed glasses were visible. "You were just promoted two quarters ago. That's phenomenal."

Stella perked up and scooted to the edge of her seat. "Our newest client—a large online vendor who shall remain nameless—provided the most amazing datasets, and I get to play with them all day. I designed an algorithm to help with some of their purchase suggestions. Apparently, it's working better than expected."

"When is the new promotion effective?" her father asked.

"Well . . ." The hollandaise and egg yolk from her crabcakes Benedict had run together, and she attempted to separate the yellow liquids with the tip of her fork. "I didn't accept the promotion. It was a principal econometrician position that would have had five direct reports beneath me and require much more client interaction. I just want to work on the data."

Her mother batted that statement away with a negligent wave of her hand. "You're getting complacent, Stella. If you stop challenging yourself, you're not going to make any more improvement with your social skills. That reminds me, are there any coworkers at your company who you'd like to date?"

Her father set his newspaper down and folded his hands over his rounded belly. "Yes, what about that one fellow,

Philip James? When we met him at your last company get-together, he seemed nice enough."

Her mother's hands fluttered to her mouth like pigeons homing in on bread crumbs. "Oh, why didn't I think of him? He was so polite. And easy on the eyes, too."

"He's okay, I guess." Stella ran her fingertips over the condensation on her water glass. To be honest, she'd considered Philip. He was conceited and abrasive, but he was a direct speaker. She really liked that in people. "I think he has several personality disorders."

Her mother patted Stella's hand. Instead of putting it back in her lap when she was done, she rested it over Stella's knuckles. "Maybe he'll be a good match for you, then, dear. With issues of his own to overcome, he might be more understanding of your Asperger's."

Though the words were spoken in a matter-of-fact tone, they sounded unnatural and loud to Stella's ears. A quick glance at the neighboring tables in the restaurant's canopied outdoor dining area reassured her that no one had heard, and she stared down at the hand on top of hers, consciously refraining from yanking it away. Uninvited touches irritated her, and her mother knew it. She did it to "acclimate" her. Mostly, it drove Stella crazy. Was it possible Philip could understand that?

"I'll think about him," Stella said, and meant it. She hated lying and prevaricating even more than she hated sex. And, at the end of the day, she wanted to make her mother proud and happy. No matter what Stella did, she was always a few steps short of being successful in her mother's eyes and therefore her own, too. A boyfriend would do that, she knew. The problem was she couldn't keep a man for the life of her.

Her mother beamed. "Excellent. The next benefit dinner I'm arranging is in a couple months, and I want you to bring a date this time. I'd love to see Mr. James attending with you, but if that doesn't work out, I'll find someone."

Stella thinned her lips. Her latest sexual experience had

been with one of her mother's blind dates. He'd been good-looking—she had to give him that—but his sense of humor had confused her. With him being a venture capitalist and her being an economist, they should have had a lot in common, but he hadn't wanted to talk about his actual work. Instead, he'd preferred to discuss office politics and manipulation tactics, leaving her so lost she'd been certain the date was a failure.

When he'd straight-out asked her if she wanted to have sex with him, she'd been caught completely off guard. Because she hated to say no, she'd said yes. There'd been kissing, which she didn't enjoy. He'd tasted like the lamb he'd had for dinner. She didn't like lamb. His cologne had nauseated her, and he'd touched her all over. As it always did in intimate situations, her body had locked down. Before she knew it, he'd finished. He'd discarded his used condom in the trash can next to the hotel room's desk—that had bothered her; surely he should know things like that went in the bathroom?—told her she needed to loosen up, and left. She could only imagine how disappointed her mother would be if she knew what a disaster her daughter was with men.

And now her mother wanted babies, too.

Stella got to her feet and gathered her purse. "I need to go to work now." While she was ahead on all her deadlines, *need* was still the right word for it. Work fascinated her, channeled the furious craving in her brain. It was also therapeutic.

"That's my girl," her father said, standing up and brushing off his silk Hawaiian shirt before hugging her. "You're going to own that place before long."

As she gave him a quick hug—she didn't mind touching when she initiated it or had time to mentally prepare for it—she breathed in the familiar scent of his aftershave. Why couldn't all men be just like her father? He thought she was beautiful and brilliant, and his smell didn't make her sick.

"You know her work is an unhealthy obsession, Edward. Don't encourage her," her mother said before she switched her attention to Stella and heaved a maternal sigh. "You should be out with people on the weekend. If you met more men, I know you'd find the right one."

Her father pressed a cool kiss to her temple and whispered, "I wish I were working, too."

Stella shook her head at him as her mother embraced her. The ropes of her mother's ever-present pearls pressed into Stella's sternum, and Chanel No. 5 swirled around her. She tolerated the cloying scent for three long seconds before stepping back.

"I'll see you both next weekend. I love you. Bye."

She waved at her parents before exiting the ritzy downtown Palo Alto restaurant and walked down sidewalks lined with trees and upscale shops. After three sunny blocks, she reached a low-rise office building that housed her favorite place in the world: her office. The left corner window on the third floor belonged to her.

The lock on the front door clicked open when she held her purse up to the sensor, and she strode into the empty building, enjoying the solitary echo of her high heels on the marble as she passed the vacant reception desk and stepped into the elevator.

Inside her office, she initiated her most beloved routine. First, she powered on her computer and entered her password into the prompt screen. As all the software booted up, she plopped her purse in her desk drawer and went to fill her cup with water from the kitchen. Her shoes came off, and she placed them in their regular spot under her desk. She sat.

Power, password, purse, water, shoes, sit. Always this order.

Statistics Analysis System, otherwise known as SAS, automatically loaded, and the three monitors on her desk filled with streams of data. Purchases, clicks, log-in times, payment types—simple things, really. But they told her more about people than people themselves ever did. She stretched out her fingers and set them on the black ergonomic keyboard, eager to lose herself in her work.

"Oh hi, Stella, I thought it might be you."

She looked over her shoulder and was jarred by the unwelcome view of Philip James peering around the door frame. The severe cut of his tawny hair emphasized his square jaw, and his polo shirt was tight across his chest. He looked fresh, sophisticated, and smart—precisely the kind of man her parents wanted for her. And he'd caught her working for pleasure on the weekend.

Her face heated, and she pushed her glasses up the bridge of her nose. "What are you doing here?"

"I had to pick up something that I forgot yesterday." He extracted a box from a shopping bag and waved it at her. Stella caught sight of the word *TROJAN* in giant capital letters. "Have a nice weekend. I know I will."

Breakfast with her parents raced through her mind. Grandchildren, Philip, the prospect of more blind dates, being successful. She licked her lips and hurried to say something, *anything*. "Did you really need an economy-sized box of those?"

As soon as the words left her mouth, she winced.

He smirked his assholest smirk, but its annoyingness was softened by a show of strong white teeth. "I'm pretty sure I'm going to need half of these tonight since the boss's new intern asked me out."

Stella was impressed despite herself. The new girl looked so shy. Who would have thought she was so gutsy? "For dinner?"

"And more, I think," he said with a twinkle in his hazel eyes.

"Why did you wait for her to ask you out? Why didn't you ask her first?" She'd gotten the impression men liked to be initiators in matters like these. Was she wrong?

With impatient motions, Philip stuffed an entire militia of Trojans back in his shopping bag. "She's fresh out of undergrad. I didn't want to get accused of cradle robbing. Besides, I like girls who know what they want and go for it . . . especially in bed." He swept an appraising gaze from her feet to her face, smiling like he could see through her clothes, and she stiffened with self-consciousness. "Tell me, are you still a virgin, Stella?"

She turned back to her computer screens, but the data refused to make sense. The cursor on the programming screen blinked. "It's none of your business, but no, I'm not a virgin."

He walked into her office, leaned a hip against her desk, and considered her in a skeptical manner. She adjusted her glasses even though they didn't need it. "So our star econometrician has 'done it' before. How many times? Three?"

No way was she going to tell him he'd guessed correctly. "None of your business, Philip."

"I bet you just lie there and run linear regressions in your head while a man does his business. Am I right, Ms. Lane?"

Stella would totally do that if she could figure out how to input gigabytes of data into her brain, but she'd rather die than admit it.

"A word of advice from a man who's been around the block a few times: Get some practice. When you're good at it, you like it better, and when you like it better, men like *you* better." He pushed away from the desk and headed for the door, his bag of condoms swinging jauntily at his side. "Enjoy your endless week."

As soon as he left, Stella stood up and shoved her door shut, using more force than was necessary. The door slammed with a hard, vibrating bang, and her heart stuttered. She smoothed damp hands over her pencil skirt as she brought her breathing back under control. When she sat down at her desk, she was too jittery to do more than stare at the blinking cursor.

Was Philip right? Did she dislike sex because she was bad at it? Would practice really make perfect? What a beguiling concept. Maybe sex was just another interpersonal thing she needed to exert extra efforts on—like casual conversation, eye contact, and etiquette.

But how exactly did you practice sex? It wasn't like men were throwing themselves at her like women apparently did to Philip. When she did manage to sleep with a man, he was so put off by the lackluster experience that once was more than enough for both of them.

Also, this was Silicon Valley, the kingdom of tech geniuses and scientists. The single men available were probably as hopeless in bed as she was. With her luck, she'd sleep with a statistically significant population of them and have nothing to show for it but crotch burn and STDs.

No, what Stella needed was a professional.

Not only were they certified disease-free, but they had proven track records. At least, she assumed so. That was how she'd run things if she were in that business. Regular men were incentivized by things like personality, humor, and hot sex—things she didn't have. Professionals were incentivized by money. Stella happened to have a lot of money.

Instead of working on her shiny new dataset, Stella opened up her browser and Googled "California Bay Area male escort service."

Which envelope should he open first? The lab results or the bill? Michael was paranoid about protection, so the lab results should be good. Should be. In his experience, shit didn't need a reason to happen. Bills, on the other hand, were a sure thing. They always sucked. The only question was how hard they'd punch him in the balls.

Tensing his muscles for impact, he tore open the bill. How much was it this month? He scanned to the bottom of the itemized invoice and located the final amount. The breath trickled from his lungs before it gusted out. Not horrible. On the scale of stinging to pulverizing, he'd put this one at merely bruising.

That probably meant he'd contracted chlamydia.

He set the bill down on top of the metal filing cabinet nestled behind his kitchen table and opened the lab results from his latest STD screening. All negative. Thank fuck. It was Friday evening again, which meant he needed to work tonight.

Time to get himself in the mind-set for fucking. Not an easy thing to do after thinking about STDs and plaguing bills. For an instant, he let himself imagine what things would be like if the bills came to an end. He'd be free at last. He could return to his old life and—shame doused him. No, he didn't want the bills to end. He never wanted that to happen. Never.

As Michael padded through his cheap apartment toward the bathroom and shed his clothes, he tried to revive his old enthusiasm for this job. The taboo nature of it had been enough in the beginning, but after three years of escorting, that was pretty much old hat. The revenge aspect still satisfied him, though.

Look at your only son now, Dad.

It would torment his dad if he found out Michael was having sex for money. A thoroughly delightful thought. Not an arousing one, however. That was what fantasies were for. He mentally sifted through his favorites. What was he in the mood for tonight? *Hot for Teacher? Neglected Housewife? Secret Lover?*

He cranked the shower knob and waited for steam to cloud the air before climbing beneath the hot spray. A breath in, a breath out, and he readied his mind. What was the name of tonight's client again? Shanna? Estelle? No, Stella. He'd bet twenty dollars that wasn't her real name, but whatever. She'd chosen to pay up front. He'd try to do something extra nice for her. *Hot for Teacher*, then.

It was his freshman year of college. He skipped all of his lectures but this one because Ms. Stella liked to drop the chalkboard eraser right by his chair. Picturing her skirt riding up as she bent down to retrieve the eraser, he gripped his cock and stroked with firm motions. When class ended, he draped her facedown over her desk and bunched her skirt up to her waist to reveal that she wasn't wearing panties. He plunged into her hard and fast. If someone walked in on them . . .

With a groan, he yanked his hand away before he could

fly over the edge. He was primed and ready to see Ms. Stella outside of class.

He kept his mind locked in the fantasy as he finished with his shower, dried off, and left the bathroom to pull on jeans, a T-shirt, and a black sports coat. A quick look in the half-fogged mirror and two swipes of his fingers through his damp hair confirmed he was presentable.

Condoms, keys, wallet. Out of habit, he reread the special comments section of tonight's assignment on his phone.

Please don't wear cologne.

That was easy. He didn't like the stuff in the first place. He slipped his phone into his pocket along with everything else and left his apartment.

It wasn't long before he parked in the underground lot of the Clement Hotel. As he strolled into the sleek, ultramodern lobby, he made sure the lapels of his coat were down and played his usual pre-meet-and-greet game where he imagined what his new client was like.

Under Client Age for tonight, it had said thirty. He sighed and corrected the age to fifty. Anything younger than forty was always a lie—unless it was a group thing, which he didn't do. Bachelorette parties paid well, but the idea of destroying young love depressed the hell out of him. Maybe it was pathetic, but he wanted to live in a world where brides-to-be only had sex with their grooms-to-be and vice versa. Besides, large groups of horny women were terrifying. You couldn't defend yourself against them, and their nails were sharp.

"Stella" could be a pampered fifty who indulged in sweets, spas, and froufrou canines, was therefore decadently rounded, and preferred to be worshipped in bed—something Michael had no problem with. She could also be a fit fifty who liked yoga, green juice, and marathon sex sessions that worked his abs better than weighted incline crunches. Or, his least favorite, she could be a hard-ass Asian go-getter who chose him because, with his mixed Vietnamese and Swedish heritage, he looked a lot like the K-drama star Daniel Henney. This last kind of woman inevitably reminded him of his mom, and after sleeping with them, he needed therapy with a punching bag.

Entering the hotel restaurant, he searched the dimly lit tables for a brown-haired, brown-eyed woman wearing glasses. Because he'd gotten through his mail without major incident earlier, he braced himself for the worst now. His gaze skipped over tables occupied by businessmen until he saw a solitary, middle-aged Asian woman micromanaging the waitress on how to make her salad. When she brushed manicured nails through her lightened brown hair, his stomach sank and he began walking toward her. It was going to be a long night.

No, this was the culmination of a semester's worth of sexual tension. They both wanted this. He wanted this.

Before he could reach her, a reed-thin older man took the seat opposite her and covered her hand with his. Confused but relieved, Michael stepped back and surveyed the restaurant again. No one was sitting alone . . . but for a girl in the far corner.

Her dark hair was pulled back in a tight bun, and sexy librarian-type glasses were balanced on a cute little nose. In fact, from what he could see of her, everything looked like it had been chosen from a sexy librarian cosplay. She wore neat pointed pumps, a gray pencil skirt, and a fitted white oxford shirt buttoned clear up to her throat. It was possible she was thirty, but Michael put her at twenty-five. There was something young and wholesome about her, though her frown was rather fierce as she scrutinized the menu.

Michael glanced about the room, searching for a hidden camera team or his friends cracking up behind the potted plants. He found neither of those things.

He closed his hands around the back of the chair across from her. "Excuse me, are you Stella?"

Her eyes shot to his face, and Michael lost his train of thought. Those sexy librarian glasses showcased the most stunning pair of soft brown eyes. And her lips—they were just full enough to be tempting without detracting from her overall air of sweetness.

"I'm sorry. I must have the wrong person," he said with a smile he hoped was more apologetic and less embarrassed. There was no way a girl like this had hired an escort.

She blinked and jostled the table as she flew to her feet. "No, that's me. You're Michael. I recognize you from your picture." She stuck her hand out. "I'm Stella Lane. Nice to meet you."

He stared at her open expression and proffered hand for a stunned fraction of a second. This wasn't how clients greeted him. They usually waved him into a seat with a sly curl of their lips and a sparkle in their eyes—that sparkle that said they thought they were better than him but were looking forward to what he could offer anyway. She greeted him like he was . . . an equal.

Quickly recovering from his surprise, he wrapped her slender hand in his and shook it. "Michael Phan. Nice to meet you, too."

When he released her, she motioned toward his chair awkwardly. "Please, have a seat."

He sat and watched as she perched herself on the precarious edge of her seat, her back straight as a board. She searched his face, but when he arched an eyebrow at her, she switched her focus to the menu. She adjusted the position of her glasses with a wrinkle of her nose.

"Are you hungry? I am." Her knuckles went white as she clung to the menu. "The salmon is good here, and the steak. My dad likes the lamb—" Her gaze jumped to his face, and, even in the dim light, he could see her cheeks go crimson. She cleared her throat. "Maybe not the lamb."

Because he couldn't resist, he asked, "Why not the lamb?"

"I think it tastes woolly, and if you . . . when we . . ." She stared up at the ceiling and took a deep breath. "All I'd be thinking about would be sheep and lambs and wool."

"Understood," he said with a grin.

When she stared at his mouth like she couldn't remember what she was going to say, his grin widened. Women chose him because they liked the way he looked. Few of them responded to him like this, however. It was flattering even as it was funny.

"Are there any things you would prefer *I* not eat or drink?" she asked.

"No, I'm pretty easy." He kept his voice light and tried to ignore the tightness in his chest. It had to be heartburn. Simple thoughtfulness wasn't doing this to him.

After the waitress took their order and left, Stella sipped from her water glass and drew geometrical shapes in the condensation with delicate fingertips. When she noticed him watching her, she drew her hand back and sat on it, flushing like she'd been caught doing something she shouldn't.

Something about that was kind of endearing. If she hadn't already paid, he wouldn't believe she actually wanted this. Why did she want this? She should have a boyfriend . . . or a husband. Against his better judgment—it was best when he didn't know—he looked at her left hand resting on the table. No ring. No white line.

"I have a proposition for you," she said suddenly, pinning him with a gaze that was surprisingly direct. "It would require a commitment of sorts—for the next couple months, I imagine. I would . . . prefer . . . to have sole access to you during that time. If you're available."

"What do you have in mind?"

"Please tell me if you're available first."

"I only do Friday nights." That was non-negotiable. Escorting once a week was bad enough. If he had to do it more than that, he'd lose his fucking mind, and he couldn't afford for that to happen. Too many people depended on him.

He never scheduled repeat appointments with the same client, either. They tended to get attached, and he couldn't stand that. But he wanted to hear what she was proposing before he declined.

"You have the next few months open, then?" she asked.

"It depends on what you're proposing."

She pushed her glasses up her nose and drew her shoulders back. "I'm awful at . . . what you do. But I want to get better. I think I can get better if someone would teach me. I'd like that person to be you."

Understanding splashed over Michael in surreal waves. She thought she was bad. At sex. And wanted lessons to improve. She wanted him to tutor her.

How the hell did you teach sex?

"I think we should do a trial run before we set anything up," Michael hedged. She couldn't actually be bad at sex, and she'd already paid. At the very least, he had to give her tonight.

Frowning, she nodded. "You're absolutely right. We should establish a baseline."

A grin tugged at his lips again. "Are you a scientist, Stella?"

"Oh, no. I'm an economist. More precisely, I'm an econometrician."

In Michael's book, that put her solidly in the brainiac category, and an odd feeling ghosted up the back of his neck. Damned if he didn't have a thing for smart girls. There was a reason why his favorite fantasy was *Hot for Teacher.* "I don't know what that is."

"I use statistics and calculus to model economic systems. Do you know how when you buy something online they usually email you with future recommendations? I help them formulate those recommendations. It's a very fluid and fascinating field right now." As she spoke, she leaned toward him, and her eyes lit with excitement. Her lips curved like she was telling him a secret. About math things. "Today's material is completely different from what I used to teach when I was in graduate school."

That odd feeling simmering up Michael's spine increased in intensity. She'd somehow gotten prettier during the course of their discussion. Brown eyes and thick lashes, pouty lips, delicate jaw, vulnerable neck. Vivid images of him unfastening the buttons of her shirt flashed in his mind.

But unlike the usual, he didn't want to do it quickly. He didn't want to skip straight to the fucking, get out, and go home. This girl was different. It was that spark in her eyes. He wanted to take his time and see if he could make her shine with a different kind of excitement. His cock dug at the fly of his jeans, dragging Michael back to the here and now.

His skin had gone hot and sensitive, and his pulse thrummed with eagerness. He hadn't been this turned on in forever. And he hadn't been fantasizing she was someone else. He reminded himself this was business. His personal wants and needs didn't play into this at all. This assignment was just like any other, and when it was done, he'd move on to the next.

He took a deep breath and said the first thing he could think of. "Were you on the math team in high school?"

She laughed down at her water. "No."

"Science club? Maybe it was chess club."

"No, and no." Her smile was a sad, barely there thing that made him wonder what high school had been like for her. Looking back up at him, she said, "Let me guess, football quarterback."

"Nope. My dad was a firm believer that sports are stupid."

Her brow wrinkled with a little frown. "I find that difficult to believe. You're very . . . athletic-looking."

"He only encouraged practical things. Like self-defense." He hated to agree with his dad on anything, but with the family business being what it was, and his helping out with it, the techniques had come in handy when shit kids teased him.

A discovering kind of smile lit her face. "What do you do? MMA? Kung fu? Jeet Kune Do?"

"I've done a little of everything. Why do you sound like you actually know what you're talking about?"

Her gaze dropped back down to her water. "I like martial arts movies and things like that."

He groaned as suspicion dawned. "Don't tell me . . . you're a Korean drama fan?"

She tilted her head as a smile peeked over her lips. "Yes."

"I do *not* look like Daniel Henney."

"No, you look better."

He settled his hands on the edge of the table as his face heated. Fuck, he was blushing. What the hell kind of escort blushed? His sisters had posters of Henney plastered all over their bedroom walls, had even established a man-beauty scale of one to Henney. They'd agreed among themselves that Michael was a solid eight. He didn't give a damn where he ranked, but it meant something that this genius girl gave him an eleven.

Their dinner arrived, saving him from having to respond to her compliment. She'd ordered the salmon, so he'd done the same. No way was he going to eat lamb. He snorted to himself. *Woolly.*

His fish was good, so he ate all of it. He suspected everything was good here. The Clement was one of Palo Alto's most exclusive hotels with rooms going for more than a thousand dollars a night. Apparently, econometricians made shitloads of money.

As he watched Stella pick at her dinner, however, he noticed that everything about her was understated. Her face was devoid of makeup, her nails were short and unpainted, and her clothes were simple—though they fit her perfectly. They had to be custom made.

When she set her fork down and wiped her mouth, her

salmon was only half finished. If they'd known each other better, he would have eaten it for her. His grandma always made him finish his dinner down to the last grain of rice.

"Is that all you're going to eat?"

"I'm nervous," she admitted.

"You don't need to be." He was a damned good escort, and he'd take care of her. Unlike most of his assignments, he even looked forward to it.

"I know. I can't help it. Could we just get this over with?"

His eyebrows twitched. He'd never heard someone say something like that in reference to a night with him. Changing her mind-set was going to be fun.

"All right." He draped his napkin over his empty dinner plate and got to his feet. "Let's go to your room."

After Stella unlocked the door, she stepped into her intimately lit suite, set her purse on the chair by the door, and arranged her high heels against the wall, almost sighing as her bare feet flattened on the carpet.

Michael sent her an amused look, and she stared down at her toes. She'd taken her shoes off on autopilot. It was one of her routines. Was it rude to do that when you had company? Maybe she should put them back on. Her stomach knotted, and her heart raced at rabbit speed.

He took the decision out of her hands by kicking off his own black leather shoes and positioning them next to hers. When he finished, he shrugged out of his suit jacket and tossed it on the chair next to her purse, revealing the simple white T-shirt underneath. It stretched over his chest and upper arms, and his jeans rode low on narrow hips. Stella couldn't help but stare.

His body was raw sculpted muscle and loose-limbed coordination. He was by far the finest male specimen she'd ever laid eyes on.

And they were going to have sex tonight.

She took a desperate breath and marched into the bathroom, where she braced her hands on the cool granite and stared at her reflection in the mirror. Her eyes were open a fraction too wide, and her face was paper pale, her lips dry. She didn't think she could go through with this. She shouldn't have picked such a good-looking escort. What had she been thinking?

Her lips twisted with a grimace. She hadn't *been* thinking. After perusing the escort files for hours, sifting through countless faces and descriptions that had blurred together, she'd taken one look at Michael and known he was the one. It'd been his eyes. Dark brown with slashing eyebrows above, they looked intense . . . but kind. All of his five-star reviews had only cemented her decision. Looking like the hottest K-drama star ever didn't hurt, either. Well, except for now, that was. There was a good chance she might throw up her dinner into the sink.

Through the mirror, she saw him step into the doorway and lean against the jamb. That motion alone was so sexy, she felt her heart trip, stumble, and scramble to continue beating. He walked into the bathroom and stopped behind her, his eyes locked on hers in the mirror. When she wasn't wearing her heels, he was more than half a foot taller than her. She wasn't sure if she liked feeling this small.

"Can I take your hair down?" he asked.

She nodded once. Within seconds, the tension on her scalp released, and her hair tumbled free. Her black hairband landed on the countertop before he eased his fingers into her hair, separating the tendrils so they fell to her shoulders and down her back. She vibrated with tension as she waited for him to initiate intimacy and send her body into nervous lockdown. It was going to happen, and then he'd see what he was working with.

A black imperfection on his bicep caught her eye, and she turned around to inspect it closer. She lifted a hand to touch it but stopped before making contact. She never touched people without permission. "What is this?"

His lips curved with a slow, crooked grin, showing off perfect white teeth. "My tattoo."

Her throat worked on an involuntary swallow, and a wave of heat swept over her. She'd never seen the point of tattoos. Until now. Michael with a tattoo was just about the hottest thing she could imagine.

Her fingers itched to pull his sleeve up farther, and she wavered over his arm until he caught her hand in his and pressed it to his skin. An electric jolt shot from her fingertips straight to her heart. He looked so perfect, like carved stone, but his skin was smooth and hot, firm but giving, *alive*.

"You can touch me," he said. "Anywhere."

Even as the invitation thrilled her, it gave her pause. Touching was such a private thing. She didn't understand how he was able to do it so well with people he didn't know.

"Are you sure you're okay with this?" she asked.

That crooked grin returned in full force. "I like being touched."

When she continued to hesitate, he drew his sleeve up himself, exposing black ink marks that swept across his upper arm, over his shoulder, and disappeared beneath his T-shirt. The tattoo had to be quite large because the shape hadn't even begun to materialize. Just how much of him did it cover?

The swell of his muscles distracted her from further investigating. She'd never touched hard rounded flesh like this before. She wanted to touch him all over. And his scent. How was it she was just noticing it now?

"Are you wearing cologne?" she asked as she filled her lungs.

He stiffened. "No, why?"

She leaned as close as she could without burying her face against his neck, seeking out more of that intoxicating scent. "You smell really, really good. What is it?"

Where was that scent coming from? It seemed to be everywhere on him, but too light. She craved a more concentrated dose.

"Michael?"

A funny look crossed his face. "It's just me, Stella."

"*You* smell this good?"

"Apparently. You're the first to comment on it."

"I want this smell all over me." As the words left her mouth, she worried she'd said the wrong thing. That statement had sounded a little too personal, a little strange. Would he notice how strange she really was?

He bent down so his lips hovered a hairsbreadth away from her ear and whispered, "Are you sure you're bad at sex?"

"What do you mean by that?"

"It means so far you're very good at it."

Her fingers flexed on his arm, and she battled the urge to press herself against him like a stripper on a pole. It bewildered her. She was not at all stripperish, and unlike him, she actively disliked touching. But she craved connection so much she hurt with it. "So far we haven't done anything yet."

"You're very good at the talking part."

"I've had sex. There isn't a talking part."

A spark danced in his eyes. "There's *definitely* a talking part."

Please, don't let there be a talking part. There was no hope for her if it involved talking. "So far—"

He gathered her hair to one side and brushed a fleeting kiss behind her ear. It happened so quickly that by the time her body tensed up he'd already pulled away. When he didn't move to repeat the caress, her muscles relaxed once again. The place where he'd kissed her burned with awareness.

Without touching her skin, he stroked his fingers over her hair. Slow, measured movements that swept from her crown, past her neck, and down her back. The motions calmed her even as they put her on edge.

"I think you should kiss me," he said in a husky voice.

Her heart squeezed tight, and her skin pricked with

panic. She was a horrible kisser. Her awkward attempts were sure to embarrass them both. "On the mouth?"

The corner of said mouth kicked up. "Wherever you want to. The mouth is usually a good place to start."

"Maybe I should brush my teeth. I can do that right—"

He pressed a thumb to her lips, silencing her, but his eyes were gentle. That touch, too, was gone before it fully registered in her brain. "Let's try this another way. Do you want to see my tattoo?"

Her mind eagerly switched gears, jumping from fear straight to excitement. "Yes."

With a small smile that was half amusement and half self-deprecating, he pulled his white T-shirt over his head and tossed it on the counter.

Stella's mouth went lax as she filled her eyes with him. A dragon's head, its mouth open in midroar, covered the entire left half of his wide, sculpted chest. The ink on his shoulder and arm formed one of the creature's claws. The intricate scales of its body worked diagonally across his abs and disappeared inside his jeans.

"It's all over you," she commented.

"It is. Here . . ." He captured her right hand and pressed it to the ink over his heart. "Feel it."

"You don't mind?" When he shook his head, she bit her lip and tentatively settled her left hand on his chest as well.

Her touch was timid at first, but when he didn't object, she grew bolder. She pushed her hands across his firm chest, enjoying the ridges of defined muscle and the smoothness of his hairless skin. Tactilely, she couldn't discern a difference between his inked skin and his unmarked skin. *Fascinating.*

Her fingertips bumped down his abdomen, and she counted under her breath, "—Five. Six. Seven. Eight." Her fingers met the waistband of his jeans, and his stomach muscles flexed and rippled as he took a breath.

"You couldn't have a regular six-pack? You had to make it eight?"

He rolled his eyes as his lips curved. "Are you complaining, Stella?"

"Nothing to complain about. I had no idea I liked tattoos until now."

"So you like it?"

She thought that should be obvious, so she didn't answer. Besides, it was getting difficult to concentrate. The sight of his perfect athlete's body and his excessive tattoo, the feel of his hot skin, and his delicious scent overwhelmed her senses.

"Can I take your glasses off? Will you still be able to see without them?"

She swallowed and nodded. "I'm nearsighted, so I won't be able to see things far away, but that's all right because—"

He slipped her glasses off. A soft clinking sounded as he set them on the counter behind her. The hotel suite and everything around her became a soft blur. Only he stood out in sharp focus. The solid feel of him against her palms grounded her.

"It might be easier to kiss me if you wrap your arms around my neck," he suggested.

Her fingers twitched as she dragged them across the decadent expanse of his stomach and over his hard chest. After looping her arms stiffly around his neck, she said, "Done."

"Closer."

She inched forward.

"More."

She inched forward again, stopping before their bodies could come flush together.

"Stella, *closer*."

Understanding broke over her, and she settled herself against him. They were touching almost everywhere. Only the thin layers of her clothes separated them. Her nerves jangled, and panic threatened, but he didn't rush her. He stood still, watching her with his patient, *kind* eyes. Against all odds, she relaxed.

"Are you still with me?" he asked.

Coming up onto her tiptoes, she aligned their bodies until they fit . . . just right. Her heart crashed in a crazy rhythm against her sternum, but she was still in control of herself—because, clever person that he was, he'd given her that control. "I'm okay."

When he closed his arms carefully around her, his heat sank through her shirt and warmed her skin. The pressure of his undemanding embrace reached deep inside her, calming her and loosening knots she hadn't known were there. Maybe she was better than okay.

She would gladly pay his escorting fee again just for him to hold her like this. This was heavenly. She burrowed her face into his neck and breathed him in. She skated her hands over his bare skin as she tried to nestle closer to him. If he could hold her a little tighter . . .

Something hard prodded her belly, and she drew her head back.

"You can ignore that," he said.

"We haven't kissed or anything. How can you . . . ?"

Hooded eyes searched hers as he lowered a hand from between her shoulder blades to the small of her back. The heat of his palm penetrated her clothes, and all the fine hairs on her body stood up. "This goes two ways, Stella. You like the feel of me. I like the feel of you."

That was a novel concept to her. Intimacy almost always was a one-way thing with her. The men enjoyed it—sort of. She did not.

She was enjoying this, however. It made her feel brave and reckless.

Her gaze locked on his lips again, and her blood raced with something new: anticipation. "Will you show me how to be a good kisser?"

"I'm not certain you aren't one already."

"I'm really not."

His mouth was inches away, but she couldn't quite push

herself to kiss it—even though she wanted to. She'd never initiated a kiss before. In the past, the men had just kind of . . . fallen on her.

"Can I tell you where to kiss me?" she whispered.

A smile slowly stretched his lips. "Yes."

"M-my temple."

His breath fanned over her ear, sending goose bumps down her neck, before he pressed a kiss to her left temple. "Now where?" The words were spoken softly against her skin, each one a caress.

"My cheek."

The tip of his nose grazed her skin as he moved lower. He kissed the hollow beneath her cheekbone. "Now?" he asked without lifting his lips.

So close. She could hardly breathe. "The corner of my m-mouth."

"Are you sure? That's very close to being a real kiss."

Impulsive impatience seared through her, and she sank her fingers into his hair, held him in place, and pressed a closed-mouth kiss to his lips. Bolts of sensation zigzagged straight to her chest. After a surprised hesitation, she did it again, and he took the lead, showing her how it was done, drawing the kisses out.

This was kissing. Kissing was glorious.

When his tongue slipped between her lips, she went stock-still. Not glorious anymore. His tongue. Was in. Her *mouth*. She couldn't stop herself from pulling away. "Is that absolutely necessary?"

He exhaled sharply, and his brow creased in puzzlement. "You don't like French kissing?"

"It makes me feel like a shark getting its teeth cleaned by pilot fish." It was weird and far too personal.

His eyes danced, and though he bit his lip, she could see a grin peeking around the edges of his mouth.

"Are you laughing at me?" Hot shame burned her face.

She ducked her head and tried to back up, but the bathroom counter dug into her spine.

The pressure of his fingertips on her chin made her face him again, leading her to believe he wanted eye contact. There were rules for that which she'd had to learn. Three seconds counted slowly in your head. Less and people thought you were hiding something. Longer and you made them uncomfortable. She'd gotten passably good at it. Now, however, she couldn't bring herself to do it. She didn't want to see what he thought of her. She shut her eyes.

"I was laughing at your analogy. You're very funny."

"Oh." She hazarded a glance at his face and found sincerity there. People said that to her sometimes, and she never understood it. She didn't know how to be funny. It only ever happened by accident.

"Instead of thinking of sharks at the dentist, think of me caressing your mouth. Concentrate on how it *feels*. Will you let me show you?"

She nodded once. That was why they were here, after all.

He bent toward her mouth once again, and she fisted her hands against his chest and braced herself. Instead of pushing his tongue between her lips, he kissed her like he had before, more drugging closed-mouth kisses. *These* she could do. *These* she liked. They rained upon her mouth in an unhurried procession. Some of her stress drained away, and her fingers uncurled.

Wet heat stroked over her bottom lip. His tongue. She knew it was his tongue, but closed-mouth kisses made her forget. Another stroke, and shivery sensations cascaded outward. More kisses. In between aching presses of his lips, his tongue caressed her, making her skin tingle.

Soon he was seducing her mouth, stroking her bottom lip, the top lip, teasing the crease. Maybe she parted her lips. Maybe she *wanted* him to go further. But he didn't. The closed-mouth kisses she'd liked so much in the beginning were no longer enough. She tried to capture his tongue, to take it into herself, but he evaded her. He brushed at her lips with maddening strokes, dipped inside for the merest second, withdrew, and she kneaded his shoulders in frustration.

Over and over again, he gave her a brief taste of salt and heat, and then retreated. Without consciously deciding to do it, she sealed her mouth with his and touched her tongue to his. His taste flooded her senses. Butterflies exploded in her stomach and sped through her veins. Her legs went weak, but his arms tightened around her, keeping her from falling.

He sucked on her bottom lip and laved the sensitized skin before taking her mouth again. The room began spinning, and she realized she'd forgotten to breathe.

Coming up for air, she said, "Oh my God, you taste good."

For a moment, he stared at her mouth like she'd taken something that he wanted back. He blinked the expression away, and a gravelly chuckle escaped kiss-reddened lips she wanted to touch with her fingertips. "Do you always say exactly what you're thinking?"

"Either that or I don't talk." No matter how she tried, she couldn't overcome it. Her brain simply wasn't wired for social sophistication.

"I like hearing what you're thinking. Especially when I'm kissing you." But instead of kissing her again, he stepped away and tugged on her hand. "Come on. I don't want to bruise you on this counter."

That was when she noticed the hard granite pressing into her back. As she let him lead her from the bathroom, she glanced at her hazy reflection in the mirror. She didn't recognize that girl with the flushed cheeks and wild hair, could hardly believe she'd kissed a man and enjoyed it. Was it possible she'd be able to conquer what came next, as well?

Michael rubbed his lips to hide a grin as Stella balanced on the very edge of the bed and folded her hands in her lap. If he kissed her right now, she'd fall to the floor. She was the kind of girl who got weak when she was hot. He fucking loved that. Every bit of effort it had taken to get past her guard had been worth it.

She'd been pretty before, but like this, she was almost too much. Freed from her tight bun, her hair framed her face in large ringlets. Arousal brightened her chocolate eyes, and her lips were swollen from his kisses. Gorgeous. He almost wished they were meeting again after tonight.

Instead of sitting next to her, he stretched out near the center of the king-sized bed, propped himself up on an elbow, and patted the area next to him. After a momentary hesitation, she crawled across the bed and lay down next to him, her body corpse-straight and her eyes staring ahead. Her pulse drummed under her jaw, and she stiffened like she was bracing herself for an attack.

That wouldn't do.

"I'm going to kiss you again." Because he sensed she needed to be forewarned, he added, "*French* kissing."

"Okay."

He leaned over her and kissed her, starting right back at the beginning with innocent brushes of their lips and teasing licks before taking her mouth once again. She really had no idea how to kiss, but it was entertaining feeling her learn. What she lacked in skill she made up for in pure enthusiasm.

She kissed him with untrained strokes of her tongue, following his mouth when he tried to pull back so he could dim the lights further. Experience told him she'd be much more comfortable with sex if the lights were low.

He tried to reach for the switch without breaking the kiss, but she buried her fingers in his hair. If there was one thing that drove Michael crazy—aside from BJs—it was having a woman play with his hair. Her nails scraped over his scalp with just the right pressure to send pleasure shooting down his spine, and he forgot about the light.

He ran his hand along the length of her body, cupped the curve of a small breast. Even through the layers of her shirt and bra, he could feel the firm ball of her nipple. He wanted to pinch it, love on it, but there was too much fabric in the way. He kissed her harder, and she arched into his body. If she hadn't been wearing a pencil skirt, he would have spread her thighs. He'd bet everything she was wet for him.

Leaning back and pulling cool air into his lungs, he assessed his handiwork. She breathed through parted red lips that glistened, and her eyes were pure sex. She was ready for more.

He fingered the button at her collar and slipped it free.

It was like flipping a switch; the change was that dramatic. One moment, her body was loose and languorous. The next, she was tense as a stretched rubber band. The color bled from her face. Her expression went from sensual to downright scared. She dropped her hands to her sides and balled them into fists.

"Stella?"

She gulped down a ragged breath and started unbuttoning her shirt. "I'm sorry. Let me get them." With uncoordinated fingers, she loosed one button, then another.

He covered her hands with his to halt her progress. "What are you doing?"

"Undressing."

"I'm not going to have sex with you when you're like this." It was wrong. He'd never had sex with a woman who wasn't one hundred percent into it, and he wasn't going to start now.

She turned onto her side to face away from him, and her chest shook. Dammit, she was crying. He lowered his hands toward her before hesitating. Would his touch help her or make it worse? Fuck it. He had to do something. He couldn't let her cry like this. Tears gutted him like nothing else. He wrapped himself around her. When she tried to shrink away, he held her tighter. What the hell? It had just been *one button*.

"I'm sorry. I didn't mean it like that. What happened? Did someone . . . hurt you? Is that why you tensed up on me?" The thought of someone assaulting her sent a murderous rage through Michael's brain, and adrenaline spiked, preparing him for a superb ass-kicking.

She dug her palms into her eyes. "No one hurt me. I'm just like this. Can you please continue and establish the baseline?"

"Stella, you're trembling and crying." He stroked tear-soaked tendrils away from her face.

She scrubbed at the moisture and took a hard breath. "No more crying."

"Other men had sex with you when you were like this?" He strove to sound gentle, but the words came out harsh. The thought of some asshole sweating over her while she was pale and terrified made his fists itch.

"Three."

"Goddamned piece-of-shit assho—"

His words dried up when she turned around to face him with a wounded expression.

"No, I'm not talking about you. You're not the problem. It's those men. Me." A wrinkle formed between her eyebrows, and he smoothed it out with a fingertip. "You need someone to go slow with you."

"You *have* been going slow with me. The others were done by now."

"I don't want to hear about the others," he bit out.

She looked away and held the folds of her shirt together. "What now?"

Michael had no idea. Whatever it was, it had to be *ultra* slow. He looked around the hotel suite for inspiration, and the large TV mounted on the wall across the bed grabbed his attention. "A movie and cuddling. We can try for the baseline afterward."

Her face became pained. "I don't really like cuddling."

"You can't be serious." All women were suckers for it. Even he liked cuddling. At least, he had back before he'd started escorting. Cuddling with clients was something he tolerated at best, but his instincts told him this was something she needed.

"I might like it with you, I suppose. It's your smell, I think. Your body wages biological warfare on me."

"So you're saying I'm your Achilles' heel?" He kind of liked the sound of that. They'd never see each other after tonight, but maybe she'd remember him. He knew he'd remember her.

Instead of smiling, as he thought she would, she searched his face. She looked into his eyes for a split second before she got out of bed and padded to the bathroom. After several moments inside, she returned wearing her glasses and holding his now neatly folded T-shirt. She set it on the nightstand, picked up the remote, and sat on the far edge of the bed, turning the TV on. As she flipped through the viewer guide, her expression was cool with concentration. Dressed in professional business attire, she could have been at a board meeting—but for the tangled, finger-swept state of her hair. "What do you want to watch?"

Her sudden distance shouldn't have bothered him. But it did. He wanted her back the way she'd been before. "No K-drama, please. My sisters force me to watch with them so they can laugh when I cry."

Her reserve melted as her lips curved, and everything was right again. "Do you really?"

"Who wouldn't? People die left and right. There are huge misunderstandings. That super cute pregnant heroine got hit by a car."

Her smile widened, though it looked almost shy. "That one is my favorite. How about something with more action and less drama?" The movie page for *Ip Man*, one of the best martial arts flicks ever, covered the screen.

"You don't have to watch this just for me."

She rolled her eyes and hit the purchase button.

"Wait," Michael said, taking the remote from her and pausing the film. "There's one more thing."

"What's that?"

"You need to take your clothes off."

S tella clawed at the unbuttoned folds of her shirt, feeling like the walls were closing in on her.

"Why?" she asked.

"Why not?"

Because she preferred being dressed, needed the tight restriction of fabric to feel safe. Because she didn't like her body. Because every time she was naked with a man, he ended up using and discarding her.

She wet her dry lips and said the most basic truth: "I'm not used to it."

Also, she was exhausted. So many new things had happened tonight, she felt shell-shocked. She desperately wanted to go home, but that would be pure cowardice. She was on a mission. Once she decided on something, she was just as single-minded as her mother—and her mascot, the pugnacious honey badger.

When his only response was the raise of an eyebrow, she asked, "Do you honestly think it will help?"

"I do." He propped the pillows up, kicked the covers down, and made himself comfortable. He looked so beautiful lying back against the pillows that for a moment Stella felt like she'd walked into a magazine cover. The shadows and light loved the striking lines of his face, the sharp edges of his man's body, and the dragon tattoo. It was difficult to believe *she'd* mussed his hair to such sexy perfection, even more difficult to believe that the place he'd reserved next to him was for *her*.

Drawing her shoulders back, she stood up and brought cold fingers to the buttons of her shirt. As the plackets came undone, her heart rate accelerated. Silence roared in her ears like jet engines preparing for takeoff. A film of sweat made the shirt adhere to her skin. After she tugged it free of her skirt and peeled it off, she shivered.

She could feel the weight of his eyes on her newly naked skin, and her hands fumbled on the side zipper of her skirt. Her fingers were so stiff it took three attempts before the small metal clasp came free. The skirt pooled around her ankles, leaving her in nothing but a simple flesh-toned bra and matching panties.

Eyes on the wall, she said, "Maybe I should have gotten better lingerie. Mine are all like this."

He cleared his throat before asking, "They're all that same color?"

"It's the most functional color."

She winced at how boring she sounded and hazarded a glance in his direction, but he didn't look put out by her underwear choices. Maybe some of his clients preferred granny panties. Those had a definite time and place. At least she wasn't wearing those right now.

"You can leave those on if you want. I'm here for you, Stella. Don't forget you have the final say on everything we're doing."

Her stomach untightened a fraction, and she adjusted her glasses and nodded. After draping her clothes on the nightstand next to his folded T-shirt—which she'd spent a good minute covertly breathing in like rubber cement inside the bathroom—she crawled onto the bed and sat next to him.

He eased an arm behind her and pulled her close so their sides came flush together. "Rest your head against my shoulder."

Once she did as he bid, he unpaused the movie. The opening credits rolled, and dramatic theme music played. She couldn't focus even though it was Donnie Yen, and, in her mind, he was better than Jackie Chan, Chow Yun Fat, and Jet Li put together. She was on the verge of hyperventilating, and her muscles were so tense, she was one large impending charley horse.

Michael ran his hand up her sweat-misted arm and stared down at her with concerned eyes. "Are you too hot? Do you want me to turn the AC on?"

Her chest constricted. "I'm sorry. I can shower."

She rocked forward to get up, but he stopped her, wrapping his arms tightly around her and settling her over his lap. Their skin was touching everywhere—her cheek on his chest, his arms around her shoulders, her side to his front—and she was achingly conscious of the dampness of her perspiration. He had to think she was disgusting. She squeezed her eyes shut as she tolerated the embrace. She didn't know how much more of this she could take.

"Relax, Stella," he whispered. "I don't mind sweat, and I like holding you. Watch the movie. He's about to have his first fight."

He clasped one of her hands in his, interlaced their fingers, and held on with firm pressure.

As he pretended to watch the movie—she somehow sensed she had his full attention—she stared down at their hands, noting the contrast of his tanned olive skin against her own. Like the rest of him, his hands were beautiful works of art with long fingers and strong veins on their backs. She frowned as her palm registered the scrape of calluses.

She found his free hand and opened it up. One large callus covered the base of his palm while three smaller ones decorated the space beneath his middle, ring, and pinky fingers. She traced her fingertips over the hard patches of skin.

"What are these from?" She couldn't imagine how escorting gave him calluses like this.

"They're sword calluses."

"You're kidding."

That lopsided grin stretched over his mouth. "Kendo. Actual sword fighting is nothing like in the movies, though. Don't get too excited."

"A-are you good at it?"

"I'm okay. It's just for fun."

She couldn't quite see him kicking ass with a face so pretty, but she had to admit the idea thrilled her. "Can you do the splits?"

"It's my secret talent."

"I'd think sword fighting was your secret talent."

"I have many," he said, running a fingertip down the bridge of her nose before lightly pinching her chin.

"What are they?"

He merely smiled and fixed his gaze on the TV. "Watch. It's getting to the part where he lays down the smack."

It was on the tip of her tongue to ask the question again, but she knew that was rude. He'd purposely refrained from answering. She realized then she knew almost nothing about him. Before, he'd said he only scheduled Friday nights. That left a whole lot of time for another life. What did he do when he wasn't escorting? Aside from martial arts. Or did he train and work out all day, seven days a week?

Maybe he did precisely that. You didn't get a body like his doing nothing. He could be one of those guys who woke up at dawn, swallowed five raw eggs, and ran stadiums. It was definitely worth it if he did—unless he got salmonella.

As pictures of him punching frozen slabs of meat flitted through her head, she forgot she was mostly naked. Her breathing evened out, and her body unwound. The pressure of his arms stayed firm, compressing and comforting, and the extraordinary events of the day caught up with her. His smell, the steady rhythm of his heart, and the low volume of *Ip Man* spanking his opponents lulled her to sleep.

Stella's eyes shot open, and she took in the bright interior of the hotel room. After groping at the surface of the nightstand, she found her glasses. The digital clock read 9:24 A.M. Her heart lurched.

She'd slept in. She *never* slept in.

When she sat up in bed, the blankets fell to her waist, and cool air touched her bare skin. She was wearing yesterday's underclothes. Alarm sirens wailed in her head as she realized she'd completely skipped her night routine. She hadn't flossed, brushed, showered, and put on pajamas. She had stuffed a dirty body into these clean sheets—well, they were definitely dirty sheets now. Good thing she didn't have to sleep in them again.

Michael stepped out of the bathroom, freshly showered with a white towel around his lean hips. His tattoo looked particularly sexy in the light of day. He grinned around his toothbrush. "Morning."

She clapped a hand over her mouth. Her breath had to be *rancorous*.

He strode casually across the room and dug through a

small overnight bag he must have retrieved from his car. It hadn't been with him last night. As he extracted fresh clothes from the bag, Stella watched the fluid bunch and play of the intricate muscles on his back, admired the twin grooves at the base of his spine. She wanted to touch her fingertips to those dents. Then she wanted to take the towel off and—

"It stops on my right thigh," he said, glancing at her over his shoulder.

It? What was *it*?

Blinking furiously to clear her mind, she noticed that his tattoo wrapped around his hip, disappeared beneath the towel, and peeked out behind his knee. The dragon had wound itself around his torso and one of his legs. She imagined she'd be doing the same thing throughout the course of their arrangement—which they still needed to discuss.

She parted her lips to speak, but the chalkiness of her mouth overwhelmed her. She jumped out of bed, only then remembering she was all but naked, grabbed the first article of clothing she saw—his white T-shirt from yesterday—and sprinted to the bathroom as she yanked it over her head.

Once inside, she lunged for her floss and ran the thread between all of her teeth. Twice. When nothing heinous came free, she breathed a sigh of relief and went about brushing at a more sedate pace.

He entered the bathroom, and she stepped aside so he could spit into the sink, feeling horribly self-conscious with toothpaste foaming from her mouth. Why couldn't she look sexy like him when she brushed her teeth? After rinsing out his mouth and patting it dry with a hand towel, he leaned toward her and kissed her cheek. He smelled of hotel soap, minty toothpaste, and . . . himself. That elusive scent still clung to him. She supposed it emanated from his pores. Lucky him. Lucky *her.*

As she continued brushing her teeth, keeping her eyes awkwardly glued to the bubbles in the sink, he left the bathroom. Pausing midbrush, she heard it: the rustle of fabric. He was getting dressed. That meant he was *naked*. Without a qualm, she rushed to the doorway and peered out.

Her lungs depressed when she saw him pulling clean jeans over his boxers. He yanked on a tight black T-shirt and sat down to pull on black socks. He had to be leaving soon.

She hurried to finish brushing her teeth and caught him just as he tied his last shoelace.

"We have to talk," she said.

The look on his face as he straightened in the chair made her stomach bottom out. He was going to back out. Last night had been a fiasco filled with panic attacks and fear sweat, and he wanted nothing to do with her now. She tightened her lips when they threatened to tremble. It had been bad, but there had been good parts. Hadn't there?

She'd thought she had a chance.

"I have something at ten I shouldn't miss." He stood, looped the strap of his bag over his shoulder, and walked to her with a loose stride. His eyes were heartbreakingly kind as he looked at her.

Or was it pity? She hated pity.

"I need you to tell me if we're moving forward with the lessons or not."

He shook his head with a sad smile. "I'm afraid not. I'm sorry."

Her heart plummeted, but she couldn't bring herself to regret last night. He'd gotten her to kiss him—*really* kiss him, not lie there and cringe as he stuck his tongue in her mouth. "I'll leave you another five-star review."

"I don't deserve it. I never sealed the deal. The agency doesn't issue refunds, but I'd be happy to return my share of the commission. Give me your account—"

"No, no refund," she said firmly. "Thanks, but no. I'm sure you had to work harder with me than most of your other clients."

"Not really, no."

She interlaced her fingers and stared down at the floor. She did *not* want to ask this, but she had to. "I know you need to go, but first, could you . . . recommend . . . a colleague who you think would work well with me?"

"After last night, you still want to go forward with these crazy lessons?"

"They're not crazy, but yes, I plan to move forward." She forced her eyes up to his stony face and took a determined breath. "Maybe if you think about it a while, you'll remember someone who's . . . patient, like you, a-and doesn't mind sweat or—"

He took a half step toward her, and his jaw worked for a moment before he said, "Girls like you don't need escorts. Girls like you have boyfriends. You need to get this idea out of your head."

Burning anger pulsed through her body, immobilizing her. He didn't know anything about girls like her. "That's completely untrue. Girls like me intimidate boyfriends away. Girls like me have never been asked out by a single boy. Girls like me have to find their own way, *make* their own luck. I've had to fight for every success in my life, and I'm going to fight for this. I'm going to get good at sex, and then I'll finally be able to entice the right person into being mine."

"Stella, it doesn't work that way. You don't need these lessons."

"I don't agree with you. Please, think about it? I trust your judgment." She rushed to her purse, extracted a business card, and scrawled her cell number on the back. Placing it in his hand, she said, "I'd really appreciate it. Thank you."

He stuffed the card into his back pocket with a hard jab of his hand. "What will you do if I don't give you a name?"

She shrugged. "My selection process was pretty good the first time around. I'll just go through the escort listings again."

"Do you know how many crack jobs there are in there? It's not *safe*." He lifted a hand like he wanted to touch her but fisted and withdrew it instead.

"Are you saying your agency's guarantee of safety is meaningless?"

He growled in frustration and raked his fingers through his damp hair, making it stand on end. "There's a vetting process with psych evals and background checks, but people can slip through the cracks. I don't want you to get hurt."

Stella tipped her chin up. "I'm not stupid. I have a Taser."

"You have *what*?"

She snatched the pink C2 Taser from her purse and handed it over.

"Holy hell, do you even know how to use it?" He stared at it with eyes so rounded she would have laughed if the situation had been any different.

"You slide the safety back, aim, and hit the button. It's very simple."

"Would you have used it on *me*?"

"I didn't, so clearly the answer is no."

When he rotated it and stared at it in horrified fascination, she grabbed it from him. *"Never aim it at yourself."* After plopping it in her purse, she crossed her arms and said, "As you can see, I have the situation under control, but I appreciate your concern."

The thought of perusing the escort ads again made her grind her teeth. None of those men interested her anymore. Once her mind was made up, it was *made up*. The only one she wanted was Michael, but she'd botched things so badly he couldn't stand to see her again. How was she supposed to get better if her problem kept driving away the people who could help her?

Her bitterness must have shown because his expression softened. "Stella, I don't do repeat sessions. Otherwise, I'd take you up on your offer."

"Why?" she asked on a frustrated exhalation.

"I used to do it in the past. A client got attached, and things blew out of control. The single-session policy has saved me and my clients a lot of grief."

"You mean you knew ahead of time you weren't going to accept?" Blackness threatened to spill over and stain her insides. She'd thought he was a potential solution to her problem. Now, it looked like it had been nothing but a one-night stand from the start.

He nodded curtly.

"Why did you stay last night, then? I was up front with you about what I wanted. All of the k-kissing and touching, my clothes, I did that for *nothing*." Her throat swelled so much that near the end, she could barely force the words out.

She pressed hot palms to her forehead, trying to deal with this betrayed feeling. The pain and shame were so unexpected, she had trouble breathing. Why had he made her do those things? Had it been a game? Had he thought it was funny?

How come she never understood people?

"I honestly didn't believe you," he said. "At most, I thought you had a confidence problem that would go away after we were together. Besides, you paid in advance. I wanted you to get your money's worth."

"You wanted to show me a good time."

"Well . . . yeah. That's why people hire me."

"But that's not why *I* hired you." She rubbed the bridge of her nose and righted her glasses, suddenly hollowed out and exhausted. "It doesn't matter. You should get going, or you'll be late."

As if from a distance, she was aware of her feet bringing her to the door and her palm gripping the handle, pulling it open.

He took a breath as if he meant to speak but ended up shutting his mouth before he could say anything. He swept past her and paused on the other side of the doorway, considering her. "I'm sorry to leave with things like this. Be safe, okay?"

She looked away from him and nodded.

"Good-bye, Stella."

He padded down the hall, and she shut the door. The locks engaged with a final click.

She should shower. She'd basically slept in her sweat last night. But when she touched her clothes, she realized she was wearing Michael's shirt. She pressed her cheek to her shoulder and inhaled his scent. After sniffing her arms and hair, she discovered it was all over her.

What did she do now?

Her body itched with the need to wash, but if she showered, that precious smell would be gone. And there wasn't ever going to be any more of it. This was it.

She sank to the floor and hugged her knees to her chest to keep the loneliness at bay. She ached so badly to be held it felt like a sickness had invaded her muscles and bones. As usual, her own arms provided little comfort. She'd give herself five minutes, and then she'd get ready for work. It was only Saturday morning, and she'd already had more weekend than she could handle. If she didn't find a way to occupy her mind, she'd spiral into something dark and bleak—was *already* spiraling.

Three quick knocks rapped on the door, and she stood up mechanically. It was probably housecleaning, checking to see if she'd left yet.

She opened the door, and Michael stared back at her with an intense gaze. His chest labored like he'd sprinted the entire way back from his car.

"Three sessions. That's the most I'll do," he said.

It took her a moment to understand that by sessions he meant lessons, but when she did, her heart sprinted so fast her fingers went numb. He was going to help her. Could three lessons possibly be enough to perfect sex? There was so much she had to learn, so much she was bad at, but what choice did she have? Maybe if they planned everything out very carefully . . .

With her limbs frozen in shock, all she could manage to say was, "Okay."

He considered her, the muscles of his jaw taut. "If we do this thing, you have to promise not to go crazy when it ends."

"I can promise that," she said through the roaring in her ears.

"I mean it. No stalking, no calling, no outrageous gifts. None of that." His fingers were tight around the strap of his bag as he awaited her response, and his expression was dead serious.

"Okay."

He unlooped the bag from his shoulders and let it fall to the ground before he stepped toward her, not stopping until her back was pressed against the open door. He flattened a hand on the door next to her face and leaned down. His gaze dropped from her eyes to her lips. "I'm going to kiss you now."

"Okay." He'd shaken her brain into malfunctioning, and apparently that was all she could say now.

He touched his lips to hers, and pleasure jolted to her heart, down her arms, down her legs. Tilting his head, he kissed her deeper. Once. Twice. Again. Until she sighed and leaned into him, tangled her fingers in his cool hair. He claimed her mouth with his tongue in a way that was new and familiar at once. She kissed him back with everything in her, trying to tell him all the things she wasn't articulate enough to say.

"God, Stella," he rasped against her lips, his dark eyes dazed and heavy-lidded. "You learned that fast."

Before she could respond, he took her mouth again. She forgot about the time, forgot about work, even forgot about her anxiety. His large body rubbed against hers, and she arched into him, reveling in his closeness.

Her phone buzzed with her mother's ring tone.

Michael tore away at once, flushed and breathing heavily. He sucked his bottom lip into his mouth as he stared deep into her eyes, looking like he was two seconds away from kissing her again.

"I should get that." She slipped inside, sat on the edge of the bed, and pressed the talk button on her phone with a shaky thumb. "Hello?"

"Stella dear, your father's—oh, hold on a second." Her father's deep voice rumbled on the other end, and Stella held the phone away from her ear as her parents discussed golf and lunch plans.

Michael approached her with a fluid-limbed gait. "I need to go, but we're on for next Friday."

"Next Friday," she confirmed with a nod.

Instead of leaving immediately as she expected, he leaned down and brushed a fleeting kiss to her mouth. "Good-bye, Stella."

She watched his departure in a dazed state. They were meeting again. In a week.

"Who was *that*?" Even with the phone several inches from her ear, Stella could hear her mother's surprise.

"That was . . . Michael." A breathless kind of nervousness filled her. She might like it that her mother had discovered her male visitor.

A brief silence ensued, followed by, "Stella dear, did you spend the night with a man?"

"It's not what you think. We didn't do anything. Other than kissing." The best kissing of Stella's life.

"Well, why ever not?"

Stella's mouth worked without issuing words.

"You're a mature adult, and you make good choices. Now, tell me all about this Michael."

Destroy. Defeat. Deceive.

Michael scanned his partner's black-clad form for weaknesses he could exploit. Right now, during the heat of the match, was the only time he gave free rein to the base, selfish instincts he battled daily. And it felt so fucking good.

No matter how hard he fought against it, at his core, he was just like his dad. The badness had been passed down in his blood.

He shoved and went for a head shot. When his partner's sword rose to block the strike, Michael pushed for that extra burst of speed and arched his weapon down. The tip of his sword cracked against his partner's side.

Clean point. Match over.

Everyone bowed and set their swords on the blue matted floor before kneeling. Michael hated this part of class, not because it meant practice was ending, but because it was time to remove his armor and return to his normal self.

This was the beauty of apparel. A suit transformed you into a certain kind of person. A T-shirt, a different kind of person. Black nightmare armor that hid your face behind an ominous metal cage, yet a different kind of person. The gear weighed thirty pounds, but he always felt lighter when he wore it.

As he shed layers, cold air touched his skin, and reality crept back into his head. Heavy thoughts stacked one upon the other like bricks, returning him to his regular burdened state. Responsibilities and obligations. Bills. Family. His day job. His night job.

After class officially ended, he put his gear in its place on the shelf along the back wall. Space was tight as fuck with five guys in the cramped changing room, and he didn't feel like waiting around, so he slipped his uniform off in the hallway. Nothing half the women in California hadn't already seen.

Two high school girls giggled and hurried into the women's room, and he rolled his eyes as he yanked a pair of jeans over his boxer briefs. Michael Larsen: now serving half the women in California plus two.

"We're probably going to have a bunch of new girl members next week now," said a voice Michael recognized as belonging to Quan, Michael's cousin and sparring partner.

"I'll let you teach them their strikes," Michael said as he retrieved a wrinkled T-shirt from his duffel bag and straightened.

"They might be disappointed."

"Whatever." He yanked his shirt on, trying and failing to ignore their contrasting reflections in the full-length mirror hanging on the wall.

Lots of girls went for Quan. With his buzzed head and the dense tattoos covering his arms and neck, he rocked that badass Asian drug lord image. You wouldn't guess he was paying his way through business school while helping his parents at their restaurant. Michael, on the other hand, was a pretty boy.

It wasn't a bad problem to have—it was paying the bills, after all—but people's responses got boring. Well, except for a certain economist someone's response. Stella's attraction to him had been obvious, but she hadn't looked at him like he was an expensive cut of meat. She'd looked at him like she saw no one else. He couldn't forget the way she'd kissed him once he'd earned her trust, the way she'd melted and—

When Michael caught the direction of his thoughts, he mentally punched himself in the dick. She was his client, and she had issues. It was fucked up to think of their sessions like this.

"If we have new students, I'll teach them. I don't mind," Khai, Quan's younger brother, offered. He still wore his uniform and practiced running strikes in front of the mirror, his pace fast but steady, like a machine.

Quan rolled his eyes. "He never minds. Even when they throw themselves at him. You should have seen the last one. She asked him out to dinner, and he said, 'No, thanks, I already ate.' 'Dessert then?' 'No, I don't eat dessert after class.' 'Coffee?' 'That will keep me up, and I have work tomorrow.'"

Michael couldn't help smiling at that. Khai reminded him a little of Stella.

As Quan shoved both of their weapons into a nearby storage box, he said, "Nice match. Bad day?"

Michael shrugged. "Just the same." He should be grateful. He *was* grateful. Everything would be fine if he could stop wanting all the things he'd given up. He didn't regret exchanging his old life for this one—he'd do it again—but at the same time, this wanting wouldn't stop. If anything, it was getting worse. Because he was a selfish bastard. Like his dad.

"How's your mom doing?"

He raked a hand through his hair. "Good, I guess. She says she likes her new meds."

"That's good, man." Quan squeezed his shoulder. "You should celebrate. Come out with me on Friday. There's this new club in SF called 212 Fahrenheit."

That actually sounded nice, and a rush of excitement burned over him. He hadn't been out without a client in forever.

The reminder of clients had him exhaling a heavy breath. "Can't. I have something."

"What?" Quan's eyes turned assessing. "Or do you mean who? You're always busy Fridays. Do you have a secret girl-friend you're scared of introducing to everyone?"

He snorted inwardly at the idea of taking a client to meet his family. Never going to happen. "Nah, no girlfriend. You?"

Quan laughed. "You know my mom. Do you think I'd subject a girl to that?"

Grinning, Michael picked up his bag and headed for the studio's front door, passing Khai, who hadn't stopped with his practice or slowed down this entire time. "Look on the bright side. If a girl meets your mom and doesn't run, you'll know you found a keeper."

As Quan followed him, he said, "No, then I'll have two scary-ass women in my life instead of one."

They both waved at Khai from the doorway, but, as usual, he was too focused to wave back.

Out in the parking lot, Quan climbed onto his black Ducati, shrugged into his motorcycle jacket, and propped his helmet on his knee before giving Michael a direct look. "You know I don't give a shit if you're into guys, right? Like, I'd be okay with that. Just so you know. You don't have to hide stuff like that from me."

Michael coughed and adjusted the position of his duffel bag's strap on his shoulder as an uncomfortable wave of heat boiled up his neck and singed his ears. "Thanks."

This was what happened when you kept secrets. People drew their own conclusions. He wondered briefly if he should just roll with it. There was no doubt in his mind his family would take that better than the truth. They didn't know about his escorting or the bills that necessitated the escorting. He planned to keep it that way.

He took a breath of air that smelled like exhaust fumes and blacktop, feeling touched by Quan's acceptance but also old and tired in his bones. "It means a lot to hear you say that, but I'm not, okay? I've just been . . . seeing . . . lots of people. No one I'd bring home, though." God no. "No one special."

As soon as that last comment came out, however, he wanted to retract it. He didn't know why, but it didn't feel right to lump his latest client in that category.

"Do me a favor and tell your mom and sisters, then. They've been gossiping about it with my mom and sister, and they keep asking me for the inside scoop. I'm going to be honest and say it was a little embarrassing telling them I have no idea what you do when you disappear." Quan kicked at a pebble on the ground, his face pensive, and Michael knew he was thinking back to times when they'd known everything about each other. Well, as much as guys ever told one another. Their moms were close sisters who had purchased homes two blocks apart and given birth to boys in the same year. As a result, Michael and Quan were closer than brothers. They used to be, anyway.

Michael rubbed the back of his neck. "I've been a crappy friend. I'm sorry."

"You went through all that shit." Quan gave him an understanding smile. "First with your asshole dad and the lawsuits and then with your mom's health. I get it. But things are better now, right? We should do stuff. Friday nights are best for me because I don't have work or class Saturday mornings. Your 'no one special' can hang with mine. Let me know." With that, Quan started his bike and pulled his helmet over his head.

After his cousin disappeared around the corner, Michael opened his car door and tossed his bag into the passenger seat. Things *were* a lot better now, but he wouldn't be double-dating with Quan anytime soon, not when he was fucking a different woman every Friday night. Well, not the next three Friday nights. Those were for Stella and sex lessons. He'd never expected to have the opposite role in his *Hot for Teacher* fantasy, but he admitted it excited him more than he would have thought.

He knew it was messed up, but Friday night couldn't come fast enough.

By the time Friday night rolled around, Stella was a jittery mess. She couldn't stop her fingers from drumming on the restaurant table as she waited for Michael to arrive. She'd arranged the appointment through the agency's mobile app—with the state-of-the-art setup, it was as easy as booking airline tickets, but without the frequent-flier miles. They'd sent a confirmation email, but that was the only indication she'd gotten that the date was still on. She couldn't help worrying that Michael had changed his mind.

She wished she had his cell phone number, but she figured he never gave that to his clients. It was too personal. Especially if his clients had the tendency to get obsessed.

Which was actually one of her main weaknesses, and a defining characteristic of her disorder. She didn't know how to be semi-interested in something. She was either indifferent . . . or obsessed. And her obsessions weren't passing things. They consumed her and became a part of her. She kept them close, wove them into her very life. Just like her work.

Going forward with Michael, she had to tread carefully. Everything about him pleased her. Not just his looks, but his patience and his kindness. He was *good*.

He was an obsession waiting to happen.

Hopefully, she could keep a cool head during the coming weeks. Perhaps it was for the best there were only three sessions. Once they were finished, she'd focus on someone she could actually have. Like maybe Philip James.

When Michael entered the hotel restaurant, she noticed right away. Tonight, he wore a perfectly fitted black suit over a white oxford shirt. No tie. His collar hung open, drawing attention to his Adam's apple and the sexy base of his throat. His gaze swept over the room and landed on her.

She looked down at the menu without seeing it, horribly aware of his slow advance toward her. *Keep a cool head.*

"Hello, Stella." He sat down across from her and folded his hands on the tabletop.

Her lungs drew in a slow breath, and she caught his light scent. Everything inside her turned over and sighed. With a sense of defeat, she lifted her eyes to his, counted to three, and looked away.

"Hello, Michael."

"Are you nervous already?"

She laughed slightly. "I've been nervous since Saturday."

"About that . . . Who was that on the phone when I left?"

Her lips tightened as she tried to suppress a smile. "It was my mom. Her name is Ann. She thinks you're my boyfriend now, by the way."

He pressed a knuckle to his grinning lips. "I see. Will that be a problem?"

"Actually, I think it's a good thing. Now that she thinks I have a boyfriend, she should stop trying to arrange blind dates for me."

"Ah, the mother-arranged blind date. I'm very familiar with those."

"Does that mean you don't have a girlfriend?" As soon as the question left her mouth, she winced. "I'm sorry. Forget I asked that."

She had no right to inquire about his personal life, but the intense curiosity burned inside her. She wanted to know everything about him. And if he *did* have a girlfriend, whoever that lucky girl was, Stella hated her guts.

"No, I don't have a girlfriend." He said it like it should have been obvious.

Thank God.

"What kind of girls does your mother try to hook you up with?"

He rolled his eyes. "Doctors, who else? And nurses. By now, I think my mom's tried to hook me up with the entire second-floor staff at the Palo Alto Medical Foundation."

Stella couldn't help being impressed. "That's really determined."

"That's nothing. You don't know my mom."

She forced a smile and focused on the menu. What did it say about her that she *wanted* to know his mom? No, wait, she knew the answer to that. It said she was nuts. Mothers were scary she-bears when it came to their sons, especially sons like Michael.

And Stella wasn't a doctor.

Enough of this. She wasn't dating Michael. It didn't matter what his mother thought of her. Stella was never going to meet the woman. She needed to get back to the matter at hand.

"Let's discuss my lessons," she said briskly.

"That's a good idea." Michael leaned back in his chair, looking at ease.

Stella tried to copy his relaxed air as she retrieved three folded sheets of paper from her purse. "Because we're pressed for time, I took the liberty of drawing up lesson plans. They're not set in stone. In fact, please suggest changes where you see fit. I have no idea if what I've written is feasible, but it helps me to keep things structured. I don't deal well with surprises."

Michael's expression went unreadable. "Lesson plans."

"Exactly." She pushed the salt and pepper shakers and candle aside. After placing her papers in the middle of the table, she smoothed the creases out with her fingertips and pointed at the first sheet, which was labeled *Lesson One*. "I put boxes next to each item so we can check things off as we go."

Eyes on the paper, he opened his mouth to speak, caught his breath, and tapped a finger to his lips. "Give me a moment."

LESSON ONE

☐ Hand Job Lecture and Demonstration
☐ Hand Job Practice
☐ Performance Review
☐ Missionary Intercourse Lecture and
   Demonstration
☐ Missionary Intercourse Practice
☐ Performance Review

Michael read and reread the clinical lesson plan, and surprise melted into amusement, which then dissipated as frustration crept over his back and up his neck. He curled his fingers and restrained the sudden urge to crumple Stella's papers into ugly balls. Irritated. He was irritated. Fuck if he knew why.

With words like *lecture* and *demonstration* involved, he should be getting off on this. It was exactly like having the teacher role in *Hot for Teacher*—except there was no "hot for" part.

"Who's going to check the boxes? You or me?"

"I can if you don't want to," she offered with a helpful smile.

A picture of her pausing in the middle of sex to put her glasses on and scribble notes on a legal pad flashed in Michael's head. Like he was a sexbot or a fucking science experiment.

"I notice there's no kissing," he said.

"I was under the impression we'd moved beyond that."

His eyebrows twitched. "How's that?"

"You said I'd picked it up, so it's best not to waste time on it. Kissing you makes it hard for me to think, and I really want to get this right. Beyond that, it feels like something people do when they're dating—which we're not. I want things to stay clear and professional between us." She took a prim sip of ice water and set the glass down, leaving a sheen of moisture on her pink lips—lips he wasn't allowed to kiss.

Her kisses weren't for him anymore. He was supposed to fuck her and let her jerk him off, but she was saving those soft lips for someone else. The thought made him almost violent, and he shoved his feelings down deep.

"You've watched *Pretty Woman* too many times. Kissing doesn't mean anything, and it's always best if you're not thinking too much in bed. Trust me," he said.

Her mouth thinned into a stubborn line. "This is too important for me not to think. I'd rather not kiss anymore if you don't mind."

Michael's irritation redoubled, and he forced his hands to relax before he popped all his blood vessels. How the hell had he gotten himself into this? Ah yes, he'd been worried about his escort colleagues taking advantage of her. Stupid of him. His life was complicated enough without worrying about his clients. This was exactly why he had the one-session policy.

He would have backed out—it was tempting—but he'd promised. He always carried through on his promises. It was his way of balancing out the universe. His dad had broken enough promises for the both of them.

"All right," he made himself say. "No kissing."

"Do the other plans look okay?" she asked.

He forced himself to read them and found them pretty similar, only she'd moved from hand jobs to blowjobs and changed the sexual positions.

Amused despite himself, he said, "I'm surprised you used the terms *doggy style* and *cowgirl*."

Her cheeks went bright red, and she adjusted her glasses. "I'm inexperienced, not clueless."

"Your plans are missing something important." He held his hand out, and she placed the pen in his palm with wary motions.

She tilted her head to the side as she watched him write *FOREPLAY* at the top of all the plans in capital letters. As an afterthought, he drew a box in front of each iteration with hard stabs of the pen.

"But why? I was under the impression men don't need it."

"You do," he said flatly.

She wrinkled her nose and shook her head. "You don't have to bother with me."

He narrowed his eyes. "It's not a bother. Most men like foreplay. I do. Getting a woman hot is satisfying as hell." Besides, he was *not* having sex with her if she wasn't ready. No fucking way.

Swallowing, she stared down at the menu. "So you're saying I don't have a chance to improve."

"What? No." His mind scrambled to figure out why she might say that and came up with nothing.

"You saw how I reacted. It was *one button*."

"And then you slept with me all night. You were basically naked, and you cling."

"Are you two ready to order?" the waitress interjected. Judging by the amused glimmer in her eyes, she'd caught the last part of their conversation.

Stella perused the dinner options, her nails picking at the fabric edging of the menu.

"We'll have the special," Michael said.

"Wise choice. I'll leave you to it." The waitress winked, gathered the menus, and disappeared.

"What's the special?" Stella asked.

"I have no idea. Let's hope it's not woolly."

A troubled frown bracketed her mouth, and she leaned forward hesitantly, meeting his eyes for the briefest second. "What exactly do you mean by 'cling'?"

Michael grinned. "It means you like to cuddle when you're asleep."

"Oh."

She looked so horrified, Michael couldn't help laughing. "I confess to liking it." Which was the truth, and unlike him. Cuddling was an obligatory thing he did for his clients because he understood they needed it. He usually spent the time counting the seconds until he could leave and go home to shower. Holding Stella had been nothing like that. They hadn't had sex, so there'd been nothing to wash away, and the trusting way she'd curled into him had made him feel things he didn't want to think about. Especially when she found it so distasteful. His irritation increased even further.

"Where does this leave us with regard to the lessons? How do we proceed when my limitations are such big road-blocks? By focusing on you, I thought I'd found a way around my problems."

"We're not going to go *around* your problems. We're going to go *through* them."

She crossed her arms and tapped out an unusual rhythm with her fingertips on her elbow. "How?"

"We're going to . . . unlock you." That made him sound like an arrogant jackass, but he hadn't gotten those five-star reviews by luck alone. When he'd lost his virginity at the ripe age of eighteen, he'd discovered he had a natural talent for fucking. Going pro had taken his skills to a whole new level.

"I don't think that's possible." She slanted her lips like she was listening to a used-car salesman.

"Did you think you'd like kissing?" And she *had* liked it—once she'd gotten over the pilot fish thing. There was hope for her. Girls didn't do that weak-in-the-knees, fainting heroine stuff when they weren't into sex. He just had to figure her out.

She tapped one of the foreplay boxes. "What happens if you try everything and I don't like it? We're under a pretty extreme time constraint."

"I don't think it'll come to that." But if it did, they'd deal with it then.

After a long stretch of silence, she said, "Let's try it your way, then."

Once the hotel door shut behind them, Michael toed off his shoes and ambled to the windows. He opened the drapes and was presented with a fine view of the medical building next door, the Palo Alto Medical Foundation. It reminded him of his mom, bills, responsibilities, and escorting commissions. Not really what he wanted to think about right now.

He yanked the drapes shut and turned around, locating Stella standing at the foot of the bed. She looked away from him and fiddled with the folded sheets of paper in her hands. Her lesson plans.

He imagined himself shredding them into confetti. He couldn't explain it, but he detested those lists. Instead of acting on the fantasy, he approached her, took the papers, and set them carefully on the nightstand. He found a narrow silver pen in the nightstand's drawer and put it on top of Lesson One. If she was clearheaded enough to check boxes tonight, he needed to analyze his technique. He dimmed the bedside lights.

"How should I—what should I—maybe I—" She gripped the collar of her shirt. "Should I undress?"

"I don't know. It's not in the lesson plan." Once the words were out, he wanted to take them back. Her lists annoyed the hell out of him, but he didn't need to belittle her. "I'm sor—"

"You're right. I didn't think to include that." She hurried past him to the nightstand. After she considered the list for a moment, she bent down and picked up the pen, demonstrating the only reason why a woman should wear a pencil skirt: to show off the perfectly rounded curves of her fine ass.

That had to be why it took so long for her cluelessness to register. She hadn't caught his rudeness or his sarcasm. Maybe she was one of those book-smart people who didn't know how to socialize, and he was being too hard on her. "If I told you your lesson plans are insulting, what would you do?" he asked quietly.

She looked at him over her shoulder with alarmed eyes. "Are there parts I should reword? I'd be happy to change things." She turned back to the lesson plan and skimmed her fingers over the lines at a thoughtful pace.

The ball of irritation in his chest loosened. He couldn't be annoyed with her when she didn't understand.

She worried the inside of her lip and tapped her fingers on the table with increasing speed before sending him an anxious look. "Should I have written something other than *Performance Review*? I hope you know when I wrote that, I meant *my* performance. There's nothing wrong with your performance. Even if there were, I wouldn't know. I'm not qualified in any way to judge—"

Before she could work herself into another panic attack, he said, "It was just a hypothetical question. Forget about it."

She seemed confused for a second, but she blinked the look away and released a relieved breath. "Oh, okay." After adjusting her glasses, she turned back to her papers and neatly wrote *Stella's* in front of each iteration of *Performance Review.*

That was a good reminder. This was about helping with Stella's performance. That was it. So what if she wasn't viewing this as the fulfillment of secret fantasies like his other clients did? He needed to take his own advice and stop thinking.

When she flipped to the second page in the pile, he shrugged out of his jacket, draped it over the arm of a chair, and unbuttoned his shirt. Tugging the tails free, he sat on the bed next to Stella. She snuck a quick glance at him, and her gaze dropped to the portion of skin revealed by his open shirt. The pen paused in midscrawl, clattered to the tabletop.

He smiled with satisfaction. Not so clinical now.

She squared her shoulders before she lifted her hands to her collar. Buttons came undone at a painstaking pace, and white fabric fluttered to the floor, followed by her gray skirt. The set of her jaw was determined as she let him look at her. And look he did.

He usually preferred women with bigger breasts, lusher hips, and rounded thighs. He liked their softness, the way they filled his hands. That was not Stella. Everything about her was modest. Wearing only a flesh-toned bra and panties, her petite body was composed of elegant shoulders and arms, a little waist that flared to gently curved hips, and shapely legs with delicate ankles. She wasn't what he'd thought he'd always wanted, but she was perfect.

"Take your bra off." His voice came out rougher than he intended, but he couldn't help it. He was dying to see the rest of her. She might not have fantasized about their time together, but he had.

Down at her sides, her hands fisted. "Is that necessary? They're not my best feature. They're small."

"Yes, it's necessary. Men like to see them even when they're small." And touch them. God, he wanted to touch them.

She grimaced, looking like she wanted to argue with him. When she reached behind herself and slid her bra off, he caught his breath.

Then he bit his lip as he grinned. Stella didn't seem to know it, but she had the kind of nipples men and babies dreamed about. Rosy-tinted areolas gave way to extravagantly protruding tips that—no question about it—had to stay pointed 24/7, hot or cold, rain or shine. Stella Lane, conservative economist, had porn star nipples. And he wanted them in his mouth.

"What now?" she asked in a near whisper.

He slipped his shirt off and tossed it on the far side of the bed. "I think you get to check a box."

She peeled her eyes from his chest and stared at him like he'd spoken another language. After several hard blinks, she shook her head and said, "Right."

Leaning over, she checked a box at the top of the list. She adjusted her glasses and paused. The glasses came off, and she pulled the tie from her hair and shook out the mass so it framed her face. Vulnerable brown eyes searched his before she focused on the wall to the side.

The air seeped from his lungs as his internal organs melted and the rest of him hardened. *So gorgeous.*

And scared. How did he ease her fear?

"Let me hold you."

She inched as close as she could get without actually touching him.

He suppressed a smile. "It might help if you sat on my lap."

Biting her lip, she crawled onto him and straddled his hips. Fuck, so close. That part of her, opened wide. He went hard in an instant but forced himself to take things slowly. This was about Stella. He expected her to sit stiff as a board until he thought up some kind of sorcery to make her relax, but she immediately settled in close and rested her cheek against his shoulder. When his arms encircled her, she released a ragged sigh and went boneless.

Seconds stretched into minutes, and he let himself savor the moment—not speaking, not fucking, not doing anything, just being with someone. The room was so quiet he heard the cars driving by outside. Talking voices passed their room, receded.

"Are you falling asleep again?" he asked finally.

"No."

"Good." He ran his fingertips down the length of her arm and smiled when goose bumps rippled outward. Nuzzling her neck, he breathed in the soft scent of her skin and kissed the sweet spot just behind her jaw. Her lips called to him, but instead of trespassing, he sucked on her earlobe and bit it, startling a shaky sigh from her.

"This is foreplay?" The breathy quality of her voice sent satisfaction curling through him.

"It is." Even though he knew the answer, he asked against her ear, "Do you like it?"

She shivered and burrowed closer to him as additional goose bumps dotted her skin. "Yes, but it's not what I expected."

"What did you expect?"

She shook her head.

"Tell me if you want me to stop or there's something specific you want." As he spoke, he threaded his fingers into her hair and angled her head back. He trailed kisses along her jawline, nipped her chin, and kissed the corner of her mouth.

Too close to the temptation of her lips. His body ached at the thought of taking her mouth in a deep kiss, and he almost did it despite everything. He'd been dreaming of that mouth all week. Feeling like he was swimming against the tide, he forced his lips down to the column of her throat.

"Touch me." He brought her hands to his chest.

She scraped her palms over him until they encountered his nipples. As if fascinated by the texture, she rubbed her thumbs on the hardening tips. His muscles tightened, and he shuddered with pleasure.

"Is that right?" she asked.

"I like that. And this." He cupped dainty breasts in his palms and pinched the nipples just so.

Her breath broke, and she gazed down at her chest. With his tanned hands on her pale skin and her decadent nipples captured between his fingers, it was an erotic sight, indeed. He couldn't resist pinching her again and enjoying her sharp intake of breath.

"Why does it feel so good when you do that?" The wonder in her voice had him grinning.

"Want to try something even better?" At her hesitant nod, he said, "Come up on your knees for me."

Her thighs flexed as she rose off his lap. Body stiff and breaths shallow, she settled her hands on his shoulders. Just as he'd planned, the new position brought her nipples to face level. Though, if she wasn't careful, she'd poke an eye out with those things. Only in his line of work was blindness by nipple assault a true hazard. To be honest, however, he didn't really feel like he was working. There was no fantasy playing in his head, and he wasn't telling himself a new lie every fifteen seconds. This moment, this woman, and his undeniable attraction to her were all real.

He smoothed his hands up and down her back until her muscles relaxed beneath his palms. That was when he gave in and kissed the underside of one breast. She curled her fingers, and her nails pricked his skin.

Pulling back, he asked, "Are you okay, Stella?"

She cleared her throat twice. "Tell me what you're planning. Please."

"I'm going to suck on your pretty nipples and lick them with my tongue."

Her grip tightened on his shoulders. "That was a bit more graphic than I was expecting."

"How would you have said it?" He ran his mouth from the underside of her breast up to the place where pale skin gave way to dark areola.

"I don't know what—"

He covered her nipple with his mouth and sucked hard.
"Michael."

The sound of his name falling from her lips was just as
unexpected as it was hot. He pulled her closer so he could
feast on her. No man could stay sane with tits like this in
his face, in his mouth, rolling on his tongue. He could play
with these for days. Relinquishing one, he licked his way to
the second.

She worked her fingers blindly through his hair, twisted
and arched her back with unconscious demand. Stella was
loving this, losing her genius mind over his caresses.

Before he knew what he was doing, he dragged his lips
up her throat, along her jaw, back toward her mouth. He
caught himself at the last second and pressed their cheeks
together as he mentally shook himself. He was seriously
fucked up. She'd said she didn't want it, and he kept—

Their lips touched. He stiffened from the electric shock of
it. She stroked his bottom lip with her tongue, and his instincts took over. He claimed her mouth like a starved man.

Her taste, her softness, her nails on his scalp, kiss after
kiss after kiss.

"I'm sorry. I know I said no kissing." She kissed him
again. "But I couldn't resist. I thought about kissing you all
week." Her words sank into him. He hadn't been the only
one, after all. Another drugging kiss. "And now, I can't
seem to stop." A murmuring sound hummed in her throat
as she kissed him yet again.

"Then don't stop."

Michael twined his tongue with hers, and her body went
soft in his arms. She undulated her hips against the aching
bulge beneath his fly and scraped her nipples over his chest.
He bit back a groan. He hadn't wanted a woman like this
in . . . Had he ever wanted a woman like this?

When he drew back, her lips were parted on soundless
gasps of desire. It took a moment for her eyes to clear enough

to focus on him, and he expected her to turn around and check another box off her list. Instead, she wrapped her arms around his neck and pressed close, holding him. She crushed her lips against his temple.

A shocking sense of being cherished spread through him. She wasn't acting like what happened between them was services rendered for payment received. She was acting like it meant something, like she cared, maybe even about him.

Another hotel room, another bed, and another client in his arms. It was a regular Friday night. Only he'd never felt so exposed, so raw, and he still wore his goddamned pants.

This was supposed to be plain fucking. There wasn't supposed to be any caring. He couldn't keep doing this if he cared. Caring would turn the escorting into cheating, and he refused to cheat. Time to shake this nonsense out of his head and get down to business.

Michael's weight settled between Stella's legs. Icy coldness dug into her belly, jolting her back to reality. Metal. His belt buckle.

They'd fallen off track. What were they supposed to be doing? She called up the list in her head. Hand jobs. It was time to learn hand jobs.

He trailed kisses to her neck, leaving her mouth free for talking, but by that time, she couldn't remember what she'd been about to say. His teeth scraped her skin, and shivers cascaded over her body. Her nipples tightened to the point of hurting, but warm palms soothed them. He flicked his tongue at one tip before he drew on her again, making her toes curl.

A rough hand skated down her stomach and slipped beneath the waistband of her panties. Clever fingers caressed her with bold strokes. He was touching her *there*. Right where she needed him to, even though she hadn't known it. Men had touched her before, but it hadn't felt like this. She only responded like this when she was alone, and never with this intensity.

"Stella, you're drenched." With each syllable, his lips grazed her stiff nipple. A hot exhalation gusted over her hungry flesh before he closed his teeth around her and bit with care.

Her body clenched hard, clenched even harder when he pressed a finger deep, filling her. He massaged her with lazy swirls of his thumb, and she started trembling. He licked her tortured nipple back into the heat of his mouth, and that was all it took. She climbed quick and sharp toward release.

And it scared the hell out of her.

She clawed at his wrist. *"Stop, stop, I'm not ready."*

As he pulled away, she dug her heels into the mattress, propelling herself to the far side of the bed. She hugged a pillow to her chest to hide her nakedness. Its coolness helped to dampen her arousal, and she took deep breaths. The impending orgasm retreated.

Michael's face was a mask of slack-jawed incomprehension as he considered her. Her cheeks burned, and shame weighed down on her chest. She had to be the worst client he'd ever had. When he lifted a hand, panic spiked and she backed up farther.

He dropped his hand. "Stella, calm down, I won't . . . touch you. Not if you don't want it."

She clutched at the pillow. "I know. I'm sorry. I just . . ."

"What did I do wrong?"

"Nothing."

His eyebrows rose in patent disbelief.

"I've never orgasmed with another person," she confessed.

He parted his lips, shook his head, started to speak, shook his head again. "Does that mean you've never . . . at all?"

Her face burned so hot, if she had been wearing her glasses they would have fogged up. "I have. By myself."

"You don't like it?" he asked in bewilderment.

"No, I do." She exhaled a tight breath and sifted through her thoughts, trying to structure a coherent explanation. "I just feel safer experiencing that alone. And I've had sex before—very bad sex. I spent the time watching as the men grunted and sweated and heaved over me. To be honest, it disgusted me. I wanted the sex to bring me closer to someone, but it only made me feel more distanced. I don't want to do that to *you*."

"Not even close. I was right there with you, loving it."

She made an exasperated sound. "I'm paying you to say those things. Well, you think that's what I'm paying for. That's not what I want."

"Do I *look* like I'm disgusted by you?" He waved a hand in the vicinity of his hips, where an impressive bulge strained at the fly of his pants.

She pursed her lips as she kept silent. If she spoke right now, chances were high she'd say The Wrong Thing. He was a seasoned escort. His body probably took commands like a show dolphin.

"You think I'm a liar." A predatory light shone in his eyes, and he crawled over the wrinkled bedcovers toward her.

She backed up reflexively.

And fell off the bed.

As she rubbed at her head, he peered at her over the side of the mattress. "Are you okay?"

Her throat clogged with embarrassment, and all she could manage was a curt "Fine."

He assessed her ungraceful, ground-crumpled form for a long moment. "I think we should call it a night."

She leaned against the wall and hugged her legs to her chest. The unchecked boxes of the lesson plan weighed on her, but she needed to understand and untangle all the emotions clashing inside her head before she could move forward. "Do you mind?"

He shook his head. Without a word, he stood, pulled his

shirt back on, and did the buttons. She swallowed a protest as he covered up skin and muscle she'd been too preoccupied and rattled to properly appreciate.

After he put on his shoes and shrugged into his suit jacket, she remembered something, jumped to her feet, and retrieved her tablet from her purse. "One second." It was difficult to cue up the page while one of her arms still held the pillow to her front, but she eventually managed and handed him the tablet.

"What's this?"

"Could you sign up for an alternate phone number, please? I think it's a good idea to be able to contact each other during the week if we need to. For logistical reasons." In case he wanted to cancel things. "I spoke to customer support at the agency and suggested they develop some kind of anonymous texting program, but in the meantime . . ."

A funny smile touched his lips as he considered the glowing screen. "You gave me your real number. I'm surprised you're not expecting mine in return."

"This is better for you, right?" Because it was definitely better for her.

Once lessons ended, neither of them wanted her calling him over and over just to listen to him hanging up on her. She couldn't see herself acting so desperate. But she'd never been obsessed with a person before, either.

Not that she was. Yet.

His facial expression was difficult to read as he said, "It is better for me. Thank you."

He fished his phone out from his jacket pocket and tapped through a series of screens on both gadgets. After a few moments, a vibrating sound emanated from her purse.

"Done," he said with a smile.

"Perfect. Thanks." She forced her lips into an answering smile.

He took a step toward the door before he paused. "We

should do something new next Friday. I could take you out."

Her heart squeezed. "Out?"

"Maybe dancing? Drinking? At a club? I hear there's this new place in San Francisco . . ."

"I don't dance." And she didn't drink. And even though she'd never been clubbing, she was certain she didn't do that, either.

"I can teach you. It'll help with lessons when we get to them later in the evening. Trust me."

Trust.

This was the second time he'd told her to trust him. What would he think if she told him how difficult it was for her to do things like dancing and drinking? Going out was supposed to be fun. For her, it was work—*hard* work. She could interact with people if she wanted to, but it cost her. Some times more than others.

In this case, was the reward worth the price?

"How will it help with lessons?" she asked.

"You think too much. It'll help get you out of your mind, make you relax. Also, I'm really good at dancing. We'd have fun. Are you up to it?"

She told herself it was the idea of *getting out of her mind*— whatever that meant—and checking boxes on the lesson plans that decided for her. But that was only a small part of it.

The biggest part was the eager sparkle in Michael's eyes. He wanted to go, and he wanted her to go with him. It was like a date. But not, of course. She knew it wasn't a date.

"I can't guarantee I'll be able to dance."

"Does that mean you'll go?" he asked with a tilt of his head.

She lifted her chin and nodded.

White teeth flashed as he smiled. "Great. I'll make plans and keep you posted. Looking forward to it." He leaned down and pressed a fast kiss to her cheek before he left the room.

Stella bolted the door and sank onto the bed in a daze. These were supposed to be simple sex lessons. Why was it getting so complicated? Why had her body betrayed her? And why did she want to please Michael so badly she'd go clubbing for him? Who was she? She didn't know herself anymore.

t's really bad to eat dessert first, you know," Stella commented.

She knew she sounded pedantic and boring, but she couldn't help the nervous chatter spilling from her mouth. Her anxiety over clubbing had been escalating exponentially during the past week, and the main event was just hours away now.

Also, Michael was holding her hand.

Her palm sweated so badly she didn't know how he could stand touching her, let alone act like it was the most normal thing in the world. Oddly, she'd handled foreplay better than this—up until the end, that was—and she'd been naked for that. She couldn't blame her reaction on her usual aversion to touch. She liked Michael's touch.

As she and Michael walked down the busy San Francisco sidewalk hand-in-hand, passersby smiled at them. An old man in a newsboy cap winked at her.

They thought she and Michael were a couple.

Stella would have laughed if she didn't feel like she was somehow taking part in a duplicitous charade. A gaggle of party girls in low-cut dresses flocked by, giving Michael double takes, then triple takes as they giggled into their hands and whispered to one another. They glanced at Stella with open envy that she enjoyed even as she knew she didn't deserve it. Wearing a slate-gray suit and black oxford shirt, he was particularly scrumptious-looking tonight.

"Here it is." Michael released her hand and held open the door for her as she walked into the old-fashioned gelato shop. Black and white tiles checkered the floor. Pink chandeliers illuminated display freezers filled with gelato and toppings. "What's your flavor?"

She could barely think about ice cream with his hand resting at the base of her spine like that. Did he know he was doing it? She'd seen men do that with their girlfriends. Stella wasn't a girlfriend.

"Mint chocolate chip," she said.

"Really? That's my favorite, too. I'll get something else, then, so we can try something new." He idly rubbed her waist as he considered the gelato flavors, and her body heated with awareness.

"Wait, what do you mean by 'we'?"

A mischievous grin curved on his lips. "You don't want to share with me?"

The college-aged girl behind the counter stared at Stella like she'd kicked a puppy.

"No, that's not it." Not entirely. After all the kissing they'd done, she knew it was silly to worry about germ transference. The fact was she'd made a detailed analysis of ice cream flavors, and she'd decided this one was the best in existence. "I just know what I like."

"We'll see about that." He tapped on the display case. "Mint chocolate chip for her and green tea for me."

Stella wanted to pay, but he dug bills out of his wallet before she could pry the credit card out from the bodice of her sapphire-blue sheath dress. Once they were seated at a black wrought-iron table by the window, he dipped his spoon into his gelato, tasted it, and grinned a slow, wide grin as he slipped the clean spoon from his mouth and scooped out more.

"Oh, that's just ridiculous," she said. "You look like you're auditioning for a Häagen-Dazs commercial. No one smiles like that after eating ice cream."

He laughed. "It really is good." His grin was out in full force, and, God forbid, did he have a *dimple*?

"Now, I have to try it." She lowered her spoon toward his bowl.

"Ah, ah, ah." Instead of letting her scoop up some herself, he held his spoon to her lips. Her eyes jumped to his, and conflicting thoughts skittered through her mind.

She shouldn't do it. This was too intimate. It was crossing a line of some kind. It felt too much like dating—which they weren't.

It was just gelato. Just his spoon. He might take it as rejection if she didn't do it, and she could never, ever in a thousand years hurt him, not even in a trivial way.

She parted her lips and let him feed her the gelato. Her heart knocked around her chest like a pinball as sweet green tea melted on her tongue. He watched her with expectation, oblivious to his effect on her.

"Okay, it's good." She tried to sound casual. This didn't mean anything. This wasn't a date. She was just another of his clients. *Keep a cool head.* She stabbed her spoon into her gelato.

"I told you so."

"I still like mine best." She put a spoonful of mint chocolate chip in her mouth. The complex combination of vanilla and mint exploded on her palate. Bits of chocolate crunched between her teeth. Perfection.

"Let me try it."

She held her bowl out toward him, but he didn't put his spoon in it. He trailed his fingers over her jaw as he tipped her head back and sealed his lips over hers. His tongue speared into her mouth, and the salt of him mixed with the flavor of the ice cream. She didn't know if she was mortified, shocked, aroused, or all three.

With a lingering lick on her bottom lip, he pulled away and grinned, his dark eyes intense and hazy.

"I can't believe you did that." Flustered, she tried to scoop herself another spoonful. Her white plastic spoon skittered onto the tabletop.

She grabbed for it, but his hands wrapped around hers. In the next instant, he was kissing her again—sweet, closed-mouth kisses that still felt scandalous. And too delicious to resist. The gelato shop dropped away. The people disappeared. In that moment, it was just her and Michael, the taste of ice cream, and their slowly warming lips.

As Michael eased his tongue between Stella's parted lips, the chilled silk and mint chocolate sweetness of her mouth drove him out of his mind. He forgot he was seducing her. He even forgot why. All he knew was her taste and the hot sighs of her breath. He wanted to devour her.

Did she know she was making those soft humming sounds as she returned his kisses? Or that her cool fingers had snuck beneath the cuff of his shirt and were caressing his wrist?

He wanted to slide his hands up her bared thighs and slip them beneath the short hem of her dress so he could touch her again. But the last time he'd done that, he'd scared the hell out of her.

Because she didn't want to make him feel the way she had with those three assholes.

Clients never worried about him like that. Why did she? He wished she'd stop. It was fucking with his head.

"Easy, man," a laughing voice interjected. "You're in a public establishment."

Stella tore away, touching trembling fingers to her red

lips. She'd surprised him today by trading her glasses for contacts and leaving her hair down in loose waves. She even wore makeup, though he'd kissed off all her lip gloss. That was fine. Like this, she was almost too beautiful to be real.

When the group of wiseasses at the next table started clapping and cheering, Michael expected her to grow flustered and embarrassed. She didn't. She ducked her head in that shy way she had and laughed along with them. Her soft smile and the luminous look in her eyes, however, were just for him, and they made him feel like he'd single-handedly vanquished an army. He was the one she saw, the one she smiled at, no one else.

His plan to seduce her out of her anxiety was working. He had no doubt that by the time he took her home tonight, she'd be ready to check the big boxes on her lesson plans. He should have done this from the beginning. Everyone knew if you wanted inside someone's pants, you didn't start in the bedroom. That was what seduction, romance, handholding, and dancing were for. That was what these ice cream kisses were for.

The problem was they were working on him, too. The more time he spent with her, the stronger his attraction to her grew—and not just physically. If he couldn't check all her boxes within the next two lessons, he'd feel obligated to extend the length of their arrangement, and that was a bad idea. He might do something stupid and fall for her.

Never once did he imagine he could spin a fairy-tale ending out of such a scenario. Not only were they worlds apart in terms of education and culture, but Stella was rich. If she learned about his dad and the shitty things he'd done to get his hands on money, she'd never be able to trust Michael. There was a reason they had sayings like *the apple doesn't fall far from the tree*, *like father like son*, and *a chip off the old block*. He fought against it and hated his dad for it, but he carried that same badness inside himself. He was a ticking time bomb, and he didn't want Stella to be around when his endurance ran out and he exploded, hurting everyone around him.

Sex was the way out of this. Check the boxes, finish the lessons, move on. Only now that he knew her better, he wanted to do more than teach her how to be good at sex. He wanted to give her the best nights of her life.

Tonight, he was giving her fireworks.

After dinner at a fusion restaurant, Stella walked with Michael down streets lined with posh department stores and skyscrapers bearing the names of large banks. Pedestrian traffic—one part tourist, one part native city dweller in Windbreakers, one part young partygoer dressed to the nines—choked the sidewalks and spilled onto the roads, where cars passed at a slow crawl.

This was the Bay Area at night, something she had never cared to experience. Surprisingly, she was having a good time. When it came to escorting, Michael was the full package. He was great both in and out of bed. His very public kisses should have embarrassed her, but instead, she'd loved them. Who wouldn't love being kissed by Michael where people could see and admire and become green with envy? He held her hand every chance he got, and he was easy to talk to. She didn't usually enjoy new things, but Michael made her feel safe. With him at her side, she was a part of this busy San Francisco night, not just an onlooker. There was something novel and wonderful about being in a crowd and not feeling alone.

They neared a set of red velvet ropes where scantily clad women and men in suits waited in long lines. A bouncer raked coldly appraising eyes over Stella's body and face, making her lean into Michael.

"Is this the club?" she asked, feeling her anxiety resurface.

He wrapped an arm around her and nodded. To the bouncer, he said, "We should be on the list. The name is—"

The bouncer tipped his buzzed head toward the entrance. "Go on in."

Michael brushed a kiss against her temple, tucked her hand into the crook of his elbow, and walked with her toward the front doors of 212 Fahrenheit. A third bouncer held the door open for them, nodding at Michael as they passed.

"They let us in because they think you'll be good for business," Michael whispered in her ear.

Her cheeks heated, and she tried not to let his words go to her head. She'd gotten her hair and makeup done for tonight. This wasn't really her.

A decent number of people milled about the interior of the club, and she fisted her hands and gave herself a quick pep talk. She'd been to benefit dinners and work galas. This shouldn't be a problem. The din of their conversations mixed with subdued electronic music and filled her ears. Thankfully, neither of those things was particularly loud. She could still think.

The space was one open room decorated in a minimalist modern style with exposed metal beams and sharp edges. A large bar occupied the back, and a DJ controlled the music from a crow's nest on the adjacent wall. Seating was sparse and came in the form of upholstered booths centered around low metal tables. There were only four such arrangements, and two were occupied.

"I want one of those tables." Her voice came out sure and steady, and the sound reassured her, loosened the knots in her stomach. She was doing fine.

"They're not free."

She slipped her credit card out from the top of her dress and handed it to Michael, laughing when he stared at her with a surprised grin. "I had nowhere else to put it."

He slid his hands up her back and pulled her close. "What else is in there?" he asked as he peered at her modest show of cleavage.

"My driver's license."

"I have pockets, you know. You could have given me your cards and phone to hold for you."

"I didn't think of that. I left my phone at home because I couldn't fit it in." But now that she knew it was an option . . . This was why women had boyfriends.

Except he wasn't her boyfriend.

Michael's fingertip tucked beneath the bodice of her dress and skimmed across the front. It brushed inadvertently across a nipple, making her blood race and breast swell before he found the license and slipped it free. From the twinkle in his eye, she realized it hadn't been an accident at all.

His expression softened as he swept his thumb over the photograph on her driver's license. In the outdated picture, she looked young and extremely shy—an accurate description for the time. She liked to think she'd gained sophistication since then. Just look at where she was now.

"That was right after I finished my postdoc."

"How old were you here?"

"Twenty-five."

The corner of his mouth kicked up. "You look eighteen. Even now, you barely look legal."

"Allow me to demonstrate how legal I am by drinking."

Feeling drunk off success and empowerment, she marched to one of the empty tables and sat, eyes peeled for waitstaff. Michael tucked a hand into his pants pocket and strode toward her with a relaxed bearing worthy of the runway. *All* of him was worthy of the runway, but there was also something about that suit. It looked expensive and excellently tailored, yet somehow more chic than anything she'd ever seen on other men.

He stretched out next to her, close enough that their thighs pressed together, and propped his arm on the seat behind her. She liked that. A lot. It made her feel like he was staking a claim on her.

"What brand is this suit? I love it." With the barest hesitation, she smoothed her hands over the lapels and crisp shoulders of the jacket.

Searching her eyes, he smiled a slow, beautiful smile. "It's custom made."

"My compliments to your tailor." She checked the inside and was even more pleased when she couldn't detect the bunching of hasty seams underneath the fine silk lining. Expert craftsmanship.

"I'll tell him."

"Maybe I should switch. Does he do women's apparel? Is he terribly busy?" As she spoke, she couldn't help running her palms down his chest, loving the firmness of his body beneath the starched cotton of his dress shirt.

"He *is* very busy."

She sighed in disappointment. "My tailor is all right, but she thinks I'm crazy. She stabs me a lot, too. I'm not convinced it's always an accident."

His muscles tensed underneath her hands, and he sat up straighter. His voice had an angry edge as he asked, "You mean she stabs you on purpose?"

Was he upset . . . on her behalf? The thought sent warmth bubbling throughout her body, and whatever grudges she'd harbored against her vindictive tailor were forgotten.

"In her defense, I'm very picky. She calls me her diva client," Stella said.

"That doesn't make it okay. She should have better control of her pins. It's not that hard. Even when I was ten, I still—" He pressed his lips together and raked a hand through his hair. "What things are you picky about?"

"Oh, well, I . . ." She drew her hands toward herself and laced them together so she couldn't tap her fingers. "I'm particular about the way things feel on my skin. Tags and scratchy, lumpy seams, loose threads, places where the fabric is too tight or too loose. I'm not a diva, I'm just . . ."

"A diva," he said with a teasing smirk.

She wrinkled her nose at him. "Fine."

A waitress in a short black skirt and a tight white top bearing the club's logo sauntered to the table.

Michael handed her Stella's credit card. "We'd like to reserve the table for the rest of the night. Water for me. Stella?"

He wasn't drinking, too? She wasn't sure she wanted to do it alone. "Something sweet, please."

The waitress arched an eyebrow but gave a professional nod. "Coming right up."

After the waitress disappeared, Michael explained, "I'm driving."

She smiled. "I like this responsible side of you."

"Michael is always responsible, aren't you, man?" A stranger appeared out of nowhere, and Stella watched in awe as he helped himself to the sofa opposite them. He wore a tight black T-shirt over bulldog-hunched shoulders and kept his hair buzzed close to his scalp. She tried not to stare rudely at the intricate tattoos decorating his muscled arms and neck, but it was difficult. She'd never seen so many tattoos up close.

Michael sat forward. "Quan—"

The stranger gave Michael a hard look. "No, I get it. You must have lost your phone or something." Switching his attention to Stella, he said, "I'm Quan, Michael's favorite cousin and best friend."

Cousin. Best friend. Her nerves jumped into high tension. She held her hand out over the table. "Stella Lane. Nice to meet you."

He stared at her hand with an amused expression before he shook it and sprawled back against the sofa. "So he does have a girlfriend, after all. Let me guess, you're a doctor."

As she opened her mouth to correct him on both accounts, Michael wrapped an arm around her and pulled her against his side. "Stella's an econometrician."

She gazed up at him in confusion until she realized he was worried she'd divulge his escorting to his cousin. Then, she mentally rolled her eyes. Her social skills were bad, but they weren't *that* bad.

Quan surprised her by leaning toward her with a bright expression. "That's related to economics, isn't it?"

"Yes."

"Has she met Janie yet?" he asked Michael.

Who was Janie?

But Michael didn't appear to hear the question. His attention was focused on a petite blond woman seated at the bar. When she patted the empty bar stool next to her, he cursed under his breath and got to his feet. "I'll be back in a second."

Stella's body went cold as she watched him stride to the bar. He sat on the indicated bar stool, and the blonde trailed her fingers down his arm. They spoke, but their words couldn't be heard above the music and the noise from the growing crowd.

When had so many people arrived? Their numbers had almost doubled since she'd entered. More continued to file into the club in a steady stream.

"I-is that Janie?" she asked.

"I don't know who that is, but it's not Janie." After glancing at Stella's face, Quan smiled slightly. "He clearly didn't want to talk to her, okay? You have nothing to worry about."

But it didn't feel like she had nothing to worry about. The blonde laughed at something Michael said and edged closer to him. Enviably luscious breasts flattened against his arm. Whatever happened next was blocked from view as people gathered around the bar.

"Are there usually this many people here?" Stella asked.

"Nah." Quan rubbed at the scruff on his head and stretched his neck side to side. "This popular DJ is spinning tonight, so it's busier than normal. The acoustics are really good here. Prepare to be blown away."

She swallowed past a lump in her throat, and a sense of foreboding settled in her gut. Since when was being blown away a good thing? Hundreds of bodies packed the room now. Far more than she'd anticipated.

A grating electronic boom erupted from speakers built into the ceiling, and Stella's heart lurched so hard her chest hurt. The room flashed red before flames began dancing up the walls. The crowd screamed with excitement while Stella struggled to breathe. Lasers and smoke. The grating receded, and ephemeral, orchestral sounds whispered over the room. Before she could attempt to relax, a beat picked up in the background, gaining speed with a slow buildup.

"Don't look so scared," Quan shouted. "That's not real fire. It's just LED lights and projectors."

The waitress appeared out of thin air and plopped a drink onto the table. She said something, but Stella couldn't hear it. In two blinks, the waitress vanished into the mass of moving bodies. The music worked toward some kind of climax, and the people grew agitated as it neared.

Stella picked up the drink and took a large gulp. Lemon, cherry, and amaretto. She wished it were vodka, or, better yet, straight ethanol. It would work faster that way.

Quan gave her an amused look. "Thirsty?"

She nodded.

Loud digital sirens screeched, silence hung over the room for a good five seconds, and a melody cascaded from the speakers. Without warning, the bass resumed at a frantic, adrenaline-inducing speed. The crowd went wild.

Her heart pounded in a dizzying rush, and fear threatened to swamp her. Too much noise. Too much frenzy. She bottled up her emotions and buried them deep inside herself, forced herself to take slow breaths. As long as she looked calm on the outside, she was winning this. The music raced, but time crawled.

The bodies shifted so she got a clear view of the bar. The blonde was playing with the collar of Michael's shirt, leaning in too close.

She sealed her lips over his.

Stella flinched like someone had slapped her. She waited for him to push the woman away. She waited for what felt like ages, waited until the crowd moved again and blocked her view.

Acid and amaretto climbed up the back of her throat.

She needed to find a place to vomit. She forced her way into the crowd, pushed through bodies swaying to the rapid tempo. The music bombarded her. Lights strobed. Sour body odor, cologne, alcoholic breath. Hard limbs and pointed joints.

Was Michael still kissing that woman?

Her eyes flooded with tears. The bodies formed a cage around her. She couldn't move. She couldn't cry for help.

A hand closed around hers.

Michael?

No, it was Quan.

He shoved people aside. A woman swore at him when he made her spill her drink. A guy shoved him back. Quan merely elbowed the guy to the side and brushed past. Through it all, his hold on her hand remained secure and steady. He led her through the people, opened a door, and cool, sweet air floated over her face.

The door clicked shut, muting the music. Someone was gasping. The flashing light was gone. She covered her eyes and sank down to the cold cement. Her trembling legs refused to take her weight.

"Thank you," she made herself say.

"Are you all right?"

"Going to throw up." Her nails clawed at the sidewalk as she tried to find a suitable place to be sick. She couldn't get enough air into her lungs.

"Easy, easy. Slow breaths." He moved as if to touch her but stopped when she flinched away. "Sit up straight. That's it. In through your nose. Out through your mouth."

Who was gasping like that? The sound was driving her out of her mind.

"Hold on. Let me go get Michael."

"Don't." She grabbed his wrist. "I'm fine." She leaned back against the side of the building and turned her face into it. The coldness felt good on her fevered forehead, distracted her from thinking about Michael with that woman. Michael *kissing* that woman.

With her mouth almost touching the wall, the sound of the gasping grew louder, and she realized it was coming from *her.*

She gritted her teeth together, fisted her hands, and tightened every muscle in her body. The gasping stopped.

"Do you need anything?" Quan asked.

"I'm fine. I'm just overstimulated." She was already feeling better, though her temples throbbed.

Quan tilted his head to the side. "My brother used to get overstimulated just like this. He's autistic."

Her chest constricted at his words. She shouldn't have used the word *overstimulated.* Most people didn't use it. Why would they? When he narrowed his eyes, she could almost see the connections being made in his mind, the question forming there.

She held her breath and hoped he wouldn't ask. She could withhold the truth, but she'd never learned how to lie.

"Are you?"

Her shoulders slumped, and her throat burned with shame. She made herself nod.

"Michael doesn't know, does he? He never would've taken you here if he knew. You should tell him."

All she could do was shake her head. Anytime people learned about her disorder, they started walking on eggshells around her. It strained the relationship until they found a way to leave. She never told people anymore. Apparently, that wasn't enough to keep some from figuring it out on their own.

"Can I borrow a hundred dollars from you, please? I want to go home." And her credit card was inside.

"You're going to leave? Michael's probably looking for you."

She doubted that. He'd been busy. As she pushed herself to her feet, she marveled at the disconnect between her body and her mind. How could her limbs still follow orders when her head felt so tired and hollow? "I promise I'll pay you back."

"Is this because that chick kissed him? I hope you saw Michael trying to peel her off. He sucks at protecting himself from women."

Hope sparked, bright and foolish. "Really?"

The door opened, and a swift techno beat radiated from the doorway.

"There you are." Michael stepped outside, and the door shut behind him, silencing the music. His gaze jumped from her to Quan and back again. "What's going on? Are you okay?"

"I needed some fresh air."

Quan's brow furrowed like he wanted to speak, and Stella held her breath.

Don't tell him. Don't tell him. Don't tell him.

He'd change. Everything would change. And she didn't want that to happen yet.

"She was trying to borrow cab fare from me. She saw you and that blonde necking and wanted to run," Quan said.

Her stomach didn't know if it should relax or knot tighter at his words. He made her sound emotional and possessive. She wished it weren't true.

"You were going to leave? Just like that?" Michael asked, his voice tinged with disbelief.

She stared down at the pavement. "I thought you and her—that you—"

"No. With you right there? Give me some credit, will you? God, Stella."

He gripped her waist and pulled her against him. His smell, his arms tight around her, his solid presence. *Heaven.* She shut her eyes and sagged against him.

"Do you want to go back in?" he asked.

"No." Adrenaline shot through her body, tightening every muscle that had relaxed in his embrace. As an afterthought, she added, "Please."

"Let's go home, then."

Stella was reserved as they walked the few blocks back to her white Model S. Several times, Michael caught her massaging her temples, but when he asked if she had a headache, her response was an unintelligible mumble. He would have thought she was doing the silent martyr act in retribution for his supposed cheating, but that didn't seem her style.

No, her style was leaving him without a single word. When Quan had told him she wanted to abandon him at the club, it'd sucker-punched Michael in the gut. The last person to leave him had been his dad. But where Michael's dad had left him with an enormous mess to clean up, Stella had planned to leave him with her car and her credit card. Who *did* that?

Even worse, he hadn't deserved it. Either time.

Tonight, he'd been busy preventing his crazy ex-client from making an enormous scene in front of Stella. Aliza was a true diva and loved drama in all forms. Now that she'd finally succeeded in divorcing her millionaire husband—and taking half of his net worth—she wanted Michael back. She was willing to pay whatever it took.

She refused to accept that Michael would rather fuck his way through splintered driftwood than return to her bed. She'd detained him for long minutes, tossing extravagant numbers at him before plastering her mouth to his.

He would forever associate the taste of cinnamon gum, cigarettes, and whiskey with Aliza.

So different from Stella, who tasted like . . . mint chocolate chip ice cream.

They piled into her car, and she activated the seat warmer, sank against the backrest, and stared out the window, absently tapping her fingers on her knees. He turned the radio on to break the silence, but she promptly turned it back off. Her fingers resumed their tapping. It was hypnotic but a little annoying.

He sent her a pointed look, but she didn't notice.

After he took them out of the city and merged into the light traffic on 101S, he broke down and said, "When you do that finger tapping, are you playing a song? Like on the piano?"

She stopped tapping her fingers and sat on her hands. "It's Debussy's *Arabesque*. I really like the combination of triplets and eighth notes."

"So you play?" When he'd picked her up from her downtown Palo Alto house, it had been impossible to miss the black grand piano dominating her otherwise empty living room. If she was artistically talented on top of being smart, successful, and gorgeous, she was officially his dream woman in the flesh. And so far out of his league as to be laughable.

Even if he didn't have all the shit associated with his dad dangling between them, he had almost nothing a girl like her could want. There was his face and his body, but anyone could have that if they paid enough. Maybe she would have been attracted to the old him, the man who had been free to pursue his passions. There'd been a lot going for that guy. Michael barely knew him anymore.

"I do," Stella said. "I started playing before I could speak."

He arched his eyebrows. Apparently, in addition to being his dream woman, she was also Mozart.

"That's not as impressive as it sounds," she said with a wry lift of her lips. "I was a late speaker."

"I have a hard time picturing that. You seem so perfect to me."

She bowed her head and released a heavy breath, but when he began to ask her what was wrong, the slow minivan in front of him caught his attention. He switched lanes and accelerated soundlessly past it. *Smooth as buttah*. He loved fast cars.

But thinking about cars always reminded him of his current car, a shiny black BMW M3, and how he'd gotten it.

"She's my crazy ex-client," he said.

He felt the weight of Stella's gaze on the side of his face. "The woman in the club."

"Yes."

She lifted a hand toward the bridge of her nose. When she couldn't adjust her glasses, she clasped her neck instead. "Did you like kissing her?"

"I *didn't* kiss her. *She* kissed *me*. But no, I didn't like it."

"Can you be very honest and answer one question for me?"

This was going to be interesting. "Yes."

"Are you a different person when you're with me?"

"You mean, if I bumped into you when you're not my client anymore, would I be a dick around you?" If she was no longer his client, she'd probably be with another man. He twisted his lips as a bad taste filled his mouth. "No."

"Are you lying just to make me feel better?"

"Stella, I've never lied to you. You're going to have to decide if you believe me."

They didn't speak for the rest of the drive. He drove up the driveway to her smart, renovated cottage, complete with rosemary hedges and solar panels on the roof, and parked in the surgically sterile two-car garage. Once he turned off the car, her eyelids fluttered open.

"You're home."

She ran a hand over her sleep-matted hair. "I'm almost too tired to get out of the car."

"I can carry you."

She aimed a sleepy smile at him, clearly thinking he was joking.

"I'm serious." The idea of carrying her to bed was highly appealing at the moment. He liked holding her, and as messed up as it was, he wanted to check boxes. He hadn't gone this long without fucking in three years, and seeing Stella in that dress was giving him full-body blue balls.

"Don't be silly." She pawed her door open and stood up with movements that were clumsy even for her. When he locked the car and met her at the door to her house, however, her eyes were steady. "I don't have energy for lessons tonight."

"It doesn't have to be lessons." He trailed his fingertips down her arm, and her skin dotted with goose bumps. Her eyelids went heavy, her eyes sensual. Beautiful Stella. "I can just make you feel good." He stroked over her palm, and her fingers unfurled, inviting him to touch. "You already paid for tonight, Stella."

Her hand fisted shut, and she turned to face the door. "I wanted to talk to you about that. Please come in."

After returning her shoes to their place in her coat closet, Stella padded past her beloved Steinway to her dining room, enjoying the feel of the cool hardwood on her aching feet. Michael followed behind her quietly, and she suspected he was noting how barren the space was.

No centerpiece adorned her dining room table. No artfully arranged place settings, either. There was nothing but . . . she didn't know what kind of wood the table was made of, but it was soft. She ran her fingers over the satiny surface as she walked to the far end of the table where she usually sat. The chairs surrounding the dining table were the only ones in her entire house.

"Did you just move in?" he asked.

She pulled a chair out for him and rubbed her elbow awkwardly. "Not really."

Instead of sitting down, he strode into the adjoining kitchen with his hands in his pockets, inspecting the gas range, the stainless-steel refrigerating units, and whatever else she had in the echoing space. Cold, gray, and cavernous, the kitchen was her least favorite room in her house. At least, it usually was.

It became a different place with Michael in it. The ambience turned intimate and inviting, and the low-hanging lights twinkled more like stars than energy-efficient LEDs. It no longer felt lonely.

"What does 'not really' mean? A month ago? Two?" He aimed a teasing grin at her as he asked, "A year?"

"Five years."

His face went slack, and he stared at her house with new eyes. "So you like it empty like this?"

She shrugged. "I'm at the office most of the time, so it doesn't bother me. Here, I have a bed, a nice TV, and really fast Internet."

He shook his head and chuckled. "The essentials."

"Is that too strange?" Like being a late talker or getting overstimulated at clubs?

"No, I think I like it," he said with a smile. "You could use some art, though, and a couch or two. Maybe a coffee table. You don't need much more than that."

A knot formed in her throat. At that precise moment in time, when she had him standing in her kitchen, in her house, she felt like she didn't need anything else in the whole world. And their time together was ending soon.

She wasn't ready for that to happen.

"Would you mind sitting so we can talk?" she asked.

With a serious nod, he rounded the oversized center island and sat in the chair she'd pulled out. His proximity drew her like a magnet, and she seated herself before she could do something distracting like touch him. She needed to stay focused. Maybe if she spoke very eloquently, he'd agree to her new plan.

She rested jittery hands on the tabletop, and within seconds, her fingers started tapping.

A warm hand slid over hers and squeezed. "You never need to be nervous with me. You know that, right?"

When he didn't remove his hand, she analyzed the way he made her feel. This was a casual, uninvited touch, the kind that normally made her want to crawl into herself. But all she registered right now was Michael's warmth and the roughness of his skin, his weight. She didn't understand it, but her body accepted him. Only him.

The realization made her mind sharpen with determination, and she gathered her courage and plowed ahead. "I'm issuing you a new proposal."

He tilted his head in a measured way. "You mean you want to extend our lessons beyond next Friday?"

"I mean I don't want lessons anymore. Our time together tonight—both the good parts and the . . . not-so-good parts—made me realize a few things. While I'm bad at sex, I'm even worse at relationships. I think I'm better off spending my time working on that. Before today, I never shared ice cream with someone or held hands while I walked down a sidewalk. I never had a dinner conversation that wasn't filled with long stretches of painful silence or those embarrassing moments when I accidentally offend people and drive them away."

He ran his thumb over her knuckles before he considered her with an unwavering gaze. "I didn't see any relationship problems—except for when you tried to abandon me, but if I'd actually been kissing her, I would have deserved it. You did fine tonight."

"That's because I was with you."

He thought that over for a pensive moment. "Maybe it's because you feel like you're in control when you're with me. Because you're paying me, there's less pressure, and you can relax."

"That's not it at all. I relax with you because of the way you treat me, because you're you," she said with certainty.

His eyebrows drew together, and he went still for several breaths. "Stella, you shouldn't tell me things like that."

"Why? It's true."

Emotions crossed his face faster than she could read them. He shook his head, swallowed. A smile hinted at the edge of his lips before he withdrew his hand from hers to rub his jaw. He cleared his throat, but his voice still came out rough when he said, "Tell me about this new proposal."

She stared down at the back of her hand, missing the warmth of his touch. "I want you to teach me how to be in a relationship. Not the sex part, but the together part. Like tonight. The talking and the sharing and the holding hands. New things are scary for me, but with you, I can handle them and even enjoy them. I want to hire you to be my full-time practice boyfriend."

His lips parted, but he didn't speak for the longest time. "What do you mean, 'not the sex part'?"

"I want to take the sex out. I don't want to be like that woman at the club and force you to be intimate with me. My hope is that if I get good enough at the together part of a relationship, a man won't mind working on the sex part with me."

"Who said anything about forcing?" he asked with narrowed eyes. "Everything I've done with you up to now has been voluntary."

She suppressed a grimace and laced her fingers together so she couldn't tap them. "The next time a man kisses me, I need him to do it because he *wants* to." Without a monetary incentive. After seeing Michael with his ex-client, everything they'd done thus far left an unsavory taste in her mouth. Her reasoning when hiring an escort to teach her sex had been oversimplified. "I know you weren't initially interested in doing repeat sessions, and my new proposal would require even more face time. Because of that, I'm willing to pay you fifty thousand dollars up front for the first month. Maybe we could try this for three to six months—at the same rate? Is that a good time frame for a practice relationship? Everything is negotiable, of course. I don't know what the industry standard is for this type of arrangement."

"Fifty thousand . . ." He shook his head like he was questioning his hearing. "Stella, I can't—"

"Before you say no, think about it," she said as her heart rate jumped. "Please."

He pushed away from the table and got to his feet. "I need some time."

"Of course." She stood up and held her breath, nervous, unsure what to do. "As much as you need."

Wrapping a hand around her upper arm, he took a half step toward her. He leaned down a few inches before he caught himself. Eyes intent on her mouth, he outlined the edges of her lips with his fingertips, sending shivers of awareness outward. "I'll tell you by next Friday. Is that okay?"

"That's fine."

He bit his teeth into his bottom lip like he was thinking about kissing her, and her own lips tingled in response. "Good night, then, Stella."

"Good night, Michael."

In a state of breathless numbness, she watched as he let himself out.

Jab, jab, cross. Jab, jab, cross. Cross. Cross. Cross.

Sweat trickled into Michael's eyes, burning him, and he swiped a forearm over his face before slamming a fist into the punching bag again. Whenever thoughts crept back into his head, he hit harder. Too many fucking thoughts, too many fucking feelings.

Jab, dodge, hook. Jab, cross.

His arms burned, and he welcomed the pain, welcomed the way it seared everything out of his brain. There was nothing but the hard resistance of the sand in the bag and the jolting impact that shocked up his arm and down his leg.

Jab, jab, jab, cross, cross, cross. Harder. Could he punch the bag straight off its chains? Maybe. Cross, cross, cross, cross—

Loud knocks distracted him midpunch, and he glared at the front door. His annoyance quickly morphed into worry. Shit, was it the landlord?

Throwing a towel around his neck, he went to open the door.

"'Sup, cuz." Quan brushed past him, set a six-pack of

beer bottles on the coffee table, and tossed his motorcycle jacket on the couch. Without pausing to look at Michael, he strode into the kitchen and began digging through the fridge. "Got anything to eat?"

"You're the one who works at a restaurant," Michael said on his way back to his punching bag.

It still swung side to side from the pummeling he'd given it, and he steadied it before he drove a fist into the faded leather. As he got back into beating the shit out of the bag, he heard a series of beeps followed by the whirring of the microwave.

"I'm eating your leftovers," Quan called out.

Michael ignored him and continued punching.

The microwave beeped, and shortly afterward, Quan carried a steaming bowl to the couch, sat, and proceeded to eat Michael's dinner. Very noisily.

When Michael couldn't take the slurping sounds any longer, he paused in his punching and said, "Most people eat at the kitchen table."

Quan shrugged. "I like the couch better." He shoved a forkful of noodles into his mouth and slurp-chewed, arching his eyebrows at Michael in a *what gives?* way.

Michael gritted his teeth and tried to find his rhythm again.

"You been hitting the weights hard lately? Your arms are bigger. They're like grapefruits, man."

Steadying the bag, Michael asked, "Why are you here?"

"You gonna apologize to me or what? Because you're the shittiest cousin ever, Michael. You really are."

He shut his eyes, exhaling. "I'm sorry."

"Yeah, I'm gonna have to ask you to try that again."

He pushed away from the bag and threw himself onto the couch next to his cousin. "I'm really sorry. It's just complicated right now, and I—" He rested his elbows on his knees and covered his face with his wrapped hands. "I'm sorry."

"I don't get why you lied about not having a girlfriend. 'No one special' my ass. You scared she won't like the family or what?" Quan asked with a sneer.

Michael resisted the urge to tear his hair out. "I don't want to talk about this."

"The fuck, Michael." Quan set his bowl on the coffee table next to the beer and grabbed his jacket. "I'll leave, then." He stalked to the door and grabbed the knob.

"Today was crappy, okay?" He began yanking the boxing wraps from his fists. "All my days are crap days, but today was worse. I thought my mom was dead. When I got there, she was stooped over in her chair, and it didn't look like she was breathing. I lost my shit."

Quan turned around, worry lining his face. "Is she okay? Why didn't I hear about this earlier? Was it like the other two times when you found her in the bathroom? Is she in the hospital right now?"

One of the wraps came off, and Michael switched to his other hand, reliving the fear and the relief and the embarrassment. "She's fine. She just fell asleep. When I went crazy, she woke up and yelled at me."

Quan's expression went from relieved to amused. "You're such a momma's boy, you know that?"

"Like you aren't."

"You should tell my mom that. Maybe she'll stop being so mean."

Michael rolled his eyes as he coiled his boxing wraps back up. "After that, someone came looking for my dad. They were trying to serve him. Not sure if it was the same person from before, or the IRS, or someone new. It's always fun seeing people's faces when I tell them yeah, I'm his son. I can see them sizing me up and making assumptions. And then when I tell them I have no idea where my dad is or if he's even alive, I get the doubt or the pity. My mom spent the rest of the day repeating old stories about how fucked up he is."

"You're the only one she tells, you know. She won't even talk to my mom about that stuff, and they're like *this*." Quan crossed two fingers. "You just gotta let her do it."

"Yeah, I know." He understood it was good for his mom to talk about it, and most times, he handled it pretty well. But lately, it had gotten harder for him. Because he was a selfish asshole.

Like father, like son.

He was tempted to take Stella up on her offer even though his gut told him he should say no. She would be better off spending her time with tech moguls and Nobel laureates—people who were actually good matches for her and could afford to be with her even when she wasn't paying them.

Not like Michael. He would give almost anything to take the money out of their equation, but the bills didn't stop, so he couldn't, either.

"You want me to go, or you want me to stay?" Quan asked from where he stood in front of the door.

Michael took two beers out of the cardboard container, popped the top off one using the other, and set the open bottle on the coffee table. "Stay."

Quan snatched the bottle on his way over and sat down next to Michael on the couch. After taking a deep swallow, he traded the beer for the noodles and took up where he'd left off, only not as loud now.

Michael popped the top off his own bottle with the edge of the table, turned on the TV, and drank as he absently flipped through the channels.

"So, about your girl . . ." Quan said. "How long you been seeing her?"

Michael took a long drag from his bottle. He needed to be buzzed if he was going to talk about this. "Stella's not really 'my girl.' It's only been a few weeks."

"Whatever, man, you've got serious pussy mojo. If you want a girl, she's yours."

Michael snorted and drank more. "I don't want a girl who likes me just because I fuck her right."

He wanted a girl who liked him for him.

"You're so full of shit." Quan swapped his empty bowl for his beer and took a swig. "She almost cried when that blonde plastered herself to your face. She's into you."

Michael's heart threatened all sorts of dramatic gymnastics at his cousin's words, and he gave himself a stern mental shake as he stared into his beer bottle. It probably wasn't what he thought. He shouldn't jump to conclusions. "That's cool."

"That's cool?" Quan arched an eyebrow. "You're not in seventh grade anymore. You should be like, that's awesome, man, thanks for telling me, I can't see from inside my ass. Do you need sex advice? Because I know shit."

Michael couldn't stop the laughter from cracking out of his lungs. "No, I'm good on the sex advice. Thanks. But if you ever need some tips . . ."

Quan fingered the raised letters on the side of his beer bottle like he had something to say but was trying to figure out how. Pinning Michael with a weighted gaze, he finally asked, "Have you ever thought she's kinda like Khai?"

Michael smiled slightly. "Yeah, just a little, though." Stella was on the socially awkward side like Khai, but she was far more expressive and sensitive. "Why do you ask?"

Quan arched his eyebrows and drank his beer. "No reason." After a moment of consideration, he pointed his bottle at Michael. "So have you two . . . you know?"

Michael took a long drag of beer. "Nope."

"Really?" Quan grimaced. "Is she a virgin? Shit, is she saving it for marriage? Run like my mom is after you."

Michael shrugged. "She needs me to go slow. I don't mind. I kinda like it." Every new response he earned from Stella felt special, just like in the old eBay commercials. *It's better when you win it.* Maybe because it had always been so easy for him before.

"Fucking liar. You're probably jacking off ten times a day."

"I didn't say I wasn't jacking off."

Quan shot forward to the front of the couch. "Oh fuck, am I sitting on your come cushions?"

"Do you really wanna know?" Michael asked with a smirk.

"You're disgusting. You know that?" Quan got up and sat on the coffee table, brushing at himself like he'd been contaminated.

Michael laughed, and the two of them spent a moment contemplating their beers.

When he couldn't hold back any longer, Michael asked, "What did you think of Stella? Did you like her?" He braced himself for the answer, realizing he cared about his cousin's opinion.

How stupid was that? Even if he did accept Stella's proposal, he'd only be her practice boyfriend. Their practice relationship would end as soon as she gained the confidence to enter a real relationship with someone better.

"Yeah, she's cute, a lot sweeter than the girls you used to go for. Your mom is going to go nuts over her."

Michael downed the rest of his beer. Not fucking likely. They'd have to meet first, and he couldn't see that happening.

"What's her last name? Stella what?" Quan asked as he pulled out his phone.

"Why?"

"I wanna see if she has a LinkedIn profile. I do this with every guy my sister dates. Aren't you curious?"

Yeah, he was curious. "Lane, Stella Lane."

A persistent buzzing dragged Stella out of yet another heated Michael dream. For this entire past week, she hadn't been able to stop thinking about him.

At work, she tried to focus on her data, but the words

and numbers turned into body parts that fit together in fascinating ways. She fantasized about his hands, his mouth, his smile, his eyes, his words, his laugh, his *presence*.

When she slept, dreams of Michael plagued her, so intense the craving of her body woke her at odd hours of the night.

Last Friday had tipped her over the line. There was no doubt about it.

Stella was officially obsessed with Michael.

And they might never see each other again. It was Friday now, and he still hadn't texted or called. Was this one of those situations where no news meant no? Her heart sank, and her limbs went heavy with sadness.

The infernal buzzing continued, distracting her. She groped at the nightstand until she located her phone. Squinting at the screen, she saw it was her housekeeper.

She coughed to clear her throat of the sound of hot dream sex. "Hello?"

"Ms. Lane, I can't make it today. My daughter is sick, and the daycare won't take her."

"Oh, that's fine. Thanks for calling. I hope she gets better soon."

"Can I make it up next week?"

"Sure, no problem." She glanced at the clock, and her heart almost stopped. It was just short of eight o'clock. She was usually sitting at her desk by now.

She'd almost hit the end button when she heard her housekeeper say, "Oh, Ms. Lane, you'll want to take your clothes to the dry cleaners since I can't do it."

"Oh, all right. Thanks for reminding me."

"No problem. Good-bye."

Stella considered skipping the dry cleaners. Not only did she not know which one she used, she didn't like the idea of ruining her morning routine by adding an extra step. It was . . . irritating and anxiety-causing. New place. New people. And after the disaster at the club, her tolerance for new things was at an all-time low.

In the end, it was the idea of having the wrong number of skirts and shirts hanging in her closet that had her perusing Yelp for nearby dry cleaners. She settled on an establishment that was ranked above all the others even though it was a little out of the way.

Off routine and harried for time—her boss would probably call the police when he didn't see her in the office first thing—she drove east down El Camino Real, leaving Palo Alto and entering Mountain View. After about five minutes, she turned into the parking lot of a small strip mall with well-maintained wooden shingle siding and oak trees along the front sidewalk. Old-fashioned signs labeled a coffee shop, a martial arts studio, a sandwich place, and Paris Dry Cleaning and Tailors.

She looped her purse and bag of clothes over her shoulder and clicked over the asphalt toward the dry cleaners. A tiny old lady with a hunched back, chipmunk cheeks, and sunken lips stood before the doors. A paisley scarf had been folded along the diagonal, wrapped around her head, and tied beneath her chin. She was quite possibly the cutest grown human Stella had ever seen.

She held a massive pair of lawn shears in her gnarled hands, brandishing them ineffectually at the oak tree in front of the store.

When Stella halted, bewildered and amazed by the sight, the old lady flipped the shears around with a dangerous swinging motion, nearly slicing her own leg off in the process, and offered the handles to her. She pointed at Stella and then the tree.

Stella looked over her shoulder, but, as she'd suspected, the old lady truly meant her. "I don't think I should . . ."

The old lady pointed at a low branch on the tree. "Cut."

Stella searched about the parking lot, but there wasn't anyone else here. She stepped onto the sidewalk and took the giant and *very heavy* shears from the lady. These things were a lawsuit waiting to happen. "Maybe we should call the landscaping company. They'd probably be happy to send someone . . ."

The old lady shook her head. Once again, she pointed at Stella's chest and then the tree. "Cut."

"Cut this?" She indicated the low branch with the tip of the shears.

"Mmmmm." The old lady nodded enthusiastically, her black eyes shining within her wrinkled face.

It appeared Stella had no choice. If she didn't do it, she feared the old lady would try doing it herself and mortally wound herself in the process. How she managed to hold the shears without slipping all the discs in her spine was a mystery.

Moving awkwardly in her high heels with her bags over her shoulder and enormous shears in her hands, she prepared to step into the landscaping at the base of the tree so she could get near enough to cut the branch down.

"No no no no no."

Stella froze with one foot in the air, her heart hopping around her chest like a Mexican jumping bean.

The old lady pointed at the landscaping, which, now that she looked more closely, was not landscaping at all. It looked like . . . an herb garden.

Teetering, Stella dropped her foot in the dirt between plants.

"Mmmmm," the old lady murmured before pointing at the branch again. "You cut."

Through a miracle or adrenaline-induced superhuman strength, Stella lifted the shears above her head, wedged them around the base of the small branch, and snipped it free. The branch fell onto the cement sidewalk like a felled bird. When the old lady set a hand on her knee and prepared to bend over to retrieve it, Stella hurried away from the tree and grabbed it for her.

The old lady smiled as she took the branch and patted Stella's shoulder. Then she eyed Stella's laundry bag, pulled the lip open so she could peer inside, and placed her hand on the strap, steering Stella toward the front doors of the dry cleaners. The old lady pushed the glass door open with surprising strength. After Stella entered, the old lady snatched the shears, hid them behind her back like no one would notice them there, and disappeared through a door behind the vacant front counter.

Stella gazed about, taking in the two headless manne-quins in the window display who modeled a precisely con-structed black tux and a form-fitting lace wedding gown. The interior of the store was calming blue-gray walls, soft white draping curtains, and lots of natural light.

A fitting was going on in an adjacent room. A respectable-looking matron in a sleeveless white jumpsuit stood on a raised platform before a trifold of mirrors.

Stella went numb with astonishment.

At the woman's feet kneeled Michael.

He wore loose jeans and a plain white T-shirt that stretched around his biceps, looking wholesome and beautiful and completely at home. A measuring tape looped behind his neck and dangled down his chest, and his sculpted wrist sported a small pincushion, replete with dozens of protruding pins. Balanced over his right ear was a blue chalk pencil.

"What kind of heels are you planning to wear with this?" he asked.

"I was planning on these, actually." The lady pulled her pant leg up to reveal regular white pumps.

"You should go open toe, Margie. And one inch higher."

Margie's lips thinned, and she angled her foot, turned it side to side. After a moment, she nodded. "You're right. I have just the pair."

"I'm going to add another inch to the hem, then. How does the waist feel?"

"It's too comfortable."

"I figured you planned to eat in this."

"My tailor thinks of everything." She pivoted and stared at the profile of her pinned-up waistline in the mirrors.

Michael rolled his eyes, but he smiled. "Remember the lipstick."

"Yes, yes, how could I forget? Fire-engine red. You'll have this ready by next Friday?"

"Yeah, it'll be ready."

"Excellent."

She slinked off to a changing room in the jumpsuit, and Michael picked up a floral print garment that had been draped over the back of a chair. He adjusted the pins and snatched the chalk pencil from above his ear to mark the fabric, his eyes focused and his hands competent.

Inside Stella's mind, missing pieces clicked into place. This was Michael in his natural state. This was what he did when he wasn't escorting. Michael was a tailor.

He shook the garment out and draped it over his arm before turning to retrieve yet another pin-strewn piece.

Catching sight of her from his peripheral vision, he said, "I'll be with you in a sec—" His eyes locked on hers, and his face went slack.

He froze.

She froze.

"How did you . . . ?" He glanced out the front windows like maybe he'd find the answer to his unfinished question outside.

Her heart pitter-pattered. This had to look really bad—stalker bad. Not fair, not fair. She'd only just realized she was obsessed with him today. She hadn't had *time* to stalk him like a fanatic. Now, she'd cost herself whatever slim chance she'd had at a full-time arrangement.

She backed up a step. "I'll go."

He strode quickly across the room and caught her hand before she could leave. "Stella . . ."

Her whole arm jumped in response to his touch, and she

wanted to cry. "I just needed my clothes dry-cleaned. I didn't know you worked here. I-I'm not stalking. I know it looks bad."

His expression softened. "It actually looks like you have clothes in need of dry cleaning." He lifted the bag of clothes from her shoulder. "Let me ring you up."

He took her things to the front counter and began counting shirts with professional efficiency. His cheeks, however, were unusually pink.

"Is this awkward?" she asked, hating that she was making him uncomfortable.

"A little. Believe it or not, this is the first time I've run into a client here. Seven shirts. I'm assuming seven skirts, too." He counted them out into a separate pile and searched her face. "Do you work *every* day?"

She nodded jerkily. "I prefer the office on the weekends."

His mouth tilted up at the corner. "You would." There was no judgment from him, no criticism, no advice that it was bad for her health and her social life. He didn't think there was something wrong with her. Stella wanted to leap over the counter and throw herself into his arms.

He began to set the laundry bag aside when he noticed there was still something inside. As he upended it, the blue dress tumbled out.

His eyes lifted to hers and smoldered.

Stella gripped the counter as ice cream memories flickered through her head. Chilled silken lips, mint chocolate chip, and the taste of his mouth. Unhurried kisses in a room full of people.

"Do you have any special directions for your clothes?" he asked in a rough voice.

Blinking away her memories, she forced her mind into the present. "No starch. I don't like the feel of it on—"

"Your skin," he finished, running his thumb over the back of her hand.

She nodded and searched for something to say. Her gaze

landed on the blue cocktail dress. "I bought this dress because I liked the color and the fabric." With its crisp silk texture and structure, it must have complemented Michael's gorgeous suit nicely . . . "The suit," she whispered. "Did you make it?"

His eyelashes swept downward, and a boyish grin covered his face. "Yeah."

Her mouth fell open. *If he could do that, then why in the world was he escorting?*

"My grandfather was a tailor. Apparently, it runs in my blood. I like making clothes."

"Would you make clothes for *me*?"

"You'd have to stand still for a long time. It's not sexy. Would you really want that?" His tone was matter-of-fact, but the look in his eyes was not. It took Stella a moment before she realized it was vulnerability.

Was it possible Michael didn't think someone could be interested in him for more than his body?

"I've had clothes made for me before, remember? I know what it's like. It's worth it to me. You're talented. I want your designs."

"That's right. I forgot." That boyish grin flashed again, looking almost shy, and she wanted to wrap herself around him and hold him forever.

"I've been expecting news from you," she whispered.

His smile faded as his expression went serious. "I needed to think about it."

"Are you accepting my proposal?" *Please don't say no.*

"Are you sure you still want to issue it?"

"Of course." She couldn't think of a single reason why she would have changed her mind.

"No sex?"

She took a breath and nodded. "That's right."

Leaning forward, he asked in a low voice, "So you can be sure the next man to kiss you or touch you only does it because he wants to?"

"Y-yes." She leaned toward him as she anticipated his answer, almost afraid to exhale.

"I accept."

She smiled in dizzying relief. "Thank—"

He tipped her face upward with a hand on her jaw and kissed her. Electric sensation crackled through her. If it weren't for the counter, she would have fallen. At her murmur, he deepened the kiss, taking her mouth with his tongue in the same way she wanted him to—

The door behind the counter opened, and someone marched out.

They tore apart like guilty teenagers. Michael cleared his throat and busied himself with the clothes on the counter. Stella pursed her lips, tasted Michael on her skin, and wiped the moisture away with the back of her hand.

From the look on the older woman's face, she'd seen everything . . . and was curious. Round-lensed glasses perched on the top of her head at a gravity-defying angle, and her black hair was pulled back in a ponytail, though several strands stood out in busy disarray. She wore a hound's-tooth sweater and green plaid pants. Like Michael, she wore a measuring tape around her neck.

The woman held out a deconstructed garment and pointed to a section of a seam. The two of them proceeded to speak in a rapid, tonal language that had to be Vietnamese.

As he bent over the garment with that sexy thinking look on his face, the woman aimed a distracted smile at Stella and patted Michael's arm. "I taught him when he was little, and now he teaches me back."

Stella eked out a smile. Had his *mother* just caught them kissing? She tried to find similarities between them, but nothing stuck out. Michael's facial features were a striking balance of eastern edges and western angles. Broad shouldered, thick, and vital, he towered over the petite woman.

Stella pushed her glasses up and smoothed her hands

over her skirt, wishing she had a white lab coat and a stethoscope.

On the other side of the open back door, racks of in-process clothes and various commercial sewing machines cluttered a large workspace. A mechanized circular rack carrying clothes in plastic wrap occupied the far left side of the room, and countless spools of thread in every shade imaginable lined the walls. The little old lady from earlier sat on a worn couch in the right corner, watching muted television on an ancient CRT. The lawn shears were nowhere in sight.

"What do you do for a living? Are you a doctor?" the woman asked with ill-disguised hope.

"No, I'm an econometrician." Stella linked her fingers together and stared at the tips of her shoes, awaiting disappointment.

"Is that economics?"

Stella's eyes darted back up in surprise. "Yes, it is, but with more math."

"Has your girlfriend met Janie yet?" she asked Michael.

Michael looked up from his garment, his expression worried. "Mom, no, she hasn't met Janie, and she isn't my—" He stopped speaking, and his gaze jumped from his mom to Stella.

His dilemma was perfectly clear. What did they call one another in public situations now?

"She's not what?" his mom asked in confusion.

He cleared his throat as he focused on the garment in his hands. "She hasn't met Janie."

Warmth splashed at Stella's body in unexpected waves. He didn't correct his mom. Did that mean they were going by boyfriend and girlfriend in public situations?

A desperate yearning gripped Stella, surprising her in its intensity.

"Who's Janie?" Stella managed to ask. She remembered that name from before.

"Janie is his sister." There was a thinking slant to his mom's eyes before she brightened and said, "You should come to our house for dinner tonight. Talk to Janie about economics, ah? She's studying that at Stanford and is trying to get a job. His other sisters will want to meet you, too. We didn't know he had a new girlfriend."

His mom's words swamped whatever giddiness she'd experienced from being called Michael's girlfriend. House. Dinner. Sisters. The words rattled around in her head, refusing to make sense.

"Just come, ah? Even if you two have plans, you still have to eat. Michael can make *bún*. His *bún* is very good . . . I forgot to ask. What is your name?"

Dazed, she said, "Stella, Stella Lane."

"Call me Mẹ." It sounded like *meh*, but with an unusual tonal dip in the middle.

"Mẹ?" Stella repeated.

His mother smiled her approval. "Don't eat anything before you come, ah? We have lots of food." With that, she brushed her hands together like business was settled, filled out the invoice slip for Stella's clothes, and handed it to her. "This will be ready Tuesday morning."

In a state of panic, Stella stuffed the slip into her purse, murmured a quiet thank-you, and walked out to her car, passing by his grandmother's herb garden—at least, she assumed the old lady was his grandmother. As she sat down in the driver's seat, his mom's words repeated in her head.

House. Dinner. Sisters.

The front door swung open and Michael jogged to her side. She opened the window, and he propped his hands on the side of the car. "You don't have to come if you don't want to." A notch formed between his eyebrows as he hesitated. "But maybe . . ."

"Maybe what?" she heard herself ask.

"Maybe it's the kind of practice you wanted."

"You'd let me practice with your family?" The fact that

he trusted her with the important people in his life touched her in ways she didn't understand, made her feel off-kilter. That yearning from earlier returned.

"Would you be good to them?" he asked with a searching gaze.

"Yes, of course." She always strove to be good to people.

"And keep our arrangement between us? They don't know about . . . what I do."

She nodded. That went without saying.

"Then I'm okay with it. If you want to. Do you?"

"Yes, I do." But not because she wanted practice.

"Let's do it, then." His eyes fell to her lips. "Come closer."

She leaned toward him but glanced at the front of the shop. "She might be watch—"

He pressed a soft kiss to her mouth. Just one. And he pulled away. "See you tonight."

13

When Michael walked back into the shop, his mom was watching him with her arms crossed. Through the display window, she had a clear view of Stella's white Tesla as it backed out of the parking lot. He was certain she'd watched the kiss. That was why he'd made it so short when what he'd really wanted to do was kiss Stella until her eyes glazed over.

She had his body tied up in so many knots, he could barely see straight, let alone think, and she'd caught him off guard here in the shop. That had to be why he'd accepted her proposal when he'd already convinced himself to do the right thing and turn her down. She hadn't teased him, and she hadn't laughed. Instead, she'd been impressed with his work and with him—the *real* him. No one wanted the real him. Only Stella. In that moment of weakness, he'd recklessly tossed his reservations aside. He'd said yes for no other reason than he wanted to be with her.

But now everything was spiraling out of control. Lines were blurring, and he couldn't distinguish his professional life from his personal life. He might not even want to. His mom thought Stella was his for real, and he liked that way too much for his own comfort. Saying yes had been a giant mistake. He already regretted it and felt how wrong it was, even if he wasn't entirely sure why. But it was too late now. It was just a month. He was a professional. He could handle a month.

"Stel-la," his mom said, like she was testing out the sound of the name.

Michael gathered up Stella's clothes and headed into the work area.

She followed right behind him. "I like her much better than that stripper you dated three years ago."

"She was a dancer." Okay, yeah, she'd also been a stripper. He'd been young, and she'd had an awesome body and all those pole moves.

"That one left her dirty underwear in a cup for me to find when I came over."

Michael rubbed the back of his neck. Even after three years of escorting, he still didn't understand the strange power games that happened between women. "I broke up with her."

It had just been about the sex anyway. His dad was a cheater, and rather than commit and hurt people, Michael had spent his early twenties keeping things impersonal. To be honest, it had been a lot of fun, and he'd gone a little crazy, pretty much fucking anyone who showed interest. His memories of the time were a rainbow haze of women's underwear.

When disaster hit and he needed money, he'd thought, why not get money for it? In his previous line of work, he'd dealt with lots of wealthy older women who propositioned him from time to time. All he'd had to do was accept. Plus, it was the perfect slap in the face to his dad—the reason for the disaster in the first place.

"That was an expensive car Stella drove," his mom noted.

Michael shrugged, put Stella's clothes with the other items that needed to be sent out for dry cleaning, and seated himself at his sewing machine.

In Vietnamese, his mom said, "She really likes you. I can tell these things."

"Who likes him?" Ngoại piped up from her place in front of the TV where she was in the middle of watching *Return of the Condor Heroes* for the millionth time—the old one starring Andy Lau where the kung-fu-fighting condor was a man in a giant bird suit.

"A customer," his mom answered.

"The one in the gray skirt?"

"You saw her?"

"Mmmm, I had my eye on her from the first second I saw her. She's a good girl. Michael should marry her."

"I'm right *here*," Michael said. "And I'm not marrying anyone." That wasn't an option when he had to escort. He could still remember all the times when his dad had left during his childhood, the way his mom cried herself to sleep, the way she fell apart but still stayed strong for Michael and his sisters and never missed a day of work. Michael would never hurt a woman by cheating. Never.

Not that Stella would ever want to marry him. Why the hell was he thinking about this anyway? They'd been on three dates. No, not dates. Sessions. Appointments. They were in a *practice* relationship. This wasn't real.

"Did I raise you to go kissing people's daughters like that if you're not going to marry them?" his mom asked.

He stared up at the ceiling in frustration. "No."

"She's good enough for you, Michael."

Ridiculous. Like he was some kind of rare prize.

Ngoại *mmmm*ed her agreement. "And pretty, too."

Michael smiled then. Stella *was* pretty, and she didn't know it. She was also smart, sweet, caring, brave, and—

His mom laughed and pointed at him. "Look at your face. Don't try to tell me you don't like her. It's clear as day.

I'm glad you finally got some good taste in women. Keep this one."

Ngoại *mmmm*ed.

Michael's smile froze in place. They were right. He did like Stella, and he wished he didn't. He knew he didn't get to keep her.

S tella parked at the address Michael had texted her and worried the flowers and chocolates she'd brought were entirely the wrong thing to bring. A Google search of Vietnamese etiquette had told her she really needed to bring *something*, though the recommendations on actual gifts had been mixed and confusing, ranging from fruit to tea to alcohol. The overall consensus appeared to be that edible was best. Thus, the Godiva chocolates in her passenger seat.

But what if they didn't like chocolate?

She'd been tempted to ask Michael, but he didn't need to know how neurotic she was or how big of a deal meeting new people was for her. And these weren't just any people. These were Michael's family, important people, and she wanted to give a good impression.

Toward that end, she'd spent the day devising conversation trees in her head so she could minimize the need for social improvising, which often ended badly for her. If she was asked what she did, she had a quick explanation and follow-up questions ready. If they asked about her hobbies and interests, she was prepared. If they asked how she'd met Michael, she'd make *him* explain. She was a terrible liar.

For several stomach-twisting moments, she ran through her list of presocialization reminders: think before you talk (anything and everything can be an insult to someone; when in doubt, say nothing), be nice, sitting on your hands prevents fidgeting and feels good, make eye contact, smile (no teeth, that's scary), don't start thinking about work, don't let yourself talk about work (no one wants to hear about it), please and thank you, apologize with feeling.

Grabbing the bouquet of gerbera daisies and dark chocolate truffles, she got out of her car and stared at the two-story East Palo Alto house. When she'd first moved here five years ago, this area had been the ghetto. With Silicon Valley's continued expansion and success, East Palo Alto land values had skyrocketed. All of the homes nearby were now million-dollar real estate—even this modest little gray house with its cracked cement driveway and scraggly landscaping that, upon closer inspection, consisted of thriving, knee-high herbs.

As she walked toward the front door where flies and moths buzzed around the bright porchlight, she ran a palm over the scratchy tops of the plants, appreciating the fresh smell. She loved that Grandma liked to keep busy.

She pressed on the doorbell button and waited. No one came. Her gut knotted.

She knocked.

Nothing.

She knocked louder.

Still nothing.

She confirmed the address on her phone. This was the right place. Michael's M3 was even parked in the driveway. Before she could drive herself crazy deciding what to do, the door opened.

Michael smiled at her. "Right on time."

She tightened her grip on the stuff she'd brought, basically having an internal meltdown of uncertainty. "I don't know if I got the right things."

He unloaded the flowers and chocolate from her hands with an odd expression on his face. "You didn't have to bring anything. Really."

Panic surged. "Oh, I can take them back. Let me put them—"

He set the items on a side table and stroked a thumb over her cheek. "My mom will love them. Thank you."

She released a long breath. "What happens now?"

The corner of his mouth kicked up. "I think the usual greeting is a hug."

"Oh." She held her hands out awkwardly and stepped toward him, certain she was doing everything wrong.

Until his arms wrapped around her, and he pulled her close. His scent, his warmth, and his solidness surrounded her. That was one hundred percent right.

He pulled away with a soft look in his eyes. "Ready?"

At her nod, he ushered her through a marble-tiled entry-way, past a formal dining area, and into a kitchen that was open to an adjoining family room. The massive boxy TV in the room grabbed her attention. A man and a woman in traditional Chinese opera attire took turns warbling out similar series of notes. After a particularly impassioned iteration, Michael's grandma clapped. Sitting next to her at the kitchen table, his mom paused in the process of peeling mangoes to voice her appreciation.

When she noticed Stella and Michael, his mom waved with her peeler. "Hello. We eat soon."

Stella worked up a smile and a wave. Bracing herself for an evening of nerve-racking social performance, she approached them and asked, "Can I help?"

A wide smile stretched over Michael's mom's face, and she set her peeler and the plate she'd used to gather mango peels in front of the empty chair to her left. When Stella unbuttoned her cuffs, Michael flashed her a grin and turned on the gas range.

As she washed her hands in the kitchen sink, she watched him heat a large wok, pour oil in, and add ingredients in the careless, yet somehow intentional manner of someone who knew how to cook. By the time she sat down next to his mom, the air was heavy with the scents of barbecuing beef, garlic, lemongrass, and fish sauce. He'd rolled his sleeves up to his elbows, and she couldn't help admiring his sculpted forearms as he stirred the contents of the wok.

It took effort to redirect her attention to the mango, and she'd just begun to peel the large fruit his mom had handed her when the tinkling of a piano in another room caught her attention. The opening notes of "Für Elise" clashed with the vibrato trilling from the TV, and Stella blinked as the sounds tore her head in multiple directions, making it difficult to think.

"That's Janie playing," his mom said. "She's good, ah?"

Stella nodded distractedly. "She is. The piano's out of tune, though. Especially the bass A." Every time that flat note rang, she winced inside. "You should get it tuned. It's bad for the piano to leave it untuned too long."

His mom's brows rose in interest. "Do you know how to tune pianos?"

"No." She laughed. The idea of trying to tune her Steinway herself was ludicrous. She'd probably destroy the instrument with her bungling. "You should never tune your piano yourself."

"Michael's dad used to tune ours," his mom said with a frown as she focused on cutting the giant seed from her peeled mango. "He did a good job. He said it was a waste of money when he knew how."

"Where is he? When can he fix it?"

His mom pushed away from the table with a tight smile. "I have something for you to try. Let me heat it up."

While Michael's mom dug in the fridge, his grandma pointed to the bowl of already sliced mango. Stella dutifully plucked a small slice from the bowl and ate it, enjoying the sweet tang of the fruit. His grandma *mmmm*ed and returned to peeling her mango.

Stella released a small breath as her stomach relaxed. She liked sitting with Grandma most of all. The language barrier made conversation next to impossible, and that was perfectly fine with Stella. "Für Elise" ended, and the tension in her head eased as the sources of sound dropped from two to one.

A youngish sister in jeans, a T-shirt, and a messy ponytail flopped into the kitchen, picked a bean sprout from a colander on the center island, and popped it in her mouth. When she noticed Stella, she waved. "Stella, right? I'm Janie." She plucked another bean sprout from the colander, but her mom slapped the back of her hand, and she yanked her hand back with a yelp. Her mom stuck a container in the microwave and shooed her toward the table with a fast torrent of Vietnamese.

Janie sat across from her with an easy grin that was higher on one side—Michael's grin. "So how do you like the Vietnamese opera?"

Stella lifted her shoulder in a noncommittal way.

Janie laughed and ate a large mango slice. "That good, huh?"

Before Stella could think up a response, Michael's mom set a plastic container on the table and opened the lid. Steam rose from a light green spongy cake. "Eat, ah? *Bánh bò*. It's very good."

Stella set her peeler and fruit down and stretched a hand toward the container when she noticed it was cheap plastic, like the kind takeout came in. "You shouldn't microwave these kinds of containers. The food probably has BPA in it now." It was basically poison as far as Stella was concerned.

His mom pulled the container close and smelled the cake. "No, it's fine. No BPA."

"Glass or Pyrex are more expensive, but they're safe," Stella said. How had no one told Michael's mom this? Did they *want* her to get sick?

"I use these all the time, and no problem." Blinking rapidly, his mom held the lid of the container to her chest.

"You wouldn't notice right away. It's repeated exposure over time. You should really invest—"

Janie snatched the plastic container from her mom and stuffed a piece of green poison cake into her mouth. "These are my favorite. I love them." Sending Stella a pointed look, Janie had a second one.

Michael marched to the table and took the container from his sister before she could eat a third piece. "It's true, Mẹ. These containers really are bad. I never thought about it. You shouldn't use them."

When he tossed it in the garbage, his mom protested in Vietnamese. Was the lady upset because Stella didn't want anyone to eat poison?

Janie pushed away from the table and left the kitchen as two girls stormed inside. They were both twenty-something with long dark brown hair, pale olive-toned skin, and lean, leggy builds. If Stella hadn't already learned the hard way that questions like this irritated people, she would have asked if they were twins.

"You fat cow, why didn't you ask before you took it and spilled wine on it? While you were making out with my boyfriend?" one girl shouted.

Stella flinched, and her already anxious heart squeezed. Fighting was her absolute least favorite thing. When people fought, it always felt like a personal attack for her. It didn't matter if she was just a bystander.

"You said you two were through, and I was curious. Also, I wouldn't have spilled all over it if it fit right. Who's the fat cow now?" the second girl shouted back.

Grandma picked up a black remote and squinted at the buttons. As vertical green lines crawled across the screen and the volume climbed, the music went from distracting to unpleasant.

"That's it. I'm taking back all the jeans I gave you." The first girl shouted even louder to be heard over the TV.

"Go ahead and take them. Show what a selfish bitch you are."

Grandma muttered and increased the volume yet again.

Stella set the peeler down with shaky hands and tried to slow her breathing. This was getting to be too much.

Two more girls walked into the kitchen. One was shorter and darker than the rest and looked to be about Stella's age. The other one was high school young. They had to all be his sisters. One, two, three, four, *five* of them.

The short one stabbed a finger in the twins' direction. "You two are going to stop fighting right now."

They scoffed and crossed their arms in almost the exact same manner.

"Ever since you moved out and left us with Mom's problems, you lost the right to say anything to us," the first sister said.

The short sister rolled forward like a tank. "Now that she's stable, it's time for me to live my life, too. Try to think of others for once in your lives."

"So now *we're* the selfish ones?" the second sister asked. "You're out hobnobbing at work parties, and we're home holding Mom's hair while she vomits after her chemo treatments."

"She's not doing chemo right now . . . Right?" The short sister looked at Michael for confirmation.

His mom snatched the remote from Grandma and maxed out the volume on the TV before she went to putter around by the sink. Stella rested damp palms on the glass surface of the table. This had to stop eventually. She just had to outlast them.

"She was, but she didn't respond well, so they switched her to a drug trial," Michael provided.

"Why didn't anyone *tell me*?"

"Because you're so goddamned busy with your important crap, why else? Mom didn't want to stress you out more than you always are," one of the twins said.

"Finding out this way is stressing me out *worse*."

"Boo-hoo, Angie," the other twin said.

As the sniping continued, a harsh beeping sounded, and

his mom took a white colander out of the microwave. Using tongs, she put steaming rice noodles into a large bowl along with the beef Michael had stir-fried and an assortment of greens.

She placed the bowl in front of Stella with a polite smile. "Michael's *bún*. You'll like it."

Stella's chin bobbed on a jerky nod. "Thank—" A suspicion rose, and she snuck a glance at the colander. She pushed the bowl away. "The colander is made of plastic. No one should eat this."

His mom froze, and a tide of red swept over her face as she stared first at Stella and then the bowl. "Let me make new noodles."

Before his mom could touch the bowl, Michael grabbed it. "I'll do it. Sit, Mẹ." His expression was strained as he removed the poisoned food, and Stella had the horrible feeling that she'd said The Wrong Thing, but she didn't know how else she could have navigated the situation.

His mom sat down and eyed Michael's sisters as they continued their argument in a loose square by the refrigerator. Sighing, she picked up her peeler and resumed where she'd left off with her last mango.

Stella kept her eyes on her own work, growing more and more nervous with every passing moment. She was painfully aware of the lack of conversation between them, and her instincts urged her to fill the silence—if *silence* was even the right word. His mom wasn't speaking, but his sisters were, and the TV had been blasting this whole time. When the piano started playing again, her nerves stretched to the breaking point. That flat A note rang one, two-three, four times. Had anything ever been so irritating?

"You really should get the piano tuned," she said. "Where is your husband again?"

When his mom continued peeling her mango without answering, Stella assumed she hadn't heard the question.

So she asked again. "Where is he?"

"He's gone," his mom said in a final tone.

"Does that mean . . . he's passed away?" Should she offer condolences? She wasn't sure what to say now.

His mom sighed, keeping her eyes on her mango. "I don't know."

The answer tripped Stella up, and she frowned as she asked, "Are you divorced, then?"

"I can't divorce him if I can't find him."

Stella stared at Michael's mom in complete bafflement. "What do you mean, you can't find him? Was he in an accident or—"

A large hand gripped her shoulder and squeezed with firm pressure. Michael. "The noodles are almost done. Do you eat peanuts?"

She blinked at the interruption. "Sure, I'm not allergic." When he nodded and went to the kitchen island, she refocused on his mom. "How long has he been gone? Have you filed a missing-person re—"

"*Stella.*" Michael's voice split through the air, a startling reprimand.

His sisters stopped arguing, and all eyes locked on her. Her heart pounded louder than the TV and the piano. What had she done?

"We don't talk about my dad," he said.

That didn't make any sense. "But what if he's hurt or—"

"You can't hurt someone when they don't have a heart," his mom interrupted. "He left us all to be with another woman. I want to divorce him, but I don't know where to send the papers. He changed his phone number." His mom pushed her chair back and stood. "Mẹ's tired. You kids eat, ah? Maybe go buy something for Michael's girlfriend if she doesn't like what we have."

His mom left, and the piano music ended abruptly. His grandma turned off the opera, leaving the room quiet but for the crackling of the TV's static discharge. The sudden quietness was a relief, but it felt ominous somehow. Her blood rushed, her head throbbed, and her breaths came in short gasps like she'd been running. Or maybe she was preparing to run.

Janie hurried into the kitchen. "What just happened? Why is Mom crying?"

No one answered, but seven sets of eyes accused her. It was worse than all the noise from before, far, far worse.

She'd made Michael's mom cry.

Stella's face flamed with embarrassment and guilt, and she jumped to her feet. "I'm so sorry. I need to go."

Ducking her head, she gathered her purse and fled.

Michael stared at the doorway Stella had rushed through, feeling like he'd watched a car accident in slow motion. A mix of unholy emotion coursed through his veins. Anger, horror, shame, disbelief, shock. What the fuck had just happened? What did he do now? His instincts urged him to chase after her.

"You better go check on Mom," Janie said.

That was right. His practice girlfriend had just put his mom in tears. What a great son he was. He went to look for her without a word. With heavy feet and a heavier chest, he climbed the stairs, walked down the carpeted hall, and paused outside his mom's bedroom. The door was ajar, and he peered around the edge, finding his mom sitting on her bed. He didn't need to see her face to know she was crying. It was written in her slumped posture and the way her head hung.

The sight destroyed him. No one got to hurt his mom. Not his dad and not his past girlfriends. Not even Stella. "Mẹ?"

She didn't acknowledge him as he entered the room and padded to her bedside.

"I'm sorry about all the things she said." He tried to keep

his voice low, but it came out unnaturally loud. "The piano, the food, Dad . . ."

He didn't know how Stella had managed it, but in just a few minutes, she'd found every sensitive spot his family possessed—their tight financial situation, his mom's lack of education, and his fucked-up dad—and poked right at them. Accidentally. That was clear as day.

Holy shit, she was bad with people. He'd had no idea how bad until tonight. When it was just the two of them, it wasn't like this.

His mom grabbed his hand. "Do you think your dad is okay?"

"I'm sure he's fine." His lips twisted as he imagined his old man lounging on a yacht in the Caribbean next to his latest wife.

"Can you email him for Mẹ?"

"No." He was never talking to his dad again.

His mom took a ragged breath and covered her face. "Your Stella was right. He could be hurt. He's so evil no one would care to help him, certainly not his new woman. She's only with him as long as the money lasts."

He fisted his hands as a familiar rage threaded through his muscles. "That amount of money should last a long time."

"Not the way he spends. He thinks he's a big shot. Nothing was ever good enough for him, remember?"

Not this again.

Michael clenched his jaw as his mom launched into another retelling of a story he'd heard a thousand times. He sat down next to her and listened with half an ear so he could make the appropriate sounds when she paused.

Words like *uses women* and *bad person* and *liar* stuck out, and he couldn't help noticing how well they applied to himself. Look at all the lies he told. Look at what he did to pay the bills. Look at him taking money from Stella for doing what any other guy would do for—

Cold horror soaked into him. This was why it had felt so wrong to accept Stella's proposal. It *was* wrong. He was taking advantage of her. What kind of man accepted money from a naïve woman to teach her things she could learn for free?

He'd finally taken the last steps and become his dad. That couldn't be right. That wasn't him. He was better.

Their arrangement had to end right now. Where was she? Fuck, was she waiting for him outside?

He shot to his feet before his mom's story was half finished. "I have to go, Mẹ. I'm sorry about . . . tonight, about everything."

"There's no need for sorry. If you love her, we'll learn to love her, too."

At the mere mention of that word, sweat broke out over his brow. "I don't." That made his actions worse, didn't it?

His mom waved his protest away. "Bring her back another day. Mẹ won't microwave the plastic when she's here."

"You shouldn't microwave it any time."

"Yeah, yeah." She said the words in such a manner that he knew she would continue doing things her way regardless of what she'd been told, and Michael swore to himself he'd throw all her plastic away and replace it with something safe. Right after he spoke to Stella.

"Good night, Mẹ."

"Drive careful."

He escaped the house in record time, but he came up short as he stepped outside.

She was gone.

He gripped one of the porch's wooden support pillars and dragged in deep breaths as his heart rate slowed and his mind cleared. Cool air, the buzzing of bugs, and the distant whir of a car's motor.

Maybe it was best that she wasn't here. He needed time to compose a decent parting speech. Something short but nice. It was him, not her, and—

No matter what he said, she was going to cry. The thought twisted his guts into knots. She'd think it was her fault. Because of how awkward she was in bed and out. Because of the unintentional debacle tonight.

He walked to his car and got inside. After he turned the ignition, he sat with his hands on the wheel. He didn't know where to go. Her place or his? They needed to talk, but he wasn't ready for her tears on top of his mom's.

The new box of condoms on the passenger seat caught his eye. He'd bought countless such boxes over the past three years. He hadn't looked forward to opening any of them as much as this one—because Stella was different. Now, he'd be back to using the contents of the box with countless Fridays of women, providing a simple service for fair payment. It didn't hurt or take advantage of anyone. That was better than what his dad did. Michael could do that and still be himself. Too bad he didn't want any of those women like he did Stella.

He pushed the box onto the floor and out of sight before heading to his own apartment. Tomorrow. He'd do the right thing tomorrow.

Stella completed her bedtime routine in a numb haze. It wasn't until she laid her head down on her pillow that she started crying.

It was over now. He'd asked her to be good to his family, and she'd made his mom cry. You couldn't undo something like that.

Her gut demanded she tell Michael the truth. Though he wasn't aware of the true extent of them, he already knew about her issues: sensitivities to smell, sound, and touch; her obsession with her work; her need for routine; and her awkwardness with people. What he didn't know was there were labels for that, a diagnosis.

But was pity any better than hatred? Right now, he thought she was insensitive and rude, but he still viewed her as a regular person who happened to have some eccentricities. With the labels, he might be more understanding, but he'd quit viewing her as Stella Lane, awkward econometrician who loved his kisses. In his eyes, she'd become the girl with autism. She'd be . . . less.

With other people, she didn't care what they thought.

With Michael, she desperately needed to be accepted. She had a disorder, but it didn't define her. She was Stella. She was a unique person.

There was no way to salvage this situation. No way to keep him.

She still had to apologize to his mom. She'd never made someone cry before, and it filled her with self-loathing. His mom's evasiveness made sense now that she knew about his dad. Stella wished she could have understood earlier, before she hurt the woman and ruined everything, but all she could control were her future actions, not the past.

As the night dragged on, she constructed and reconstructed her apology, recited it over and over in her head. When the sun rose, she dragged herself out of bed and got ready to tackle the day.

She drove to the same strip mall she'd gone to yesterday and parked in front of Paris Dry Cleaning and Tailors. As soon as they flipped the sign, she'd apologize and leave.

A night of sleeplessness had left her head clouded, and her heart ached from the relentless pressure of her anxiety. Her fingers had been clenched around the wheel so long the joints were locked. She was drained and wanted to get this over with so she could go to the office and lose herself in work.

Five minutes before nine, the sign flipped from *Closed* to *Open*. Taking a deep breath, Stella picked up a second box of chocolates and a bouquet of peach roses and exited her car. Inside, Janie sat behind the front counter.

She lifted her attention from the textbook on her lap and blinked in surprise at Stella. From the tense set of her mouth, it was not a good kind of surprise. "Hi, Stella . . . Michael doesn't work on Saturdays."

"I wasn't looking for him." What was the point? They were done. She held up the roses and chocolates. "I brought these for your mom. Is she here?"

Janie's expression softened. "Yeah, she's here."

"May I speak to her, please?"

"She's working in back. I'll take you there."

She followed Janie into the backroom and stopped in front of a green commercial sewing machine, where Michael's mom was busy feeding fabric beneath the sewing foot with quick efficiency, her glasses perched on the tip of her nose.

Stella's muscles tensed, and her heart thundered. It was time to do this. She hoped she didn't screw it up. She hoped she said the right thing.

Janie murmured something in Vietnamese, and Michael's mom looked up. Her gaze jumped from Janie to Stella.

Stella swallowed and forged ahead. "I came to apologize for last night. I know I was rude. I'm not . . . good with people. I wanted to thank you for inviting me over to your house." She held out the flowers and chocolates. "I got these for you. I hope you like chocolate."

Janie snatched the truffles before her mother could touch the box. "I do."

Michael's mom accepted the flowers and sighed. "We still have a lot of food left over from last night. You should try to come again."

Stella looked down at her feet. Michael would be horrified if he saw her at his mom's tonight. "I need to go. I'm truly sorry about last night. Thank you again."

She turned around to leave but caught sight of Michael's tiny grandma at the couch. The old woman nodded at her, and Stella fumbled on something that was half curtsy, half bow before she left.

Michael walked into the studio and tossed his duffel bag on the blue matted floor next to the other two bags.

The fighters in the middle of the room broke apart, took five steps back, switched their swords to their left hands, and bowed.

"Look what the cat dragged in," said the fighter on the right. It was Quan. A helmet obscured his cousin's face, but Michael knew it was him by his voice and the name embroidered in white on his black sparring gear. Also, Quan was an inch shorter than his baby brother.

Khai waved a gloved hand at him and seamlessly switched from sparring to strike drills using his reflection in the mirror. Ten whip-fast head strikes, ten wrist strikes, ten rib strikes. Then back to the beginning. Ten more head strikes . . . When Khai worked out, he *worked out*. There wasn't downtime. His single-minded focus was impressive. And reminded Michael of Stella. He released a heavy sigh.

"Don't usually see you Saturdays. What's up?" Quan asked.

"I wanted to get some sparring in," Michael said as he scratched an ear. He usually spent Saturdays running and lifting weights—things he could do alone since he was tired of people after what he did on Friday nights. Today, however, he didn't want to be by himself. He knew he'd just think about Stella the whole time. After deliberating through the night and most of today, he still didn't know how to break things off without hurting her. It had to happen, though. And soon. He should call her after he finished sparring and arrange a meeting. Face to face was best.

"Suit up, then," Quan said. "Class starts in an hour. Teacher took the day off, so loser leads class—little kids' class."

That was the perfect incentive to win. Children brandishing sticks were horrifying. You'd think smaller kids were less dangerous, but they were actually the worst. They spun around the studio like tornadoes, hitting beneath your armor or stabbing you in the balls, all by accident. They didn't know any better. Kind of like Stella in social situations.

And Khai.

As Michael put his gear on, his eyes kept gravitating toward Khai as he methodically worked through all his strikes ten at a time. Always the same number and always the same order. If Stella ever took up kendo, Michael could see her doing the exact same thing. After last night, there were a lot more similarities between her and Khai than he'd originally thought. Khai never noticed when he tripped upon sensitive conversation topics, either. He was also horribly honest, creative in strange ways, and . . .

His gaze jumped to Quan as an unexpected suspicion rose. "You asked if I thought Stella was like Khai."

Quan undid the laces behind his head and pulled his helmet off. Dark eyes regarded him steadily. "Yeah, I did."

"Did she tell you something I should know?" He remembered that night, how it had felt like he'd interrupted something when he'd found them outside the club together.

"After she finished hyperventilating from overstimulation, yeah. She told me something," Quan said.

"She was hyperventilating?" he heard himself ask. His stomach dropped, and coldness prickled over him. What kind of ass was he that he hadn't known and hadn't been there for her? He should have been the one. Not Quan.

"Too many people, Michael. Too much noise, too many flashing lights. You shouldn't have taken her there."

Everything clicked together then. "She's autistic."

"You disappointed?" Quan asked with a tilt of his head.

"No." The word came out hoarse, and he cleared his throat before he continued. "But I wish she'd told me." Why hadn't she told him? And why had she let him pressure her into going to the club? She must have known what it would do to her.

And *last night*. Shit, it must have been awful. The TV blasting, the piano, his sisters shouting, everything new . . .

"She just wants you to like her."

The words punched Michael in the stomach. He *did* like her, and knowing this didn't impact that at all. She was still the same person. Except he understood her better now. At least, on a conscious level, he did.

Subconsciously, he felt like he'd always known. Because

he'd grown up with Khai, he knew how to interact with her. He didn't even have to think about it. That had to be why she could relax with him when she couldn't with others . . .

A strange charged sensation buzzed through him, tensing his muscles and putting his hairs on end. Maybe he didn't have to end their arrangement.

Maybe accepting her proposal wasn't taking advantage of her. Because she was autistic, maybe she really could use a practice relationship before she entered a real one. Maybe he was the perfect one for her to practice with. Maybe he could help her for real.

He didn't have to take the entire fifty grand. Come to think of it, he didn't have to take any of it. He had credit cards. He could make up the difference next month. By helping her without financial motivation, he'd finally prove he wasn't his dad.

He yanked his gear off and tossed it on the floor in a careless heap. "Put that away for me, will you? I have to go."

Stella's phone beeped, dragging her out from the world of her data. Her office materialized, her desk, the computer screens with the command prompt and all the clever code she'd written, her windows, the darkness beyond them.

The alert on her phone said, *Dinnertime*.

She opened a desk drawer and pulled out a protein bar. Her mother would be angry if she saw Stella eating one of these for dinner, but she didn't care. She just wanted to work.

Absently chewing on the cardboard-y chocolate mixture, she made small adjustments and refinements in her algorithm. It was good. Maybe some of her best work.

Her phone buzzed, and the screen lit with a text message from Michael.

Is that your office on the 3rd floor with the lights on at 6PM on a Saturday?

She dropped her protein bar and stood up to look out the

window. A familiar form leaned against a lamppost in the parking lot. She immediately dodged out of view, too humiliated to be seen.

Her phone buzzed with another message. Come down. We need to talk.

She sank back into her chair. This was it. He'd come to end it. Her thumbs shook as she composed a short response. Just tell me via text message.

I want to talk to you in person.

She threw her phone onto her desk and crossed her arms. She was tired and embarrassed. She didn't need to witness the dissolution of their arrangement in person. Or were there additional things he wanted to talk to her about? More things she'd done wrong?

Maybe she shouldn't have apologized to his mom? Had that been creepy and intrusive? Why couldn't she get *anything* right?

She ran her hands over her hair and attempted to slow her breathing. Did she have to apologize for apologizing?

The phone buzzed yet again, and she flipped it over with the tip of a trembling finger so she could read it.

I'm going to stay out here until you come down.

She rubbed at her temple. Her head throbbed, and sweat glued her clothes to her body. She needed to go home and shower.

Might as well get this over with.

She tossed her once-bitten protein bar into the trash, saved her work, and powered down her computer. Tossing her purse over her shoulder, she shut the lights off and left the room.

The empty halls and low-lit cubicles usually comforted her. Tonight, they made her lonely and sad. As she strode to the elevator, she wondered how long it would be before this feeling went away. A week? A month? She wished everything could go back to normal—like before she'd met Michael. These highs and lows in emotion were exhausting.

The click of her heels on marble echoed through the reception area, and she made herself push the front doors open and walk outside.

Michael shoved away from the lamppost and dug his hands into his pockets, looking like his usual gorgeous self in the glow of the streetlights. "Hi, Stella."

"Hi, Michael." Her chest tightened and began aching. She drummed her fingers against her thighs until she caught him watching and fisted her hands.

"My mom told me you stopped by the shop."

That was it. She'd really done the wrong thing. Her heart plummeted, and her face threatened to crumple. She schooled her features into place. "I'm sorry if I shouldn't have done that. I couldn't bear knowing I'd hurt her. I never mean to hurt people, but I do it all the time. I'm working on fixing this, but it's so complicated, and I just—I just—I just . . ."

He stepped toward her until they were separated by an arm's length. "What are you talking about?"

She stared down at her shoes. She was *so tired*. When would this be over so she could go home and sleep? "You're angry. Because I went to see your mom. That's intrusive."

"I'm not, actually."

She lifted her gaze and found him watching her with sad eyes. "Then . . . I don't understand."

"As your practice boyfriend, shouldn't I be here? It's getting late."

She took a surprised breath. "After everything I said at your mom's, you still want to have a practice relationship with me?"

"Yeah. Things are complicated with my family, and I should have prepped you ahead of time. I'm sorry I didn't think to do that."

When he wrapped an arm around her waist and pulled her close, she was too stunned to speak. *He* was apologizing to *her*?

"Are you okay? You look like you're going to pass out."

She tensed at his nearness, unsure what to do. "I'm fine. Don't worry."

"When was the last time you ate?"

"I don't remem—oh, I ate something right before you texted."

"What was it?"

She was *not* telling him. He'd probably act like her mother and chastise her. That was the last thing she needed right now.

He brushed his fingers along her jaw before clasping her face in his palm and tipping her head back. A butterfly-light kiss teased her lips. "You smell like chocolate. Did you have candy for dinner, Stella?"

"Not candy. A protein bar. There are vitamins and stuff in it."

"You're coming with me. Don't argue. I'm going to feed you." He walked her to her car, which was parked not far away, and by that time, she was simply too tired to protest.

The doors unlocked when they sensed the key fob in her purse, and she sat in the passenger seat. She fumbled for the seat belt, but he caught it and buckled her in with sure movements. He got in on the other side and pulled out of the parking lot.

The motion of the car lulled Stella into a drowsy half slumber, and it was several minutes before she realized he'd left downtown and headed across the freeway. "Where are we going?"

"Back to my mom's."

A surge of adrenaline burned the sleepiness out of Stella's head, and she sat up in her seat, wide awake. "What? Why?"

"There's a lot of food there. My mom had me cook for like a hundred people last night."

She adjusted her glasses as her heart started ramping up for takeoff. "I'd really like to go home."

"Do you have anything to eat at your place?"

"I have yogurt. I'll eat it. I promise."

He shook his head as he released a tight huff of breath. "I'll feed you quick and then take you home."

Before she could think up a suitable response, he pulled into the driveway of the little gray house. When he opened the door, she could hear the same music carrying faintly on the wind. She gripped her seat belt like a lifeline.

"I can't handle the TV tonight," she confessed in a pained whisper. After last night, her usual tolerance was gone. She'd fall apart and scare everyone. Michael would change his mind about the arrangement—she still couldn't believe he didn't want to cancel. Or he'd start walking on eggshells around her, which was worse.

"Hold on a minute." He dug his phone out of his pocket and typed in something on the screen.

Within moments, the music stopped.

"You made them turn it off? Won't your mom and grandma be unhappy they can't watch their shows?" Her entire body flamed with embarrassment. She despised it when people had to make changes for her.

He gave her a funny look. "It's just TV."

"I don't like it when people have to act differently for me."

"We don't mind." He walked around to her side, opened the door, and held his hand out. "Will you come in?"

When Stella's small hand landed in his palm, the hard knot of tension in Michael's gut loosened, but an awful brew of guilt and sadness continued to eat at him.

She looked terrible. Her bun was off-center, and messy strands framed her drawn face. Her normally bright, expressive eyes were dim, swollen, and shadowed. His heart dipped when he realized she must have cried a lot to make them that way. *He'd* made her cry.

This was not his Stella.

Well, the sweatiness of her hand was all Stella. He squeezed gently and led her to the front porch.

When he opened the door and prepared to enter, she stiffened and dug in her feet. "I forgot to bring something. Google says I'm supposed to bring something. Let me go and—"

"It's fine, Stella." He wrapped an arm around her waist and propelled her into the house.

Inside the entryway, she shut her eyes and took a breath. He could see her absorbing the silence, feel her body relaxing against his arm.

"You know you can always tell me when things bother you, right? Like the TV last night . . . or the club last week."

Her eyelids fluttered open, but instead of looking at him, she stared off to the side, suddenly tense all over again. "Did Quan say something to you?"

Michael hesitated to answer. Something told him it was extremely important to her that he didn't know, so he did what he'd learned from his dad even though he hated it. He lied. "Only that the noise and crowd were too much for you. Why didn't you tell me? I wish you had."

"I already told you I don't like it when people have to act differently for me."

"We could have done something else," he said in exasperation. The last thing he wanted was to hurt her or make her uncomfortable.

"Why are there oranges here?" she asked, indicating the plate of oranges next to the urn of incense and bronze Buddha statue on the table in the entryway.

"Don't change the subject."

She sighed. "Fine. It embarrasses me. A lot."

All that self-torture . . . because it embarrassed her to admit she was different? His insides melted down, and he grabbed her hand and squeezed.

"Can you tell me about the oranges now?"

He smiled at her single-mindedness. "It's an offering for the dead. Supposedly, they get hungry in the afterlife," he said with an uncomfortable shrug. As a scientist type, she had to think this was silly. He did, too, but it was something Ngoại and his mom liked to do.

A small smile played over her lips. "Do you give them other kinds of food, too? I'd get tired of fruit all the time, myself. How about candy?"

He laughed. "You've had enough candy today."

"What do you do with the fruit now that it's been offered? I assume the dead don't actually rise and consume it . . ."

"We eat it. I'm not entirely clear on how long you're supposed to wait, but at least a day or so, I think."

"Hm." She inspected the Buddha statue, angled her head so she could see behind it. Judging by her expression, she was fascinated, and he recalled that she loved martial arts films and DramaFever. She did not look condescending or bored or imposed upon. She did not look like his dad.

"Do you feel like you've entered the set of an Asian drama? Is that what's going on here?" he asked.

"This is better. This is real life." She pointed to the box of incense hidden away behind the statue. "Can I light one? Will you show me how to do it? I've always wanted to."

He rubbed the back of his neck. "I don't actually know how. I mean, I don't remember the order of the lighting and the bowing and all that. When I was little, I refused to do it, and Ngoại stopped requesting it."

"Does it take very long?" she asked with a frown.

The corner of his mouth tipped up sheepishly. "I don't think so, no. Let's go say hi to my mom and grandma, and then I'll feed you. Okay?"

"Okay."

She followed him through the dining room and into the kitchen where Sophie and Evie were dishing rice noodles, shredded mint and lettuce, and barbecued beef into large bowls. They looked to be back on speaking terms. Considering their track record of enemies one day, best friends the next, that was about right. Ngoại and his mom were slicing up heaps of mangoes at the informal seating area where they did all their eating—the formal dining table was for presentation only. Ngoại was dressed in her favorite black knit cardigan, and his mom wore a Christmas sweater even though it wasn't holiday season.

"Hi Ngoại, Mẹ," Michael said.

His mom nodded at him before considering Stella. "Welcome back. Dinner's ready soon. Sit and eat, ah?"

Stella smiled, but her grip on his hand was fierce. "Sure, thank you. It looks good."

"These two are Sophie and Evie. They're not twins," he said, bringing her to the kitchen island that was covered with food stored in brand-new Pyrex containers. "Sophie— the one with that red stripe in her hair, God, when did you get that?—is an interior decorator, and Evie is a physical therapist."

"Hi, Stella," they said at the same time. Mom must have told them about Stella's apology because it looked like they wanted to make a fresh start.

Stella gave a tiny wave. "Hi."

"Is Angie here?" he asked.

"Nope. More work stuff," Evie said.

"On a Saturday," Sophie added with a sneer.

"Because people work—"

"On *Saturdays*—"

"All the time."

The sisters faced one another and traded knowing glances.

Michael whispered in Stella's ear, "They've been finishing each other's sentences since they were little. I think they're aliens."

Stella's lips trembled into another smile, and she leaned into him. Poor shy girl. His family had to be overwhelming for her, and this wasn't even all of them. He tightened his hand around hers and fought the desire to kiss her. Something about the way she turned to him like he was her safe place satisfied caveman needs Michael hadn't known he possessed.

He cleared his throat and asked, "Where are Janie and Maddie?"

"Upstairs doing homework. They'll come down when they're hungry. They both have tests soon."

"They're the two youngest," he explained to Stella. "Maddie is the baby. She's a sophomore at San Jose State."

"I'm going to forget everyone's names." She looked so worried—Michael melted a little. Why did she care? These people couldn't be special to her. They were just his family.

"That's okay. I wish I could."

"Very funny, Michael," Evie said with a roll of her eyes. "You only have to remember me. I'm a PT, so if you get carpal tunnel or something, you know who to look for. Posture is everything."

"Why couldn't you be a doctor, then, E?" his mom asked as she peeled her tenth mango. "All I wanted was a doctor in the family, and not one of you could do that for me."

"Stella's a doctor," Michael said with a grin.

Her eyes rounded into giant buttons. "No, I'm not."

"Yes, you are. You have a PhD. That makes you a doctor. And you went to the University of Chicago, the best school for economics in the U.S., probably the world. You graduated magna cum laude."

As he'd known would happen, his mom perked up with interest. "That's fantastic."

Stella blushed, bringing much needed color to her cheeks. "How did you . . ."

"Google stalking."

Her eyes searched his, and a surprised smile hinted at the corners of her mouth. "You stalked me?"

He shrugged. It was his turn to feel awkward now.

"Okay, lovebirds, dinner's ready. Come eat," Sophie

said. She set down a bowl filled with noodles that had been cut short with scissors and ultra-thin sliced meat in front of Ngoại and kissed her temple like she would a baby.

Once they'd seated themselves at the table, Michael watched as Stella carefully mimicked Sophie's food preparation ritual, adding chili sauce, pickled daikon and carrots, bean sprouts, and fish sauce to her bowl of noodles, greens, and beef.

"Have you ever had this before?" he asked.

She shook her head absently as she mixed everything together and took a bite. Her eyes opened wide, and she grinned as she covered her mouth. "You're a good cook."

"Michael is very good with his hands," his mom said with a proud nod.

Sophie rolled her eyes before she smirked suggestively and asked Stella, "Do you agree? Is he 'good with his hands'?"

His mom scowled at Sophie, but Stella merely smiled and nodded. "I think so."

Sophie arched her eyebrows and sent Michael an *is she for real?* look.

As dinner progressed, Michael watched Stella through a new lens provided by his recent discovery. He didn't notice so much when it was just the two of them, but she had trouble with eye contact. She rarely spoke unless someone asked her a direct question, and then her answers were short and to the point. When she listened, however, her focus was the kind of stuff she probably used on complex economic problems. She frowned, hanging on every word like it was of utmost importance.

These people mattered to her because they mattered to him.

"Where did you grow up, Stella?" his mom asked after they'd moved from *bún* to mangoes.

"Atherton. My parents still live there," Stella provided.

His mom's eyebrows climbed at the mention of the wealthiest zip code in California. "Do you like babies?"

Michael almost dropped his fruit, and his voice was gruff with horror when he said, "*Mẹ.*"

She shrugged innocently.

"You don't have to answer that," he said to Stella.

She met his eyes like she hadn't with everyone else. Her facial muscles relaxed, but the intensity of her concentration didn't. Her beautiful mind focused on him. Michael admitted to himself he loved it.

Stella lifted a shoulder. "I don't know if I like babies. I haven't been around that many. My parents want grandchildren, though. My mother, mostly."

"That has to be why she keeps setting up blind dates for you," Michael said.

Stella nodded. "I think so."

"Meddling mothers."

At his comment, Stella's lips curved into a smile, and her eyes shined. He forgot what they'd been talking about. If he couldn't kiss her soon, he would go mad.

"When you get to my age," his mom said, crossing her arms over her chest, "you want to play with babies. It's natural."

Sophie jumped to her feet. "Help me with the dishes, Stella?"

"Sure, I'd love to help," Stella said. "Is there a particular way you do it?"

"Just whatever way gets them clean."

Evie cleared the table as Sophie and Stella piled things into the sink. His mom and Ngoại stared at him with serious expressions. He braced himself for something bad.

"She won me at the shop today. It's important to know how to admit when you're wrong. You should keep her," Mẹ said in Vietnamese.

He shook his head and thinned his lips. "It's not that easy."

"Why?"

"We're too different. She's really smart and makes loads of money."

"*You're* smart," his mom insisted.

He rolled his eyes.

"You're not like your dad wanted, but that doesn't mean you're not smart. And you don't make as much because you're busy helping me at the shop. I told you I don't need you anymore. You let so many opportunities pass because of me. I don't want that for you, Michael, and I don't want you to lose this girl, either. She's a good one. *Keep* her."

"It's not that simple."

"It is. She likes you. You like her."

If he had less control, he would have pointed out his mom's relationship with his dad, but that was hitting below the belt. His dad loved his mom—in his own way. But he also loved cheating. Michael would never understand why his mom took his dad back every single time.

"Just promise to try, all right? I like this one," his mom said.

Michael could have laughed. Of all the girls he'd ever brought home, she liked the one he couldn't have. His client. His rich, highly educated, beautiful client, who was paying him to help her learn how to get someone better.

"You're just saying that because she's doing dishes."

Michael knew the way to his mom's heart, and it wasn't food. It was cleaning, doing dishes. He didn't have to do dishes because he cooked. For whatever reason, none of the women in this house cooked. He'd had to learn in order to survive.

"She doesn't mind working," his mom said. "That's important."

"Mmmmm," Ngoại agreed.

For a moment, the three of them watched as Stella washed bowls, rinsed them, and handed them to Sophie to dry. She'd rolled her sleeves up and worked with great attention, listening and smiling distractedly as Sophie chatted with her.

"Take her home," Ngoại said. "She looks tired."

His mom nodded. "Take her home."

He pushed away from the table and went to wrap his

arms around Stella's waist. Because he couldn't resist, he ran his lips down her neck so she shivered. The soapy sponge paused in midscrub, and her expression was confused as she gazed at him over her shoulder. He slid a hand down her delicate forearm and hijacked the sponge from her. He finished washing the frying pan and the rest of the dishes with her in front of him, occasionally pausing to kiss her ear, her neck, or her jaw.

Sophie slanted him a *go get a room* look as he handed her the last colander—one of many that he'd made his mom promise never to stick in the microwave again—and he could tell she was dying to say something dry and caustic but was holding back because she didn't want to embarrass Stella.

Stella's eyelids had gone heavy, and her nails dug into the tile counter as she tried unsuccessfully not to respond to him.

"Ready to go home?" he whispered.

She nodded.

They said their good-byes and piled into Stella's car, and he pressed the Tesla's on button.

Before Stella could buckle her seat belt, he asked, "What are you seeing in terms of living arrangements and frequency of visits?"

"What do most couples do when they're in committed relationships?"

"They live together, and they see each other every day. Is that what you want?" It was strange hearing himself say the words out loud. These were things he'd spent his entire adult life avoiding, but with Stella, he might be ready for them. If she wanted them, too.

She rubbed her cheek on her shoulder. "I want that, then. I have a guest bedroom you can use. But if you're uncomfortable staying with me, I understand. Not all couples live in the same house."

"What if I want to share your bed, Stella?" he asked in a low tone.

Despite how much he wanted to help her and prove he wasn't his dad, he wasn't sure he could do this if sex was off the table. He wanted her too much. Besides, most of her problems stemmed from lack of confidence. Bed was a great place to work on that.

"You don't have to do that," she said.

"That wasn't the question. I know I don't have to."

Staring out the passenger window, she said, "My bed is open to you if you want it, but you know where my skill levels are at. That hasn't changed since our last time together."

He smiled at that. She sounded worried about pleasing him. Something his clients almost never cared about.

"Let's seal the deal."

"Oh, all right." She pulled a hand out from under her thigh and held it out toward him.

"We're going into a practice relationship. I think we should kiss on it."

She locked eyes with him as her lips parted in surprise, and that was all the invitation he needed. Leaning across the center divide, he kissed her. He meant for it to be a seductive, slowly enflaming kind of kiss, but the sighing sound she made drove him straight out of his mind. He took her mouth with hungry strokes of his tongue. She wound her fingers through his hair, scraped them down his chest and abdomen, and tucked them into his jeans. *Yes.* Finally, they could get back to checking boxes—

Knuckles rapped against the driver's-side window. A muffled voice spoke incoherent words.

He launched himself back into his seat before powering the window down.

Sophie crossed her arms and tapped her bare foot on the pavement before she bent down, narrowed her eyes, and clearly mouthed the word *pervert* at him. "Mom wanted me to remind you your headlights are lighting up Ngoại's room so she can't sleep."

"Sorry, forgot. We'll head home now."

Peering into the car, she said, "Good night, Stella. Hope we see you again soon."

Stella swiped at the loose hairs falling over her face and cleared her throat with a cough. "Good night, Sophie."

Sophie sent him one last reproving look and sauntered back into the house. Seconds later, his phone lit up with rapid text messages from Sophie.

Geez Michael, go easy on her.

You'll scare her away, and we all really like her.

Honestly, in the DRIVEWAY? What are you, 13?

He choked on a laugh and handed the phone to Stella so she could read the messages.

She bit down on the tip of a fingernail as she grinned. "I'm not scared."

He ran a hand through his hair, took a deep breath, and adjusted the painfully stiff flesh rising against his fly. "Let's get you home."

He drove with gratuitous disregard of the law through the empty residential streets, envisioning himself peeling her librarian clothes off and pinning her against the wall, the floor—he didn't care where.

It was going to be so good with Stella, spectacular even. He was going to—he glanced at Stella, trying to decide what to do first, and his hopes plummeted. He was going to carry her into her house and put her to bed.

In the scant minutes since they'd left his mom's, she'd fallen fast asleep. Her head lolled to the side, and her glasses sat on her nose at a crooked angle. She didn't so much as flinch when her garage cranked open and her tires squeaked over the epoxy floor.

He tried to shake her awake, but she didn't react. Her breathing remained deep and even, her body relaxed. With a sigh, he lifted her out of the car and headed toward her bedroom—*their* bedroom as of tonight.

Stella awakened by slow degrees. She registered the sunlight on her face, the distant barking of a neighborhood dog, and Michael's delicious smell. It was all around her, warm and concentrated, and she burrowed into the sheets with a happy sigh.

A heavy weight over her side kept her from rolling the sheets around her like a burrito, and she frowned. What was that? She lifted the blankets and stared in shock at the muscular arm wrapped around her waist. Her *naked* waist. She'd slept in her bra and panties last night.

And she hadn't gone through her night routine. She was covered in nastiness. Her *mouth*. It was probably forming an ecosystem for antibiotic-resistant strains of bacteria. She shot up in bed, her entire being focused on running straight to the bathroom. Floss, brush, shower, pajamas. Floss, brush, shower, pajamas.

Michael yanked her back down and kissed her nape. "Not yet."

"I'm gross. I have to get clean. I—"

He sucked on her neck and pulled her hips back as he

rocked forward, making her achingly aware of the firm flesh prodding against the backs of her thighs through his boxers.

Her body went into total system failure. Her limbs weakened. Between her thighs, she flushed and tingled with wanting. The intensity of her desire frightened and embarrassed her. She needed to be in control of herself and her body. Control was gone.

"Good morning." His voice was a husky rasp that sent shivers down her spine.

"G-good mor—" A hand dipped inside her bra and cupped her breast. He stroked the tip until it ached and pinched, sending a burst of sensation straight to her core. When he headed downward, smoothing a hand over her belly, her stomach muscles clenched.

"I want to touch you here." He palmed her sex with a bold grasp, and the heat of his touch spread through the cotton of her panties, searing her.

She gripped his wrist, fully intending to pull him away, but her hands refused to cooperate. His forearm was firm with defined muscle, his skin smooth, utterly distracting.

"Is that permission?" he whispered.

She'd given him permission last night. She wanted this, but she didn't know how to handle this side of herself. Her body told her to say yes. Her mind told her to say no.

Her body won the fight, and her hips arched against his hand. He edged the crotch of her panties aside. He kissed her nape as he traced the slick entrance to her body with his fingertips. A sharp breath tore from her lungs. Panic and pleasure collided.

"You're wet already, Stella. You're like a Lamborghini. Zero to sixty in two point seven seconds."

"You like Lamborghinis?" She tried desperately to cling to coherent thought. She needed to think at all times, to weigh her actions and her words. When she let go, she *always* made mistakes. She did the wrong thing, hurt people, mortified herself.

He continued touching her lightly, trailing around and around her opening in maddening circles. His teeth scraped against her neck before he licked and kissed her. Goose bumps spread over her skin.

"Yes, I like them. No, don't get me one," he said.

"Why not?" She rubbed her feet against his shins, dug her fingernails into his arm. *Push him away. Pull him closer. Regain control. Let go.*

"It doesn't suit my lifestyle, and my mom would be very, very curious how I got it." He emphasized the word *very* with barely there strokes over her clitoris. Her sex spasmed and trembled at the edge of release.

He bit her earlobe. "You're about to go off, aren't you? That's all it took."

"It's because I've been fantasizing about you ever since last Friday." Oh God, what had she just said?

He removed his touch and sat up. His expression was soft as he brushed tendrils of hair away from her face. "What does Fantasy Michael do?"

"Everything."

He laughed before his eyes went intense. "Does he make you come with his mouth? Real Michael wants to do that."

She squirmed as the need to please him warred with her inhibitions. That was one thing Fantasy Michael hadn't done. "I'm more interested in giving oral sex than receiving it."

"Maybe we should work on it," he said in an unusually subdued tone. "I'm not the only guy who loves going down on women."

She sank her teeth into her lip and fisted the sheets. Women. Plural. For a regular man, that meant anywhere from one to ten, maybe twenty. For Michael . . . hundreds. It might even be thousands, for all she knew. A new type of anxiety weighed down on her. Could she possibly measure up against all of his past clients?

"I don't want to disgust you."

"You won't."

"How do I make it good for you? Are some women better at receiving oral sex than others? What do they do?" She badly wanted to be good at it. She wanted to blow all the others out of the water—but there had been *so many of them*.

"What is going on in that beautiful brain of yours?" he asked in bafflement.

"I just—I want—I need—I think—"

"No more thinking," he said as he touched a thumb to her lips.

He ran warm hands from her shoulders down to her wrists, interlaced their fingers and squeezed their palms together. Her muscles tensed as she worried she wasn't responding the right way. What was she supposed to do? Now that she understood he wanted her to feel pleasure, she wanted to give it to him, wanted to make him happy.

"Stella, you're locking up on me." His eyes searched hers, worried now.

"I'm sorry." She felt the sweat between their hands and fingers and winced. Her heart pounded. She was screwing this up.

He gathered her in his arms and held her, smoothing a hand through her hair in slow sweeps. "This is because of oral sex? We don't have to have it."

Stella pressed her forehead to his neck and breathed in his scent. By slow degrees, she relaxed into his embrace. "I'm very competitive."

He brushed a kiss against her temple. "Okay, but how does that factor into anything?"

"It means I want to please you more than all your other clients have."

"Stella, *I'm* the one who's being paid to please here."

"I'm not paying you for sex anymore, remember?"

He made a frustrated growling sound and held her tighter. "What am I going to do with you? I have you hot and naked in my arms, and you're still not ready."

She sighed and rested against him. She idly traced the

dragon scales on his bicep. "We could floss, brush, shower, and dress."

He threw the covers off. "Let's do it, then."

D on't you have any casual clothes?"

Michael swept her damp hair to the side and kissed her neck as she stared at her wardrobe, trying to make her clothing selection for the day.

"I didn't need them when I started working, so I gave them all away," she said.

"You had them, though? Or were they all knee-length skirts and button-downs?" As he spoke, his arms stole around her bathrobe-clad waist and hugged her to his naked chest. Her body couldn't decide if it wanted to relax or stiffen.

She suspected he was seducing her. It was almost working. It was definitely making her mind fuzzy, but that was a good thing. He was distracting her from her headache and the fact that she was terribly off-schedule today, something that normally filled her with irritation and frustration until she could start over and do things right.

"They *were* skirts and button-downs. How do you know me so well?"

His hot breath fanned over her ear as he chuckled. "You are my favorite puzzle lately. I want to see you in sundresses, Stella."

"I don't have any."

"It's Sunday. We could go shopping."

She turned around, feeling a spike of anxiety at the thought of going out in public, going somewhere new, and worst of all, trying on itchy, scratchy clothes that were probably dusted with rat feces from warehouse floors. "Can you make me sundresses? I was serious when I said I wanted custom Michael designs. I'll have to get anything I buy seriously altered before I can wear it, anyway."

Instead of answering, he pulled a pink shirt off its hanger

and inspected the inside seams. "French seams. The fabric is . . ." He rubbed it between his fingers. "It's plain cotton."

"I love cotton. Silk, too. I don't mind synthetic fabrics like acrylic and Lycra, as long as they're soft, but I can't stand crisp denim or wool or cashmere or angora."

A pleased smile curved over his mouth as he continued to check out the construction of her shirt. "My practice girl-friend might know more about textiles than I do. Impressive."

His compliment made her feel warm and bubbly, but her mind snagged on her "practice girlfriend" title. She didn't like it—namely the "practice" half—but she knew she had to be realistic about what she could and couldn't have. Better to focus on the irony of her tactile defensiveness leading them to a common interest. She restrained herself from reading off fabric types and qualities like an encyclopedia.

He hung her shirt back up neatly and stepped in front of her, resting his hands on her hips. "I really want you in sundresses, Stella. I love the pencil skirts. They do fantastic things to one of my favorite parts of you, but they've also been torturing me."

"How? Why?"

"They don't let me do this." Watching her with heated eyes, he drew the end of her bathrobe up. It made a brush-ing sound against his jeans as he bared her thighs to the cool air. His palm scraped up the outside of her leg, paused at her hip, and reached behind her to squeeze her rear, mak-ing need shock through her body.

The brown curls between her thighs were visible, and she caught him eyeing them darkly. Without asking, with-out hesitating, without giving her time to think, he slipped his hand over her hip and down to her pelvis. Daring finger-tips threaded through the hair and massaged the peak of her sex.

Her skin burned where he touched her, and her knees weakened. She braced herself on his shoulders.

"That's my girl," he whispered as he leaned down to kiss her.

The taste of his clean mouth was heavenly, and a high-pitched sound hummed from her throat as she kissed him back. She tried to kiss him as well as he'd taught her, but she couldn't concentrate. His fingers were doing diabolical things to her. It was all she could do to stand, and she wasn't doing a good job of it. Each stroke of his fingers melted her a little more. She was starting to tremble.

Without breaking the kiss, he picked her up and carried her to the bed. The feel of her back sinking into the down blankets brought her to reality. They were finally going to do this. Sex. Without structure, without a plan. She was going to be bad at it, and he'd have to show her what to fix, how to improve, and she'd try very hard to take the criticism in stride even though it humiliated—

He tore her bathrobe open, and his mouth fastened on her nipple, drawing deeply. She arched into him with a gasp that turned into a moan when his hand slid between her thighs again and stroked her. Her sex clenched so hard it hurt.

"Shhhhhh," he whispered against her breast.

One long finger slipped into her, and grateful sighs and murmurs tumbled from her lips. That was exactly what she needed. He worked a second finger in, and the stretching sensation had her head falling back. No, *this* was what she needed. Her heels dug into the bed as she pushed into the penetration. His fingers eased in and out, curling against her to breathtaking effect.

When he removed his touch, she couldn't bite back a protesting sound. "Michael, more, I—"

He lifted his glistening fingers to his lips and sucked them into his mouth. The intensity of his eyes coupled with his devilish grin had her bunching the blankets in her hands as her core tightened on itself.

The caresses resumed with deep, slow thrusts. It was

good, so good, but he wasn't touching her where she needed it. Her hips writhed as she tried to relieve the growing ache. When he withdrew again, she stroked her hands down her stomach in rampant frustration, but her own touch did nothing to excite her.

He gripped her knees, pulled them apart to bare her sex to his eyes. His chest expanded on a sharp inhalation, and his dragon tattoo rippled. His throat worked on a loud swallow. "I should have known you'd have the prettiest little—"

"Michael, don't say it," she said quickly.

He paused, considered her with a naughty glint in his eyes. "You mean . . . pussy?"

Flames burned her face, and she wanted to hide inside herself.

The corner of his mouth kicked up. "No wonder my mom likes you so much. It's very Vietnamese to be modest about sex. I didn't even know the correct Vietnamese word for girl parts until I was twenty. Most people call it a little bird. My aunt refers to it as a sweet potato. Those aren't the right words for yours. You have a pussy, Stella."

Her face burned even hotter, and the blush spread down her neck to her chest, touching everything. "That's a cat. They purr and catch mice. Me—that part—it doesn't—the image is so ridiculous—I can't—"

"It's a pussy, Stella, and it's wet for me, and I want to eat it." Focusing a dark look between her legs, he traced her folds, dipped inside briefly, and began circling the part of her that wanted him most. "And this, this is your clit. It wants my mouth so bad it's bright red. Put us both out of our misery, and let me taste you. If you hate it, I'll stop."

It hit her then that he truly wanted this, her. He liked what he saw. His unabashed craving for her most private parts was real. And dirty. And . . . exciting. A secret Stella woke up and stretched, drawn to Michael and his words.

"Will you be disappointed if I don't like it and I don't respond like other women?" She wanted to like it, wanted to orgasm for his mouth like so many other women had, and because of that, her arousal started fading away as performance anxiety took its place.

"If you don't like it, then we'll move on." Running his hands down her inner thighs, he spread her wider. The tip of his tongue pressed against his gorgeous upper lip.

He bent down close to her wet flesh, making her nervousness spike to heart-pounding levels, and took a deep breath. "I'm beginning to understand your addiction to my smell. It's a good thing you don't smell like this everywhere, though. I'd have a constant hard-on for you. I'm having enough trouble as it is."

A gentle closed-mouth kiss landed on her clitoris, and her entire body stiffened. That was not what she'd expected.

"Hate it?" he asked.

"I—I . . ."

Another kiss, followed by a slow tasting. He hummed his approval and covered her with his mouth, sucking with slight pressure as his tongue laved her. Soft and warm and delicious. Stella's body went limp as heat bloomed inside her.

"I can tell you don't like it," he rasped. "Just let me . . ." His tongue stroked into her, lapping at the moisture that flooded from her. "One last taste." He returned to her clitoris, scraping his teeth against the sensitive nerves before he kissed her again, sipped at her, licked her.

She buried her face in the blankets as pleasure concentrated low and deep. His tongue was so clever, but release stayed just out of reach. This was too new. Her body was in a state of shock from the sensations bombarding her. When he stopped she was going to cry.

Two fingers worked into her, and her eyes rolled back into her head. He began a steady rhythm as his tongue flickered over her, and she couldn't prevent her hips from rising to meet his thrusts. Oh God, she was riding his hand, smothering his face with her sex. That had to be bad. She told herself to stop. She couldn't.

Somehow, she found her hands tangled in his short hair. Her body was coiling tighter, grasping at his fingers, so wet now she could hear the slippery sounds every time he drove back into her.

"I'll stop, Stella. Clearly . . ." His tongue rubbed over her fast and hard, and she clenched helplessly around his fingers. "Clearly, you hate this."

"Michael." That breathy, needy voice was hers. She didn't care. She rubbed her hungry flesh against his tongue, nearly sobbing when he took her back into his mouth.

He sucked with perfect pressure, and she came apart with strong, wrenching convulsions. He rode out the orgasm with her, dragging out the pleasure with soothing flicks of his tongue. As the aftershocks spaced out, he pressed a parting kiss to her sex and rose over her to blanket her with his body. She buried her face against his chest, feeling more exposed and vulnerable than she'd ever been.

She'd let him do that to her. She'd made all those sounds, lost all control.

"You came on me like a porn star, Stella. I almost spilled in my jeans."

"Did it take me too long? Was that a lot of . . . work?" It discomforted her that she'd been the only one to derive pleasure from that act. She much preferred to be on the giving side of things.

He laughed softly. "I drew it out on purpose, Stella. You were sexy as hell." Peeling away from her, he sat back on his heels and extracted a small foil from his pocket. "Do you want to?"

She pushed herself up, and the bathrobe slipped off her shoulders. She stifled the reflex to cover her nudity but couldn't bring herself to meet his eyes. Her pulse was out of control. "Yes, I want to." She took the foil from his hand and tore it open with shaky fingers.

He got down from the bed and unbuttoned and unzipped his fly. His muscles bunched and shifted, and the dragon tattoo winked at her as he stepped free of his pants with masculine grace. This was Michael in all of his naked glory. He was perfection. Even *that* part of him.

Oh God, *especially* that part of him. His erection stood at attention, thick and veined, in flawless proportion to the rest of his beautiful body. She'd just had the most intense orgasm of her life, but she wanted more. She wanted that. It made her mouth water, and she'd never given a man oral sex.

She couldn't remember how to breathe as he kneeled on the bed and wrapped one of her hands around him. He was so hot, satiny soft, but rigid underneath. *Want, want, want.* In any way she could. In whatever way he liked.

"Stella, the look on your face." His voice was hoarse, almost a groan. He guided her fist up and down his length, saying, "This is my cock. When you want it, when you need it, that's the word I want you to use."

Unable to speak, she nodded. Secret Stella loved the idea of demanding his . . . cock . . . and him providing it, though she didn't think she'd ever be able to get that word past her lips. Not unless they were talking about farm animals. Probably not even then.

"Do you want to put it on me?" he asked, indicating the forgotten condom in her other hand.

She licked her lips and cleared her throat. "Yes."

Her hands weren't steady, so she and Michael ended up doing it together. When they finished, he pulled her close, and she shivered at the feel of their skin coming in contact. Her nipples grazed his chest, and his solid length burned against her lower belly. He swept his hands up and down her back as he angled his head, trying to catch her gaze.

"Why won't you look at me?"

She trained her eyes on the notch at the base of his throat and hunched her shoulders forward. "I'm feeling very self-conscious."

"We're both naked."

She didn't know how to explain that it was on the *inside* that she was feeling naked. If he looked into her eyes, he'd *see* all of her, the person she kept hidden away. No one wanted to see that. This was supposed to be fun and educational, not soul-baring.

He tipped her chin back, and she caught a glimpse of tender eyes before she squeezed her own shut.

"Kiss me, please," she said.

Warm lips took hers, tasting of her and him and sex. His hands grew urgent as he caressed her. He grabbed her thigh and hooked her leg around his hips, opening her to him. With a flex of his hips, he stroked over her sex. The friction sent blood pooling fast and hot.

"Now, Stella."

She wrapped her arms around the barrel of his chest and pressed her lips to his neck. "I'm ready."

He lowered her to the bed, and his body covered her. He nuzzled against her jaw and ear, pressed soft kisses to her cheek, the corner of her mouth, her lips. "You have to talk to me, okay? If something hurts, if you don't like it, if you want something more, if it's perfect. Say everything."

Eyes still shut, she said, "I'll . . . try."

Unexpectedly, he flipped her around so she was on her hands and knees. "I think you'll feel less self-conscious this way."

She opened her eyes, taking in the rumpled pillows and wooden headboard. He was right. This *was* better. He couldn't see her. She immediately relaxed. "Will it be good for you this way?" The other men had all preferred the missionary position.

"No, it's going to be excellent." Rough hands glided down her back and massaged her with voluptuous motions. His firm chest brushed against her shoulder blades as he propped an arm on the bed next to her. Reaching in front of her, he slid a hand up her inner thigh. He searched through her folds and sank his fingers deep, working her until her hips were rocking and fresh moisture drenched the both of them. Withdrawing, he teased her clitoris with gentle touches.

"Michael . . ."

"Stella," he replied, breathing heavily in her ear.

Something hard prodded at the entrance of her body and pushed inside slowly. Stella stopped breathing. Sex had hurt in the past, but there was nothing now but a sensuous stretching that went on and on until Michael seated himself fully inside her. She tried to swallow, to talk. Couldn't. They fit perfectly.

For long moments, Michael remained immobile. Sensing the tension in his body, she looked at him over her shoulder.

"Michael?"

His face was drawn as if in pain. "I've been wanting this too long. It's too good. You feel . . ." He exhaled. "If I move, I'm going to lose it."

She couldn't stop herself from smiling. She wasn't alone in this. "Move." She arched her back and rocked against him. The motion pushed him in even deeper, filled her.

A raw groan escaped his throat. "Stella, I'm serious. Give me a moment to cool down. This is our first time. I want fireworks for you."

Our first time. He made it sound like there would be lots of times. The thought made her so happy her heart wanted to burst. She didn't need fireworks. She just needed him.

Wet kisses landed on her neck, interspersed with teasing nips and greedy licks. He traced the folds stretched tightly around him before sliding his slick fingertips higher. When he rubbed her there, she clenched on him and moaned.

Only then did he begin moving. He withdrew, thrust back into her, retreated, returned, picking up a driving rhythm. The twin assaults of his fingers and invading sex kindled flames beneath her skin that spread outward in widening rings.

"Stella," he said with a groan. "You feel too good. Sweet Stella, my Stella."

His words soothed and excited. She tried to speak as he'd asked her to, but all that came out were gasps and sighs of pleasure. Instead, she communicated how she felt with her body. She spread her thighs wider and writhed to match him thrust for thrust. Did he like that? Or was she being too debauched? The hand propped against the mattress captured hers, and he interlaced their fingers.

"Just like that," he whispered. "Perfect."

Her sex fisted tight. For a timeless moment, she hovered on the brink, breathless, possessed, loved. The orgasm crashed over her. She rippled around him as he drove into her relentlessly. She attempted to meet his thrusts, but the strong convulsions gripping her body stole her coordination.

His lips traveled from her neck to her jaw, and when she turned toward him blindly, he captured her mouth, stroking his tongue deep. The caresses between her legs did not ease, and before the last orgasm had finished, she felt another building. Her muscles fluttered around his impalement, clamped down, and exploded yet again. With a hoarse groan, he surged into her one last time.

He rubbed his jaw against her cheek and neck and lowered her shaking body to the bed, held her close like she was his. She stroked clumsy hands over the strong arms wrapped around her and held him back.

Until she remembered sex didn't mean anything to him, and she loosened her grip somewhat. Michael enjoyed physical intimacy. That was all.

Emotion clogged her throat, anyway. If this was just practice, she never wanted the real thing. How long could she live in a fantasy?

As Michael embraced a boneless, contented Stella, his heart stumbled around his chest like a drunken man.

That hadn't been practice fucking for a practice relationship or pro bono fucking to prove he was better than his dad.

He'd fucked hundreds of women, but he'd never been so in tune with one woman's body. He'd never been so desperate to please or so elated when she cried his name and came for him again and again and again.

He didn't know what that had been, but it sure as hell hadn't been fucking.

She hugged him tighter, pressed sloppy kisses to his shoulder and neck, and grinned up at him. She arabesqued her fingers on his chest—apparently this was not always a bad sign—and it tickled like hell.

He flattened her fingers against his heart to still their tapping and tried to put himself in a professional state of mind. "Look at you. I'm expecting another five-star review."

"Six stars." Her grin widened, and chocolate eyes shone at him and forgot to dart away, letting him really look at her for the first time that morning. It made him feel like he'd won something priceless, kicked the breath straight out of his lungs.

"You're bad for my ego. It's big enough as it is," he made himself say in a light tone.

"You don't act egotistical. You're very modest but confident. It's one of the many things I love about you."

Love?

Sharpness panged inside his chest.

She could never love him. He felt the certainty with every fiber of himself. Love required trust, and only a fool would trust him. He was his father's son.

But he could prove he was more if he did this right. That was all he could ask for. He glanced at the clock and was amazed to see it wasn't even ten yet. The events of the morning had felt life-changing, but they'd only been awake for two hours.

"I'm starving, and I need coffee," he said. "I also need to get my car. All of my clean clothes are in there."

Mostly, he needed some space. She was getting too close, and he needed to put distance between them. He got out of bed and pulled on his jeans, fully aware of his audience's appreciative gaze. He felt a little ridiculous about it, but maybe he did it slowly. Maybe he flexed his abs and biceps as he zipped his fly and buttoned his pants. Because really, putting on pants required a lot of muscle.

"Hurry up and get ready, Stella."

Her brow furrowed. "Why?"

"We're going shopping. Couples do that on Sundays."

Stella pursed her lips as she stared at her reflection in the mirror. Michael had just opened up an entire new branch of apparel to her.

Yoga clothes.

In particular, yoga *pants*.

She was very possibly in heaven. The pants didn't itch at all, and they were tight. She loved clothes that hugged her. Even better, they made her legs and butt look outstanding. She looked like a dancer. Or a yogi. Or some hybridized version of the two.

"Come out so I can see," Michael said from outside the changing room.

Biting her lip to hide her smile, she opened the door and stepped out.

His crooked grin came out in full force, and his rare dimple winked. "Knew it."

"Do you like it?" She smoothed a hand over her tummy and turned in a slow circle.

He stood up from the waiting chair and approached her, running appraising eyes over her curves. He slid a hand down the length of her neck to her shoulder and across the tight-fitting long sleeve so he could interlace their fingers. "I love it."

"I'm sexy in this."

He wrapped an arm around her waist and drew her near. "Very sexy." He brushed his lips over hers and tickled his way to her ear and neck, making her squirm and bite back giggles that would have been decidedly unsexy.

From the corner of her eye, she caught a shopgirl watching her with open envy. The girl mouthed the words *So lucky*, and Stella grinned even though she had mixed feelings. None of this was real. She was paying for it. Not that she minded the expense. Michael was worth every penny.

"I assume you're going to buy them?"

"One of every color."

"I have to put my foot down. Not the fluorescent orange with yellow spots. It hurts me," he said with a wince.

"No fluorescent orange and yellow, got it. Oh, they have dresses." Her eyes rounded at the possibilities.

When they stopped for lunch at a small French bakery in the Stanford Mall, three enormous bags of apparel took up the space on the pavement by their feet. He insisted they had the best non-Asian sandwiches in California, which Stella found interesting because she hadn't even known Asian sandwiches were a thing.

She expected the sandwiches to be stacked high with deli goodness, but when he brought lunch to their outdoor table, it was plain baguettes with turkey, Swiss, and butter. At least he'd bought an almond croissant, too. To her surprise, her first bite of the baguette was delicious.

"The secret is really good bread and butter. All you need is strong basics," he said with a wink, and she got the feeling he was talking about more than food.

As light afternoon shopper traffic passed by and the sun shone down through the trees, Stella decided she might want to do this again. Her regular Sunday schedule was shot, but she was open to developing a new weekend routine. She was adaptable, especially when things involved Michael.

Dressed in casual khakis and a white button-down open at the collar and rolled up to his elbows, he looked magazine delicious—as usual. It occurred to her they'd spent the entire morning shopping for her. How selfish and self-absorbed of her.

"Do you want to look at men's attire?" She considered the shops around them, wondering if any of them appealed to him.

He shook his head with a funny smile. "No, thanks."

"Are you sure? Would you let me get you something?" When his expression went uncomfortable, her heartbeat picked up, and she tried to make light of the situation by adding, "Since you won't let me get you a Lamborghini."

He sent her a searching look. "Would you really get me a Lamborghini if I wanted it?"

She stared down at the crumbs on her sandwich wrapper and nodded. "I can afford it, if that's what you're asking. I don't really know how to talk about money matters, but I make a lot, and there aren't many things I want to spend it on. I would love to get you a car. Especially if—" She cut herself off before she could say something that would make him angry.

"If what?"

"I'd rather not say. I'm pretty sure it's not appropriate."

He tilted his head to the side, and his expression grew shuttered. "I'd like to hear it."

"I was going to say . . ." She took an uncomfortable breath. "Especially if another woman got you the one you have."

He focused on folding his sandwich wrapper into a neat square. "Are you asking if the car was a gift?"

She was pretty sure it was, and it infuriated her. "Yes."

"It was, actually."

"From the blonde at the club."

His brow wrinkled. "How do you know that?"

"She's the client who won't leave you alone." The memory of the woman kissing him flashed in her mind, and Stella's hackles rose. Not only that, but he'd had sex with her—probably multiple times. She dug her nails into the glass surface of the table as her breathing went fast and bitter.

He settled a hand on top of hers, and her heart rate eased. "I don't like getting those kinds of gifts. Please don't, okay?"

"Okay." But she couldn't help feeling he kept the gift because he liked the woman who'd given it to him. Wasn't that what you did when someone meant something to you? You kept the things they gave you?

She wanted him to keep something from her. The fact that he wasn't allowing her to give him anything made her feel almost desperate.

"You've got your work cut out for you if you're going to start getting jealous of my past clients, Stella," he said, his eyes level and his voice somber, like his escorting was a sad reality they had to accept.

Question after question piled on her tongue. If he didn't like it, why did he do it? He was so talented with clothes.

Why didn't he make more of it instead of dry cleaning and altering it? What did he use his escorting money on? Did he have some secret addiction? Was he in danger?

Why couldn't he be hers for real?

He was hers for now, though. He didn't want the blonde. He hadn't been with the blonde this morning.

As they finished up with lunch, the question from before persisted in the back of her mind.

Why *couldn't* he be hers for real?

There was only one plausible reason she could think of: He didn't want her back.

Things like that weren't written in stone, though. At the beginning of all of this, she'd been prepared to learn skills that would aid her in seducing a man—possibly Philip James. But why should she settle for Philip when maybe she could have Michael? Could she use what he taught her . . . on him? Could she seduce her escort?

She was supposed to be working. The online underclothes project was interesting. Normally, she'd have finished by now. But she simply could not look at underwear, even the word *underwear*, and not think of Michael.

The desk drawer where she kept her phone beckoned to her. She wanted to text him. Was that . . . allowed? Aside from that night at her office, they'd only texted for logistical purposes.

She tapped her fingers on the surface of her desk before she fisted her hand. How was she supposed to seduce him if she couldn't get up the nerve to send him a simple text message? She dug her phone out.

Hi.

She deleted the message before sending it.

I miss you.

Just the sight of those words made her palms sweat. Too direct. Delete.

I wanted to confirm our plans for tonight.

She hit send and placed the phone on her desk as she stared at her computer monitors without seeing a single thing. The screen on her phone went black from inactivity. He was probably busy.

Her phone vibrated, but instead of buzzing once to indicate she'd gotten a text message, it kept buzzing. A phone call.

She peeked at the screen, and her heart jumped when she saw it was Michael. She hugged the phone to her chest before answering it. "Hello?"

"Hi, Stella." In the background, his mom gabbed in Vietnamese and a sewing machine whirred. "I need both hands so I decided to call you back instead of texting. We're still on for tonight. That Thai place in Mountain View."

"Okay, I'll meet you there."

"Perfect."

The sewing machine paused, and silence hung in the virtual space between them. She willed him to speak. She wanted to hear his voice again.

"Remember clothes. For my place. Unless you don't want to stay there. You don't have to," she said in a rush.

"No, I'm fine with that. I just forgot. Thanks for reminding me." He chuckled, and Stella's hands tightened on the phone. She really, really missed him, and it had only been a day since she'd seen him last.

His mom said something, and he sighed. "I have to go. Looking forward to tonight. Miss you. Bye."

Her breath caught before she murmured, "Miss you, too." The line had already disconnected, however, and she said the words to herself.

How did other people get through their day when they missed someone like this? She wanted to *see* him.

She tapped on her phone's photo bank, and found it, as she'd known it would be, empty. Feeling impulsive, she texted Michael again.

I want a picture of you for my phone.

Please.

She waited.

When she lost hope that he'd respond and set her phone on her desk, it vibrated.

It was a quick selfie, a close-up of his face with his eyebrow raised. He looked goofy but still utterly delectable. She sighed and ran her thumb over his cheek.

Her phone buzzed again with text messages from him.

Where's mine?

I want your hair down.

She released a disbelieving laugh. Are you serious?

Hair down. Selfie. Now.

Undo your top two buttons, too.

Feeling silly, she gripped the rubber band holding her hair back and tried to pull it free. It caught, and when she pulled harder, it snapped, unraveled from her hair, and landed on the floor. She worked the strands apart with her fingers and then loosened the top buttons of her shirt. Her face peered at her from the phone screen, but she looked . . . different. She didn't look like regular Stella. She looked like Secret Stella, the girl who was going to see her lover tonight.

Her finger accidentally hit the camera button, capturing her face as understanding hit. That was what they were. They were lovers. She liked the sound of that, quite a lot.

She sent the picture to Michael.

Almost instantly, her phone vibrated.

Damn, Stella.

Sexy. As. Hell.

A laugh bubbled free, and she was half tempted to send him something really sexy. Except she had no clue how to go about it. There was probably an art to the camera angle and body positioning, and her office was surrounded by windows. Either her colleagues would get an eyeful or she'd have to figure out some way to stuff her phone inside her fitted clothes.

She set her phone down in defeat and made herself focus on her work, which she still loved. As she waded through the data, she ran across an interesting finding: The vast majority of married men didn't buy underclothes—not even for themselves. Their wives did. Screening and filtering the data, looking back through the many years of numbers provided, she discovered they quit purchasing underclothes even before public records announced their marriages.

What was going on there? What kind of anthropological phenomenon was this?

The thrill of a new puzzle simmered through her veins, captivating her. She plotted the data against several different variables, analyzed the curves and seemingly random scatter graphs, looked at the statistics. She could not figure it out. She *loved* when she couldn't figure it out.

Her phone buzzed, and the screen read, *Dinner with Michael.*

She sent a longing glance at her computer monitors, but she didn't let her hands touch her keyboard again. There was no such thing as five more minutes for her. If she went back to work, the next time she surfaced from the data would be well after midnight. That was why she set the alarms.

Also, Michael was just as interesting as the data, and he made her laugh. He smelled good and felt good and tasted good and . . . She hugged herself as her feet danced over the carpet. This was almost too much perfectness. Exciting work during the day. Exciting Michael at night. She wanted this every day, forever.

She saved her work, powered down her computer, and gathered up her things. Walking down the hallway while people were still in the office was something she did rarely, but her coworkers didn't usually think much about it. Tonight, however, the unusual attention she got as she passed by confused her. The top econometricians in their offices paused in the middle of writing formulas on their whiteboards. The younger analysts in their cubicles gave her startled looks.

As she strode past Philip's office, he looked up from the

papers on his desk and did a double take. She waved at him and went to the elevator banks. Just as the doors began to close, Philip jumped inside.

"You're heading out early today," he said.

In the process of adjusting her glasses, she realized her hair was down. This was why everyone was acting so funny. She rolled her eyes. It was just hair. "Dinner plans."

Philip's light eyes tracked over her in a thorough sweep. "Meeting someone?"

She tucked her hair behind her ear. "Yes."

"Took my advice, huh?" he said with his usual smirk.

"I did, actually. Thanks."

He blinked, and his eyebrows climbed. "You're surprising, Stella, and you look good with your hair down."

The appraising nature of his gaze made her thoroughly uncomfortable, and she itched to refasten her top two buttons. "Thanks."

"So who is he? Do I know him? Is it *serious*?"

She tapped her fingers on her thighs. "I don't think you know him. I hope it's serious. It's serious to me."

"Don't ask him to marry you too soon, okay? That scares the crap out of guys."

She scowled at him.

He cleared his throat. "Sorry, that came out wrong. Just go slow. That's what I meant to say."

When the elevator dinged and the doors slid open, he pressed a hand to the door sensor to keep it open. "Ladies first."

She marched out, hoping a fast gait would help her leave him behind, but he speed-walked to her side.

"Where are you two going?"

"A Thai place." She spotted her car in the parking lot and wished she could teleport herself directly inside. She was never wearing her hair down at work again.

"So you like spicy food?"

"I do. I'll tell you if this place is any good, and you can take Heidi there."

"Not dating Heidi anymore. She really is too young for me. No common ground. She said I have to work on how I communicate with people. Apparently, I come across condescending. It's frustrating. I can't help it if I know things." He coughed. "Forget that last part."

That gave her pause. She knew what it was like to have trouble communicating. Did that mean Heidi had broken things off? Underneath his obnoxious exterior, was Philip sad? Was he capable of being sad? "I see."

"You and I have common ground." By the look in his eyes, he meant it. He was actually interested in her now.

Stella stopped at her car. "We do."

Her mother thought they were perfect for one another. If he hadn't inspired her toward out-of-the-box thinking with his asshole advice, she might actually be interested back. At the very least, she might have let him be her fourth disastrous sexual encounter.

Not any longer. The only one she wanted now was Michael.

"I have to go, or I'll be late."

He stepped back. "Have a good night, Stella. Not too good, though. See you tomorrow."

After she got inside her car and buckled up, she caught sight of him getting into his own vehicle. A brand-new, bright red Lamborghini. Not her style at all. She would have hated it on sight if it weren't for the fact that Michael liked them.

Sighing, she headed to meet him. The drive was quick, and it wasn't long before she walked into the humid interior of the restaurant. He was waiting for her at a table for two by the window, looking edible himself in black slacks, a striped button-down, and a black silk vest that fit his trim waist to perfection.

His eyes twinkled, and he tapped his lips with an index

finger as he watched her walk between rows of tables toward him. When she reached the table, he stood up and wrapped her in a tight embrace, pressing his lips against her neck as he wove his fingers into her loose locks. "All this hair. My Stella looks gorgeous tonight."

She breathed him in and molded herself against him. A sense of rightness locked into place, and her resolve hardened. She was going to seduce him. If she could just figure out how. "My rubber band broke when I took it out earlier. Now everyone at work thinks I've taken up stripping."

His shoulders shook as he laughed.

The waiter approached, and they reluctantly broke apart to sit.

"You could, you know. You've got the body," he said with a teasing grin.

"With my coordination, I'd concuss myself on the pole."

He stayed wisely silent on the topic of her coordination.

"Is this another Michael original?" she asked, indicating his vest, which she loved to distraction.

"Of course. By the look in your eyes, you want to touch it. My work is complete."

That was when she noticed she was reaching across the table toward him. She pulled her hands back and sat on them, adjusting her glasses with a wrinkle of her nose.

"You can look at it more closely later." He held a palm out on the table and cocked his head to the side, waiting, and she realized he wanted to hold her hand.

How was she supposed to seduce him when he seduced her so well?

She withdrew her hand from underneath herself and settled it in his. He closed his fingers around hers and stroked his thumb over the back of her hand.

"H-how was your day?" As the words left her mouth, she recognized it was the first time she'd asked him that. It wasn't the first time she'd wanted to know. Was it too personal? Could she ask him things like that?

His lips twisted with something between a smile and a grimace. "It's prom season. Not my favorite time of year."

"Lots of alterations?"

"And squealing teenaged girls."

"They must all crush on you instantly." That had to get pretty exhausting.

"I have my mom do most of those fittings, so it's not so bad. But I am going cross-eyed from all the spaghetti-strapped gowns. Your picture was the highlight of my day."

That sounded terrible. Her picture hadn't even been that good. "Do you wish you could work with more menswear, then?"

The thought that he wasn't doing what he loved felt like a sharp bur in her side. She would need therapy if she had to do work she detested all day, every day, every week.

He shrugged, but his expression was thoughtful. "I prefer the creative side of the work, making something new. I don't mind the actual constructing and altering, but it's not very challenging."

"Have you thought of starting your own line?" She covered her mouth as the idea occurred to her. "You could go on one of those reality TV fashion contests. You would win."

He smiled down at their joined hands, but it wasn't a happy smile. "Three years ago, I got selected for a spot on one of those. I think they liked my face better than my portfolio, but whatever. An opportunity is an opportunity. Stuff happened, though, and my mom got sick. I had to turn it down."

The blood drained from Stella's face as her chest broke open. Of course, he would do that for his mom.

He glanced up at her, and his expression went tender. "Don't look so sad. She's doing really well lately."

"It's . . . cancer?" She vaguely recalled hearing his sisters mention chemo while they were fighting, but she'd been so overwhelmed she hadn't fully absorbed the information. How had that gotten past her? What kind of person was she?

"Stage four, incurable, inoperable, lung cancer. No, she's never smoked. She just has bad luck. The latest treatments are working for her, though. Things have been good," he said with an encouraging smile.

She squeezed his hand tight as she gazed at him. Did he have any idea how indescribably wonderful he was?

The waiter arrived, and Michael asked her, "Want me to order?" When she nodded, he rattled off the names of a few dishes without looking at the menu.

"How was *your* day?" he asked.

"Fine."

He grinned and pinched her chin. "Details, Stella."

"Oh. Well . . . I've encountered an interesting puzzle with my work. There is this fascinating phenomenon I can't expl—why are you looking at me like that?"

His head was tilted to the side, his smile particularly fond. "You are adorably sexy when you talk about your work."

"Those things don't go together."

He laughed. "They do with you. Continue, puzzle fascinating phenomenon."

"I'll tell you when I figure it out. Which I will. Let's see here. What else happened? Oh, my boss is pressuring me to hire an intern. And I took my first selfie today." She left out everything relating to Philip. There was no need to mention that uncomfortable encounter.

"Does your boss think you're working too much?"

She shrugged. "Who doesn't think that?"

"It's not too much if you love it. Like you do."

"Precisely. Please tell my mother that."

"If I see her, I will," he said. But judging from the tone of his voice, he thought the likelihood of his seeing her mother was low.

"That would be in about a month at the benefit dinner she's throwing. If you want to come with me, that is. You don't have to," she added quickly.

The muscles in his jaw worked as he considered her. "Do you want me to come?"

She nodded. "She's threatened to matchmake if I don't have a date." And she only wanted to be with Michael. No one else.

"Very dire, indeed. When is it?"

"A Saturday evening. Formal attire. That shouldn't be a problem for you."

The corner of his mouth kicked up, but the tension around his eyes remained. "All right, I'll mark it on my calendar. I'd be happy to go."

"Really?"

"Yeah."

She bit her lip, hesitated, but decided to go ahead and say it. "Will you make my dress?"

He searched her eyes for a long moment. "Okay."

"I'll pay for it, of course—"

"Wait until you see it first," he said, bringing her hand up to his mouth so he could kiss her knuckles.

"I'm going to love it."

He shook with another laugh. "I think you will."

Dinner arrived, and conversation—real conversation—continued at a steady pace as they ate food spiced with lemongrass, makrut lime leaves, basil, and red chili peppers that burned her lips. She asked Michael about his favorite designers—Jean Paul Gaultier, Issey Miyake, and Yves Saint Laurent—and learned he'd gone to fashion school in San Francisco. He asked when she'd discovered her love of economics—high school—and when she'd had her first boyfriend—never. He'd gone steady with a girl in fourth grade, spending time with her primarily on the school bus. Stella ate more than she normally would have. She wanted to drag this out.

When the bill came, she grabbed for it, but Michael handed the waiter his credit card with adept smoothness. She narrowed her eyes.

This wasn't the first time he'd insisted on paying for things with her, and it made her intensely uncomfortable. Living expenses like these were inconsequential to her, and he clearly had money troubles. Why wouldn't he let her pay? How could they work around this? She had no idea how to discuss monetary things without insulting him.

On their way out of the restaurant, Michael said, "I need to stop at my place to pick up my clothes. I forgot about it until you reminded me."

"Does that mean I can see it?" Or was she making assumptions by thinking they were spending the night together?

"If you really want to. It's nothing special." He rubbed the back of his neck, looking charmingly ill at ease.

"It can't be worse than my place."

"What do you mean by that?"

"My place is empty and . . . sterile." People called her that when they thought she wasn't listening.

He ran his fingers across her cheek and down her hair. "It just needs furniture. Come on, then. It's really close to here."

By *really close*, he might have said he lived in the apartment complex right next door. It would have saved her from trying to find a place to park. After circling the packed parking lot unsuccessfully, he told her to take his assigned spot, and he parked a ways out on the street as she waited for him by the complex's water garden.

Taking her hand, he led her up a set of outdoor stairs to his third-floor apartment. "I didn't clean before I left, so expect the worst. Don't have a heart attack, okay?"

She braced herself. "I promise."

Michael held his breath as Stella walked into his one-bedroom apartment. It wasn't dirty—he was actually a super neat person—but it wasn't very nice, either.

He tried looking at the space through her eyes. A small brown Ikea sofa sat against one wall of the living room across from a modest-sized flat-screen TV. At the back of the room were his workout bench and an arrangement of organized free weights. His punching bag hung near the corner in flagrant violation of his rental agreement.

The kitchen was a cramped area with laminate counter-tops, an electric range, and a small wooden table with four matching chairs. He kept a plant in the center of the table for color because, yeah, he liked that sort of thing. A metal filing cabinet was pushed against the back wall with bills and things on top he hadn't gotten around to yet.

Stella removed her high heels and set them next to his other shoes. Her purse she placed absently on his couch as she inspected the DVDs lined up inside the TV console.

Leaning over for a closer look, she gave him a gratuitous view of her luscious ass. "You *alphabetize* them."

He couldn't help laughing. She never acted the way he expected. "Am I rocking your world, Stella?"

"What is this? *Laughing in the Wind*?" She opened the glass door and pulled out the one-inch-thick DVD case.

"Only the best *wuxia* television series ever."

She glanced up from the box with her lips parted, looking like she'd found the Holy Grail, and it took effort not to grin like hell. None of his previous girlfriends had known what *wuxia* was, let alone shared his secret dorky obsession.

Trying to stay cool, he kicked his shoes off and placed them next to hers. "You can borrow it if you want."

She hugged her treasure to her chest. "Okay, thanks."

"Be careful, though. It's really addicting, and there are eighty episodes or something." He rubbed the smile off his mouth and ran his fingers through his hair. "Feel free to look around while I pack my stuff."

But instead of staying behind when he went to his bedroom, she followed him and perched on the edge of the bed, smiling at him before checking out the plain space with curious sweeps of her eyes. Dressed in her expensive business clothes, she looked so out of place inside his cheap apartment that he wondered why the fuck he'd brought her here.

To torment himself, probably.

This was a no-client, no-woman zone, a place where he went to get normal in his head. How was he going to set his mind straight when things ended if he had memories of her sitting on his bed, waiting for him, smiling in the way that was just for him?

He escaped to his walk-in closet and stared at his suits and shirts, letting the sight remind him of a time when he hadn't lived with a noose around his neck. He mentally picked out which garments to bring to Stella's and retrieved a black sports bag from the top shelf. On his way out of the closet, he deliberated over the number of socks and boxers to pack. A week's worth should—

Stella was curled up in his blankets, burrowing into his pillow with an expression of pure ecstasy on her face. It was strange as hell. It shouldn't have aroused him.

But it did.

He dropped his bag to the ground and leaned over her. "Now that you've found my pillow and sheets, you don't need me anymore. Is that it?" he whispered.

Her eyes popped open, and she blushed. "They smell so good."

"Aren't you concerned they're dirty?"

She widened her eyes and tossed the blankets away from her chest. She looked like she might be sick, looked almost betrayed.

Before she could start hyperventilating, he lay down on the bed and gathered her against himself. "I'm the only one who sleeps here, Stella. I was kidding. And I shower at night." He had to wash his clients away before he slept. No way would he bring them into his bed.

Well, except for this client. None of his rules had ever applied to Stella.

She pounded her fists against his chest without force. "That's not funny, Michael."

"I'm sorry." He smoothed the hair away from her face and straightened her glasses for her. "I was only teasing you, and I didn't think about . . . the others . . . until you reacted that way."

"You really haven't brought any of them here?"

Was she jealous? Did he *want* her to be jealous? Fuck yes, he did. "Never."

She pursed her lips like she was biting the inside. "I should leave. I barged my way in here, didn't I? Thank you for showing it to me. I like it. I should get a plant."

She prepared to get up, and he told himself to let her go. This space was not for clients, and he didn't need more memories of her in his bed.

Let her go.

His arms refused to listen. They pulled her close so their bodies lined up in that perfect, custom-made way.

"In my mind, I don't group you with them, Stella."

"You don't?"

She looked so hopeful, Michael couldn't stop himself from saying, "No. You're not just another client to me."

"In a good way, right?" she asked with a wobbly smile.

"In the best way." He stroked her loose hair, and she shut her eyes as she leaned into his caress, trusting him in a way that humbled him.

When he slipped her glasses off and set them on the nightstand, she opened her eyes and swallowed, drawing his attention to the wildly beating pulse point beneath her jaw. Her cheeks bloomed with color. She wanted him. He'd never loved being wanted this much.

"So pretty, Stella."

He brushed his thumb across her bottom lip, and she sighed and kissed it before she surprised him by sucking it into her mouth. She stroked her tongue over him before she bit him, sending a sudden fire burst of sensation directly to his cock.

"Where the hell did you learn that?"

She released his finger. "I just wanted to do it. But I plan to research erotic finger biting tomorrow."

"You could ask me, you know." He lifted her small hand to his mouth and bit the base of her palm.

Her fingers twitched, and her breath came out in a long, ragged exhalation. "I want to know all the things you love most." She captured his hand and brought it to her mouth. White teeth nipped at his skin, and the hairs on his body stood up.

"I love kissing you," he admitted.

She trailed her fingertips lightly over his lips. "Does that mean I can kiss you?"

"You don't have to ask." She was the only one who ever did. Maybe that was why he was so crazy about her.

"I have permission to kiss you whenever I want?" She watched his mouth like what he said was too good to be true.

"Yeah."

She brought their lips together and kissed him like he was oxygen and she was short on air. He ran his hands down her back to her hips, cupped her sweet ass, pulled her into his hardness. She struggled to get closer, threaded her fingers through his hair as she poured herself into the kiss.

So soft, every part of her. But covered by clothes. Michael loved clothes, but they locked Stella away. He'd never felt the urge to tear at buttons like he did now. Breaking the kiss, he captured a hand and loosened the cuff around her elegant wrist.

"Clothes off," he growled.

After he'd unbuttoned her cuffs, she wordlessly went to work on his, and he realized this was her first time undressing him. He'd been undressed by hundreds of different people. In that moment, he couldn't remember a single one of their faces.

There was only Stella.

They worked together, their arms crisscrossing and intertwining as they unbuttoned each other's shirts and his vest, tugged the tails free. She stroked pale hands over his chest and grazed the disks of his nipples, making his skin burn.

He trailed his fingers from her collarbone, down the valley between her bra-covered breasts, over her flat belly, to the waistband of her skirt. After he undid the hook fastening at the side, he eased the zipper over the sweet curve of her hip.

"Skirt off, Stella. If I can't touch you, I'll go crazy." He needed his hands between her legs, needed to taste her.

She sat up on her knees and lowered her skirt. Sitting back down, she pulled the skirt all the way off and set it on the nightstand. She peeked at him from beneath her eyelashes as she curled her legs under herself and fiddled with her open cuffs. Her unbuttoned shirt exposed her skin-tone bra and panties and flawless creamy skin.

"You're still wearing too many clothes," he said.

She drew her shirt off with a shy shrug of her shoulders and unhooked her bra, letting it fall from her breasts. Michael almost groaned at the sight of her stiff nipples. When she ran her palms over her breasts and rubbed the tips with restless motions, he did groan. That was fucking hot, and she had no clue.

"It makes them ache when you look at them like that," she whispered.

"Like what?" he rasped, wondering if she'd say it.

"Like you want t-to . . ."

"Lick them? Suck them?"

Her face went bright red, but she nodded.

"Come here."

She crawled to him and pressed herself to his front, nuzzling his neck as her hands snuck behind him under his shirt and grasped his back. The hard tips of her nipples grazed his chest, and Michael couldn't resist cupping her tits and tweaking the pebbled flesh with his fingers. Her breath was a ragged sigh against his throat before her teeth scraped at his skin.

"You're wearing a lot more clothes than I am, Michael."

"Then take them off for me."

Her eyes brightened, and a smile curved on her lips. As he'd known she would, his Stella really liked the idea of undressing him. She brushed her hands over the black silk of his vest before she pushed it over his shoulders and set it on the nightstand carefully—because it was his work, and she respected that. Such a simple thing, but it made him want to wrap her up and never let her go.

His shirt came off, was draped over the nightstand as well, and when her attention returned to him, she lost her focus. She ran greedy hands over his arms, chest, and abs, traced his tattoo. She kissed the dragon's eye, licked it.

"I love your tattoo."

"You don't strike me as a tattoo girl."

"It's yours, Michael," she said simply.

He pulled her hips against his and arched into her so she could feel what she did to him.

Her head fell back, and her body softened. Michael was good, but he'd never been this good. It was like Stella was made for him, specially designed to respond to him. Only him. The thought filled him with fierce possessiveness.

His hands grew rough as he touched her body, molding her to him as he claimed her mouth. The kiss was a savage thing of teeth and tongues, but she didn't protest. Instead, she matched him roughness for roughness, kissed him until she was gasping.

He was unprepared when she stroked over the fly of his pants. Pleasure coursed through him in a heated wave. His cock jumped, and a hoarse groan tore from his throat. His stomach muscles flexed as he tried to catch his breath.

"I love this part of you," she whispered with another stroke. "Show me how to make you feel good."

Some vague sense of self-preservation told him to deny her, warned that he shouldn't arm her with tools that would lead to his downfall, but as always, he couldn't refuse her. He unbuttoned and unzipped his pants and withdrew the hard length of his cock, almost losing it when her eyes went dark with naked longing.

"Like this." He wrapped her fingers around himself with a groan and taught her the rhythm he preferred, the pressure that drove him out of his mind, things he'd never shown his clients. They'd only cared about themselves.

Stella was different. Her entire being was focused on pleasing him. Because she wanted to learn how to do this for someone else or because he mattered to her like no one ever had? He knew which one it was. He still wanted her anyway.

He eased his hands down the swan line of her spine and hooked his thumbs in the elastic of her panties, pushed the material down her thighs. They were soaked clear through, and the scent of her arousal pushed him to the edge of his control. He almost spilled into her palm. She might be pleasuring him as part of her sex ed, but she was loving it, too. You couldn't fake this kind of evidence.

After settling her back onto the bed, he tore her panties off, balled them up, and brought them to his nose to inhale her scent. "I'm keeping these."

"They're not—they're—"

He spread her thighs wide and took in the sight of her beautiful pussy. Wet, swollen folds flushed deep pink and blossomed wide open for him. His fingers rubbed over her of their own volition and pushed into her.

Fuck, the heat, the tightness. So perfect for him. His body became one enormous ache of wanting.

"Stella, do you have any idea how hot your—"

"Michael," she whined, bending her legs restlessly. "Don't say it."

He paused. Her words said no, but her body . . . Her chest heaved on ragged breaths, and she was clenched tight around his fingers.

"I think you like it when I talk dirty to you," he whispered.

She shook her head frantically. "It's embarrassing."

"Your pussy doesn't think so. You're milking my fingers, Stella."

She clenched even harder in response and arched her hips against his hand, driving him deeper.

"It's y-your fingers. I love when you touch me." She shut her eyes and ran her cheek over the sheets.

With his free hand, he caught her clit between his fingers and stroked, slow and sure. She pressed the back of her hand to her mouth and tightened around him. But not as violently as before.

His Stella liked to be spoken to. A lot.

That was fine. Michael liked to talk.

"I think it's the words," he said as he continued to stroke her with both of his hands. "It's a shame you can't see what you look like right now. My fingers are all the way inside your pussy, and you're drenching my palm. Does it feel good?"

She bowed her back and bunched the sheets in her hands as she called out his name.

Her nipples caught his attention, and his tongue curled in his mouth as he remembered her taste and texture. "Do those candy nipples ache?"

She nodded, bumped her hips against him, and slid her hands up her belly to her tits. A frustrated sound tore from her throat as she pinched at the tips. She dropped her hands to her sides. "It only feels good when you do it."

Because Stella's mind needed to be seduced as much as her body, and apparently, her genius brain really liked Michael. He was just her practice boyfriend, but she responded to him like she'd never responded to anyone else.

He put them both out of torture and sucked a decadent nipple into his mouth. "You're made of candy, Stella. Sweet, sweet, sweet."

She rocked against his hands with increasing speed.

"Are you going to come for me so soon? I haven't even licked your pussy yet."

A whimpering sound escaped her lips, and her expression went pained. She locked down so hard he thought that was it, but after a breathless moment, her muscles eased.

"Maybe I should try out other words," he whispered as he trailed his lips down her belly.

Tiny muscles fluttered around his fingers, and he knew she was close. She sank her teeth into her bottom lip as she threw her head back, inhaling sharply.

He touched his tongue to her clit before asking, "Is it your . . . box?"

"No."

"Your . . . Lady V?"

She smiled into the blankets. "No."

"Beautiful vagina."

Her smile widened, and she shook her head.

He licked her again, sucked on her with the faintest pressure, and she arched against his mouth. Still, she hovered on the brink, exactly where he wanted her.

"I know." He kissed her inner thigh. "It's your . . ." He accented each word with a kiss upon her damp skin. "Wet. Hot. Sweet potato."

She burst out laughing, and the sound worked into him and around him, fanning embers of happiness into full flame. He loved the sound of her laughter. He loved her smile. He loved—

He cut off that train of thought before it could finish. Now was not the time for thinking. It was time for feeling. He licked her clit into his mouth, and her laughter turned into a long moan. She wove her fingers into his hair, undulating against his face, and he willfully lost himself in her taste, her scent, her erotic sounds, and the feel of her on his tongue. Nothing was this good.

When she gripped his shoulders and pulled insistently, he looked up in confusion.

"Michael, I want it. I need it. Now. Please," she said between heavy pants for breath.

"It?" Fuck, was she going to talk dirty to him?

She continued trying to drag him up over her. "I'm aching for you, Michael."

Too shy, after all, but her words hit him just as hard. He had to take a moment to focus on breathing and not spilling all over the sheets before he climbed off the bed, turned her over, and pulled her hips to the edge of the mattress. This was the way she needed it. It was too personal for her to do it with him face to face. Maybe with her next man, she'd—

He distracted himself from that shitty image by running his hands over her generous ass. Their relationship was just practice for her, but this moment, right now, was real. "I love your bed, but it's too low to the ground. There is something mine is perfect for."

She buried her face in his sheets. "Now, please."

But when he patted his pocket, it was empty. He groaned in disbelief. Forget blue or indigo. Violet. His balls were violet. "I don't have a condom." He was an escort, for fuck's sake, and he'd forgotten a condom. He'd been too eager to see Stella to go through his regular pre-session checklist.

"Don't tease me like that, Michael." She arched her hips, presenting him with a glimpse of her swollen pussy. *God.*

He wanted to press into her so badly he hurt.

"Not teasing. I left the box in my car."

She stared back at him with tormented eyes.

"I'll be right back."

With that, he adjusted his painfully hard flesh, zipped and buttoned his pants, and ran from his apartment.

S tella collapsed onto Michael's bed. After her first three sexual encounters, she'd been convinced intercourse wasn't for her. It had been messy, at times painful, and extremely uncomfortable. Right now, it was all she could think about.

Her body throbbed from the force of her craving, aching to be filled, and held, and . . . spoken to.

She grinned as she recalled what he'd said. Did other people laugh during sex?

She tapped her fingers on the bed as she waited, but patience had never been one of her strong suits. She was a person of action. She hated wasting time. And she hadn't finished investigating Michael's apartment.

She lowered her feet to the floor, grabbed her glasses, and pulled his shirt on, smiling to herself when the tails fell to her knees. The non-French seams bothered her skin, but his smell made up for the irritation. Besides, she wouldn't be wearing this for long.

A peek inside his closet filled her with vast contentment. Yes, it rocked her world. All of his beautiful suits and shirts were perfectly lined up, organized by color, fabric sheen, and stripe width. She trailed her fingers over the sleeves of his suit jackets before she turned and considered his dresser. She wanted to open the drawers and see how he kept his socks, but that seemed intrusive. What if he caught her snooping? Would he think she was searching for something? *Was* she searching for something? Maybe she was, but not for anything in particular. She just wanted to understand him better.

She padded out of his bedroom, walked past his TV—she'd already seen most of the titles there and had stuffed *Laughing in the Wind* in her purse—tracked her fingertips over the cold surfaces of all the ordered dumbbells on the rack by his workout bench, slammed her fist into his punching bag, and then rubbed at her knuckles because that had hurt.

A look in his fridge told her he cooked regularly. It was filled with Asian cooking sauces with mysterious labels, fresh produce, and all sorts of healthy things Stella had no idea what to do with. There were a few containers of the yogurt she liked, though.

As she ambled over to admire the plant on his dining table, the papers on top of his metal filing cabinet caught her eye. Bills, from the look of them.

And Michael had money problems.

She snuck a glance at the front door, but it remained shut. She perked her ears, listening for the sound of his footsteps. Nothing.

Her heart pounded. She knew this was a violation of privacy. She shouldn't.

She unfolded the top bill and read it as fast as she was capable. Just an electric bill. Less than a hundred dollars a month. She was about to fold it back up when she noticed the name on the bill. Michael Larsen.

A strange pain pierced her chest. He hadn't trusted her with his real name.

She grimaced. If she didn't know who he was, she couldn't stalk him after things ended. She put the bill back the way she'd found it, but even with how bitter she felt, she couldn't help scanning the other one on the file cabinet. A medical bill from the Palo Alto Medical Foundation. It wasn't addressed to him, however. The name on it was Mrs. Anh Larsen.

Stella snatched it up and read the itemized list of procedures: CAT scan, MRI, X-rays, blood draws, blood tests, et cetera. The total came to a staggering $12,556.89.

Wasn't insurance supposed to cover these things?

She pressed an unsteady hand to her forehead. Had his mom gotten sick without health insurance? Was Michael paying her medical bills? How was he paying . . .

Her breathing went erratic, and her stomach twisted and sank. Michael didn't have a drug addiction or a gambling problem.

He just really loved his mom.

The room went blurry as her eyes watered. She straightened the bills back to the way she'd found them and swallowed around the knot in her throat. He'd slept with all those people, with her, because his mom was sick.

She pressed a fist to her lips as she curled up on his couch. The door swung open.

Michael took one look at her and rushed to her side. "What's wrong?"

She opened her mouth to speak, but nothing came out.

He scooted onto the couch and wrapped her up in his arms, kissing her temple, wiping the tears from her cheeks, running his hands down her back. "What is it?"

What did she do now? How did she solve this? She didn't know how to cure cancer. Maybe she should have gone to medical school after all.

She locked her arms around his neck and kissed him.

He tried to back away. "You need to tell me—"

She kissed him harder. He softened slightly and kissed

her back for one drugging second before he pulled away again.

"Tell me what's going on," he said firmly. "Why are you crying? Did I go too fast again? Did I do something you're not ready for?"

She didn't know how to communicate what she was feeling. Her chest was bursting with emotion. It was too much, too intense . . . Terrifying.

"I'm obsessed with you, Michael," she confessed. "I don't want just a night or a week or a month with you. I want you all the time. I like you better than calculus, and math is the only thing that unites the universe. When you're done with me, I'm going to be that crazy client who stalks you just so I can see you from a distance. I'm going to call you until you're forced to change your number. I'll buy you an extravagant car, anything and everything I can think of, so I can feel connected to you. I lied when I promised I wouldn't get obsessed with you. That's my nature. I have—"

He sealed his lips over hers, and his urgency seared through her. He grasped her with rough hands, but she didn't care. She clawed at his pants until she could free his length. Then she tore away and worked her way down his body to take him into her mouth.

She sucked and laved him with clumsy strokes of her tongue. She had no idea what she was doing, but he didn't seem to mind. He rocked his hips into her mouth with sinuous movements. She stroked his tattoo, caressed his strong thighs. By the tenseness of his body and the increasing speed of his motions, his hoarse sounds, she knew he was close. It fueled her own arousal, made her press her legs together as moisture coated her thighs.

"I want inside you," he said, trying to tug her away from his erection.

But Stella didn't want to stop. She needed to feel him filling her mouth, needed to taste his completion.

He groaned as she resisted his persistent attempts at

freedom. When she finally relented, letting him slip from her mouth, he kissed her hungrily and rolled her into the couch. After sitting up, he dug into his pocket. His chest worked on deep gusting breaths as he tore the foil open and rolled the condom on.

He lowered himself over her and kissed her mouth, her jaw, her neck. Hard flesh prodded at her sex. As he slid into her, their eyes accidentally met and locked. Panic spiked. Too raw, too exposed. She tried to look away until she realized the vulnerability she saw was *his*. Dark eyes gazed deep, seeing her seeing him.

Their bodies picked up an elemental tempo. Hips surged and retreated, claimed, gave. He searched between their bodies until he could touch her right where she needed it. She burned and wound tighter and tighter. Moans tumbled from her lips as she arched into him. Through it all, their gazes held. He saw it all, heard it all. She would have been embarrassed if it weren't for his smile, the tender way he brushed the hair from her face before his free hand tangled with hers. The most incredible feeling of being loved washed over Stella.

Release seized her. Hard wrenching spasms stole her ability to move, speak, and think. The hand interlaced with hers tightened. His motions sped up. With one last deep thrust, he joined her in falling apart.

The world stopped.

All was silence but for their hearts trying to synchronize their crashing.

Whispering her name and kissing her softly, Michael eased out of her body and carried her into his bedroom. He settled her on the bed and pulled the covers up to her chin. He disappeared into the bathroom, and water ran. Before she could start to miss him too much, he returned and crawled into bed so they were facing each other.

He ran his fingers down her cheek and pinched her chin. "Does my Stella want to stay or go home?"

She felt a grin forming on her mouth. When had he started calling her that? *My Stella*. Did he know there was nothing she wanted more than to be his? She wanted to ask what he meant by it but was afraid he'd stop saying it.

"I can stay the night here?" In his apartment, in his bed where clients weren't allowed? Was she rubbing off on him, then? Maybe there was hope. Maybe he really could be hers.

"If you want to. None of your things are here, though. You'd have to use my toothbrush, and you don't have any pajamas. You might have to sleep naked," he said with a suggestive arch of an eyebrow.

Those things bothered her, true. She'd probably sleep terribly and feel off all day tomorrow. But it would be worth it to be with him. And to put her mark on his apartment like wild animals did—probably even the pugnacious honey badger.

"I want to stay."

His smile alone made her decision worth it.

Over the next week, Michael learned Stella's rhythms. In bed, she responded best when he went slowly and whispered dirty things in her ear, but if he wanted something more intense—anything—she was game and eager to please. He couldn't have asked for a better lover. The irony of the situation was not lost on him.

Out of bed, she thrived on routine. She got up at the same time every day, showered away evidence of their morning sex—he loved starting the day off right—had yogurt for breakfast, and stayed at the office until six o'clock. Her evenings belonged to Michael. When they weren't messing around like hormonal teenagers, they filled the time with long dinners, meandering conversation, and companionable silences that Michael had never experienced with a real girlfriend.

Saturday night, after spending the day perusing one of the San Francisco museums and taking turns making outlandish comments about the art, they watched another episode of *Laughing in the Wind* in bed. Well, *she* was watching it. He was watching her as he combed his fingers through her long hair.

She rested her head against his shoulder, eyes on the large screen mounted on her bedroom wall. From time to time, she gasped or stiffened in reaction to the film, and her bare legs shifted beneath the hem of the oversized white T-shirt she wore—his T-shirt from the very first night they'd spent together.

He didn't know how to describe the way he felt seeing her in his clothes, knowing she'd kept his shirt and had been wearing it to sleep all this time, but it was really good. He'd been feeling like this a lot lately—basically, anytime Stella smiled, demanded a kiss, or crossed the room to be near him, but also when they weren't together. He'd spent the entire past week in a euphoric high, grinning for no other reason than he was thinking of her.

No doubt about it.

Michael was stupid in love.

He knew this was temporary, knew it wasn't real, knew it couldn't possibly end well, but he'd done what no escort should do anyway. He'd fallen for his client.

"So she saved his life, but now she's hiding behind that curtain pretending to be a grandma. Is he ever going to see her face?" Stella asked, drawing his attention back to the screen. "Is she the one he falls for?"

"Do you really want me to tell you?"

She thought about it for several seconds before nodding. "Yes. Tell me."

He laughed as he pulled her closer and kissed her temple. So thoughtful and serious but so quirky, too. He loved that about her. "Too bad. You'll have to watch it to find out." Because he couldn't help it, he kissed her jaw and nipped at her ear. God, it felt good having her near. He'd been made to love her.

She crossed her arms. "Why won't she let him see her? It's clear she likes him."

"It's because she knows they can never be together."

"Why not?"

"Her dad is a villain." Which reminded Michael of himself and his own fuckhead of a dad and shredded his insides to pieces.

"*She* isn't bad, though," she said stubbornly. "They can work it out."

He said nothing. The heroine in the movie wasn't a bad person, but the jury was still out on Michael. He tried to be good, but when things got hard and he felt like his life was strangling him, awful, seductive thoughts ran through his head. Shortcuts, easy ways to freedom, clever sneaky things. He knew people. It would be so easy to take advantage of them. There was very little preventing him from doing exactly that, nothing but a shaky code of ethics and the desire not to follow in his dad's footsteps.

If he were a better person, he'd tell Stella about his past and let her take the necessary precautions, let her leave. But he couldn't bring himself to end this. He wanted more of her, not less. And their relationship was helping her. He could tell. Day by day, her confidence grew, and she smiled, laughed, and even joked. Soon, she'd decide she was ready to move on.

Until then, Michael was determined to enjoy every moment with her. Nuzzling her sensitive neck, he swept a hand up her silk-smooth thigh and underneath *his* shirt. Then he groaned as his body hardened.

"No underwear? Trying to tell me something, Stella?" he whispered in her ear, loving the way she shivered and parted her legs to allow him access. She never turned him down, was just as starved for him as he was for her.

"You always throw them somewhere, and it takes me forever to find them. I figured I'd just—" She gasped when he massaged her clit, and her head fell back against his shoulder.

"Watch the show. You might miss something." Fuck, she was wet already. Hot moisture licked over his fingertips as he traced her folds, and his cock strained against his jeans like it had been weeks since he'd last had sex, not hours. He wanted her again, that closeness, that connection, that unbelievable, mind-exploding pleasure. No amount was enough.

She tried to follow directions—she always did—but it wasn't long before she gave in and pulled him down for a wild kiss, which led to another, and another, and another . . .

The next time he noticed the TV, it had returned to the main menu. The entire DVD had played while they were busy with other things. After washing up and turning off the TV and lights, he climbed into bed. Stella murmured as he gathered her against his chest, but she pressed a drowsy kiss to his throat.

Possessiveness mixed with tenderness, and he brushed the hair away from her face and trailed his fingertips over a smooth shoulder illuminated by moonlight.

His Stella.

For now.

Until she decided she'd had enough practice. Or she found out about his dad.

When Stella got home from work midway through the next week, an empty house greeted her. Michael had texted her that he was running late, so she'd been expecting this. What she hadn't expected was this gaping sadness, this cold aloneness.

They'd only been in this practice relationship for a week and a half, but she'd already grown accustomed to him. Michael was part of her routine now, part of her life, and his absence sparked unrest in her being. When things ended, she'd have nothing but this emptiness.

If things ended.

If she failed at seducing him. There was nothing left on her original lesson plans. Not a single thing. She'd checked. It was time to move into full seduction mode.

She wished Michael could teach her how to do that, too,

because she had no idea what she was supposed to do. Google searches provided conflicting advice, and very little of it was useful in a situation like hers where they were already in a monogamous relationship of sorts. One particularly obnoxious article had advised women to focus all their time and effort on improving their looks and then lower their standards.

Well, Stella's standards were locked at eleven on the one-to-ten scale. Only Michael would do. As for her looks, she couldn't bring herself to wear contacts or makeup except for special occasions. If his insatiability in bed was any indication, Michael didn't mind her the way she was.

Her inner muscles clenched as she recalled what he'd done that morning—the way he'd kissed her, caressed her, the things he'd said. She swept a hand from her chest down to her thigh, wishing he was touching her right now. But even if he never slept with her again, she still wanted him. The nonbedroom side of Michael appealed to her just as much as the lover side, if not more. He made her laugh, and he listened to her, even when she wasn't saying anything particularly interesting. He was comfortable around her, and that made her comfortable around him. Sometimes she convinced herself that her labels didn't matter. They were just words. They didn't change who she was. If he learned about them, he wouldn't care.

Maybe.

Out of habit, she walked to her piano. She sat on the bench and lifted the fallboard, and the cool smoothness of the keys beneath her fingers calmed her. For years, music had been her main method of coping with emotions—good ones, bad ones, and those in between. Rich chords sang from the strings, called forth by muscle memory alone, and she gave herself up to the music, let everything she was feeling pour into her fingertips. When the song ended, she kept her hands on the keys, listening as the notes faded.

"I knew you played, but I didn't know you could play like that," Michael said from directly behind her.

She couldn't help grinning as she looked at him over her shoulder. "You made it back."

His smile was tired, but it reached his eyes. In a mere fraction of a second, everything was right again. The coldness vanished. Missing pieces settled back into place.

"What song was that? I feel like I've heard it before," he said.

"'Clair de Lune' by Debussy. It's my favorite song."

He rested his hands on her shoulders and brushed a kiss over her nape. "It's beautiful, but so sad. Do you know anything happier?"

Sad. Her lips wrinkled on something that didn't feel like a smile. That was a common theme for the pieces in her repertoire. "Well . . . maybe this."

She bit her lip and picked the familiar melody from the piano, wondering if this was what he meant by *happy*.

He surprised her by sitting down on the bench next to her and saying, "I thought 'Heart and Soul' was a duet."

She shrugged. "I've only ever played it solo."

He captured her right hand and put it in his lap. A smile curved over his lips as he nodded his head toward the keyboard.

"You play?" she asked.

"Only a little, but I know this one."

Breathlessness overtook her. Her fingers stumbled on the first notes, but she got into the swing of it pretty quickly. The bass half of the song was a simple repetition, a pattern, and second nature for her. When Michael wove the melody seamlessly with her accompaniment, startling warmth cascaded up her spine, and her body flushed with pleasure. She'd never played a duet with someone other than her piano instructor, and those occasions had been technical exercises, nothing special.

"You're good at this," she commented, glancing up at him as she continued to play.

His smile widened, but he kept his attention on his fingers. "With six of us wanting the piano at once, we had to learn to share. Also, none of us could ever figure out how to play your half with only one hand. You're really good."

"It's just practice." And necessity.

The sight of their hands side by side on the keys mesmerized Stella. The contrast was stark and beautiful: large to small, tan to pale, masculine to feminine. So different, but in perfect rhythm. They were making music. Together.

The song ended, and she let her fingers slip away from the keyboard and averted her eyes. That naked feeling was back.

He kissed her neck and smoothed his fingers along her jaw before gently urging her to meet his gaze. She thought he would speak, but he didn't. He only smiled.

She wanted to ask if he liked being with her, if he liked *this*, but she struggled to muster the courage. What if he said no?

"Are you hungry? Let's eat," he said, and the moment disappeared.

She'd ask him later. After she'd had the opportunity to appropriately seduce him.

A week later, Stella still had no idea what she was doing in terms of seducing Michael. He *seemed* happy—she knew she was—but the end of their first month was coming up, and she had no confidence that he'd want to sign on for more.

That night, his mom was having her over for dinner again. Stella racked her brain for clever ways she might ask his family for advice regarding Michael. If anyone knew him, it would be them. But how could she ask without them suspecting something was strange about her relationship with Michael? They thought she and Michael were dating for real.

As he'd instructed her to do, Stella let herself into his mom's house and set her shoes against the wall next to Michael's. Her black heels looked tiny next to his leather loafers, but she liked seeing them sitting next to each other. It pleased her on a fundamental level.

She placed a box of pears on the front table next to the bronze Buddha, and grunts and heavy breathing drew her attention to the sitting room to the right. She padded over and stared at a pretzel formation of limbs on the carpet by the upright piano. It seemed to contain Michael and another girl. Stella would have been jealous, but the whole ordeal looked really uncomfortable.

"Just give up and say it," Michael gritted out.

"No, I had that armbar. You only got out because of your steroid abuse."

"I do *not* use steroids, and you only got the armbar because I didn't want to crush your boobs."

"Going for your balls next time."

Looking closer, Stella saw they both had their arms locked around each other's throats. Like anacondas in a death match, neither was willing to let go.

"Maybe call it a draw?" Stella suggested.

"Hi, Stella," a voice chirped. His sister's face was covered in a curtain of dark hair, and Stella had no idea which one it was. There *were* so many of them. "Your girlfriend is here, Michael. Give up."

"Dinner is ready in ten minutes." The red hue to Michael's face was rather concerning but completely self-inflicted, as far as Stella could tell. "I'll be with you in a second."

"Only if you're giving up. Who's your daddy?" his sister said as she flexed the impressive arm wrapped around his neck.

"Not some little brat."

The two rolled on the carpet, kicking and flailing their legs.

"I'm going to say hi to your mom and grandma, then," Stella said. She would have preferred Michael's company when she greeted them, but this thing between Michael and his sister looked like it was going to take a while.

Neither of them responded. They probably couldn't spare the oxygen for talking.

She meandered through the house, which was actually quite enormous—you wouldn't guess from the outside. His mom and grandma were seated in the family room, peeling grapefruit meat from their individual segments as they spoke in musical Vietnamese. Two men in a monkey suit and a pig suit flew across the screen of the muted TV.

"Hi . . . Wai?" She bowed her head awkwardly. She could not wrap her tongue around the pronunciation of the word for *grandma*, *ngoại*.

Michael's grandma smiled and waved her to the empty space on the aged leather sofa. As usual, she had a scarf wrapped around her head and tied under her chin. Adorable grandma. Was she staying away from the lawn shears lately?

Nodding at his mom, she said, "Hi, Mẹ," and sat in the indicated spot, feeling her stomach knot and her muscles tense. Even though she'd seen his mom a handful of times by now, she was still horribly nervous around the woman. Every word had to be measured before Stella could let it out of her mouth, every action considered. She didn't want to mess up again. This was Michael's mom—the most important woman in his life since he didn't have a real girlfriend. All thoughts of asking for advice with Michael evaporated in the face of her anxiety.

His mom held out a bowl of perfect, skinless yellow-green grapefruit slices. Stella had never seen grapefruit peeled quite like this, and she took a slice out of a mixture of curiosity and fear of insulting her. Once she bit into the fruit, sweetness exploded on her tongue, untarnished by the usual bitterness of the skin.

She covered her mouth in surprise. "It's really good."

"Have more." His mom smiled and set the bowl down in Stella's lap. Today she was wearing a striped pink button-down and floral print jeans. Her glasses perched on the top of her head at a distracted angle. "Get salt if you want. E likes it with salt."

"No, thank you." Stella ate one more, two more before she made herself stop. It looked like a lot of work peeling them this way. In an effort to keep her hands busy, she picked up half of a grapefruit and tried to copy his mom's technique, all too aware of the stilted silence in the room.

His mom watched her peel the fruit with a tiny nod. "Michael is making *bún riêu* tonight. It's really good. Has he made it for you yet?"

Stella shook her head as she trained her eyes on the grapefruit. "No, he hasn't." Did his mom know Michael had been spending nights at her place? Did she disapprove?

"Mommy, when is the *bún riêu* ready?" Janie trounced into the room and paused, smiling at her. "Hi, Stella."

Stella returned her smile. "Hi. Michael said ten more minutes."

Janie flopped into a scuffed armchair, throwing a jean-clad leg over the arm. "Starving and all I had for lunch was some crackers. I've been doing homework since ten this morning."

Stella silently held out the bowl of peeled grapefruit while Mẹ glowered at her daughter. "You're getting too pale." Turning to Stella, she asked, "Can you see how pale she is?"

Janie snatched the bowl and inhaled piece after piece. Stella's jaw almost dropped. Did she know how much time it took to peel the things?

"Maybe a little pale?" Stella said.

Mẹ spoke to Ngoại in Vietnamese, and Ngoại cast a disapproving look Janie's way. Stella didn't understand what she said when she spoke, but it sounded ominous.

"Thanks for throwing me under the bus, Chị Hai." A crooked grin almost identical to Michael's flashed as Janie winked, and Stella's chest turned to mush.

"What does *Chị Hai* mean?"

Mẹ smiled as she focused on peeling fruit.

Janie popped the last grapefruit slice into her mouth. "It means Sister Two. Michael is my Anh Hai, which means Brother Two. I'm down by the bottom with number six because I had the poor luck to be fifth born. We don't start at one, by the way. I think one is reserved for parents or something. That's South Vietnamese interfamily naming convention. You get his number because you're his."

A goofy grin teased at Stella's lips as her heart did clumsy flips and flops. She loved the idea of getting Michael's number. It made them a pair. Like the shoes by the front door and their hands on the piano.

Janie laughed and said something in Vietnamese to her mom and grandma. They both looked at Stella and laughed as they voiced their agreement.

"Michael's been really happy this month," Janie said. "Like embarrassingly happy. The general consensus is it's because of you."

She caught her breath. "Has he really?"

"Yeah. He's *obnoxious* when he's happy."

Stella bit her lip to hide her smile. All of the emotion boiling inside her chest made her feel like it would rupture open, spewing rainbows and glitter. "He's never obnoxious."

Janie snorted. "I bet he doesn't make *you* smell his socks."

She choked on a laugh.

"What's going on here?" Michael asked from the doorway.

His hair stood up in complete disarray, and his face was still flushed from beating up on his sister. He wore a wrinkled white button-down over a plain T-shirt and faded jeans. He was gorgeous.

"Telling her about the socks, dickhead," Janie said with an evil smirk.

Mẹ sent her a sharp narrow-eyed look, and Janie shrank into her chair.

"I mean, Anh Hai," she mumbled.

"That's right. Give me my respect." His smile was superior and lofty and . . . obnoxious. Stella loved it. "Come on, dinner's ready."

Out in the kitchen, his mom went about dishing rice noodles into giant bowls and ladling soup over the top. Janie took the first bowl and brought it to the table where Ngoại sat, cutting everything into little pieces with a scissors before squeezing in lime.

Michael pulled her to the side. "Hi." He swept his eyes over her and ran his hands down her back, pressing her close. "I like this dress on you. Are the seams bothering you?"

"No, they're fine. The problem is in the front."

"What is it? Want me to fix it?" He unbuttoned her black cardigan and inspected the construction of the tight-fitting Lycra dress with a frown. "I don't see anything obvious."

"Can you sew a-a-a . . ." She glanced at his family as they set bowls at the table and dropped her voice. "Can you sew a bra into it?"

A wicked smile spread over his mouth, and he opened her cardigan wide to look at the hard points of her nipples. "I could, but I'm not going to."

He pulled her into the dining room and leaned her against the wall. When he palmed her breasts and tweaked at her nipples, she gasped as her body softened in a jolting flash.

"This is a very high-fashion look, you know." He bent down and brushed his lips against her temple, her cheek, and finally her mouth—a whisper-light touch that left Stella wanting. "You know how I feel about fashion."

She snuck her fingers underneath his shirt to touch the hard ridges of his belly. "It's indecent."

He kissed her again, deep and slow this time, and pulled away with hooded eyes. "You'd be cold without the cardigan, anyway. No bra." He rubbed her nipples in exactly the right way to make her limbs melt. "Look at you getting weak in the knees for me. So hot, Stella."

He captured her lips and stroked his tongue into her mouth. When he pulled her hips flush against his arousal, heat arrowed through her body and made her toes curl. She shouldn't want him again. Their morning had been particularly acrobatic today, and she'd barely made it to work on time.

The tension on her scalp loosened, and her hair tumbled free. He worked a hand under her dress and gripped her inner thigh.

"Ugh, get a room." One of his sisters stomped by.

Michael broke away with laughing eyes and high color. "You're just mad because you didn't win."

"You're a dick," Maddie said.

After his sister disappeared into the kitchen, Michael ran his fingers through Stella's hair. "Are you okay? Too embarrassing getting caught?"

She shook her head. She didn't care if she was caught as long as it was with him.

He planted his hands on the wall behind her and lined his body up against hers so they fit just right, hardness to softness, curves to hollows. "Sexy Stella."

Their lips joined for another breathless kiss.

"Oh my God, get a room."

Stella jumped at the brusqueness of Sophie's voice, and Michael laughed as he broke away. Without looking at them, Sophie marched into the kitchen.

"Let's eat." He grabbed Stella's hand and led her to the two empty seats at the kitchen table.

When everyone cast knowing glances at them, she blushed and stared down at her bowl. Slices of tomato and green herbs floated atop an orange soup thickened with something that looked like scrambled eggs.

"You should wear your hair down more often, Stella," Sophie said. "Might want to pull it up to eat, though. It'll get dirty." She held a jar of brown-colored *something* out to her. "Want some?"

Stella reached for it. "What is—"

Michael snatched it and set it on the table. "She'll faint if she smells it, Soph. Her nose is super sensitive."

Sophie shrugged. "Stinks but tastes good."

The label was mostly Chinese, but at the bottom it read *Fine Shrimp Sauce.*

"I like shrimp," Stella said.

Michael pushed the jar to the other side of the table. "Not this kind of shrimp. Even I can't eat this stuff."

"Let her try it, Michael," Sophie said.

When Stella's gaze fell upon Janie and Maddie, both girls shook their heads in matching horror.

With an impatient sigh, Mẹ grabbed the jar and put it in front of Stella. "This is *mắm ruốc*. The correct way to eat *bún riêu* is with *mắm ruốc*."

Stella closed her fingers around the jar. Feeling a lot like Snow White with her apple, she brought it to her nose. On the first whiff, her eyes watered. It was fishy, shrimpy, and potent. Upon her second and third sniffs, however, the smell lost some of its force. "You just put it in the soup?"

Mẹ spooned a dollop into Stella's bowl. "Like this. And lime and chili sauce." She squeezed lime in and added a spoonful of red spicy-looking sauce.

As she picked up her chopsticks and soup spoon, Michael watched her with wide, apologetic eyes. She mixed everything together, twirled the noodles around her chopsticks, and placed them in her spoon with broth like she'd seen Sophie do. Then she put it in her mouth.

It tasted . . . good. Salty, a little sweet, a little tangy. She grinned as she had another spoonful. "I like it."

"It's good, right?" Sophie asked. "High five, you."

Stella high-fived Michael's sister, feeling silly but also like she'd made up for refusing to eat the BPA-laced food. His mom was smiling, Ngoại was *mmmm*ing, and Janie and Maddie were muttering to themselves.

"They refuse to try it," Mẹ said, pointing to the two youngest.

"It smells like death," Janie said.

Maddie nodded emphatically. "Dead bodies."

Mẹ blasted them with a harsh string of Vietnamese, and both girls cowered.

Under the table, Michael squeezed her leg. He leaned toward her to whisper in her ear. "Do you really like it? You don't have to eat it. I can get you something else."

"I really do." She'd still eat it even if she hated it, though.

His mom looked proud and vindicated. And it wasn't poisoned. Not that she knew of.

He brushed his lips over hers once before pulling away with a cough and a laugh. "I can smell it on you."

She stuffed another spoonful in her mouth, glaring at him as she swiped the hair away from her face with a forearm.

"Here, let me get your hair." He unlooped her rubber band from his wrist and gathered her hair away from her face in a ponytail.

"Thank you."

He smiled and pinched her chin. By the look in his eyes, she knew he would have kissed her if his family hadn't been watching—and she didn't smell like Fine Shrimp Sauce and dead bodies.

"Gross, stop undressing her with your eyes," Sophie said.

"Seriously," Maddie chimed in.

"And since when do you keep rubber bands handy for her hair? Whipped much?" Janie added.

Stella contemplated diving into her soup bowl.

Michael merely shrugged and grinned. Then he wrapped an arm around her shoulders and kissed her temple.

Dinner passed in a blur as his sisters alternated between bickering and teasing. His mom interjected now and then with firm mediation or withering glances, but Stella had a feeling the woman was content. Once everyone had finished their soup and filled themselves with skinless grapefruit, Mẹ ordered Janie and Maddie to clear the table and wash the dishes.

Michael took her hand, preparing to take her home, but his mom waved them toward the family room.

"Stella, I have something to show you."

Michael groaned. "Mẹ, no, not today."

"What is it?" Stella was helplessly curious.

"How about next time?" Michael asked.

"He was really cute," Mẹ said.

"Baby pictures?" Stella all but danced in place. "Michael, I want to *see* them."

He grudgingly followed as she towed him after his mom into the family room. Mẹ handed Stella a fat picture album, and mother and son sat on either side of her on the couch.

She smoothed her fingers over the velvet cover of the album. The one her mom kept for her was almost identical to this one. It was the kind with sticky pages and the thin plastic cover sheet that peeled off. The first page was a grainy ultrasound printout and a picture of a wrinkle-faced infant who looked like he was a thousand years old. As the pages progressed, however, he cuted up quickly.

There were pictures of Ngoại holding him, of him learning to walk and trying to pick up a watermelon. In one picture, chubby toddler Michael wore a little suit—was it his *first suit?*—in between a young couple. The woman was a very young, very beautiful version of his mom wearing a white traditional Vietnamese dress with pink flowers embroidered on the front. The man had to be his father. He was tall and blond and had Michael's crooked grin.

"You were beautiful, Mẹ," Stella said, running her fingertips down the flowing dress. "I love the dress."

"I still have that *aó dài*. You can take it home with you tonight if you want."

"I can really have it?"

"It doesn't fit me anymore, and Michael's sisters aren't interested. They only fought over the jewelry, but that's all gone." Mẹ's voice was subdued, and her eyes lingered over the blond man's face. "This is Michael's dad. Very handsome, ah?"

Michael turned the page without a word.

His chubbiness was gradually replaced with gangly limbs and male beauty. He smiled often and was full of life and fun. There were dozens of pictures of him and his baby sisters surrounded by passels of full-blooded Vietnamese cousins. He looked out of place next to them with his paler skin and non-Asian features, just as he must have looked out of place next to all of his peers at school for the exact opposite reasons. What had it been like not fitting in anywhere?

Maybe it hadn't been that different from her own experience growing up.

There were pictures of early teens Michael playing chess with his dad, his face creased in intense concentration, pictures of him frowning over science projects, pictures of him dressed in full kendo-sparring gear like a little badass, where the front flaps of his uniform displayed his last name in caps: *LARSEN*.

When he flipped the page quickly and shot her an alarmed look, she kept her face blank, pretending she hadn't seen it. She wasn't good at lying, but she knew how to pretend she was okay. She'd been doing it around people since she was little.

She hated doing it with him.

Was it that important to him that she didn't know his real name? What did he think she'd do with the information? The knowledge that he didn't trust her dimmed the warm glow the evening had given her. Was she foolish for hoping she could make him hers?

When she surfaced enough from her thoughts to notice the photos again, they'd almost reached the back of the album. The pictures showed off a nearly full-grown Michael who was so gorgeous she couldn't help sighing. He stood next to his beaming father, chess tournament trophy in hand, kendo tournament trophy in hand, science fair trophy in hand.

"That's a lot of trophies," she commented.

"Dad liked it when I won, so I tried really hard."

"Michael was valedictorian at his high school," his mom said, looking at Michael with boundless love.

Stella smiled. "I knew you were smart."

"It was just hard work. I figured out how to test well. You're way smarter than me, Stella."

She searched his closed-off face, wondering why he discounted himself like that. "I wasn't valedictorian. I only did well in math and science."

"My dad would have preferred that."

Michael flipped to the last page.

There, he graduated from the San Francisco Fashion Institute. His shoulders were squared, his expression determined. His parents were in the picture, his mother visibly bursting with proud happiness while his father looked like he'd been forced into the photograph. His hair had gone mostly white over the years, and while he was still an attractive older man, he looked worn and cynical. The crooked grin was gone.

"He didn't want you to go to design school."

Michael shrugged. "It wasn't his decision." His voice was flat, his usually vivid eyes dull.

Stella covered his hand with hers and squeezed. He turned his hand over, interlaced their fingers, and squeezed back.

"Michael is very talented. When he graduated, he had five job offers. He worked for a big designer in New York before we needed him at home because his dad left." Mẹ gazed off into space, the set of her mouth bitter, before she blinked and focused on Michael. "But I'm glad I called you home. You were ruining yourself. Too many women, Michael. You don't need a hundred women. Just one good one."

His mom patted Stella's leg, and Stella felt a terrible, deep wanting well up inside. Right now, she was considered a good woman. What would his mom think if she knew about the labels Stella had been purposefully withholding? Would she suddenly become unsuitable for her son? What kind of mother wanted an autistic daughter-in-law and possibly autistic grandbabies?

And since when had she started thinking about *marriage and babies*? She and Michael weren't in a real relationship. *Would* he date her if he didn't need the money? If he were free to be with whomever he wished, would he pick her?

"Okay," his mom said briskly. "That's all of the pictures. Michael, come help Mẹ with my iPad while I find the *aó dài*."

Michael gave a resigned sigh and stood.

"Can I look at these pictures longer?" Stella asked.

Mẹ smiled and nodded, but Stella had only looked at the pictures for a minute or two when Janie wandered into the room. She held a meaty textbook in her hands.

"So is it true you're an economist?" Janie asked. She shifted her bare feet on the carpet until her knees pointed together.

"It's true. You're in your third year at Stanford, right? That's a really good program." Stella remembered now that Michael's mom had wanted her to speak to Janie about her work. "What's the textbook for? Do you need help with your homework?"

Janie hugged the book to her chest and sat down in the armchair she'd occupied earlier. "I was more hoping . . ." She took a breath. "I was hoping you could help me get an internship? Maybe send my résumé to colleagues who are hiring? I'm having a hard time getting interviews. I have no experience, obviously, and I did really bad my first year. My GPA hasn't recovered. But I know my stuff. This is what I want to do."

"Do you have a copy of your résumé handy?" As soon as the words left Stella's mouth, she wanted to recall them. She sounded like she was in interview mode, and Janie looked nervous.

Janie pulled a sheet of paper from her textbook—an international macroeconomics tome—and handed it to her.

The résumé described her passion for economic theory in concise language, listed relevant coursework and skills, and displayed her grade point average. In her major, it was 3.5. Cumulative, it was 2.9. Definitely not the numbers she needed to get into brand-name institutions, even as a Stanford student.

As gently as she was capable, Stella asked, "Can I ask what happened in your first year?"

Janie stared down at her textbook. "It's when Mom was really sick. It was a hard time for everybody. We had to take turns taking care of Mom and running the shop, and we were already overwhelmed with the repercussions of the separation and all that. I didn't balance my time well. Honestly, I didn't care about school at that point, which is stupid because it's so expensive and we were hurting for money."

Wait, why had they been hurting for money? Did it have something to do with Michael's dad? From the outside, they looked well off. The shop seemed to do well. They owned this house. She wanted to ask so badly, her fingers clawed at the edges of the photo album, but that was rude. She might feel like she knew these people, but it hadn't been that long since she'd first met them.

And the last time she'd pried, she'd put Michael's mom in tears. She never wanted to make someone cry again.

Lamely, she said, "I see."

"Do you think I have a chance of getting an internship with those grades? Is there anything I can do to make my résumé more attractive?"

With Janie's grades, her résumé was easy to overlook. However . . . The beginning of an idea took root in Stella's mind, and she tilted her head, looking at Janie in a new light. "Are you interested in econometrics?"

Stella had filled out half of the necessary forms to open up an internship position in her department—of which she was the sole employee—when her phone buzzed. She dug it out of her desk and smiled at the message from Michael.

What is my Stella doing?

She texted him back. Paperwork.

Can you take a long lunch?

She hugged her phone and spun her desk chair in a circle before replying. Yes.

Never mind the untouched lunch sitting next to her keyboard that she'd had delivered. She could put it in the fridge for tomorrow.

His response had her smile widening.

Head over to my mom's shop when you can.

She gathered the internship papers into a neat pile and prepared to leave. It was lunchtime on Friday, and everyone had left for the various restaurants downtown. She walked through the hallways and entered the elevator, expecting to make a clean getaway.

Philip stepped between the doors as they started to close.

"Are you actually heading out for lunch today? Care if I join you?" he asked.

"I'm meeting someone."

"The same guy?"

She nodded.

"Lucky guy."

She stared at the floor level indicator, wishing it would go from three to one much, much quicker.

"I heard you're planning on taking an intern."

"That's right."

"My cousin is a good fit."

Her eyes jumped from the numbers to Philip's face. "I already have someone in mind."

He put his hands in his pockets and shrugged. "All right."

"Wait . . ." She sighed. "Send me your cousin's résumé." As much as she wanted to hire Janie, she had to be fair about this. There was such a thing as professional integrity. The spot needed to go to the most qualified candidate.

Michael would understand. He didn't let his sister win when wrestling just because she was younger and smaller and weaker. Stella had to go through the proper vetting process. She had a feeling, however, Janie was her girl. When you loved something—like she and Janie did—you were good at it. If you weren't good right away, you *got* good at it.

Philip released an amused huff of breath. "All right, then."

The elevator dinged, and she strode through the lobby. Frustratingly, Philip followed her to her car.

"Are you going to that charity benefit tomorrow?" he asked.

"How do you know about it?"

"My mom and yours are on the planning committee. I know, small world, right? Anyway, I was wondering if you have a date. My mom is going to find me one if I don't get one on my own." He smiled and hunched his shoulders in a way that made him seem far more approachable than normal.

Their situations were so similar, Stella couldn't help sympathizing. "Mine threatened the same thing."

"Look, Stella, I know you're seeing someone, but . . . Before, you said you *hoped* it was serious, kind of like you weren't sure. Is he your boyfriend or not?"

She looked down at the blacktop in the parking lot. "It's complicated."

"What does that mean?"

"I need to go. I don't want to be late." She gripped the door handle to her car.

He lowered a hand toward hers but stopped before making contact. Did he sense she needed her space? Maybe he really did understand her.

"Does it mean you're just having sex? Because you're better than that. I hope you know that. All that stuff I told you before about needing practice—it was crap. You intimidate the hell out of me, and I was trying to make myself seem more worldly. It's stupid. All that matters is connecting with the right person. I think you can be that person for me, Stella. I've liked you for a long time."

"Why are you telling me this *now*? We've worked together for *years*." She could hardly believe her ears. He'd liked her all this time? Her?

"Because I have issues, and my tongue ties up when I'm with you and all that comes out is asshole garbage. I was waiting for you to ask me out because I'm insecure, but I'm asking you now. The idea that you're seeing some guy who doesn't appreciate you makes me crazy. You're a ten for me, Stella."

He thought she was a ten? *Someone thought she was a ten.* Her chest caved in, and her eyes stung. "I'm not a ten. I have . . . issues, too."

"I know. Your mom told my mom. She told me. I have a whole slew of problems that change names every time I switch therapists. We're perfect for each other. You're still a ten for me."

But he wasn't *her* perfect ten. He might have been, though, if things had been different. There was a time when she would have been interested in exploring whether there was a nice guy inside him somewhere. She couldn't fault him for sounding condescending when she often came across the same way. Besides, she wanted him to be good underneath it all. The idea gave her hope for herself.

"I'm sorry, Philip. I already asked him to go to the benefit with me. I can't uninvite him. More than that, I don't want to. I'm obsessed with him."

A stubborn look crossed Philip's face. "Obsessions pass."

"Not for me, they don't."

"I assure you he's just a phase. You're not in love," he said with certainty.

Her lips parted. Love? Was that what this feeling was? Was she in love with Michael?

"How can you be so sure it's not love?" she asked.

"I know because *I'm* the one you're going to fall in love with. *Me*," he insisted.

"Philip, don't do this, whatever this is."

"You need to give us a try."

With that, he stepped forward and bent toward her.

She tried to back away, but her car was right behind her, preventing escape. She turned her face to the side. He didn't wear overpowering cologne, but his smell was wrong. She pushed her hands against his chest. The feel of him was wrong. He wasn't Michael.

He touched his lips to hers. Dry skin on dry skin. A wet tongue slimed into her mouth, and her heart skittered. Her body went into lockdown. It was like her first three encounters all over again.

Wrong wrong wrong.

She twisted away and dragged her sleeve over her mouth. Dirty, black feelings grated over her skin, inside and out.

Philip grimaced and set his jaw, fisted his hands. "You just have to get used to me, Stella. You acclimated to that bastard."

She shoved at his chest, pushing him away. "Don't ever do that again."

Heart pounding and hands shaking, she got in her car. By the time she reached the shop, she'd mostly calmed down, but that unclean feeling persisted. She wanted to brush her teeth.

Inside, she located Michael kneeling in the fitting area at an older gentleman's feet, pinning the hem of his pants. Michael wore jeans and a black T-shirt. Measuring tape, pincushion, and chalk pencil were in place. She loved him in work clothes. He must have dressed similarly when he designed in New York City, sketching patterns over lighted architect tables and draping cloth over ungrateful mannequins.

As if sensing her, he glanced up, caught sight of her, and smiled.

She started to return his smile, but the bad taste in her mouth reminded her of what had happened in the parking lot. What if Michael kissed her now? She'd get Philip all over him. *Disgusting.* "Bathroom. I need the bathroom."

He stood up with a troubled frown. "Back there."

She ran into the back, spotted the door to the bathroom, and rushed to the sink. After turning on the water, she soaped her hands and scrubbed at her lips and her tongue. She splashed water into her mouth, swished, spit, repeated over and over.

Michael opened the bathroom door and watched as Stella rinsed out her mouth like she'd eaten something nasty. Was she sick? His insides twisted as his mind automatically jumped to the worst-case scenarios he was far too familiar with.

The door swung shut behind him as he closed the distance between them and swept his hands down her tense back. "Hey, what's wrong?"

Please, be okay.

For several long moments, the room was silent but for the rush of the water in the sink. A deep frown creased her brow as she watched the water swirl around the drain. Meeting his eyes in the mirror, she cranked the water off and said, "A coworker kissed me."

Everything inside Michael stilled, and a cold rage spread outward. With the training he did, he wasn't the kind of person who could pick fights. But he could sure as fuck end them. He would enjoy ending this one. His knuckles cracked as he fisted his hands.

"What's his name? What does he look like? Where can I find him?" The questions came out in a hard monotone. The motherfucker was going to enjoy himself a trip to the hospital.

She whipped around to face him, her eyes wide. "Why?"

"No one forces you, Stella."

"Are you planning to do something to him? I don't want you to get in trouble."

"You just washed your mouth out for a whole minute. Now I'm going to wash his out." With blood.

She wrung her hands as she searched for words. "I'm okay. As you can see."

"If you weren't okay, he'd be a dead man," he growled.

"Can you drop this? Please?"

He shook his head in disbelief. Someone had touched her, kissed her, stuck his fucking tongue in her mouth. "How can you be so calm about this? Did you *want* him to kiss you?"

"No, but . . ." She looked away from him. "Maybe there was a time when I did."

A horrible thought entered his head. "Is he the reason you hired me? You wanted to practice for this guy?"

Her cheeks flushed with color. "M-maybe? He seemed like a good candidate at the time. But I don't want him anymore, which is ironic because—" She stopped talking with a grimace.

"Because what?"

"He told me today he's liked me for a long time, that— surprise—I'm a ten for him." She sent him a searching gaze as she said, "He told me he doesn't care about how different I am."

He couldn't stop himself from dragging her against his chest then. He hadn't said those things, but that didn't mean he didn't feel them. "That's because you *are* a ten. All the things that make you different make you perfect."

"I'm not perfect, Michael. I'm really not," she said in a pained voice.

"Did you kiss him back?" At this point, that was the only thing that could make her imperfect for him. Maybe not even that.

She shook her head. "No."

"Did you like it? When he kissed you?" Because he had to know.

"Not at all," she whispered.

"Why? Did he do it wrong? Was he a bad kisser?"

"It felt wrong."

"Why?"

"Because he wasn't you." The soft look in her eyes killed him. He would do anything for that look. Anything.

He angled her head back with a hand against her jaw, trying to be gentle despite the violence raging in his veins. "Going to kiss you." He had to. If he didn't, he would go crazy.

"Don't. He's in my mouth. I can still taste him. I can't get him out."

He released a fierce growl. "I need this, Stella."

At her small nod, he crushed their mouths together and kissed her deeply. He needed to erase every last trace of that piece of shit, needed to mark her as his. She went weak and sank into him, and he closed his arms around her, stroking her roughly.

"Can you still taste him?" he rasped against her lips.

"No," she said on a gasp.

He worked her skirt open and slipped his hand into her panties, almost groaning from the liquid heat that met his fingers. Who was that for? Him or her coworker?

"Michael."

His name on her lips soothed a place deep inside him, and the urgent need to hear it again and again claimed him. He pushed her skirt until it pooled around her ankles and ripped the fly of his jeans open, freeing his cock. Then, he dug a foil from his pocket, tore it open, and rolled the condom on.

When she began to lower her panties, he shook his head. He looped one of her legs around his hip as he lifted and pressed her against the tile wall.

She made an impatient sound. "Don't tease me, Michael. I need you."

He pulled the crotch of her panties to the side and thrust hard and fast, burying himself inside her. Her breath broke, and she moaned his name. So fucking hot. He stroked his tongue over every inch of her mouth, claiming it as he angled his hips to hit her clit.

The tight grip of her body, her sweet mouth, her legs around him, her breaths on his neck—perfection. He reveled in every part of Stella. His heart thundered, and his blood rushed. His need grew desperate, but he held back, determined to wait for her. When she shattered and convulsed around him uncontrollably, he pumped into her harder.

He grasped at her hips, her thighs, pressed their foreheads together so he could see into her beautiful, dazed eyes and drove into her one last time, letting everything that he was pour into her, losing himself. As the breaths sawed in and out of his chest, he held her tight. He never wanted to let her go.

When he finally found the strength to pull away, he settled her on her feet and went to toss the condom in the toilet. He wiped himself off, aware of the appreciative way she watched him and loving it. She didn't look at anyone else like this. Just him.

After living with her for the better part of a month, he could say that with certainty. There were parts of her—many parts, the best parts—she only shared with Michael, and it had helped him forget their relationship wasn't real.

But he needed to remember. She hadn't wanted her co-worker's kiss, but if she had, there was no reason why she shouldn't have done it. They weren't monogamous. He wasn't her boyfriend or her fiancé or her husband. She was his client, and he was her . . . vendor. That sounded awful as fuck, but it was true. He had no right to defend her and no right to be possessive. She was paying him to help her—at least she thought she was—and he needed to stay detached and professional.

Too bad he'd gone and fallen for her, instead. When they eventually separated, it would break him. But she'd be better off. She'd know how to be herself with another person and what to expect out of a relationship, what it felt like to be loved. He hoped she never settled for less.

Drawing on years of escorting experience, he slipped on a smile and said, "I'll have to buy you a new pair of those."

When a confused expression crossed her face, he nodded toward the torn side seam of her panties that she'd been absently fingering all this time.

She smiled and flattened her palm over her hip. "That's okay. I can do it."

"I don't mind. Though for most couples, women buy all the underwear."

She tilted her head to the side. "Why?"

He shrugged. "I think it's because they do a lot of shopping and like to take care of the people they love."

As he said the words, Stella drew in a surprised breath. A discovering look lit her face before she stared off into space, focusing on things inside her head.

"Where did you go?" He waved a hand in front of her

until she refocused on him. It was such a Stella thing to do, he grinned despite the emptiness in his chest. He loved how brilliant she was. Everything about her did it for him. Every single thing. "You're thinking about work, aren't you? Here I am talking about replacing the underwear I tore having hot bathroom sex with you, and you're zoning out to think about econometrics."

She straightened her glasses with a wrinkle of her nose. "I-I'm sorry. I can't help it all the time. I try to be present, but—"

"I'm teasing you. I love your genius brain," he admitted. Because he couldn't help it, even when he was sad, he kissed her soft lips once, twice, and one last time again. "Come on, Ngoại will probably have to use the bathroom soon, and I want to show you something."

Stella covered a gasp when Michael pulled a hanger from a hook on the wall, revealing a little white dress of creamy fabric. "Is that for me?"

"I had to guess at your dimensions, so the fit might be all over the place. Try it on for me?"

She stared at the garment in wonder. Her own Michael Larsen dress.

After closing herself in the mirrorless dressing room, she undressed in a hurry. Of course the dress was strapless so she couldn't wear a bra, but the inside was lined in soft silk. There wasn't a single exposed seam to bother her skin. She was dying to see what it looked like on.

Holding the bodice to her chest, she walked out and turned around. "Can you zip the back for me, please?"

His lips brushed against her nape as the zipper closed with an intimate *zzzzip*, sending a shiver down her spine. It felt like it fit her perfectly. It hugged her body better than her yoga clothes, and she loved her yoga clothes. When she turned around, Michael assessed her with a critical eye, his sexy arms crossed over his chest.

"Can I look?" she whispered.

A small smile formed on his lips, and he nodded toward the raised area in front of the mirrors where he did fittings.

She stepped onto the dais and felt her heart stutter, reboot, and resume. The dress was a smooth ivory sheath that followed the lines of her body from her knees to her chest. The fabric of the bodice fluted just off center in such a way that it gave the impression she was a curvaceous calla lily. Her nipples were *not* visible.

It was perfect. Simple. Modest but daring. *Her.*

She ran her hands over her hips, turned around, and gasped at what the expert construction of the dress did to her behind. Her butt had never looked so pert and voluptuous. She settled a hand over the ripe curve of one cheek, and Michael cleared his throat.

He stepped onto the dais and trailed his fingers down her sides. "I'm happy with the fit. My hands knew the size of you."

"I love it. Thank you, Michael."

"My gift to you. For all the birthdays when I didn't know you. When *is* your birthday?"

Warmth effervesced inside her like champagne. A gift. From Michael. That he'd made with his own hands. Each seam, each thread, each piece of fabric had been chosen just for her. "The summer solstice, June twenty-first. You?"

"June twentieth. But I'm two years younger than you."

"Do you mind that I'm older?" She knew men often liked younger women.

He grinned. "Not at all. I crushed on older women when I was growing up. I can still see Ms. Rockaway bending over in her tweed skirt to pick up the chalkboard eraser."

"Who was she?" Unpleasant emotion speared through Stella.

"Chemistry teacher sophomore year. I hope you're jeal-

ous, so you know how I feel about Dexter kissing you,"
he said, his face thoughtful as he ran his fingertips down
her arm.

"Dexter?"

"Maybe Stewart. That's a good name for the kind of guy
I'm picturing."

"Don't picture him."

"Mortimer."

She laughed. "No."

"Niles."

"*Michael.*"

"Don't tell me his name is Michael."

"It's not. You're my only Michael. Do you really want to
know his name?"

He was quiet for a moment before he released a heavy
breath and said, "It's better if I don't. Since you don't want
me to beat the shit out of him." When she stiffened at his
language, a hard smile touched his lips.

She caught her breath, unsure what to say. It wasn't Philip
she cared about. It was Michael. If he went after Philip, there
could be awful consequences. Lawsuits, jail, HR claims.
Even though she would have liked to see Michael in action,
one nasty kiss wasn't worth all that.

"I'm glad you like the dress," Michael said with a soft-
ening expression. "I'm looking forward to seeing you wear
it tomorrow."

After a lunch of catfish soup with pineapple and celery
over rice, Stella rushed back to the office. She wanted
to look at the data again.

Philip lifted a hand at her when she passed by, but she
didn't have time to deal with him. She strode past his office,
tossed her purse in her desk drawer, and sat down, clicking
through screens on her monitors until she came to the func-
tion she'd formulated to model men's purchasing behavior

with regard to high-end boxer shorts. It was an elegant equation with five key variables that included things like age and income bracket and several minor variables.

She'd boiled the termination of male purchasing of boxers down to a single binary variable, β, and had found markers that led to its activation, things like increased spending on fine dining and luxury gifts. It seemed counterintuitive to Stella that in a time of decreased price sensitivity, men suddenly quit buying their underwear. Even luxury boxers weren't *that* expensive.

Now, as she looked at the math and the numbers, Michael's words trickled through her brain. *Women like to take care of the people they love.* Somehow, some way, Stella had used market data, math, and statistics, to quantify love into a single variable.

β was love.

β was a zero or a one. A yes or a no.

And it was overwhelmingly linked to the time when men quit purchasing their own underwear. It wasn't an absolute, of course. People were people, and they hated to be entirely predictable. But it was a visible trend. You could gamble with this data and win more than you lost.

If a woman purchased underclothes for a man, it meant she loved him.

Stella was fully capable of purchasing underclothes.

She left work early that day to go shopping. When she returned home with her find, she wrapped it in a red bow and hid it at the bottom of the drawer Michael had appropriated for his underclothes. If he stopped buying boxers now, it meant he loved her back.

If he loved her, her labels wouldn't matter. She'd tell him everything.

Michael raked a hand through his hair as he stared at the suits hanging in Stella's closet, trying to pick out the one he'd wear to the benefit tonight. He was going to meet her parents. Every nerve in his body told him it was going to go terribly, but he would still drag himself there.

Stella had asked him to come.

She peeked into the doorway, grinning. "Can't decide which one?"

"You pick."

Shyly, she stepped into the closet. She was holding the dress he'd made to her chest. "Zip me first?"

Because he couldn't resist, he kissed her neck, sucking on the sweet skin as he searched underneath the loose bodice and palmed her tits. When he pinched her nipples, her breath hitched in the sexiest way.

"We're going to be late if you keep that up."

"Everyone's late to these kinds of things." He bit her nape as he stroked a hand over her belly and prepared to slip into her panties. He loved touching her there, loved the way she responded.

"My parents are never late. They want to meet you."

His hand froze in mid-descent. Because he couldn't bring himself to say he wanted to meet them—why would he want to meet people who were bound to disapprove of him?—he said, "It should be interesting."

"Thank you for coming with me. I know you'd rather do other things."

He'd rather do prom fittings, but he didn't say that. "You know how I like to wear suits." That, at least, was true. He withdrew his hand from her dress and pulled the zipper up.

"A three-piece. I love you in three-piece suits."

"The black one, then. It'll look good with your dress."

She grinned as she turned to face him. "Everything looks good with my dress. People are going to ask where I got it. Can I tell them it's a Michael Larsen original?"

He hesitated as he heard his full name on her lips. "You know my real name."

Her eyelashes swept downward. "It was on your electric bill and the uniform in your picture. Are you mad?"

"Are *you*?" Had she Googled him or his family? There were articles in the local papers that outlined in detail all the shit his dad had done. Had she read them? No, she couldn't have. She wasn't looking at him with veiled suspicion. It was only a matter of time though.

His heart crashed, and his skin went hot. *Tick, tock. Tick, tock.* But the clock wasn't ticking down to the time when he exploded and hurt everyone. Now, it was ticking down to the time when she learned everything and it was over between them.

She lifted a shoulder, but she didn't look at him, and she didn't speak.

"You *are* mad," he said in realization.

"*Mad* isn't the right word."

"What is the right word?"

"I don't know. I felt like you didn't trust me." She hugged her arms around her middle. "Like you were making sure I won't be able to find you when things end between us."

"No, I trust you. I was just . . ." Afraid of losing her. "I hate my last name." That, too.

"Why?"

"It's my dad's."

She searched his face with her eyebrows drawn together. "Why do you hate your dad? Because he left your mom?"

He swallowed hard. If he answered that question truthfully, he'd lose her today, right now.

The badness in his heart advised him to lie. It would be so easy just to lie. That was what his dad always did.

"I'm sorry," she said in a rush. Blinking rapidly, she adjusted her glasses and rubbed at an elbow. "It's too personal, isn't it? Forget I asked."

"Stella, you can ask me things," he said, feeling an ache start in his chest and spread outward. It wasn't a relationship if they couldn't talk to each other. "I hate him because of the *way* he left, because he's a cheater and a bad person. I haven't seen him in years, but I'm certain he's out there cheating on other women, hurting other people, leaving them in the worst way. It's what he does."

"He left you, too?" she asked with sad eyes.

"Yeah, and all of my sisters."

His mom had told Michael not to hold what his dad did to her against him, to forgive him, but how did you forgive someone who wasn't even there? As fathers went, as long as they weren't abusing you, a shitty one was still better than none. Michael had none. And trying to hold the family together by himself was breaking him apart.

She threw herself into his arms and hugged him tight, saying nothing, and Michael kissed her forehead. With each breath, her sweet Stella scent reached into him and soothed him. He needed this. He needed her. When people heard about his dad, they cursed him, and they empathized with his mom. None of them thought about what it meant to Michael. No one but Stella.

He knew he should tell her the other half of the story about his dad, but he couldn't. He hadn't loved her enough yet.

Setting her away from his body, he said, "We should get ready."

The benefit was at an exclusive club a ways down Page Mill Road, amid lighted tennis courts, putting greens, and glowing blue swimming pools. Michael parked Stella's Tesla in front of a large building with modern lines and the ugly brown façade typical of Palo Alto architecture.

After he helped Stella out of the car, she stared at the windows of the club. Her nervousness was obvious, but the golden light spilling from the windows made her look dreamily beautiful. Her hair was pulled up in a loose side knot, pinned in place with a white silk rosette. She hadn't needed to bring a purse—Michael had her phone and cards in his pocket—and her empty hands arabesqued on her thighs.

"If I start talking about work, will you stop me, please?"

He took her hand in his and squeezed, feeling the cold sweat on her palm. "Why? Your work is interesting."

"I get carried away, and I take over the conversation. It bothers people."

"I like it when you get carried away." That was when she was at her most captivating, when her eyes twinkled. He brought her hand to his lips and kissed her knuckles.

Her mouth wobbled into an uncertain smile as she looked up at him. "That's part of why you're so wonderful to me."

"I'm glad you know it."

She laughed as he led her to the front doors. Once inside, the din of hundreds of casual conversations enveloped them. The banquet room was filled wall to wall with round tables of Silicon Valley's finest, and a live band played low-key jazz from a stage at the back of the room. A wall composed almost entirely of windows showcased the lap pool and lighted golf course outside.

"How are you dealing with all this noise?"

She turned to face him with a startled look. "Is it bothering you, too?"

"I'm fine. You're the one I'm worried about." He didn't want her to end up hyperventilating outside again.

"The noise isn't terrible. I'm more nervous about the seating arrangements. My mom likes to surround me with new people. I've gotten better at the talking, but it's still a lot of work."

He tilted his head as he absorbed that. For him, talking was . . . talking. There wasn't a work part. "You overthink it."

"I *have* to think really hard when I talk. Otherwise I blurt out rude things, and I alienate everyone."

"It's because you're so honest."

"People don't like honest. Except for when you're saying good things. Figuring out what people think is good is tricky, especially when I don't know them. It makes conversation a minefield."

A woman who had to be Stella's mother sailed forward in ropes of pearls and a loose, off-white dress that fell over slender curves to midcalf. Her dark hair was gathered in a bun identical to the one Stella usually wore, accentuating a facial structure Michael was very familiar with. This elegant midfifties woman was Stella in another twentysome years. Stella's future husband was a lucky fucking bastard.

She hugged Stella and pulled back to admire her with maternal pride. "Stella dear, you look lovely." Her attention switched to Michael, and she smiled. "And there he is. So good to see you, Michael. I'm Stella's mother, Ann."

She held her hand out, knuckles up, and he lifted it to his mouth to brush a quick kiss over the back. He knew he was in upper-crust territory when hand kissing was an expected greeting.

"Good to see you, Ann."

"And his voice is beautiful, too. I just can't get over this dress, Stella. Wherever did your personal shopper find it? You look like a flower."

Stella beamed at him. "Michael is a designer. This is one of his creations."

And didn't that sound perfect coming from her lips? The only problem was he hadn't designed much in the past three years, and he didn't see himself getting back to it anytime soon. His mom said she didn't need him at the shop, but with her sickness, he needed to keep an eye on her. He'd run across her unconscious body in the bathroom twice. If he hadn't, who knew what would have happened.

Ambition could wait. He only had one mom.

If he felt stifled and suffocated in the prison of his life, that was his problem. This wasn't going to last forever. He didn't want her to die. He loved her. But it was an unavoidable truth that her passing would set him free.

Love, he found, was a jail. It trapped, and it clipped wings. It dragged you down, forced you to places you didn't want to go—like this club he didn't belong in.

Ann clasped her pearls. "Oh, isn't that perfect for you, Stella. Did he make this himself?" She fluttered around Stella, checking the zipper, peeking inside at the construction of the dress. "Concealed seams. No tags. And it's so soft."

Ann looked up at Michael with glassy eyes before she whispered in Stella's ear and kissed her cheek, making Stella blush.

"Well, come on and let me introduce you to her father." Ann looped her arm around his and steered them toward a half-occupied table far from the band.

A middle-aged man with a bit of a potbelly, gray hair, and wire-rimmed glasses sat next to four empty seats. He was carrying on an animated conversation with the goodish-looking blond guy at his side.

"Edward, this is Michael. Michael, this is Edward, Stella's father."

Stella's dad stood up and shook hands. It was a civil handshake, firm without fighting for dominance, but the light brown eyes behind his lenses examined Michael like a laboratory specimen of unknown origin. Michael felt like he had on prom night meeting his date's dad for the first time, like he should have brought his résumé and latest STD screening results. He stifled the impulse to shake out his hands and feet like he did before he sparred in competition.

"Nice to meet you," Michael said.

"A pleasure," Stella's dad said with a stiff smile that reminded Michael a lot of his own dad—well, if his dad had been remotely normal.

"This is Philip James," Ann said, indicating the blond guy. "Philip, this is Michael, Stella's boyfriend."

Philip stood up and straightened a black suitcoat that fit his athletic frame in a way that would make any tailor proud. "Pleased to meet you." The guy held his hand out politely. When Michael shook it, however, his fingers were tightened in a painful vise. What the hell? Philip's hazel gaze was flinty as he sized Michael up. "Stella told me about you at work."

At work? Michael glanced at Stella, and she looked away uncomfortably. The kiss. *This* was Dexter Stewart Mortimer Niles.

Michael released Philip's hand before he gave in to the urge to slam him onto the table. "Philip," he said with a terse nod.

This piece of shit had put his tongue in Stella's mouth. He was not at all what Michael had expected. He should have been thinner, with bad posture and less muscle. He definitely should have had glasses, nice thick ones that looked like binoculars.

Seemingly oblivious to the tension thickening the air, Ann continued introducing the well-dressed people seated around the table: a single nerdy guy who fit Michael's original perception of Philip to a T and happened to own a well-known tech company, a highly educated Indian couple, and a white-haired older woman in a lavender skirt suit whose neck, ears, and fingers dripped with enormous diamonds.

He unbuttoned his jacket and sat down between Stella and the table's last empty seat with a composure that three years of escorting had taught him.

"So, Michael, tell me about yourself," Stella's dad said, crossing his arms and leaning back in his chair on a calculating gaze. Yep, this was prom night all over again.

Michael knew exactly how this was going to go.

"What would you like to hear?" Michael asked.

"For starters, what do you do?"

Philip watched him with sullen interest.

Michael's dad had wanted him to be an astrophysicist or an engineer. Near the end, his dad had settled on architect. That was still respectable. "I'm a designer."

"Oh, how interesting. What do you design? Or does your security clearance not allow you to say?"

When he unraveled that, he almost laughed. "No, I'm not a defense contractor. I design clothes."

"He designed Stella's dress, honey," Stella's mom said with a gentle smile. "He's remarkably talented."

Edward's face wrinkled in distaste, but he rallied, giving Michael the benefit of the doubt. "That must be a difficult business to get successful in. Are you working under one of those New York designers?"

"Not currently."

"You must be creating your own line. That's exciting," Ann said.

"I've taken some time off, to be honest."

Stella began to speak, but he grabbed her hand and

shook his head slightly. He really didn't need these people to know he did dry cleaning and alterations all day. It was bad enough it was the truth.

No, it wasn't bad. He wasn't ashamed of it. It was good, honest work—fuck it. What sense was there in lying to himself? Sitting next to all these people with their fancy educations and exorbitant wealth, yes, he was ashamed. He wasn't the kind of man anyone would pair with someone like Stella.

"So . . . you do *nothing*?" Philip asked with a look of disbelief.

Michael schooled his features into nonchalance and shrugged. "More or less." His mom's illness was none of their fucking business, and he didn't want the whole table looking at him with pity.

Matching grimaces crossed Edward's and Philip's faces, and Michael clenched his jaw. They probably thought he wanted to marry Stella for her money. Didn't they know Stella was too smart for that kind of shit? When she fell in love, it would be with someone who was her match.

"I'd go crazy with boredom." Philip's expression turned thoughtful as he looked at Stella. "You can't stand inactivity, can you, Stella? You're driven, and you like knowing your work has an impact on the world. It's why we get along so well."

"It's true I like working," Stella allowed, but she cast a worried look at Michael.

"Ed, you should have seen what she did with the last project we worked on together," Philip said. "She came at the problem in a way I'd never seen before and is single-handedly revolutionizing the way online vendors market to their customers."

"I'm sure she couldn't have done it without your help, Phil." Stella's dad grasped Philip's shoulder fondly. So these two already knew one another? Were they golf partners or some shit? Fifteen different ways to chuck a man flitted through Michael's mind. And what was this about her *needing* Philip? Stella didn't need anyone. Not even Michael, not anymore. He wasn't sure if she ever had.

A genuine smile curved over Stella's lips. "That's actually true. We work well together."

Really. He hated the idea of her working with Philip and liking any part of it. The bastard should have irritated her as much as he did Michael. He was hit by the juvenile desire to kiss her publicly and stake his claim on her, and he removed his hand from hers before he could act. She didn't notice. She was still smiling at Philip—her real smile, the one he usually got to himself. Fuck if that didn't hurt like getting one of his balls torn off.

"She's one of the few who can tolerate me. I know I'm an asshole. I have standards, and I can't stand laziness and ineptitude." Philip sent a telling glance Michael's way.

Michael took a deep breath and released it slowly. He searched the walls of the room for a clock. How much more of this did he have to withstand?

The conversation at the table veered down the path of economic theory and advanced statistics, and he watched with a sinking sensation as Stella opened up and began talking. She had said to stop her if she started talking about work, but she was loving it. It was so clearly her passion in life. Michael didn't want to deny her. Philip, for all his supposed assholishness, kept up with her in a way Michael never could.

He was reminded of that kiss. She'd said she hadn't liked it and that Philip was annoying, but she certainly wasn't minding interacting with him now.

Michael couldn't help observing that Stella and Philip made a good-looking couple. With their similar interests and backgrounds, they were nauseatingly perfect for one another. He remembered that it was Philip who had inspired Stella to hire an escort in the first place. She'd wanted to make Philip hers. Maybe—fuck, he hated thinking this—maybe she should.

At the end of the day, what Michael and Stella had was physical. They didn't connect in this cerebral manner, and he knew how important it was that Stella's mind was stimulated.

It sucked admitting it, but he wasn't enough for her. On several different levels. She could never love him. Michael really was nothing but practice. As the economics conversation continued, a heartsick, organ-shredding feeling gripped him. Everything felt wrong. Even his skin felt off-size.

"Oh, I'm so glad Philip's mother was able to make it," Ann said.

A red-nailed hand rested on the back of the chair next to Michael, and a familiar combination of scents assailed his nose. Cinnamon and cigarettes. Ice cubes clinked before a lowball glass half-filled with whiskey was set on the table.

"Hello, darlings. Sorry I'm late." A petite woman with long bleached blond hair and a tight black cocktail dress lowered herself into the empty seat. Her profile was turned to him, but Michael recognized her. He'd kissed that jaw. "I had to make a quick stop before—" She faced him, and her expression went as surprised as the Botox allowed. "Well, well, well, hello, Michael."

"Hello, Aliza." What an *excellent* time to bump into his least-favorite former client.

Y ou two are acquainted? How wonderful is that." Her
mother clapped her hands together.

Stella felt like she was going to vomit. Philip's mom was
the woman from the club. She'd given Michael his car. The
one he drove every day. The one he wouldn't let Stella replace.

Michael reclined in his seat with a cool smile, looking
casual, perfectly comfortable, and drop-dead handsome in
his black suit. "We go a ways back."

Aliza released a husky laugh and stroked her hand down
his arm. "We do."

When he didn't so much as flinch at the contact, Stella's
throat knotted. Michael liked older women—he'd said so.
With her large breasts, tiny figure, whiskey-smooth voice,
and sophisticated seductiveness, she was sex incarnate. Stella
reminded herself he'd ended things with Aliza. Today, he
hadn't given Aliza three glorious orgasms with his beautiful
mouth before making love to her like he couldn't get enough.

"Please do tell me, *who* did you come here with?" Aliza's
eyes swept over the table and considered Stella's mother before they went back to Michael's face.

"He's here with me." Stella scooted closer to him and covered his hand with hers. She expected him to flip his hand over and interlace their fingers like he usually did. When he remained immobile, her stomach dropped. What did that mean?

Aliza picked up her whiskey and considered Stella over the glass's rim. "Well, aren't you wholesome-looking. Your daughter is beautiful, Ann. I can see why Phil likes her so much. It's a shame she isn't single."

Her mother smiled, but Stella could see from the tension around her eyes that she was worried. "Thank you, Aliza. These two look very happy. It's no shame at all."

Stella squeezed Michael's hand tighter as she stared up at his profile. Before tonight, they had been happy. What was wrong? He remained impassive, his gaze trained on Aliza. Stella was touching him, but he felt miles away.

"So it's *serious*?" Aliza looked at Stella's parents before she smirked and sent Michael an amused glance. "Meeting the parents now, Michael? Would you have met mine for the right price?"

"What are you talking about?" Philip narrowed his eyes as he looked from his mom to Michael and back again.

Aliza took a healthy drink from her lowball glass and smiled suggestively. "We used to . . . go on dates."

"You've got to be kidding me." Philip stared at Michael in rising disgust. "You've slept with *my mom*?"

"Not exactly," Michael replied with a tight smile.

Aliza chuckled. "There wasn't any *sleeping* involved, if I remember correctly."

"Oh, for Pete's sake. I need a drink." Her father pushed away from the table.

"Get me another whiskey on the rocks while you're at it, darling," Aliza said, shaking her glass.

"You've had enough." He fled toward the cocktail bar in the back corner.

Aliza's throaty laugh floated over the table before she drained her glass of the amber fluid and set it down. "Never."

Because Stella was sitting so close to Michael, she saw when Aliza's red nails brushed over his thigh. He didn't move. He merely stared at the woman as her hand stroked leisurely upward, coming closer and closer to the fly of his pants. Why wasn't he stopping her? Did he want her to touch him?

Standing up abruptly, he said, "I'm going to get some air. Excuse me."

Before Aliza could pursue him, Stella jumped up and followed him through the back doors. The air outside smelled of nighttime, cut grass, and chlorine, and the coolness sent goose bumps over her bare shoulders and arms.

"Michael," she called out.

He paused next to the blue glowing swimming pool. "You should go back in, Stella."

She walked to his side. This distance between them was making her panic. How did she bring them back together again? She took his hand and wrapped him around her waist as she pushed her body close. "But I'll miss you."

His eyes softened, and he tightened his arms around her. She sighed and rested her cheek on his chest, breathing him in. If he could hold her like this, everything was still okay.

"You were having a good time before my past sat at the table." He swept his hand up and down her back.

"I would rather have stayed home with you." She brought herself closer to him and kissed his throat. "Why did you let her touch you like that? It drove me crazy." He was hers.

"Did it?" He skimmed his lips over her jaw, brushing light kisses upon her sensitive skin.

"Yes."

"It's a bad policy to make a scene with former clients. Even if they don't appreciate it at the time, they come to later on. I'll do my best to afford you the same courtesy in the future."

In the future. After they separated. "I don't want that."

He was part of her life now, one of the best parts. He couldn't leave.

"That makes things easier for me," he said.

"No, that's not what I meant."

"What *do* you want, Stella?"

"I want . . ." She licked her lips and took a breath. Could she say she wanted *him*? Could she say she loved him? She smoothed her hands over his chest and gripped his shoulders, and he watched her with rapt attention. She wished she were better with words. She wished she could let her body speak for her. Her body always knew how to communicate perfectly with his. Even now, she found herself responding to his nearness, leaning in close, fitting against him just right.

His Adam's apple bobbed, and he pulled away. "Come on, then. Let's get back to your place. Unless you want to try it in the car?"

"What are you talking about?"

"Sex, Stella." The words were hard and clipped in the night air.

Her lungs constricted so tight she could barely breathe. "That's not what I was going to say."

"Then we need to end this farce. Because I don't have anything else to give you."

"But you do. You listen to me and talk to me and—"

"I will never be able to talk to you like that asshole in there. I don't even want to. I'm too stupid to give a shit about math and economics."

"That's not true. You are smart."

"I've amounted to nothing. I've gone nowhere. I fuck people for money, and when that's not enough . . ." He met her eyes with a steady, serious gaze. "I think about stealing it. I plan it out in my head, who I'd take it from, the lies I'd say, how I could cover my tracks. Because I'm just like my dad."

She shook her head. What was he talking about? He would never steal. She had no doubt of it.

"You wanted to know why I hate him. I'll tell you the whole reason." He paused for a heavy second before saying,

"He's so good at cheating he's famous for it. He was in the news a while ago. Haven't you heard of him? Frederick Larsen."

"I don't . . ." But even as she spoke, the familiar sound of the name dredged up memories. She drew in a sudden breath. "The con artist. He seduced women and . . ."

"Stole from them. He told everyone he owned a software company. He was gone so often on 'business trips.' My mom knew he cheated, but he always came back. Until three years ago when he disappeared and his other wife showed up on my mom's doorstep looking for him. It turned out every dollar he earned came from some swindled woman. And he swindled my mom the worst. Before he left the last time, he cleared out her bank accounts and cashed out on enormous loans in her name. She had to mortgage everything to the teeth to pay them off, but even that wasn't enough. She was going to lose the shop and her house she'd worked so hard for. My sister was going to have to drop out of school because we suddenly couldn't pay for it."

He turned away from her and began unknotting his tie with violent jerks of his hands. "The job I'd been so crazy about—the one I'd traveled across the country for, thinking my family was home safe with my dad—paid such a small amount I had to quit. I didn't have any skills that paid quickly, not like you. So I took this thing my father gave me, my body that's the same exact height as his, my smile that looks just like his, and I sold it. I fucked half of California with it, day and night for months, and I used that money to help make everything right. But by that time, my mom got sick, and she . . ."

The tie fluttered to the ground, and he loosened his top buttons like his shirt was suffocating him. He covered his eyes with his palm as he breathed raggedly.

Stella stepped toward him hesitantly. She placed her hand on his face, finding it drenched with hot tears. Her throat was too swollen to speak, so she wrapped her arms around his neck and held him with all her strength. He buried his face in her hair and held her back.

"It's not your fault your dad did that horrible thing, and you're nothing like him," she whispered. How could he possibly believe that?

"If I'd *been* there, I might have noticed what he was doing, and I might have stopped it."

"Shhhh." She smoothed her fingers through his hair. "Even if you'd been there, you wouldn't have found anything until it was too late. He fooled tons of people. That's what he's good at."

He tightened his arms a fraction and pressed a kiss to her cheek. When he spoke, his voice was rough and intimate, bare. "The crazy thing is, even after all he's done, even with how much I'm ashamed of him and hate him, I still miss him. He's my dad. My dad is a lying, cheating criminal, and I love him."

Stella had no words for Michael at that point, so she continued to hold him. What did you say when someone hurt like this? All she could do was rest her beating heart next to his and hurt with him.

After a moment and an eternity, Michael pulled away. Wiping at the tears on her cheeks, he said, "I accepted your proposal because I wanted to help you with your issues, and it's clear we've worked through them. You're ready for a real relationship now. If some bastard doesn't want you because you're autistic, he doesn't deserve you. Do you hear me? You have nothing to be ashamed of."

The blood drained from her face, and her heart stopped beating. "You know?"

He smiled slightly. "I figured it out after that first night at my mom's."

He'd known all this time? Was that good or bad? She didn't know. "You want to leave?" she heard herself ask.

"It's time for me to move on, Stella. We're not giving each other all the things we need."

She understood at once he meant her, that *she* wasn't enough for *him*. Because of who and what she was, her impairments and eccentricities, her label.

Black hopelessness dragged her down. It had been naïve of her to hope she could seduce him. Her chin quivered, and she bit the inside of her lip to still the motion. "I see."

He brushed his fingertips across her cheek, tucked tendrils of hair behind her ear. "You need more than sex, and I can't give you those things."

She looked down at her shoes. Maybe it had just been sex for him, but for her, as pathetic as it sounded, it had felt like love.

He smoothed warm hands down her cold arms and squeezed her hands. "Thank you for these past months. They were special to me."

Not special enough.

"Thank you, Michael. For helping me with my anxiety issues."

"Promise you won't be hiring more escorts after this."

"No more escorts. I promise." There was only one escort she wanted.

"Good girl." He breathed a kiss into her hair. "I'm going to go now."

"I can drive you home." She didn't want them to part yet.

"I'd prefer to call a cab. I want to clear my things from your place, and it's better if you're not there when I do that. Take care, okay?"

"Okay."

He dug her key fob, phone, and cards from his pockets and handed them to her. "Good-bye, Stella."

"Good-bye, Michael."

Statue-still and numb, she watched as he left. Then, she turned around and walked inside. Her preference was to go home, but he wanted to collect his things in peace. All other exit strategies were out, as well. The thought of passing by him in the parking lot or on the road filled her eyes with fresh tears.

Better to return to the dinner. It was the last place she wanted to be right now.

After going to the bathroom and fixing her makeup as well as she knew how, she seated herself at the table.

"Where's Michael, Stella dear?" her mother asked quietly.

"He left. We just broke up."

Philip smirked.

Aliza cast Stella a pitying glance from the other side of Michael's empty chair and placed a hand on Stella's shoulder. "Men like him need to be free, darling."

Stella pushed Aliza's hand off without a word.

Her father narrowed his eyes in displeasure. She knew how he felt about any kind of rude behavior. "It's all for the best."

For once, her mother had nothing to say. She merely watched Stella with concerned eyes.

"You can do much better," Philip added. The directness of his gaze said that by *better* he meant *him*.

Stella's knuckles went white as she curled her fingers around her knees. Emotion boiled inside her chest, screaming to get out, but she bit it back.

"I agree," her father said. "I saw nothing good in that man."

Sharpness lanced her insides, and her control dissolved. "Then you weren't looking closely enough. He's not doing nothing. He's not lazy. Sometimes there are more important things than passion and ambition. He put his career on hold so he could take care of his mom, who's dying of cancer. He's the kind of person who will give up everything for the people he loves, *everything*. He's nothing *but* good."

And he didn't want her.

Her father's face darkened. "Then why didn't he say so?"

"Why would he want to share that with people who are looking down on him?"

"I wasn't—"

"That's enough, Edward," her mother snapped. "It was

obvious what you were thinking. You want her to be with someone driven and career-focused, someone who can take care of her. You don't seem to realize she's driven enough on her own, and she doesn't need someone to take care of her financially. Stella dear, let's get out of here. The noise is getting to me."

Her mother held out her hand, and Stella took it, letting herself be led to an empty seating area just outside the banquet room. A massive bouquet of willow branches and calla lilies dominated the low coffee table.

Stella traced the edge of one of the flowers before she sat down and shut her eyes. It was much quieter out here, and some of the tension in her head eased. But the ache in her heart didn't abate. Instead, it spread outward and intensified, crushing her with hopelessness and defeat. The soft weight of her mother's hand on her leg had her eyes drifting open.

Her mother embraced her, pulling her into ropes of cool pearls and Chanel No. 5. Stella still didn't like that strong scent, but in that moment, its familiarity calmed her. She relaxed and let her mother hold her like she had when she was little, not realizing she was crying until her mother hushed her and began rocking side to side.

"I'm so sorry, dear. I've always wanted an artist for you, someone sensitive who would put you first. Later, we can think up a strategic way to find the perfect person. You should really try Tinder, dear."

Even now, her mother was still in honey badger mode. She never gave up.

Stella released a long, ragged breath. "That person was Michael."

"Don't get stubborn on me now, Stella. There are billions of people on this planet, and you can't force love. You'll find a better fit than him if you stay focused."

Stella said nothing. Michael was mint chocolate chip for her. She could try other flavors, but he'd always be her favorite.

Her differences always did this. They left her most alone when she was surrounded by people. Usually, she didn't care. She didn't need people. She was happiest when she had the space and time to focus on things that interested her. But Michael interested her, and she didn't feel alone when she was with him. Far from it. The knowledge that it was all one-sided *hurt*.

"Do you think, Momma, that you could shelve the husband-hunting and grandbaby discussions for a while? I want to make you happy, but I'm really tired right now."

Her mother squeezed her tighter. "Of course, forget all about grandchildren. I didn't mean to pressure you. I just want you happy."

Stella sighed and shut her eyes. She didn't care about being happy. All she wanted at the moment was to feel nothing.

The silence in Stella's house was absolute. Funny how Michael had never noticed it before. When he was here, he was usually busy talking to Stella, listening to her quirky observations, cooking in her massive kitchen and feeding her, kissing her, making love to her . . .

He was going to miss this house. He was going to miss *Stella*. A lot. He already missed her. He was breaking into pieces from missing her. Ending their arrangement had been the right thing to do, though. She didn't need his help anymore, and she deserved someone better than him. Someone smarter who didn't have a criminal for a dad. Someone who could impress her parents and didn't run into past clients when they went out to dinner.

That reminded him that he'd be back to regular escorting next Friday. The thought held absolutely no appeal. He wasn't even sure if he could get a hard-on for someone else at this point. All he wanted was Stella smell and Stella taste and Stella skin. His body had tuned itself to fit her, and nothing else would do. The old fantasies that used to interest him were now dull and boring. He'd developed a new kink, and it involved a shy girl who daydreamed about economics.

He sat down on Stella's bed and rested his face in his palms. This was his last time sitting here. Fuck it all, another man would be sleeping in this bed soon. Wretched ugly feelings rose. Stella was his to kiss, his to touch, his to love. He wanted to tear the blankets off the bed and shred everything to pieces. If he couldn't have it, no one could. She could get a new fucking bed.

Fisting his hands, he made himself go to the closet before he could lay waste to her bedroom. He stuffed T-shirts and jeans into his sports bag before moving to the underwear drawer. He wanted to get this done so he could leave. Socks piled into the bag, followed by neatly folded boxers. At the bottom of the drawer, he encountered an unopened package. The exact brand and size of boxers he used, though he usually purchased navy blue and these were red. A bow was tied around it.

Stella had bought him underwear.

It was the first gift she'd given him. How funny. Had she thought his were getting worn out? Maybe they were. He tossed the package into his sports bag and zipped it up. They weren't very expensive, and she certainly wasn't going to use them herself. She'd bought them for him, and he was going to keep them.

On his way out of her room, he slipped his billfold from his pocket, fished out a folded slip of paper, and set it on her nightstand. There, proof that he wasn't his dad.

But maybe that wasn't why it felt so right to do this. Maybe it felt right because he was in love.

He strode through the empty house, turning off lights as he went. After he locked the front door, he tucked his key under the welcome mat, said a quiet good-bye, and left.

When Stella reached for her glasses the next morning, her fingers encountered a piece of paper. Frowning, she picked it up and held it close to her bleary, tear-swollen eyes. A check. *Her* check. For fifty thousand dollars.

She sat up in bed and ran trembling fingers over the surface of the check. What did this mean? Why hadn't he kept it and cashed it?

His words from last night whispered through her head.

I accepted your proposal because I wanted to help you.

Not because he wanted to be with her, not even for money, but because he pitied her.

Because she was autistic.

Awful emotion spread through her like poison, and she covered her mouth to muffle the sounds coming from her throat. She'd thought she was rubbing off on him. She'd thought she was special. She'd thought he could love her back. But every time they'd been together, it had been nothing but charity. All those kisses, all those moments, all charity. And now that he'd done his good deed, he was moving on.

The pain crushed and tore, destroying her from the inside. She wasn't a good deed. She was a person. If she had known how he felt, she never would have issued that proposal. She was *not* a charity case. Her money was just as good as anyone else's. Why couldn't he have just taken it?

Swiping at her face angrily, she told herself she was tougher than this. She wasn't going to fall apart over a man who didn't want her.

She made the bed with angry jerks of her arms and stomped into the bathroom to floss her teeth. She worked the mint string so forcefully her gums bled. When she closed her hand around her toothbrush, something reckless made her let go and hop in the shower instead. Very deliberately, she reversed her shower routine, scrubbing herself from bottom to top. She wasn't a robot or a walking diagnosis. She was herself. She *was* enough. She could be anything. She could *make* herself into anything. She could prove everyone wrong.

By the time she left the shower, she was breathing heavily. She was going to do this and do it well. When she was done, she'd be new and fresh and fantastic. She deserved to be those things.

She dried herself off with brisk rubs of her towel, purposefully walked past her waiting toothbrush, and went into the closet, where she pulled on the black dress Michael loved. She didn't bother with a cardigan. Let people look.

Gazing in the mirror over her sink as she finally allowed herself to brush her teeth, she found her eyes ablaze with determination. Her hair was a wild mess, but she didn't plan to tame it. She wasn't in a tame mood. Other women let their moods dictate their actions, change their routines. Stella was going to be the same.

After she choked down a slice of dry toast, she stared at her empty house. What now? Her body raged with the need for action, for change, for violence. There would be no working today. People didn't work on Sundays. Once the shops opened, they went out. They ran errands. They did things together.

There was no more *together* for Stella.

She sat down before her glossy black Steinway and lifted the fallboard away from the keys. She automatically played the opening chords for "Clair de Lune," but the song was too slow and too romantic, and it reminded her of Michael. She broke from the melody after the first crescendo. Instead of letting the music ebb back into gentleness, she took it higher, poured melodic anguish into it. Her throat swelled, and her heart bled into the notes.

That wasn't enough. She gave the piano her rage. She pounded chords onto the keys in quick succession like storm waves crashing on cliffs. Wave after wave after angry wave. Still not enough.

She did something she'd never done before. Stella had always been gentle. She spoke softly. She didn't hurt anyone intentionally. She loved music and order and patterns.

She slammed her hands on the keyboard, producing clashing off-key jumbles of notes. A mess of chaos. Loud, loud, louder. Over and over again until her palms hurt, and her teeth were gnashing, and her body shook from sound overload. At that point, she hit harder, warring against the noise and herself.

A snapping deep within the piano traveled up her fingers and into her arms. Only then did she let her shaking hands fall away from the keys. She lifted her foot from the sustain pedal, dampening the residual ringing of the strings. The pained stuttering of her heart filled her ears.

The piano needed to be tuned.

She'd worry about it later. The stores were opening soon, and she wanted to go shopping. For perfume.

The shop was closed on Sundays, but something made Michael go there anyway. He unlocked the front door and stepped inside. After passing by the empty fitting room, he entered the work area in back. There, he scanned the mechanized rack where they hung the dry-cleaned clothes, the walls of multicolored thread, and the green commercial sewing machines.

This place was his mom's livelihood, and she was incredibly proud to be the owner of such a thriving business. Of all their extended family, she was one of the most successful. Well, she would have been, if not for his dad.

To Michael, this place was a prison. He didn't want to do tedious fittings and alterations and dry cleaning. He wanted to create something from scratch.

He went to the bureau at the back of the room and pulled out the small drawer he reserved for his sketchpads. The book on top felt cold and familiar under the pads of his fingers, the paper soft. He sat at one of the worktables and opened the book to a blank page, set his pencil tip down.

Usually, he started the clothing design first, the collar and shoulders, sometimes the waist if that was the focal point of everything. The face was usually just an impression, a profile, the curve of a jaw. Hands and legs were quick pencil strokes, just vague ideas. Today, he started with the face. It was the only thing in his mind.

Those eyes and the heavy fringe of lashes. Arching eyebrows. That nose. Those kissable lips. When he finished, Stella stared at him from the page. He'd captured the essence of her perfectly. His hands knew her every line.

Her likeness was enough to make the blood rush to his throat, and he dug his phone out of his pocket and checked it for messages or missed calls.

Nothing. Just like the other ninety-nine times he'd checked today.

She'd said she would stalk and call, and he was messed up enough to want it. If obsession was all he could have from her, he wanted the works. The more drama, the better. Maybe they'd have no choice but to get back together.

The screen on his phone blacked out, and cold reality sank into him. Her obsession hadn't been strong enough to stand up in the face of his family's criminal past, not on top of all his other drawbacks. It really had been just practice and sex.

His phone buzzed with an alert from the agency app. Someone had booked him for this Friday. For a second, he thought it might be Stella, and bright happiness flooded his being. Even knowing everything about him, she still wanted him. He clicked through the screens on his phone as fast as he could, but when the app loaded, he saw it was someone new. His stomach dropped.

There'd been a time when he'd liked the variety his escorting assignments provided. Now, his body crawled with revulsion at the mere idea of touching someone else, let alone kissing or having sex with them. He felt . . . permanently pair-bonded, like a goddamned swan. Only the swan he'd chosen hadn't pair-bonded back with him.

Why would she have?

Look at all the people he'd fucked. What had he accomplished with his life? What had he really done? A lot of dry cleaning, that was what. He was nothing. Good for a test drive, but not to take home. He should be proud he'd helped bolster Stella's confidence and proven he was better than his dad, but he was a selfish ass, and all he wanted was more of her.

In the foreseeable future, she'd be pleasuring another man—that shit Philip—in the precise way that drove Michael out of his mind. Her hands would touch another body, her mouth would—

He crammed his palms into his eyes and breathed away his gut-churning nausea. If she was going to fuck other people, he would, too. He'd go right now. He started to stand, but paused. It was Sunday morning. Not trolling time.

And he physically could not.

Touching another woman right now would make him vomit. Or worse, cry like a baby.

He was having a hard enough time keeping it together as it was. His eyes burned, and his throat ached, and he hurt everywhere. No women. Not unless they had soft brown eyes and a shy smile and loved economics and made the sweetest breathless sounds when they kissed him and—

Fuck. Enough already. He clawed his fingers through his hair and tried to squeeze thoughts of Stella out of his head.

Toughen up and soldier on.

But he was tired of being tough and soldiering on. He'd been doing it for three endless years. He was trapped here, trapped in his life, trapped in never-ending debt. Trapped by love.

That was his problem. He always loved too much. If he could just tear his heart out and stop feeling, he would be free. A frenzied kind of madness gripped him as he stared down at his sketchpad.

Whispering a silent apology in his head, he ripped out the picture of Stella and tore it straight down the middle before shredding it. The pieces floated to the ground like leaves from a dying tree. Then he flipped to the front of the book. Sun-saturated mornings with Stella had inspired the white and yellow dress on the page. It was his absolute favorite. He tore it out and destroyed it. And the next design. And the next. All of them. Then he went to the bureau in back, grabbed all his sketchpads, and threw them in the trash. After that, he opened the large bottom drawer where he kept the projects he'd been working on in secret. Gritting his teeth, he ripped the fabric apart, seam by seam, garment by garment, dream by dream.

When he'd finally destroyed everything that could be destroyed, he stared at the carnage on the floor and spilling from the garbage.

It had worked. He felt nothing now.

He walked to the sewing machine he usually used, sat down, and considered the pile of unfinished clothes next to it. A few pairs of pants needed hemming, dresses needed to be taken in, and a jacket had a torn inner lining. They were all clothes someone else had designed. Someone else's vision.

Might as well finish all of it. Maybe he could give his mom more time off this week.

He started to sew.

Later that week, Sophie manned the shop and watched Ngoại while Michael took Mẹ to the doctor for her monthly checkup and bloodwork. It was a short drive, but it felt like forever with his mom crossing her arms and boring holes into the side of his head with her eyes. He cranked the music volume up and focused on the road.

She turned the radio off. "I can't take it anymore. You walk around all day like a cat who's lost his mouse. You don't talk. You scare the customers. And you're working like you're dying. Michael, tell Mẹ what's going on."

He tightened his grip on the leather steering wheel. "Nothing's going on."

"How is Stella? Tell her to come on Saturday. Grapefruit was on sale, so we have a lot."

He said nothing.

"Mẹ is not stupid, you know. Did you break up with these people's daughter?"

"Why are you so sure it wasn't the other way around?" Stella would have done it eventually. When she decided she'd practiced enough.

"Clear as day, she's passionate for you. She would never do that."

He clenched his jaw against a fresh surge of unwelcome feeling. Stella had liked him well enough, but the only place she'd been "passionate" for him had been in bed.

"I met her parents, Mẹ."

"Oh? Were they nice people?"

"Her dad didn't think I was good enough," he said with a bitter twist of his lips.

"Of course, he didn't."

Michael snapped his attention from the road to his mom's profile. "What do you mean 'of course, he didn't?'" He was her only son. She never talked about him like this.

"You're too proud, just like your dad. You have to be understanding. He only wants what's best for his daughter. She's his only child, right? What do you think it was like when I married your dad?"

"Grandma and Grandpa love you."

"They do. Now. They didn't approve of me at first. Why would they want him marrying a Vietnamese girl with only an eighth-grade education who barely spoke English? They refused to come to the wedding until your dad threatened to cut ties with them. I had to work to convince them. It didn't happen overnight. But it was worth it."

"I didn't know that . . ." It made him look at his grandparents in a new, rather unfavorable light.

"When you love someone, Michael, you fight for them in every way you know how. If you put your mind to it, her dad will come to like you. If you treat his daughter right, he'll love you."

"I think it would be very selfish of me to fight for her. There are men who are better suited to her. They're richer, more educated, and more . . ." His words trailed off as she slowly turned to face him, her eyes narrowed in a ball-shriveling stare.

"You sound just like your dad. If you can't stand being

with a woman who's more successful than you, then leave her alone. She's better off without you. If you actually love her, then know the value of that love and make it a promise. That is the only thing she needs from you."

"You think I'm like Dad? You think I'd do what he did?" His mom's words submerged him in frigid water and stopped his lungs. Fuck, his own mom thought—

"You would never do that," she said with a dismissive wave of her hand. "He has no heart. You do, and it steers you in the right direction. But you think you need to be best and do everything yourself. You and your dad both have that problem."

"No, I don't—"

"Then why are you still working at the shop? And why did you do all my sewing? You think this old woman can't sew a straight line?" she asked in exasperation.

"No, I—"

"I can't stay at home anymore. I know I'm not as fast as I was, but I do a good job. I'm feeling better. The drugs are working. You kids have to stop trapping me in the house, and you, Michael, you have to stop coming to the shop. I don't want you there anymore, especially in this black mood. You're bad for business."

"Me, I can't leave you alone, and you won't let anyone who's not family work with you." It was an inescapable truth he'd had to come to grips with, one bar of the cage he voluntarily lived inside. Because he loved her.

"You think you're the only one in the family who knows how to sew? How many cousins do you have? What about Quan? He came to the shop on Saturday to use the machine to fix his jacket zipper. He knew what he was doing, and he doesn't like working for his mom. She yells too much."

Michael flinched back in his seat as his brain scrambled to understand what she'd said. "You'd let him work in front? With all those tattoos?"

She pointed at Michael's arm where black ink peeked

out from underneath the sleeve of his T-shirt. "You have it, too. Don't think I didn't notice. I have no idea why you young people do that to yourselves."

He dropped his left hand away from the steering wheel so his arm lowered out of view. "Girls like it."

"*My* Stella likes that?"

"Well, yeah." She'd kissed the dragon so many times it probably missed her as much as he did by now. It occurred to him Philip James was probably bare as a baby under his clothes. A satisfied smile spread over his lips.

And since when had his mom started calling Stella hers?

"She's not as innocent as you think," he added, trying to mitigate his mom's eventual disappointment.

She slanted him an *are you kidding me?* look before focusing on the buildings passing by. "Like a girl would stay innocent long with my son. Besides, every mother wants a daughter-in-law who can get down to business. I want to hold babies again."

Michael choked and coughed.

"Don't miss the turn." She pointed to the front drive of the Palo Alto Medical Foundation.

He dropped her off at the door and went to park in the underground parking structure. His mind was a mess of loud thoughts as he left the elevator and went to look for her in the waiting area outside the oncology suite.

His mom said his heart steered him in the right direction, and she didn't think he'd ever do what his dad had. She wanted him to fight for Stella. She thought love was enough.

But love wasn't enough if it was only one-sided.

His favorite receptionist, Janelle, flagged him down. "She already went in. Before you go looking for her, I need your signature on some paperwork over here."

He strode up to the reception desk with a feeling of dread. In his experience, paperwork was not a good thing. Bills were paper.

"Since you have power of attorney, you sign here and here," Janelle said.

He frowned down at the papers. They didn't look like regular medical paperwork at all. "What are these for?"

"The foundation has recently started a new program that provides assistance for households with insufficient insurance coverage who haven't been approved for federal or state assistance for various reasons. Your mom was one of the lucky few who were approved for full aid from here on out. That's got to be a relief, huh?"

Michael snatched up the papers and started reading the fine print as fast as he could. The more he read, the more stunned he became. His skin tingled with disbelief. "Is this really real? It's *all* covered?"

"This is the real deal. Just sign the papers, Michael honey." Janelle's eyes were warm and understanding, and Michael didn't know how to react. This was too good to be true.

No more medical bills. No more bills. No bills. Was that possible? Michael didn't have this kind of luck. *Bad* things happened to him. Life for him was seeing how he could handle the punches and keep going. This had to be a scam.

"How were we selected?" He almost couldn't hear himself speak through the desperate cacophony of his heart.

Janelle shook her head with a smile. "I'm not familiar with the selection process, but the program has made several families really happy today. Believe it, honey. It's all official, and it's happening." She squeezed his hand before handing him a pen with a plastic daisy taped to the end.

He read over the print one more time, picking up phrases like *recognition of financial hardship* and *full medical coverage*. There were no red flags, no requests for payment, no contingencies, no confusing clauses. This was legit. His gut told him it was legit. The tip of the pen rested inside a yellow highlighted area in the document.

"How is this program funded?" he asked.

"Private funding. You know this area and all the large philanthropic organizations. Go on and sign it already. You're making me nervous."

His heart slowed, his hands steadied, and he scrawled his signature on the highlighted lines of page after page of legal verbiage.

She gathered the papers together, filled a small paper cup with water from inside her office, and handed it to him. "Drink this. You're looking faint. Go on back now and break the news to your mom. She's in her regular exam room."

He tossed the water back and marched into the suite of exam rooms, going straight to the second room from the end. His mom was stretched out on the exam table with wires sneaking out from underneath her sweater to link to an EKG. A nurse printed readouts from the machine and made notes on his clipboard before he helped his mom peel the sensors off her chest.

"How's everything looking?" Michael asked as he sat down.

"I'll let the doctor tell you when she comes in." The nurse smiled, gathered up his papers and machinery, and left the room.

"It's going to be good news." His mom straightened the lilac cashmere sweater that actually matched with her pants—plain white—for once. "Mẹ feels good."

This seemed like too much good news for one day, but there was color in her cheeks, and the smudges under her eyes weren't as pronounced.

"Have you gained more weight?" he asked.

"Three pounds."

That loosened some of the tension in Michael's body. "That's great."

"Stop worrying and trust Mẹ."

A knock sounded on the door, and his mom's doctor stepped inside, a curvaceous woman with sandy shoulder-length hair and a demeanor that instantly put people at ease.

"So it's good news. I know I've shocked you again, Michael. Your mom is doing really well," she said with a laugh before her focus returned to his mom. "Your last scans were stable, and we're going to start spreading them out even further. We'll keep your current dosages the same and do blood-work every month. Of course, if anything changes, we want to see you right away, but I don't think that's likely."

"Tell my son it's okay if I work more. He and his sisters are trying to trap me at home."

Dr. Hennigan eyed him with an understanding smile. "If she wants to work, let her work, Michael. It's healthy to stay active—both physically and mentally."

Michael crossed his arms. "Maybe instead of working, she should start dating."

"Oh no no no no no. No more men for me." His mom made emphatic motions with her hands and shook her head. "I'm done."

The doctor's eyebrows rose in a considering way. "He's right. You could start dating, Anh. Might be fun."

His mom sent him a withering glance, and he couldn't help but laugh.

They left the exam room shortly thereafter and walked by the reception desk. Janelle grinned warmly, and his mom gave her a distracted wave.

"Is she in shock?" Janelle asked.

His mom frowned. "He wants me to get a boyfriend. *Me*. I'm almost sixty."

Janelle nodded sagely. "It's never too late for true love."

"Bah. I just want to work. Money is better than men. I want a Hermès handbag."

"Well, maybe you can afford it now," Janelle said with a wide grin.

Michael ushered his mom out of the office before they could go into why she could afford it. As they got into his car and pulled out of the parking structure into the sun, he wished he could tell her about the program, but then he'd have to come clean about all the lies he'd told her regarding her excellent but nonexistent health insurance and how he'd been paying her medical bills all this time.

The only one who would understand was Stella, but she was gone. No, he'd have to keep this to himself.

Stella rested her forehead in her palm and methodically went over the attributes in herself she associated with her disorder: her sensitivities to sound, smell, and texture; her need for routine; her awkwardness in social situations; and her tendency toward obsession.

Over the last week, she'd tackled all of them but the last two. She didn't know how to tackle those. She could listen to awful music as she worked, wear perfume, take kitchen shears to the French seams of her shirts, and destroy her routines, but she couldn't suddenly talk to people with ease, and she couldn't *not* be obsessed with something she loved.

Her mind spun around and around in circles, trying to figure out how to solve the problem. While she wasn't great at talking, she had made marked improvement over the years. If she focused and watched what she said, she was able to interact with people without making them uncomfortable—mostly. That left obsession.

How did one not obsess over something wonderful? How did one like something a reasonable amount? If she was being realistic with herself, she had to admit this simply wasn't a possibility for her. She couldn't like something halfway. She'd tried that with Michael and failed miserably. Did that mean she had to abstain completely from things she enjoyed?

She supposed she could give up piano, martial arts movies, and Asian dramas. But what about her greatest passion? Econometrics?

Giving that up would be the biggest sign of her commitment. Her work was such a pivotal part of her life that if she resigned, everything would change. She really would be a new person.

She set her glasses on her desk and covered her eyes with her palm, giving up on the data on the screen. Her mind was simply too overwrought to focus. If she couldn't do her work, maybe she *should* resign.

Maybe she should devote herself to something with more concrete benefits to society. Like the medical field. She could be a doctor if she tried hard enough. She didn't love physiology and chemistry, but what did that matter? Most doctors probably focused on the end results of their labor instead of the daily reality of their work. Truth be told, it was better if the work bored her. She wouldn't obsess over it then.

That was it. She had to quit her job.

With stiff fingers and feverish determination, she began drafting a letter of resignation to her boss.

Dear Albert,

Thank you for the past five years. Being a part of your team was an invaluable experience to me. I cherished the opportunity not only to study fascinating, real market data but to effect measurable change in the economy through the application of econometric principles. However, I must leave because

Because what? Albert would not understand any of the reasoning filling her brain right now. He was an economist. All he cared about was economics.

If she told him she was autistic, he wouldn't care. It didn't impact her effectiveness as an econometrician in a negative way. If anything, her obsessive tendency to hyperfocus for long periods of time, her love of routines and patterns, and her extremely logical mind that couldn't comprehend casual conversation made her a *stronger* econometrician.

It was a shame those same things made her unlovable.

A discreet knocking sounded against the door, and she checked the clock before turning around to see Janie walk into her office. Right on schedule. She hurried to minimize the letter of resignation and stood up to face her internship candidate.

Janie smiled, and though her lips trembled with nervousness, the action still reminded Stella so much of Michael that her heart squeezed.

Belatedly, she shook Janie's hand. "I'm so glad to see you. Please, have a seat."

Janie brushed her hands over her black skirt suit and sat. She tapped her toes for several seconds before she crossed her ankles. "Good to see you, too, Stella."

In the awkward silence that ensued, Stella absently scratched her neck. The opened seams of her shirt felt like lines of ants crawling on her skin.

"How are you?" she asked, trying to distract herself from the itching.

"Me? Er, I'm fine." Janie wore her long hair loose today, and she tucked a dark brown tendril behind her ear as she looked down at her leather portfolio on Stella's desk. "Michael is not fine."

Stella's chest tightened, and the skin on her face prickled. "Oh no, why? What happened? Is your mom okay?"

"My mom is fine. Don't worry," Janie said, making calming gestures with her hands. "Well, she's upset with Michael. She wants him to quit coming to the shop, but he won't. On top of that, he's been intolerably grouchy lately, and he's working nonstop. It's like he's possessed. We're all worried and annoyed."

"I don't—I don't understand why he should be unhappy." He couldn't possibly be unhappy for the same reason she was. Hopelessness mixed with the abrasion of open seams on her skin, making her want to tear her shirt off and scream.

"It's *you*. He misses you."

She shook her head. That was impossible. Hearing her deepest desire said out loud filled her with bitterness that verged on anger. "How about we get this interview started?" She gathered up the case study documents she'd prepared and handed them to Janie.

Instead of looking at them, Janie set the papers on top of her portfolio. "Why did you two break up?"

Because they'd never really been together to start with. Because she'd only ever been a charity case to him.

Stella busied herself digging through her file drawer as her eyes glassed over. After several precarious moments of furious blinking, the danger of tears passed. She swallowed, cleared her throat, and said, "That's not relevant for this interview. I'll give you five minutes to read the case study and then we can talk about it."

"I think you two need to talk."

"We *had* a lengthy talk." One Stella didn't want to go through again. If she heard him say she wasn't enough again, she'd lose it.

"Well," Janie said. "Being apart clearly isn't working for either of you. You need to talk again."

Stella rubbed her temple, caught a concentrated whiff of the perfume she'd sprayed on her wrist, and felt her lunch crawl up her throat. She yanked her hand away from her face and breathed through her mouth. "I can't."

"Come on, Stella. I know he probably screwed up somehow, but give him another chance. He's crazy about you."

"It wasn't Michael who screwed up. It was me." She'd screwed up by being herself.

"I have a hard time believing that. Michael is really bad at relationships. He has issues."

That gave Stella pause. She was the one with the issues. Wasn't she? "What kind of issues?"

"Are you kidding me? He hasn't told you this stuff?" Janie looked up at the ceiling, muttering to herself before she said, "My dad made him feel like crap for turning down all the engineering schools he got into. He said Michael would amount to nothing, said he'd be poor and he'd have to earn a living off his pretty face because he was good for nothing else. He cut Michael off and made him pay for his fashion degree himself. Michael is super talented, and he *acts* confident. But you're the first girl he's dated who is actually good enough for him."

After Stella absorbed that information and set it aside for later consideration, she forced her lips into a smile. "That's a really nice thing to say. I appreciate it."

"Oh my God, you, too? Clearly, you guys are made for each other. Well, my reason for coming here was an entire flop, then. I'll head out." Janie prepared to get up.

"You don't want to interview?"

Janie tucked her hair behind her ear again. "Isn't it nepotism since we know each other?"

Stella smiled. "You'll be speaking with six of us, and the decision to hire you has to be unanimous. I think that should eliminate your concerns regarding fairness. Also, even if we don't hire you, I think you'll learn something from the interviewing process. There are some really brilliant people here. Take some time to read the case study, won't you?"

"All right." Janie hunkered down over the papers, reading with an intent expression that reminded Stella very much of Michael.

As the interview progressed, Janie nailed question after question, even displaying unique, out-of-the-box thinking that would aid her in the future. Though she'd stumbled during her freshman year, it was clear she'd brushed herself off and hit the ground running.

"One last question," Stella said. "Tell me why you chose to pursue a career in economics and math as opposed to other fields."

Janie's eyes sparked as she leaned forward. "That's easy. Math is the single most elegant thing in the universe, and economics is what drives the human world. If you want to understand people in a sophisticated manner, I believe economics is the way."

"But why do you want to understand people better? You have a large family and, I assume, lots of friends."

"I do have lots of friends and family." Janie shrugged. "But they're just a small subset of society, not entire markets or nations. And, frankly, they're not that interesting. They don't fascinate me. They don't make the world fall away. I would die for them, but I can't live for them. I can live for economics. It's my calling, just like it's yours."

Watery-eyed and emotional for reasons she didn't understand, Stella got up and shook Janie's hand. "I think everyone here is going to like you quite a bit."

Janie grinned, and Stella walked her to the next interview and wished her luck. When she returned to her office, she stared at the last, unfinished sentence in her letter of resignation: *However, I must leave because*

Why was she thinking of giving up her life's calling?

Because of Michael. Because of a man.

She swiped her nails through her hair, tearing strands from the tie. There was no point in working to snare a man who didn't love her as she was. No one benefited from that, least of all her. It wasn't fair, and it wasn't honest. It wasn't her.

This crusade to fix herself was ending right now. She wasn't broken. She saw and interacted with the world in a different way, but that was *her*. She could change her actions, change her words, change her appearance, but she couldn't change the root of herself. At her core, she would always be autistic. People called it a disorder, but it didn't *feel* like one. To her, it was simply the way she was.

She had to accept the fact that she and Michael simply didn't fit. Sawing away at herself to force a match was pure foolishness. *Quitting her job* was pure foolishness, and she wasn't going to do it. Setting her jaw, she closed the letter of resignation without saving it.

She gathered her things and prepared to leave early. She needed to get out of this ruined shirt and wash the perfume off. Her behavior of the past week disgusted her.

Yes, she was lonely. Yes, she had a broken heart. But at least she had herself.

A soft ding sounded, alerting Michael that the front door of the shop had opened. He looked up from his sewing in time to see Janie explode into the workroom.

"I got an offer."

He set his sewing aside. "Hey, that's great."

His mom squealed and ran to hug her. "Mẹ is so proud. Good job."

"I didn't even know you were interviewing," Michael said. "What company is it?"

A combative glint shined in Janie's eyes as his mom patted her head and returned to her sewing machine. "Stella's company. Advanced Economic Analytics."

Silence roared in his ears. "What?"

"I asked her to help me find an internship, and she did. I start work in a couple weeks. I'm so excited." Janie danced in place, her smile going from ear to ear.

"She got you a job?" He had to have misheard. Stella wouldn't have gotten his sister a job.

"You never told me she works for AEA. Even my professors are envious I'm interning there. When they like you, they fund your research in grad school and postdoc. I've got it made—if I don't mess this up."

"You need to call her and thank her, Michael," his mom said in a serious tone. "This is a big thing she did."

Did people do that when their exes got jobs for their siblings? Wait a second. How could there be a precedent? Exes didn't do that. Only Stella. How was he supposed to stop loving her when she did things like this?

Janie puffed out her chest and blew on her fingernails. "In my defense, I killed those interviews. I spoke to all six of their senior econometricians, and they have to decide unanimously when they make an offer."

He realized then that Janie had seen Stella. Recently. His heartbeat sped up. He had to know.

"How was she?"

With that question, Janie's eyes hardened. "She's fine. She looks really good, actually."

"That's . . . good." It didn't feel good, though. It felt shitty. He should be happy she was doing well, but he wasn't. He wanted her to be sad without him, as sad as he was without her.

She'd really moved on. Fuck, a knife in the ribs would be better than this.

"That's right. It *is* good," Janie said.

His mom sent Janie an admonishing look, but Janie merely crossed her arms and jutted her chin out.

Michael pushed away from his sewing machine. "Since you're here, I'm going to take off early."

He got into his car without a destination in mind. All he knew was he needed to leave the shop.

Janie would be starting her first job soon. His mom's health was good enough for her to start dating. Stella was moving on.

Everyone was moving forward with their lives but him.

What was stopping him? The bills were gone, and he didn't need to escort anymore. His mom wanted him to stop working in the shop. All the bars of his cage were gone, but he was still sitting in his old place, afraid to move.

Maybe it was time for him to change that.

He pulled his car into the parking lot outside a Vietnamese restaurant in Milpitas that specialized in noodle dishes. Bells on the door jingled as he stepped inside. Quan cleared dirty eatware into plastic bins on a roller cart and wiped down the tabletops with a wet towel. The lunch crowd had left, and he was the only one in the front of his parents' restaurant—aside from the assortment of freshwater fish that lived in the tank covering the entire back wall of the place.

He glanced up at Michael, paused a second, and said, "You look like shit."

Michael rubbed at the back of his neck. "Haven't been sleeping much." After sharing a bed with Stella for so long, he was having trouble transitioning back to solitary sleeping. When he did manage to fall asleep, he dreamed of her. And came all over his sheets. That reminded him he had to do his goddamned laundry. Again.

"Barely seen you lately. How's it going with your girl?"

Michael stuffed his hands in his pockets. "We broke up."

Quan's tattooed arm froze in midswipe along the tabletop. "Why?"

"Wasn't working."

"Why the fuck not?"

"Look, I came to ask for your help with something else."

Quan's eyebrows shot up. "So *this* is why you look like shit. What did you do that she broke up with your ass? Did you try, you know, saying sorry? Getting flowers? Stuffed bears? Chocolate? Chicks dig those things. I shouldn't have to tell you this."

"I was the one who ended it."

Quan tossed his cleaning towel on the table. "What the hell, man. Why?"

Michael raked a hand through his hair, grimacing as the knife in his ribs twisted. Because he wasn't good enough for her. And even if he could *get* good enough for her, she wasn't into him, anyway. She'd moved on.

A tight breath punched from Quan's lips as he watched Michael's reaction. "Well, what did you need help with? Are you finally thinking of getting a bike?"

"No, no bike. I'm . . . looking for my replacement at the tailor shop." Saying the words out loud made him sweat.

"And you're telling me because . . . ?"

"You can sew, and . . ." Michael snuck a glance at the swinging door leading to the kitchen and lowered his voice to say, "You hate working for your mom, but you get along with mine. Most importantly, I trust you. I can't go if my mom's not in good hands."

"What are you planning to do? Are you moving back to New York?"

"No, I'm staying here—I need to stay close even if I'm not there, you know? I'm thinking of starting my own line."

It had been his dream since forever, but he'd been forced to put it off. All this time, the ideas and the concepts had grown in his head, getting bigger and harder to suppress, but now . . .

"About time." Quan punched him in the shoulder as he grinned.

"So will you do it? Will you work at the shop?"

Quan gave him a funny look before saying, "I could do it short term if you needed it, but not permanently. Alterations bore the shit out of me. Yen is looking for work, though, and she likes sewing. As long as she can bring the baby in, that should work out for everyone."

Michael felt a strange lightness take over his body. "That sounds perfect."

"You should have asked a lot earlier. There's always someone in our family who's out of work. No one could understand why you stayed at the shop this long. It's pretty obvious you hate it. You're not alone, you know. Family's got your back."

As Michael searched his cousin's earnest face, he realized he'd never once considered asking for help before now. The entire problem with his parents and his mom's health had been his own personal cross to bear. *Why* had he thought that? Because he was guilty over leaving in the first place? Maybe he'd felt he needed to atone for his selfishness. And maybe, like his dad, he was too proud.

"You're right. I should have asked earlier." Ideas arranged themselves in his head, and he said, "I could use your help now with my line, actually. I'm a designer, not a businessperson, and I know you're getting that MBA . . ."

Quan crossed his arms over his chest with a serious look. "Are you asking if I wanna go into business with you?"

Michael returned his cousin's serious gaze. "Yeah. I think I am. Fifty-fifty."

Quan continued wiping down the tables. "I gotta think about it."

"Sure, yeah. I'll send you my designs."

"You don't need to do that," Quan said as he focused on his work.

"Oh, okay." Michael took a hesitant step back. Maybe he shouldn't have asked, then. They'd spoken about partnering up in the past, but maybe it had just been talk.

Quan glanced up at him with an impatient look. "I know what you can do, Michael."

Michael released a pent-up breath, and he went from worrying that his cousin had too little faith in him to worrying he had too much. "Of course, we'd draw up official contracts and stuff and arrange it so I can't screw you over like my dad did to my mom."

Quan rolled his eyes as he straightened. "How about just a handshake?" He held his hand out.

Michael's attention switched from his cousin's hand to his face several times. "What's that for? You decided? Just like that? It hasn't even been two minutes."

"You wanna do this or not?"

As Michael clasped his cousin's hand in a firm grip, he couldn't stop a grin from taking over his face. It looked like everyone trusted him but him. "Yeah, let's do it. Fifty-fifty."

Instead of letting go, Quan pulled Michael close for a hard, one-armed hug. "You're such a shit, you know that? Been waiting for you to ask me. Took you long enough."

Stella stopped outside Philip's office, took a breath, and knocked on the door. He turned away from his computer screens. As soon as he recognized her on the other side of the glass window, he came to open the door.

"Hi, Stella." He smiled, but his eyes were guarded.

"I'm on my way out. Want to get dinner with me?" The last thing she wanted to do right now was spend time with Philip, but she'd told her parents she'd consider him, and she took her promises seriously. Her parents both liked him. Maybe she could bring herself to like him, as well. Also, she was one hundred percent certain he was not the kind of guy to be with her out of pity. That was important.

"I'd love to." The wattage on Philip's smile increased to blinding levels. "Just give me a second to save my work."

As they traveled down the well-lit sidewalks toward the downtown restaurants, Philip settled his hand at the base of her spine. She did her best to ignore it, but after a minute or two, she put distance between them.

She clenched her fingers around her purse straps. "I'm not ready for that."

He let his hand drop to his side. "Still hung up on him, I see."

"I'm working on it." She'd given her housekeeper permission to wash the sheets this week. No more Michael smell.

"He slept with my mom, Stella. That should help you get over him faster."

She stared at his bitter profile. "You slept with Heidi."

"Heidi isn't . . . old."

"Neither is your mom."

He rolled his eyes.

"If you hit on our new intern, I'm going to be very unhappy with you. She's practically a baby. She's Michael's sister, by the way."

"That hottie Janie is his *sister*?"

"She was the best candidate."

"She was," he admitted grudgingly. "She had a strong understanding of regression analysis and statistics. I can't believe she's his sister."

When they seated themselves in the restaurant, he was still muttering about Janie under his breath.

"It's only been three years since she was in high school, Philip."

"So?"

She released an exasperated breath. Instead of bringing up how hypocritical he was, she said, "Let's talk about hobbies. Do you have any? What are they?"

That lightened his mood immediately. "I'm pretty serious about golf. I'm not bad, either. And I like going to the gym."

He sipped from his water glass, and his gaze swept over the posh interior of the restaurant.

Stella waited for him to ask about her. He tapped his fingers on the table in time to the classical guitar music playing in the background. He took another drink of water.

"I alternate between lap swimming and running every day," he added.

"No martial arts?"

"Eh. I took a fencing class in college, but it seems silly in this day and age."

That meant Michael would probably trounce him in a match. She'd kind of enjoy seeing that.

"I like martial arts movies," she said.

"That's so unlike you. I'm more of a documentary person, myself."

As Philip droned on about the latest documentary he'd seen, Stella's mind wandered. She found herself reimagining the night of the benefit dinner. In her fantasy version of that night, Michael didn't break up with her. Instead, he declared himself helplessly in love with her. Enraged beyond all reason, Philip challenged him to a duel, and the men faced off outside next to the pool. Because they didn't have swords on hand, they used golf clubs.

When she smiled at her fanciful thoughts, Philip interpreted that as encouragement, and he grew more animated as he spoke of his fascination with exposés and political commentary.

Stella wondered what a match between a kendo artist and fencer would look like. It would probably be pretty funny if they were using irons and putters—assuming they had enough control not to bludgeon each other to death. They really needed a scene like this in a K-drama. She'd watch it over and over.

The hero didn't even have to win. All he had to do to get the girl was fight for her. If he lost, she'd kiss him better.

When they stepped out of the restaurant onto the crowded sidewalk, Philip smiled at her and captured one of her hands. "I think we get along really well, Stella. We should do this again."

Then he leaned down to kiss her.

As Michael walked with Quan toward his favorite Korean BBQ restaurant on University Avenue, he couldn't help scanning the sidewalks for glimpses of Stella. Her house was only blocks away. While it was unlikely she'd be out doing late-night shopping, it was possible.

Even so, he was unprepared when he saw her standing outside a Mediterranean restaurant across the street. Her hair was up in its usual bun, her glasses were in place, and she wore her regular oxford shirt, pencil skirt, and pointed pumps. His Stella, his brainy, sweet—

Was that Philip James? Was he about to *kiss* her?

Michael saw red.

His muscles tensed, and he lunged. Quan's firm grip on his arms drew him up short.

"Easy, man."

Before Philip's lips could touch hers, Stella turned her face away and took a step back. She pulled her hand out of his grasp, saying words that couldn't be heard from this distance but were clearly rejection.

Instead of taking it like a man, Philip advanced toward her with a predatory glint in his eyes.

"Okay, he's asking for it," Quan said.

Quan let him go, and Michael crossed the street without consciously taking a single step. If there were cars in the way, he didn't notice them. He plowed straight through them for all he knew. Before the bastard could touch his dirty lips to Stella's side-turned face, Michael yanked him away and slammed his knuckles into Philip's eye.

As Philip staggered back, Michael drew a stunned Stella into his arms. Beneath the angry surging of his heart, a sense of rightness settled in place. The feel of her, the smell of her, *his.*

"Are you okay?" he whispered.

She blinked at him in bemusement. "Did you really just punch him in the eye?"

"That little shit was about to force himself on you. Again. No one forces you. Ever."

Philip lowered the hand from his quickly swelling eye to stab a finger in Michael's direction. "We're on a date. There was no forcing involved."

Stella pushed away from Michael and adjusted the purse straps on her shoulder. "I'm going home now. Alone. Good night."

"Stella, wait." Philip tried to follow her, but Michael stepped in his way.

"You heard her. She's going home alone."

When Philip looked like he might press the issue, Quan came up beside Michael. His hands hung loose at his sides, but he was poised for violence, his eyes cold. "Do we have a problem here?"

Philip took in the barricade formed by Michael and Quan and backed off. His mouth worked like he wanted to speak, but in the end, he clenched his jaw shut, glanced longingly in Stella's retreating direction, and left.

Michael squeezed Quan's shoulder. "Thanks."

Quan's lips quirked, and he tipped his head toward Stella. "You should go check up on her."

"Get a table. I'll find you there."

He ran after Stella and fell in step beside her, but instead of slowing down, she increased her pace, keeping her gaze focused straight ahead.

"I had the situation under control. Don't forget I own a Taser."

Her abruptness and impersonal tone snuck right underneath Michael's guard and irritated the shit out of him. He still dreamed about her daily, and she was seeing other people. It hadn't even been two whole weeks.

"Couldn't wait to test your new skills out, I see."

She grasped at her purse straps and walked even faster. The sidewalk ended, and her heels clicked over asphalt as she marched down the now-residential street toward her house.

"If you wanted to sleep with him, you were going about it all wrong. You should have let him kiss you. Why didn't you? Nerves?"

"Go away, Michael."

"I want to know why you didn't kiss him. He's what you want. Isn't he?"

She froze in her tracks. Her chest worked on rapid breaths

as she stared to the side. "Why are you following me and talking to me? I don't know how to deal with this. I don't know how I'm supposed to act or what I'm supposed to say."

"We can't act like friends?" He'd thought they were that, at least.

She met his gaze. Beneath a mixture of streetlights and moonlight, her eyes looked watery and vulnerable. "We're friends?"

"I hope so."

"That doesn't work for me." She stepped away, her jaw stiff and her eyes narrowed. He thought she was angry until tears started tracking down her face. "I don't want to be your pity friend."

His chest constricted at the sight of her tears, and he quit breathing. "Who ever said anything about pity?"

She swiped at her cheeks as her chin quivered. "You did. You said you were done helping me but I still wasn't enough. You said it, and you meant it. You can't take it back now."

"I never said *you*. I said *we*." He swallowed hard. "You never once thought I meant *me*? That *I'm* not enough for *you*?"

Guileless eyes searched his face, wide from her lack of understanding. "Why would I ever think that?"

"Because I'm a prostitute, and my dad is a criminal."

Her lips turned down, and she took a step away from him. "I don't care about those things. None of that impacts who you are or how you treat me. You're using those things as excuses because you don't want to hurt me. But I want you to know I can handle the truth. If I'm not enough for you, that's fair and I accept it. I'll get over you eventually. I don't want to be coddled or lied to because of what I am. I don't need your *pity friendship*."

With that, she breezed past him and sailed down the street. Her walk was fast and all business. There was no seductive swaying of hips, no grace; this was no runway walk. He loved it.

He loved *her*.

And she was trying to get over him.

In order to get over him, she had to have fallen for him first. She knew about his escorting, his financial situation, his education, and his dad, and she still loved him.

That changed everything.

Determination coursed through him. He'd been so blinded by his insecurities that he'd pushed her away and hurt her. What he should have been doing instead was fighting for her.

The fight started now. If she could trust and accept him as he was, then he could, too. She deserved that kind of man. For her, he was going to be that kind of man.

He followed Stella from a distance to make sure she made it into her house safely, and then he ran to find Quan. He needed help devising a battle plan.

A knock on her office door distracted Stella from the new algorithm she was formulating. As she swiveled around, the door opened, and an enormous bouquet of calla lilies walked into the room.

Their lead receptionist, Benita, a curvy brunette in her early forties, set the vase on the desk and exhaled through her mouth. "Okay, that was heavy. It looks like you have an admirer."

Stella plucked a card out from between the blooms. She recognized Michael's bold scrawl immediately.

For my Stella. Thinking of you. Love, Michael.

"I don't know what this means." She stared at the note sitting in the palm of her hand.

Benita craned her head to the side to read Michael's script and grinned. "Michael is the honey you're dating, isn't he? He's quite the looker."

"We broke up."

Benita's grin turned sly. "Looks like he wants to get back together. Are you going to give him another chance?"

Before she could reply, Philip stalked past her door. After a split second, he reversed and glowered at the bouquet on her table. An impressive black eye decorated the right side of his face.

"That son of a bitch." He barged into her office, headed for her flowers.

She threw herself in front of them. "What are you doing?"

"I'm going to throw those in the Dumpster where they belong."

"No, you're not! They're mine." This was her first bouquet from a boy ever.

"I'll get you better ones," he said through his teeth. "Those have to go."

"I don't want you to get me flowers."

"We're dating, remember?"

"We're not dating. We went on one date, and I don't want another. We're not compatible at all."

Benita pursed her lips and watched Philip with raised eyebrows, obviously enjoying the drama.

He approached Stella with tensed shoulders and clenched hands. "And you're compatible with *him*?"

She curled her fingers around the card. Was it still compatibility if it was one-sided?

"I was really happy when he and I were together. He's a good listener. More than that, he wanted to know about me, my day, what I was doing, and—"

"All I care about is whether or not he's good in bed," Benita interjected.

Stella bit her lip and blushed down at the carpet. The word *good* didn't do Michael justice. *Phenomenal* was more like it.

"You lucky duck." Benita turned to Philip and grabbed his arm. "Come on, PJ, let's go to the kitchen. You need to ice that eye."

PJ?

Philip grumbled under his breath and stared a few daggers at her lilies before he allowed Benita to pull him out of

Stella's office. As the two of them walked down the hall, he settled his hand at the base of her spine, slipped it lower, and squeezed. Instead of smacking him as Stella thought she would, Benita brushed the light hair from his brow and clucked over his bruise.

That was . . . interesting.

Apparently, Benita didn't care that Philip was a complete hound when it came to women. That worked out just fine for Stella. She didn't have to feel bad for not asking him out again.

She rotated the flower vase and fiddled with the stems. Flowers had always seemed pretty senseless to her. They stank, they wilted, and then you had to clean them up. But these were from Michael.

Her phone buzzed repeatedly, and when she retrieved it from her desk drawer, she saw it was him. She considered letting it go to voice mail, but her thumb hit the talk button on its own.

"Hello."

"Did you get them?" he asked.

"Yes . . . Thank you."

"How's Philip Dexter's eye looking today?"

"Purple."

He made a satisfied sound, and she could almost see his evil smile. She barely refrained from sighing like a schoolgirl. His barbarism shouldn't please her like this.

"It'll start turning green in a few days," he said.

"You really shouldn't have given him a black eye." But she loved that he had. It made her feel special in a way she'd never known. She was a bloodthirsty villainess.

"You're right. Next time, I'll double-punch him in the balls. If anyone's going to kiss you, it had better be me." After an awkward pause, he asked, "Will you have dinner with me tonight?"

Her foolish heart leapt at the thought of seeing him

again, but she forced it into submission. She didn't understand why he was doing any of this, didn't trust it. "No."

There was a long silence before he said, "Good. I like a challenge."

"I'm not trying to challenge you."

"I know you're not. You're trying to get over me, which is worse."

"Michael . . ."

"I have stuff to do. Talk to you later. Miss you." The call disconnected.

She paced about her office with increasingly agitated steps. He didn't want her to get over him. How irritating. What was she supposed to do? Pine over him for eternity?

This burst of outlandish courting had started immediately after he saw Philip trying to kiss her when she didn't want it. Michael was trying to warn Philip off because he didn't think she could protect herself.

She was still his charity case.

Breathing heavily, she picked up his note, crumpled it into a misshapen ball, and tossed it in the trash. That was what she thought of his pity.

If she wanted to get over a man, she was going to get over a man.

She sat down and read over the last few lines of code on the programming screen. Her brain was too distracted to concentrate. She kept thinking about Michael. Her body still yearned for his caresses and his dirty words. More than that, she missed *him* and the routines they'd made together.

He couldn't really want her back, but it would be wonderful if he did. When she noticed the hopeful direction of her thoughts, she scolded herself and told herself to focus on the data. It didn't work. Making a frustrated sound, she fished his note out of the trash, smoothed it out, and stuffed it in one of her drawers.

Each day that week, he called and asked her out to dinner. Each day, she refused. She didn't need or want his help. She could take care of herself just fine.

As of Friday evening, her desk sported the vase of still lovely calla lilies, another vase of roses ranging in shade from bloodred to pink, a bundle of balloons, and a fuzzy black teddy bear in a karate gi. She was far too old for stuffed animals, and the sight of it embarrassed her. Michael's extravagance was making her the talk of the office. She had to figure out a way to make this stop.

When it was time to leave, she powered off her computer, grabbed her purse, and headed for the door, snatching Karate Bear on the way out. She didn't want him, but the thought of him sitting alone in her office all night made her heartbreakingly sad.

She squished the bear under her arm, making him as small as possible, and exited the building. No one needed to see her walking around with a stuffed animal in tow.

"Heading home?" The solitary voice came from behind as she crossed the empty parking lot, and her heart leapt into her throat.

She whipped around with a hand on her chest.

Michael pushed away from the wall of her office building, thumbs hooked into his pockets. He wore a fitted black vest over an oxford shirt that was unbuttoned at the throat and dark slacks. Too gorgeous. She dragged her eyes away and went to pick up her bear from his abandoned location on the blacktop.

Brushing off the bear's fur, she said, "This can be interpreted as stalking, you know."

He ducked his head with a sheepish smile. "I know."

"You need to stop all of this."

"It's not just a little romantic? I don't have a lot of experience with courting, so you'll have to excuse me if I come across too strong."

She pursed her lips. With his looks and charisma, she was sure all he generally had to do was crook his finger and wait for women to crawl to him. She didn't want to be one of those foolish women anymore. "Cut it out, Michael. We both know you're not courting me."

His shoulders stiffened. "What do you mean?"

"You don't need to protect me from Philip anymore. He's switched his attention to the receptionist."

"None of this has been about Philip." He stalked toward her, his brow furrowed and his jaw tight.

Her instincts told her to back away as he neared, but stubbornness had her digging her feet in. She lifted her chin. She wasn't scared of him. "I'm done being your charity case. I don't want—"

Clasping the sides of her face in his hands, he kissed her. Sensation shocked through her, ending her struggles before they began. The cool silk of his lips on hers felt like heaven. As he stroked his hot tongue into her mouth, his salty taste and familiar scent intoxicated her. She gripped his shoulders and pressed her body to his. He surrounded her with his arms and aligned their hips, her softness to his hardness. Liquid aching pervaded her limbs.

"Look at you melting for me," he rasped against her mouth. "I've *missed* you."

He kissed her again, a deep, slow tasting that curled her toes and made her sigh against his lips. Her hair loosened, and she shivered as he threaded his fingers into the mass.

"Pretty Stella," he whispered, running his hands over her loose locks. "I might not have the hang of courting, but I kiss you right."

That snapped her out of her kiss-induced haze immediately. She jerked free of his arms and wiped a sleeve over her mouth. "Don't kiss me. Don't touch me. I don't want you doing anything with me out of pity."

"Why do you keep talking about pity? I never said I pitied you," he said with a frown.

"Then why didn't you take my money?" Without waiting for his response, she retrieved the bear from the ground for the second time. She wanted to hug it close, but she made herself hand it to him. "This past week was nice, but I've had enough. I'm asking you to stop. Please."

"Does that mean you no longer have feelings for me?"

A film of moisture glossed over her eyes, and she spun away from him blindly. "I'm going to go now."

"Because I have feelings for you."

She froze, felt his hand close around hers and pull until she faced him once again. He tipped her chin up, and her tears threatened to spill free. Had he really said that? With her heart drumming in her ears like this, she must have misheard.

He took a breath, released it, took another. "I didn't take your money because I'm in love with you. I told myself you needed me, that helping you would prove I wasn't like my dad, but those were just excuses to be with you. You don't need me, and I don't have to prove I'm not like my dad. I know I'm not. I ended things because I was certain you didn't love me back. But when you said you were going to get over me, you gave me hope."

Her skin flushed with heat—her hands, her neck, her face, the tips of her ears. He didn't pity her. He loved her. Had she heard correctly? Was it true?

He swallowed once. "Could you say something, please? When a guy tells a girl he loves her, he doesn't want silence in response. Was I too late? Are you over me?"

"Are you wearing the underwear I got you?"

Laughter cracked out of him. "Sometimes, the way your mind works is a complete mystery to me."

"Are you?" She transferred the bear underneath her arm and tucked her fingers into the waistband of his pants above his leather belt.

Lips curving, he unfastened his belt, unbuttoned his pants, and drew the zipper down. "If we get arrested for lewd acts in public, they better let us share a cell."

She pulled his shirttails out of the way, and even in the poor lighting of the parking lot, she could see the red plaid of his boxers. She lifted her eyes to his as effervescent warmth pervaded her body, filling her heart and spreading to every extremity. He *did* love her. And her theory was confirmed. Michael's β had changed from one to zero. For her. "You're wearing them."

"I don't like to go commando. Chafing."

Trying to suppress a goofy grin, she straightened his pants and belt. "Women buy underwear for the men they love. It's economics. Data supports this claim."

"Are you telling me you love me, Stella?"

She hugged Karate Bear tight and nodded, suddenly overcome by shyness.

"You're not going to give me the words?" he asked.

"I've never said them to anyone but my parents."

"You think I run around telling women I love them?" He pulled her close and pressed their foreheads together. "I'm going to get the words out of you. Tonight."

"Should I be worried?"

"Yes."

"What are you going to . . ." The heat in his eyes stalled her words.

"Let's go home."

"Okay."

Instead of leading her down the street toward her house, he brought her to a small silver Honda Civic and opened the passenger door for her. "I traded in my car," he said with an awkward shrug.

She sat and buckled her seat belt, taking in the clean, nonleather interior of the car. Nothing about it reminded her of Aliza. "I like this better."

"You would." He smiled as he got behind the wheel. "I'm partnering with Quan to start a clothing line, and I needed startup funds. Since I quit escorting, there was no reason to keep that car."

He was finally doing it—quitting escorting, taking chances, and making a name for himself. In that moment, he was so perfect to her she wanted to launch herself across the gearshift and kiss him until he was breathless.

"That's great. I'm so happy for you, Michael." But the thought of him selling his car because he needed money bothered her, especially when he'd returned her check. "Do you still have some of your mom's medical bills to pay? Did the foundation's medical assistance program fail to cover everything?"

He tilted his head as he frowned at her. "How do you know about my mom's bills or the program?" After a moment's hesitation, his eyes widened. "Was it *you*?"

She averted her eyes.

"It *was* you," he said in a discovering voice. "How did you know about my mom's lack of insurance?"

"That night at your apartment, I saw the bills, and I made the connection between the cost of her treatment and your escorting fees. I think . . . that's when I fell all the way in love with you."

A boyish grin spread over his lips. "I was going to get those words out of you in the most delicious way." But then his smile vanished, replaced by a thoughtful line. "It must have cost a fortune. You started an entire medical program. Just how rich *are* you?"

She worried her bottom lip as she continued to hug the teddy bear. "I'm not that rich anymore. Well, I'm kind of rich. It depends on how you define it. You're probably not going to like it. Are you sure you want to know?"

"Out with it, Stella."

"I had a trust fund. There was about fifteen million dollars in it," she said with a shrug. "I donated it to the Palo Alto Medical Foundation to start that medical program."

"You gave away your entire trust fund? For me?"

"That's kind of what you're supposed to do with money like that, isn't it? Give it away? I can support myself with my salary. It's just money, Michael, and I couldn't stand the idea that you were being forced into escorting. If you want to do it, that's one thing. But if you don't . . ." She shook her head. "I was determined to give you a choice. Besides, we're helping lots of families now. It's a good thing."

"We?" He leaned forward and kissed her cheek, the corner of her mouth. "That was all you. That money was not mine." He pressed a series of kisses to her lips. "Thank you for giving me that choice so I could pick you. Thank you for being you. I love you."

She couldn't help smiling then. She didn't think she'd ever get tired of hearing him say that. "Now I can say my boyfriend is a designer with complete confidence. That is, if you *are* my boyfriend. Are you?"

Instead of answering right away, he started the engine and drove out of the parking lot. Eyes on the road and voice casual, he said, "I better be your boyfriend. Since I'm asking you to marry me in three months."

Stella's jaw dropped as shock washed over her in waves that alternated between hot and cold. "Why are you telling me this?"

A small smile played on his lips as he darted a quick glance her way before focusing on the road once again. "Because you don't like surprises, and I figured you'd need time to get used to the idea."

He was right about that, but before she could dwell on it too much, he dropped one of his hands from the wheel and caught hers, interlacing their fingers the way he always did.

Saying nothing, she let the moment wash over her, the uncertainty, the breathless hope, the anxiousness, and the shimmering contentment. The sight of their intertwined hands pleased her. So different, but still five fingers and five knuckles, the same general blueprint.

She tightened her grip, and he squeezed her back. Palm to palm, two lonely halves found comfort together.

EPILOGUE

Stella strolled down a quiet sidewalk in San Francisco's warehouse district, a discreet corner of town inhabited by several West Coast–based fashion businesses. After opening an unmarked door, she entered an industrial space consisting of steel walls, cement floors, and exposed ceilings.

A photo shoot was in progress on the far side of the room, and Stella smiled as she took in the models showcasing Michael's latest designs. It was barely autumn, but the models presented his winter line. Children ranging in age from preschool to tween posed in exquisitely tailored, miniature suits, vests with matching newsboy caps, sweater dresses, and fur-trimmed mantles.

Quan saw her first. "Hi, Stella." He waved at her absently before continuing an animated discussion with the camerawoman.

Michael paused in the middle of tying the golden ribbon on a little girl's white chiffon evening dress and glanced up at her, brightening. "You're early."

"I missed you."

His smile widened, and he patted the little girl on the shoulder and directed her toward the set, where a coordinator was positioning the children and the props. As he walked to her, he tucked his hands into the pockets of his slacks and swept an appreciative gaze over her navy-blue skirt suit and the scarf loosely wrapped around her neck. She knew he was admiring his clothing selection for her today, and her lips thinned as she suppressed a smile. The things that made him happy . . .

When he reached her side, he leaned down and kissed her on the mouth before trailing his hands down her arms and capturing her hands. He brought her knuckles to his lips and brushed a thumb over the fingers on her left hand, drawing her attention to the respectable trio of diamonds sparkling on her ring finger.

"I still can't believe you went into debt to buy me this," she said.

Even so, she had to admit she loved everything it represented. She'd never been into jewelry, but she caught herself gazing at her ring more often than she'd expected and, invariably, thinking of Michael. When people at the office caught her grinning for no apparent reason, they rolled their eyes and muttered under their breaths.

"I needed to announce how 'taken' you are. Also, as of this morning, I'm officially out of debt. Quan got us the venture backing. We're opening three new stores by Christmas."

She mentally ran the numbers, and excitement bubbled inside of her. "That's really fast. You're doing even better than the high-growth trajectory I developed for you."

"We are. Your analytics are part of what convinced the venture capitalists, actually."

"I think it was your designs and aggressive marketing strategy."

"Okay, that may have had something to do with it." He laughed, but the look in his eyes was soft. "Having you with me this whole time has meant everything to me, though. I hope you know that."

"I do." The past few months had been busy for the both of them, but together, they'd made it work. "It's the same for me."

His expression went serious. "You said you were having the meeting with the partners at your firm today. How did it go?"

"They offered me a promotion again. Principal econometrician. Five direct reports in addition to my trusty intern."

"And?"

She took a breath before saying, "I accepted it."

His lips fell open, and in the next moment, he crushed her in a fierce embrace. He pressed a kiss to her temple. "Do you regret it?"

She burrowed closer to him and breathed in his scent. "No. I'm nervous about it, but mostly, I'm happy."

"So proud of you."

She smiled so big her cheeks ached. "The promotion comes with a large bonus. I'm warning you in advance I'm buying you a new car."

When he pulled back, she worried he was upset. She couldn't read the shuttered look on his face as he said, "I can buy myself a new car."

She bit her lip to keep from frowning, but she understood if he had to earn his own way. She didn't need to spoil him. She just wanted to.

"But I want the same model as yours," he continued. "And I like black."

She tilted her head to the side and drew in a slow breath. "Does that mean . . . ?"

"It means if you want to buy me a car, I want to drive it." His lips curved with a suggestive grin, and his eyes danced. "If you want to buy me boxers, I want to wear them."

Her chest filled with lightness, and she grabbed his hand

so she wouldn't accidentally float away. "It means you love me."

He interlaced their fingers the way he always did and squeezed. "That's right. It's economics."

THE END

Author's Note

The first time I heard of "high functioning" autism, previously known as Asperger's syndrome, was in a private discussion with my daughter's preschool teacher. I was completely shocked by the teacher's suggestion. While my girl was a handful, she didn't fit my preconceptions of "autistic" at all. In my eyes, she's always been just as she should be—a sweet little thing with a firecracker personality. I came home and did some quick research on the Internet, and my findings didn't seem in line with my girl's traits. Just to be sure, I asked my family members and her physician for their opinions, and results were unanimous: She was *not* autistic. They had to be right, and I let it go.

At least, I thought I did. Real Life Me let it go, but Writer Me was fascinated. You see, a gender-swapped *Pretty Woman* had been niggling at the back of my mind for quite some time, but I hadn't been able to figure out why a successful beautiful woman would hire an escort. One autistic trait from my quick Internet research stuck with me: trouble with social skills. That was certainly something I could empathize with—and a compelling reason to hire an escort. What if my heroine was autistic like my daughter wasn't? I needed to learn about this character.

I started to research in earnest, and I discovered the most interesting thing: There are books specifically for *women* on the spectrum. How come women need their own books? We're all people. I figured men and women should be the same. I purchased *Aspergirls* by Rudy Simone.

The strangest feeling settled over me when I started reading her words, and it only got stronger as I delved deeper into the book. Apparently, there's a major difference in the way autism is perceived between men and women. What I'd previously read described autistic *men*, but many autistic women, for a variety of reasons, *mask* their awkwardness and *hide* their autistic traits to be more socially acceptable. Even our obsessions and interests are generally tailored to be socially acceptable, like horses and music instead of license plate numbers that start with three. Because of this, women often go undiagnosed or are diagnosed later in life, frequently after their own children receive diagnoses. Women with Asperger's exist in what people call the "invisible part of the spectrum."

As I read Rudy Simone's book, I found myself looking back at my own childhood and remembering a million little things, like how someone at school told me my facial expression was scary, and I spent hours and hours afterwards practicing in the mirror. Or how sometimes I got through the day by mimicking my favorite cousin's mannerisms and speech patterns because she was popular and that had to be the right way to be, only it was *so exhausting*. Or how I used to tap my fingers one-three-five-two-four over and over in that pattern when I was nervous or bored, but I realized it annoyed people, so I started doing it on my teeth so no one could see or hear, and now I have early onset periodontal disease, but I can't stop to save my life. Or the George Winston obsession that led me to teach myself to play the piano when I was a tiny thing and is still going strong decades later. Or, or, or . . .

What started as mere research for a book became a journey of self-realization. I learned that *I am not alone*. There are other people *just like me* and very possibly my daughter, too. As I pursued and eventually attained a diagnosis (at age thirty-four), Stella, my autistic heroine, was born on the page. It has never been so easy for me to write a character. I knew her intimately. She came from my heart. I didn't have to filter my thoughts to make her socially acceptable, something I'd been unconsciously doing for ages. And this freedom allowed me to find my voice. Before this, I'd been using every other author's writing style, trying to be someone else. When I wrote *The Kiss Quotient*, I became myself, and I've been unapologetically myself ever since. Sometimes instead of confining you, a label can set you free. At least, that was the case for me. I've started therapy to help with struggles I hadn't known were common to people like me.

That said, I feel the need to point out that everyone on the spectrum has their own valid experiences, impairments, strengths, and points of view. My experience (and, therefore, Stella's) is just one among many and cannot be taken as "standard." There is no standard.

For interested parties, I found the following resources on autism spectrum disorder and Asperger's to be informational but not boring:

Aspergirls by Rudy Simone (geared toward women)

Everyday Aspergers by Samantha Craft (geared toward women)

Look Me in the Eye by John Elder Robison

The Reason I Jump by Naoki Higashida

YouTube videos featuring clinical psychologist Tony Attwood

Autistic Women's Association (facebook.com/ autisticwomensassociation)

All the best,
Helen Hoang

Acknowledgments

They say writing is a solitary task. And that's true. You sit down, and you write alone. But this book never would have come so far without the help and support of many, many, *many* people.

This book, in this form, would not exist if I hadn't had the opportunity to participate in Brenda Drake's Pitch Wars contest. Thank you, Brenda and the Pitch Wars team. You're doing an amazing thing. (If you're an unpublished fiction writer, you should really check out pitchwars.org.) The contest connected me to my wonderful mentor, Brighton Walsh, who has had an immeasurable impact on my life. Not only did she help me improve my writing, but she guided me through this wild journey toward publication and became a true friend. Thank you, Brighton, from the bottom of my heart.

Thank you so much to all my critique partners for taking time to read my work. Ava Blackstone, you were my very first writing friend. You gave me courage and confidence, and I'm super lucky to know you. Kristin Rockaway, you read the first crappy draft of this book, and your feedback helped me get into Pitch Wars. Michael and Stella's first kiss is better (more awkward, lol) thanks to you! Gwynne Jackson, you fantastic human, thank you for being there. You are honest, patient, and kind, and I'm keeping you forever. Suzanne Park, I don't know where to start with you. You are a truly generous person, so damn funny, and you get me. Jen DeLuca, I'm grateful I got to have a mentee sister during Pitch Wars and super glad it was you. I am envious of your incredible writing and try to emulate it. ReLynn Vaughn, thank you for your honesty and encouragement and including me in Viva La Colin so I could meet Ash Alexander and Randi Perrin. You ladies are so fun. A. R. Lucas, I'm endlessly entertained that I wrote your doppelganger in Stella. Shannon Caldwell, thank you for telling me you read the whole book in one night—I walked around grinning for hours. Jenny Howe, thank you for letting me send you my progress updates to stay on track. C. P. Rider, we need to go to Denny's again!

Thank you to the Pitch Wars mentee class of 2016. You are an incredible group of people. Right now as I work on these acknowledgments, a few of you are writing with me in our Am Writing Group. Ian Barnes, Meghan Molin, Rosiee Thor, Laura Lashley, Tricia Lynn, Maxym Martineau, Alexa Martin, Rosalyn Baker, Julie Clark, Tracy Gold, Tamara Anne, Rachel Griffin (I still want to name a book *Calculust*!), Nic Eliz, Annette Christi, and so many others have been there to flip virtual tables over rejections and cheer for successes. You guys make this writing thing even better. Thank you to Pitch Wars mentor Laura Brown. I wasn't your mentee, but your kindness has always stuck with me.

Thank you to the San Diego chapter of Romance Writers of America. Demi Hungerford, Lisa Kessler, and Marie Andreas, a lot of my writing and revising gets done during sprints with you. Tameri Etherton, Laura Connors, Rachel Davish, Tami Vahalik, Tessa McFionn, and Janet Tait, you are one awesome pack of women, and you always make me feel welcome. Extra thanks to HelenKay Dimon for leading our chapter's April Writing Challenge, during which I wrote most of the first draft of this book.

Thank you to the Autistic Women's Association for helping me meet other autistic women like myself. The people I've interacted with in our Facebook group are some of the sweetest, most considerate individuals I've ever known, and it's an incredible experience knowing I'm not alone, that there are others who share my same challenges and eccentricities. Harriet, Heather, Elizabeth, and Tad, among many, you ladies were a great support as I learned more about myself and autism, and eventually attained a diagnosis. Thank you for your friendship.

Special thanks to my incredible agent, Kim Lionetti, for being patient with me, fighting for me, and making dreams come true by finding *The Kiss Quotient* a home.

Thank you, Cindy Hwang, for seeing potential in this book and being absolutely wonderful. Kristine Swartz, Jessica Brock, Tawanna Sullivan, Colleen Reinhart, and others, you have been a pleasure to work with. Thank you, Berkley, for helping me share another perspective with readers and literally fight hate with love.

THE

Kiss

QUOTIENT

{HELEN HOANG}

DISCUSSION QUESTIONS

1. Prior to reading this book, how would you have imagined an autistic woman? How does Stella compare to this vision?

2. Stella was surprised when she heard her coworker Philip James had been asked out by their new intern. When it comes to heterosexual relationships, do you think men should be the initiators? What does it say about a woman if she asks out a man?

3. Does it surprise you to see an autistic person exploring a sexual relationship? If so, why?

4. With regards to autism, people are divided between using person-first language (i.e., "person with autism") and identity-first language (i.e., "autistic person"). One of the main arguments for person-first language is that it separates a person from their mental disorders. Many autistic people, on the other hand, prefer identity-first language because they believe autism is an intrinsic part of who they are and have no wish for a "cure." Which do you think is right? Do you think it can depend on each person's individual circumstances and

preferences? How did you feel when Stella tried to make herself fresh and fantastic? Why did you feel that way?

5. What do you think of a man with Michael's Friday night profession? How does that compare to your impression of a woman with that profession? If gender makes a difference, why is that?

6. How does Michael's daytime profession affect his attractiveness?

7. Throughout the book, Michael worries he's inherited his father's "badness," that it was passed down in his blood. Do you think this is illogical? Are you able to empathize with him? If so, how?

8. *Is* love alone enough? Can people with different cultures, education levels, and wealth be together in the long run? How can they make it work?

Read on for a special look at Helen Hoang's

THE BRIDE TEST

On sale now

Scrubbing toilets wasn't usually this interesting. Mỹ had done it so many times she had a streamlined routine by now. Spray with poison everywhere. Pour poison inside. Scrub, scrub, scrub, scrub, scrub. Wipe, wipe, wipe. Flush. Done in less than two minutes. If they had a toilet-cleaning contest, Mỹ would be a top contender. Not today, though. The noises in the next stall kept distracting her.

She was pretty sure the girl in there was crying. Either that or exercising. There was lots of heavy breathing going on. What kind of workout could you do in a bathroom stall? Knee-ups maybe.

A strangled sound was issued, followed by a high-pitched whimper, and Mỹ let go of her toilet brush. That was definitely crying. Leaning her temple against the side of the stall, she cleared her throat and asked, "Miss, is something wrong?"

"No, nothing's wrong," the girl said, but her cries got

louder before they stopped abruptly, replaced by more muffled heavy breathing.

"I work in this hotel." As a janitor/maid. "If someone treated you badly, I can help." She'd try to, anyway. Nothing rankled her like a bully. She couldn't afford to lose this job, though.

"No, I'm fine." The door latch rattled, and shoes clacked against the marble floor.

Mỹ stuck her head out of her stall in time to see a pretty girl saunter toward the sinks. She wore the highest, scariest heels Mỹ had ever seen and a skintight red dress that ended right beneath her butt. If you believed anything Mỹ's grandma said, that girl would get pregnant the second she stepped foot on the street. She was probably pregnant already—from the potency of a man's child-giving stare.

For her part, Mỹ had gotten pregnant by messing around with a playboy from school, no skimpy dress and scary heels needed. She'd resisted him in the beginning. Her mom and grandma had been clear that studies came first, but he'd pursued her until she'd caved, thinking it was love. Instead of marrying her when she'd told him about the baby, however, he'd grudgingly offered to keep her as his secret mistress. She wasn't the kind of girl he could introduce to his upper-class family, and, surprise, he was engaged and planned to go through with the wedding. Obviously, Mỹ had turned him down, which had been both a relief and a shock for him, that son of a dog. Her family, on the other hand, had been heartbroken with disappointment—they'd pinned so many hopes on her. But as she'd known they would, they'd supported her and her baby.

The girl in the red dress washed her hands and dabbed at her mascara-streaked cheeks before tossing her hand towel on the counter and leaving the bathroom. Mỹ's yellow rubber gloves squeaked as she fisted her hands. The towel basket was *right there*. Grumbling to herself, she stalked to the sinks, wiped off the counter with the girl's hand towel, and launched it into the towel basket. A quick inspection of the sink, counter, mirror, and neatly rolled stack of towels confirmed everything was acceptable, and she started back toward the last toilet.

The bathroom door swung open, and another girl rushed inside. With her waist-length black hair, skinny body, long legs, and danger heels, she looked a lot like the previous girl. Only her dress was white. Was the hotel having some kind of pageant? And why was this girl crying, too?

"Miss, are you okay?" Mỹ asked as she took a tentative step toward her.

The girl splashed water on her face. "I'm fine." She braced her wet hands on the granite countertop, making more mess for Mỹ to clean up, and stared at her reflection in the mirror as she took deep breaths. "I thought she was going to pick me. I was so sure. Why ask that question if she doesn't want that answer? She's a sneaky woman."

Mỹ tore her gaze away from the fresh water drops on the counter and focused on the girl's face. "What woman? Pick you for what?"

The girl raked a certain look over Mỹ's hotel uniform and rolled her eyes. "You wouldn't understand."

Mỹ's back stiffened, and her skin flushed with embarrassed heat. She'd gotten that look and tone of voice before. She knew what they meant. Before she could come up with a suitable response, the girl was gone. And, forget the girl's grandpa and all her other ancestors, too, another crumpled towel lay on the counter.

Mỹ stomped to the sink, wiped up the girl's mess, and threw the towel into the basket. Well, she meant to. Her aim was off, and it landed on the floor. Huffing in frustration, she went to pick it up.

Just as her gloved fingers closed around the towel, the door swung open yet again. She looked heavenward. If it was another crying, spoiled girl, she was leaving for a bathroom on the other side of the hotel.

But it wasn't. A tired-looking older woman padded to the sitting room on the far end of the bathroom and sat on one of the velvet-upholstered love seats. Mỹ knew at first glance the lady was a Việt *kiều*. It was a combination of things that gave it away: her genuine granddaddy-sized Louis Vuitton handbag, her expensive clothes, and her feet. Manicured and perfectly uncalloused, those sandaled feet had to belong to an overseas Vietnamese. Those people tipped *really* well, for everything. Money practically poured out of them. Maybe today was Mỹ's lucky day.

She tossed the hand towel in the basket and approached the woman. "Miss, can I get you anything?"

The lady waved at her dismissively.

"Just let me know, miss. Enjoy your time in here. It's a very nice bathroom." She winced, wishing she could retract the last words, and turned back toward her toilets. Why they had a sitting room in here was beyond her. Sure, it was a nice room, but why relax where you could hear people doing bathroom stuff?

She finished her work, set her bucket of cleaning supplies on the floor by the sinks, and performed one last inspection of the bathroom. One of the hand towels had partially unrolled, so she shook it out, rerolled it, and set it on the stack with the others. Then she repositioned the tissue box. There. Everything was presentable.

She bent to pick up her bucket, but before her fingers could close around the handle, the lady said, "Why did you fix the box of Kleenex like that?"

Mỹ straightened, looked at the tissue box, and then tilted her head at the lady. "Because that's how the hotel likes it, miss."

A thinking expression crossed the lady's face, and after a second, she beckoned Mỹ toward her and patted the space next to her on the sofa. "Come talk to me for a minute. Call me Cô Nga."

Mỹ smiled in puzzlement but did as she was bid, sitting

down next to the lady and keeping her back straight, her hands folded, and her knees pressed together like the virginest virgin. Her grandma would have been proud.

Sharp eyes in a pale, powdered face assessed her much like Mỹ had just done to the bathroom counter, and Mỹ pressed her feet together awkwardly and beamed her best smile at the lady.

After reading her name tag, the lady said, "So your name is Trần Ngọc Mỹ."

"Yes, miss."

"You clean the bathrooms here? What else do you do?"

Mỹ's smile threatened to fade, and she kept it up with effort. "I also clean the guests' rooms, so that's more bathrooms, changing sheets, making beds, vacuuming. Those kinds of things." It wasn't what she'd dreamed of doing when she was younger, but it paid, and she made sure she did good work.

"Ah, that is— You have mixed blood." Leaning forward, the lady clasped Mỹ's chin and angled her face upward. "Your eyes are *green*."

Mỹ held her breath and tried to figure out the lady's opinion on this. Sometimes it was a good thing. Most of the time it wasn't. It was much better to be mixed race when you had money.

The lady frowned. "But how? There haven't been American soldiers here since the war."

Mỹ shrugged. "My mom says he was a businessman. I've never met him." As the story went, her mom had been his housekeeper—and something else on the side—and their affair had ended when his work project finished and he left the country. It wasn't until afterward that her mom discovered she was pregnant, and by then it was too late. She hadn't known how to find him. She'd had no choice but to move back home to live with her family. Mỹ had always thought she'd do better than her mom, but she'd managed to follow in her footsteps almost exactly.

The lady nodded and squeezed her arm once. "Did you just move to the city? You don't seem like you're from around here."

Mỹ averted her eyes, and her smile fell. She'd grown up with very little money, but it wasn't until she'd come to the big city that she'd learned just how poor she really was. "We moved a couple months ago because I got the job here. Is it that easy to tell?"

The lady patted Mỹ's cheek in an oddly affectionate manner. "You're still naïve like a country girl. Where are you from?"

"A village close to Mỹ Tho, by the water."

A wide grin stretched over the lady's face. "I knew I liked you. Places make people. I grew up there. I named my restaurant Mỹ Tho Noodles. It's a very good restaurant in California. They talk about it on TV and in magazines. I guess you wouldn't have heard about it here, though." She sighed to herself before her eyes sharpened and she asked, "How old are you?"

"Twenty-three."

"You look younger than that," Cô Nga said with a laugh. "But that's a good age."

A good age for what? But Mỹ didn't ask. Tip or no tip, she was ready for this conversation to end. Maybe a real city girl would have left already. Toilets didn't scrub themselves.

"Have you ever thought of coming to America?" Cô Nga asked.

Mỹ shook her head, but that was a lie. As a child, she'd fantasized about living in a place where she didn't stick out and maybe meeting her green-eyed dad. But there was more than an ocean separating Việt Nam and America, and the older she'd grown, the larger the distance had become.

"Are you married?" the lady asked. "Do you have a boyfriend?"

"No, no husband, no boyfriend." She smoothed her hands

over her thighs and gripped her knees. What did this woman want? She'd heard the horror stories about strangers. Was this sweet-looking woman trying to trick her and sell her into prostitution in Cambodia?

"Don't look so worried. I have good intentions. Here, let me show you something." The lady dug through her giant Louis Vuitton purse until she found a manila file. Then she pulled out a photograph and handed it to Mỹ. "This is my Diệp Khải, my youngest son. He's handsome, ha?"

Mỹ didn't want to look—she honestly didn't care about this unknown man who lived in the paradise of California—but she decided to humor the woman. She'd look at the picture and make all the appropriate noises. She'd tell Cô Nga her son looked like a movie star, and then she'd find some excuse to leave.

When she glanced at the photograph, however, her body went still, just like the sky immediately before a rainstorm.

He *did* look like a movie star, a man-beautiful one, with sexy, wind-tossed hair and strong, clean features. Most captivating of all, however, was the quiet intensity that emanated from him. A shadow of a smile touched his lips as he focused on something to the side, and she found herself leaning toward the photo. If he was an actor, all the aloof dangerous hero roles, like a bodyguard or a kung fu master, would be his. He made you wonder: What was he thinking about so intently? What was his story? Why didn't he smile for real?

"Ah, so Mỹ approves. I told you he was handsome," Cô Nga said with a knowing smile.

Mỹ blinked like she was coming out of a trance and handed the picture back to the lady. "Yes, he is." He'd make a lucky girl even luckier someday, and they'd live a long, lucky life together. She hoped they experienced food poisoning at least once. Nothing life-threatening, of course. Just inconvenient—make that *very* inconvenient. And mildly painful. Embarrassing, too.

"He's also smart and talented. He went to graduate school."

Mỹ worked up a smile. "That's impressive. I would be very proud if I had a son like him." Her mom, on the other hand, had a toilet cleaner for a daughter. She pushed her bitterness away and reminded herself to keep her head down and go about her own business. Jealousy wouldn't get her anything but misery. But she wished him extra incidences of food poisoning anyway. There had to be some fairness in the world.

"I am very proud of him," Cô Nga said. "He's why I'm here, actually. To find him a wife."

"Oh." Mỹ frowned. "I didn't know Americans did that." It seemed horribly old-fashioned to her.

"They don't do it, and Khải would be angry if he knew. But I have to do something. His older brother is too good with women—I don't need to worry about him—but Khải is twenty-six and still hasn't had a girlfriend. When I set up dates for him, he doesn't go. When girls call him, he hangs up. This coming summer, there are three weddings in our family, *three*, but is one his? No. Since he doesn't know how to find himself a wife, I decided to do it for him. I've been interviewing candidates all day. None of them fit my expectations."

Her jaw fell. "All the crying girls . . ."

Cô Nga waved her comment away. "They're crying because they're ashamed of themselves. They'll recover. I had to know if they were serious about marrying my son. None of them were."

"They seemed very serious." They hadn't been fake crying in the bathroom—that was for sure.

"How about you?" Cô Nga fixed that assessing stare on her again.

"What about me?"

"Are you interested in marrying my Khải?"

Mỹ looked behind herself before pointing at her own chest. *"Me?"*

Cô Nga nodded. "Yes, you. You've caught my attention."
Her eyes widened. *How?*

As if she could read Mỹ's mind, Cô Nga said, "You're a good, hardworking girl and pretty in an unusual way. I think I could trust you with my Khải."

All Mỹ could do was stare. Had the fumes from the cleaning chemicals finally damaged her brain? "You want me to marry your son? But we've never met. *You* might like me . . ." She shook her head, still unable to wrap her mind around that. She *cleaned toilets* for a living. "But your son probably won't. He sounds picky, and I'm not—"

"Oh, no, no," Cô Nga interrupted. "He's not picky. He's *shy.* And stubborn. He thinks he doesn't want a family. He needs a girl who is more stubborn. You'd have to make him change his mind."

"How would I—"

"*Ơi,* you know. You dress up, take care of him, cook the things he likes, do the things he likes . . ."

Mỹ couldn't help grimacing, and Cô Nga surprised her by laughing.

"*This* is why I like you. You can't help but be yourself. What do you think? I could give you a summer in America to see if you two fit. If you don't, no problem, you go home. At the very least, you'll go to all our family weddings and have some food and fun. How's that?"

"I—I—I . . ." She didn't know what to say. It was too much to take in.

"One more thing." Cô Nga's gaze turned measuring, and there was a heavy pause before she said, "He doesn't want children. But I am determined to have grandchildren. If you manage to get pregnant, I know he'll do the right thing and marry you, regardless of how you get along. I'll even give you money. Twenty thousand American dollars. Will you do this for me?"

The breath seeped from Mỹ's lungs, and her skin went cold. Cô Nga wanted her to steal a baby from her son and force him into marriage. Disappointment and futility crushed her. For a moment, she'd thought this lady saw something special in her, but Cô Nga had judged her based on things she couldn't control, just like the girls in the skimpy dresses had.

"The other girls all said no, didn't they? You thought I'd say yes because . . ." She indicated her uniform with an open palm.

Cô Nga said nothing, her gaze steady.

Mỹ pushed up from the sofa, went to collect her bucket of cleaning supplies, opened the door, and paused in the doorway. With her eyes trained straight ahead, she said, "My answer is no."

She didn't have money, connections, or skills, but she could still be as hardheaded and foolish as she wanted. She hoped her refusal stung. Without a backward glance, she left.

Ready to find
your next great read?

Let us help.

Visit prh.com/nextread